THOUGH MY HEART IS TORN

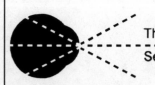

THOUGH MY HEART IS TORN

JOANNE BISCHOF

THORNDIKE PRESS

A part of Gale, Cengage Learning

GALE
CENGAGE Learning·

Detroit • New York • San Francisco • New Haven, Conn • Waterville, Maine • London

GALE
CENGAGE Learning®

Copyright © 2013 by Joanne Bischof.
The Cadence of Grace Series #2.
All Scripture quotations are taken from the King James Version and the New King James Version®. Copyright © 1982 by Thomas Nelson, Inc. Used by permission. All rights reserved.
Thorndike Press, a part of Gale, Cengage Learning.

LIBRARY OF CONGRESS CATALOGING-IN-PUBLICATION DATA

Bischof, Joanne.
    Though my heart is torn / by Joanne Bischof. — Large print edition.
      pages ; cm. — (The cadence of grace series ; #2) (Thorndike Press large print Christian historical fiction)
    ISBN 978-1-4104-6313-5 (hardcover) — ISBN 1-4104-6313-3 (hardcover) 1. Marital conflict—Fiction. 2. Life change events—Fiction. 3. Domestic fiction. 4. Large type books. I. Title.
    PS3602.I75T46 2013b
    813'.6—dc23   2013026613

Published in 2013 by arrangement with Multnomah Books, an imprint of Crown Publishing Group, a division of Random House, Inc.

Printed in Mexico
1 2 3 4 5 6 7 17 16 15 14 13

To those who hurt, and to the One who holds them, this is for you.

Have not I commanded thee? Be strong and of a good courage; be not afraid, neither be thou dismayed: for the Lord thy God is with thee whithersoever thou goest.

JOSHUA 1:9

PROLOGUE

September 1901
Rocky Knob, Virginia

Joel Sawyer stared at his unwelcome guests in disbelief, the roomful of faces blurring. He stumbled back and sank onto the bench. His head fell against the wall behind him. "This can't be," he muttered.

"I'm afraid it is." The reverend's voice trembled worse than the shanty walls, which shook in the evening wind.

Joel closed his eyes. His jaw clenched, and heat rose up his neck. Gideon O'Riley was a dead man. If the task were up to him alone, he would see it done. Wanting to strike the boy, he curled his fingers against his leg, forming a fist so tight it threatened to turn his hand numb.

Opening his eyes, he tipped his chin and stared at the young woman who sat across from him. *Cassie Allan, pretty girl.* Her brown hair was stuffed into a tidy knot at

9

the nape of her pale neck, hints of unruly curls tugging free. A glance into her eyes confirmed the trait ran deeper than appearances. Yes, *unruly* was the word. If only his daughter were as cunning. He chewed the inside of his cheek until it burned.

He glanced at the reverend. "So what's to be done?"

The question hung heavily on the thick silence. On a bench near the fire, Bill O'Riley lowered his head, hat dangling between limp hands. Defeated. He'd yet to speak, and Joel doubted he would start now.

Reverend Gardner shifted in his seat, bringing Joel's attention back to the old man who was too short for his weight. *More like a mole than a man.* Joel disregarded the thought and forced himself to focus on the matter at hand. The reverend had stuttered his way through the unwelcome news and now sat fumbling with his hat, making Joel wish he could snatch it away, ring the sweat out, and hand it back.

The bedroom door creaked open, and Maggie emerged from the darkened room. Huddled on the bed, his children, shadowed in the light of a single candle, made scarcely a sound. Never had there been so many people in his house. It was crushing. Maggie stepped from the bedroom and closed the door softly behind her. She offered him a weak smile.

He ignored her.

"I apologize for the church's oversight." The reverend's droning words were unsteady, and Joel's mind hunted for the vital points. "We'd like to put this embarrassment behind us . . ."

Joel coughed. He tried to focus.

"There is no other choice but to remedy this. Gideon and your daughter must return . . . if we're to repair the Allans' honor."

Glass clanged against metal. The reverend stopped and nodded to his hostess. With her eyes down, Maggie ducked her head and lit the oil lamp, fingers quick. After silently sliding the glass over the flame, she slipped from the room. The door closed without a sound behind her. One less person. If only Cassie and her pa would leave. Take Bill O'Riley and their horrid news with them.

Joel felt the reverend's gaze on him.

"We must find them." In the candlelight, shadows haunted his face.

Leaning forward, Joel rubbed his hands together. Grit ground between his palms. The mistake was Gideon's — his foolish son-in-law who had deceived them all. The reverend rambled on, and Joel warred with the urge to backhand him. *The church's*

11

oversight. Hah!

It bordered on criminal.

But Joel could not turn back time. Lonnie was already married to the scoundrel. And now they were asking him to get them home. Now.

"And my daughter" — Joel ran a hand along the scruff of his jaw — "what's to become of her?"

An unwelcome voice invaded the conversation. "It's beside the point."

Henry Allan. Joel glared at Cassie's father. "Watch yourself."

"Gentlemen, please." Gardner's quivering hands reached for the space between the men.

Henry leaned back in his chair, his face filled with a brokenness that was beyond Joel.

Supper sat untouched on the table, and though the fire in the cast-iron stove had dwindled to meager coals, the smell of roast chicken still hung in the air. A cruel reminder of his empty stomach. If that weren't rude enough, now Cassie's father was giving him lip. At least Bill O'Riley was silent where he sat. The man hadn't an argument to his name. Their children were heathens, the pair of them. The truth made Joel shift in his seat, disgust sliding through his veins.

12

Joel rubbed his knuckles together to loosen the tension that swept through the rigid muscles in his arm. "Lonnie's my oldest girl, and —"

"And what of my oldest girl? Abandoned." Henry's last word slipped out in a pained whisper, and he stood, sending his chair tilting. His hands, now balled into fists, shook with each word. "Think of the pain my Cassie has endured these last months."

The young woman rolled her eyes, the wayward motion tipping Joel's head back. If she were his daughter, he'd smack the look off her face. But Henry Allan was too busy gaining the reverend's sympathy to notice. Let him have it. Joel had no desire to fight for Lonnie's innocence. It didn't exist. They had all been fooled.

He should have expected it from Gideon. The wretch whom less than an hour ago he had still considered family. And look where it landed him. Joel glanced at the reverend, ignoring the man who hovered angrily beside them. He was finished with Henry Allan for the evening.

They should pass it off, wash their hands of this disgrace. "Surely this situation is better suited for the law."

The reverend cleared his throat, and Joel realized he'd spoken his thought aloud.

"We would. But we wanted to bring it to you first." As if he'd mustered some unseen strength, Reverend Gardner's beady eyes bored so deep into Joel's that Joel found himself shifting. Again. "It seems that if all parties involved can come to an agreement of peace, we needn't bring in any outside aid . . . and the trouble it would bring. We need only resolve the matter and see that the proper documents are in the hand of the circuit rider the next time he journeys on courthouse business."

"So, now I need to get them home. Is that it? Is there anything else I should know?" Joel clipped the words off, not caring if his mood leaked through. "What of the child?" he nearly spat.

The reverend's eyes filled with sorrow as they met his. "Will be your responsibility, I'm afraid."

He should have known.

The reverend's face grew somber. "It must be done. You must send word . . . bid them home immediately." He slid his hat on and rose slowly. "Or the Allans will indeed involve the law. Something, I believe, neither of us wants." His fat throat worked. "I'd imagine that having the law knocking on your doorstep, asking questions, isn't desired." Firelight drew the shadows long across his face. "The law has a way of . . . unearthing things."

Joel wanted to wring that fat neck.

Irritation shot through him that the reverend knew of the accusations. The rumors. Joel would deny the stories until his last breath. But still . . . a man of the law knew how to hunt for truths best left buried deep. He had no desire to test that.

He stepped toward the door, which was rattling on its hinges in the windstorm that beat against the house. With a single nod, Bill O'Riley rose from his bench and quickly bid the room goodnight in a husky voice.

The reverend held the door open and, with a stiff nod, motioned for the Allans. Cassie stepped out first, clutching her shawl, which fluttered and slapped with a life of its own. Joel caught the glint of her eyes in the moonlight. Her pa followed close on her heels. The wind howled. Henry Allan glanced back over his shoulder, pinning Joel with a fierce stare before pulling his hat over hair the color of dirty snow.

The reverend hesitated and turned toward Joel. A gust of wind burst into the house, clawing its chilly fingers through Joel's thin shirt.

"Mr. Sawyer. Again, please know that I am sorry. This, uh, sort of thing does not happen . . . often."

"Well, I should think not," Joel snapped, not wishing for an apology but for an empty house. He wanted nothing more than to collapse in bed and forget this evening had ever taken place.

"But it must be remedied." Reverend Gardner's words choked to a raspy whisper.

Joel knew the Allans were as unhappy with the revelation as he was. The reverend's gaze shifted between his eyes.

The small man continued. "You do know —"

"Yes!" Joel yelped, then lowered his voice to a bitter growl. "Of course I know."

Cassie Allan had three brothers. Three grown brothers. Each a good shot and skilled with a knife. Joel watched Henry Allan descend the steps, his coat whipping in the wind. Joel did not want trouble. Perhaps for Gideon, but not for himself. There was nothing else to do but comply with the Allans' wishes. They had the law on their side, which was more than could be said for his fallen daughter and her miserable husband.

Retreating from the doorway, the reverend nodded once. He started down the steps, and the door creaked closed.

Joel stepped back and turned to see faces peeking out from behind his bedroom door.

"You can come out." His sons, Sid and Oliver, slipped out of the bedroom and hurried into the lean-to where they collapsed on their cornhusk mattress. With Charlotte tangled in her embrace, his wife led Addie out by the hand, and Joel watched with little emotion as Maggie helped the five-year-old crawl into the bed that filled the corner of the room. The bed that had once been Lonnie's. Maggie lifted Charlotte in and smoothed the quilt over the two girls.

With quick movements, she snatched up a pair of plates and tossed the remains into the pot. She glanced up, concern laced across her aging features. "What have you decided?" she whispered.

"I'll tell you when you come to bed."

Maggie nodded and stepped aside for him to pass in front of her. All but one of the candles were quickly snuffed out and the oil lamp extinguished to save the costly, precious oil. Maggie worked quietly on the other side of the wall, dishes thunking in the washbasin. The darkness of the bedroom wrapped around him like a shroud, and Joel suddenly felt more consumed by the situation than ever.

ONE

Gideon's boots crunched dried leaves as he made his way from the farm toward Apple Hill and the grove left by settlers long ago. The trees, which had seen many more summers than he, stood stark against the gray sky. Their gnarled, rough-skinned branches held the year's harvest of crimson fruit.

With a grunt and a full heart, he leaned into the weight of the wheelbarrow that would have been empty if it weren't for his wife huddled in the metal bin, plaid skirt tucked around her knees. Lonnie threw her head back and laughed breathlessly as he struggled to scale the steep hill. A smile lifted his cheeks.

"Someday I'm gonna plant an orchard closer to the house," he panted.

She chuckled. "Am I inspiring you?"

"You're heavy!" He gasped for breath.

Lonnie's voice seemed to float along the cool September breeze. "Keep going; you're almost there!" She laughed, her long braid bouncing, and her nose, still dusted in summer's freckles, wrinkled.

Tempted to tip his cargo over into the dry grass, Gideon grumbled playfully and dug his toes into the moist earth. Lonnie's fingers clung to the side of the wheelbarrow when it faltered, and her squeal made him think the better of it. The rusted wheel squeaked one last turn, and Gideon dropped the handles. The muscles in his arms burned. He flexed his hands to calm the blood that pulsed through his veins. He could scarcely breathe, and when Lonnie tumbled out, broken bits of laughter drained his lungs.

She brushed leaves from her skirt. "See," she said, "that wasn't so hard."

With his hands free, Gideon tore off his coat and used it to wipe his forehead. "Speak for yourself." He chuckled, draping the coat over the handle of the wheelbarrow. The autumn air collided with his damp skin, cooling him instantly through his shirt. He lifted a bucket from Lonnie's grasp and ran his thumb under her soft jaw.

With a rosy-cheeked smile, she slipped her arm through the crook of his elbow. Her bare feet fell into a slow rhythm with his worn-out boots, and they circled the small

20

grove of trees as they decided on the best place to start. He handed her the pail and then reached for the ladder leaning against the nearest trunk. Untouched for nearly a year, the sun-rotted wood seemed to have become a part of the thick bark. Clouds challenged one another in front of the sun, dimming the orchard, cooling the air.

He lifted the ladder over his head and settled it into place, cobwebs trailing. "Ladies first." He wiggled the end into soft soil that was thick with rotted leaves.

She hesitated, and he glanced at her.

"You give me a funny smile every time I say that." He squinted into the sun when it broke through the clouds.

"I do?"

"You do." With a firm grasp, he held the ladder steady. One hand clutching her bucket, Lonnie grabbed the nearest rung and started up the rickety ladder. It never wavered as Gideon held it fast.

"I suppose . . ." She stopped when they were eye level. His green eyes were wide, wondering, and in an instant she remembered the man he had once been. A shiver crept across her shoulders but faded just as quick. Those days were gone. She plucked an apple. Then a second, her thoughts distant. "It just makes me happy. That's all."

Slowly, he added another apple to the bucket. A clear pain tugged his brows together. "It was that bad, wasn't it?"

The regret she saw in his face put a stitch in her ever-mending heart.

Lonnie drew in a deep breath, knowing she could speak nothing but the truth, and her silence was truth enough. As the memories formed themselves anew, Lonnie pictured an unhappy young man standing at the front of the church, her unwanted hand inside his. If he could have wished her away, he would have. Hovering on the brink of a life of despair, she had made her marriage vows to the one man she despised most.

The man who had tried to steal her innocence one starry night.

His mouth was drawn, eyes sad as he watched her remember. Lonnie blinked quickly, shaking the icy memories from her heart. It was long ago. Her pa's merciless grip on her life, further gone still.

The breeze tousled Gideon's flannel shirt, pulling it tight across his shoulders. "It's good to remember, I suppose." He plucked an apple and held it in his broad hand, studying it. "It's best not to forget what once was." He smoothed his thumb over the dusky red skin. "It's hard to think on it.

Believe me, I'd rather not." His voice was muted, chin to chest. "But" — he glanced up at Lonnie, his hair unruly in the morning dew — "forgetting seems unsafe."

"Unsafe?"

He gently lowered the apple into the pail and made no move to reach for another. He squinted at her. "If I forget . . . who I was. *What* I was." He shook his head, throat working. "I just don't want to get comfortable. Do you know what I mean?"

She kissed his forehead, inhaling his scent, and lingered when his eyes closed. "I do. And thank you." Her fingers grazed his hair. "That means the world to me."

Gideon's lopsided grin warmed her. He took the bucket from her and gently tipped it; the apples rolled inside the empty wheelbarrow. He faced her. "You're too good for me, Lonnie Sawyer."

"It's O'Riley now." She laughed and climbed higher.

He winked at her. Peering up at her through branches, he spread his arms out wide, his familiar form silhouetted against a rising sun. "So I got all of this. A second chance. A wonderful wife. And a son."

Lonnie put a hand up to shield her eyes.

"And what do you get?" His face was maddeningly serious.

Lonnie tugged another apple free. "You still don't know, do you?" Before she could change her mind, Lonnie motioned him forward. Her bare feet lowered her down the rungs until she stood level with his tall frame.

His eyes widened, and the freckles sprinkled across his nose made him look more like a boy than a man of twenty-three. Placing one hand and then the other on his shoulders, she marveled at the solid flesh beneath his faded work shirt. "I'll tell you, but only if you don't tease me about it."

"I promise," he said in a throaty whisper. His Adam's apple bobbed.

An unavoidable smile warmed her lips, and Lonnie delighted in the effect she had on him. "I got the only man I've ever loved. There was no one before you, and there will be no one after you. I could never ask for more. In fact" — she pressed fingertips to her chest, so full was her heart — "I think God was smiling down on me the day I married you." She paused, remembering the rest of God's grace.

Gideon smiled, joy flooding his face.

It was enough to fill Lonnie's heart to overflowing.

Gideon noticed Lonnie blush as they

ducked into the warm kitchen. Elsie glanced up from her chopping block and turned out a bowl of dough. The heavy cutting board wobbled, knocking wood against wood, as Elsie's pudgy hands began to knead.

Gideon lowered a loaded pail at her feet.

"We have your apples." Lonnie reached for her apron. She twisted the ties into place and began to hoist the bucket. It scarcely budged.

With a smirk, Gideon lifted it for her.

"Now do I get my pie?" Gideon set the bucket on the table with a *thunk* and ran his hand over his smooth chin, the bare skin a foreign feeling beneath his rough hand.

"Only if your wife stops standing there blushing like a nervous schoolgirl and starts slicing apples." Elsie winked, and Gideon watched the color in Lonnie's cheeks brighten.

"I'm not blushing." Lonnie took her place at the kitchen table, paring knife in hand. "I thought we were supposed to stick together, Elsie."

When Gideon flashed her a disarming smile, Lonnie swatted him away. "Whose side are you on, anyway?"

His hand grazed her sleeve in passing. At the sound of Jacob's cries above, Gideon strode through the parlor, then took the stairs two at a time. He found the little boy in his cradle, a bundle of blankets around him. Gideon scooped him up, and Jacob pressed a sleepy head to his shoulder, rubbing a tiny fist against his eyes. Gideon kissed his hair and savored the scent of his son as he went back down the stairs.

"Well, look who's awake." Elsie held out her hands as an offer to take him.

Gideon hoisted Jacob higher against his chest. "I've got to finish a few things out in the barn. Thought he might just come with me."

A coil of red skin fell into Lonnie's lap, and she set a bare apple aside. "He'd like that."

Stepping out into the crisp autumn air, Gideon straightened Jacob's thick socks and tugged his wool pants down around pudgy ankles. He strode toward the barn, the door already propped open. Gideon ducked into the dim building, and the homey smell of animals and fresh-cut wood met him. Jebediah worked quietly at the bench. He glanced up with a nod when Gideon came in. Jacob flapped his arms. Gideon set the boy down on his tummy on a tattered blanket where a pile of small, smooth blocks would keep him busy for quite some time. Jacob struggled to pick up a block.

Jebediah worked silently, the man never needing to fill empty space with words. He'd been that way for as long as Gideon had known him — since the day Jebediah had rescued Lonnie from a life of sorrow. Laying down the challenge that Gideon could be more than a man of anger. From that moment on, Jebediah had walked every day with him, through the struggles, through the blessings. All for Lonnie. She'd been worth every moment of it.

Sitting on the workbench was a trio of wooden buckets. Gideon had already made and sold a dozen. Though they didn't fetch much, he had a little silver in his pockets for his family. Come a sugar snow, they would be in higher demand. Made of cedar and white ash so that the sap would retain its sweetness, the buckets were stout and tightly formed, and if Gideon were still a betting man, he'd reckon they'd last many a winter.

With steady hands and a watchful eye on his son, Gideon fitted two pieces together. Not quite right. His chisel made nary a sound in the hard wood. He sighed, enjoying the peace of his work.

"Headed to town tomorrow," Jebediah said. "Gonna pick up our supplies before it gets too late in the year. Also need to get

27

the mail. It's been too long."

Gideon glanced up.

"Elsie and Lonnie have given me their lists. Anything else you need?" Jebediah slid a crinkled paper forward.

Gideon took it, studying their feminine script. Lonnie had written "4 yards of gray flannel," and Gideon remembered the skirt she'd wanted to make. He penciled in a few items, then thought a moment. He knew she also wanted a new blouse but wouldn't admit it. He jotted down one last item. "I have the money inside. I'll get it to you when we go in." He slid the paper back to Jebediah.

Jebediah eyed it. "Didn't you pay any attention in school?"

Gideon chuckled. "It's legible."

Jebediah squinted. "Hardly." With a laugh in his gray eyes, he folded the paper and tucked it in his pocket.

"That's two yards. And make sure you let Mr. Cramer's wife help you pick that out." Gideon tugged at his flannel shirt. "Something pretty. Not one of those backwoods patterns you always take to."

The older man's mustache tilted skyward in a broad grin. He strode over and scooped up Jacob. "You watch it." A laugh carried on his husky voice.

Ducking his head, Gideon eyed the pieces of ash, now resting snugly together. "How long will you be gone?"

"Two days. Maybe three if I get held up." Jebediah's broad hand patted against Jacob's small back. The little boy pressed his head to his shoulder.

"I'll keep up on all the chores."

"I know you will. And I appreciate it."

Gideon worked his chisel through another wooden slat. Shavings curled and fell. "Lonnie will be pleased to receive word from home."

Jebediah stepped toward the doorway and leaned against the jamb. Sun glinted off his boots. "Not you?"

Gideon shrugged, set his chisel down, and reached for Jacob when the boy lunged toward him. "There's nothing back there for me."

Two

At the sound of horses, Cassie lifted her head. Her pa moved to the window. Her ma lowered her knitting to her lap, and the rocking chair stilled. "Who is it, Henry?"

Chatter subsided, and several pairs of eyes blinked up at their pa.

He stuck his tongue in his cheek and stared out into the night. Silent moments ticked by without a word. Finally, he stepped away from the window. He glanced at his wife before turning his gaze to Cassie. "It's Bill O'Riley."

Cassie gulped. She was going to be sick. But her ma's face brightened.

"Oh, Henry" — she smoothed the collar of her dress — "do you think he could be bringin' news?" She looked at Cassie. "Perhaps he knows of Gideon. Perhaps he's received word of some sort."

Cassie's pulse quickened as she stared at the dark window. *He could be here for another reason.* But Mr. O'Riley was not a close friend of her pa's, and she knew it. Surely his visit had one purpose and one purpose only.

Samuel grunted and pulled his pipe from his mouth to whisper something to Eli, who sat beside him. Her oldest brother lowered his paper long enough to chuckle. Cassie glared at her older brothers. She knew how they despised Gideon, and as much as she wanted to blame them, she couldn't. Their friendship had long since ended. Samuel and Eli's anger was justified. Cassie fiddled with the locket around her neck. Gideon had once been everything she'd thought she wanted. And in a moment of weakness — no, stupidity — she'd sealed her fate. Did she love Gideon? Cassie glanced toward the dark window. He had made her feel alive. He'd made her feel loved. He'd been all she had wanted and more. And now? Now he was married to Lonnie. He hadn't wasted much time, had he?

Her heart lurched.

To everyone else, it mattered little what she thought. Besides, her parents only saw black and white. And all they saw was a soiled daughter. There were few remedies for what had been done. No gaining back what had been lost. Yet her parents clung to

31

the hope that perhaps her honor could be salvaged.

Cassie circled her thumb and fingers around her wrist when it began to shake, then clutched her apron. Could she go through with this? How she wished her feelings were as easy to read as the paper Eli was studying. When it came to Gideon O'Riley, her desires were a basketful of confliction. Yearning, frustration, uncertainty. She dropped her apron in a whisper of fabric.

Flanked by his brothers, Eli sat back in his chair and crossed one ankle over the other. He tugged at his short beard and rubbed the scruff with the back of his fingers. Samuel flashed Cassie a confident grin, but she didn't share his certainty — his hunger for revenge. She only wanted to get out of this unscathed.

A shoulder bumped hers, and Cassie's hand grazed against her sister's. At thirteen, Libby knew nothing of her older sister's reckless behavior and would have no suspicions about Mr. O'Riley's sudden appearance.

When the waiting became too much to bear, Cassie rose on her tiptoes and slid the last of the clean glasses onto the top shelf. Supper had long since ended, and with four grown men to feed, the pot of venison stew had been picked clean. Cassie pushed the scrap bucket aside and tucked a dangling carrot top in. She snatched up a chipped plate and ran a water-soaked towel over it.

Mr. O'Riley knocked. Cassie nearly jumped.

Her pa paused, his hand hovering against the knob. His shoulders rose and fell in a single sigh. He opened the door and tipped his head. "Evenin'."

Mr. O'Riley's boots thudded into the fire-lit room. His hair was tidy, combed off to one side. "Evenin'," he nodded cordially. His mossy eyes flickered over the dark space, landing on each member of the Allan family.

Cassie stepped back, stomach churning.

Her pa peered over his shoulder at his three sons. "Jack. Samuel. Eli. Outside." Without complaint, they rose in a chorus of shuffling and whispers.

Her pa glanced back at his guest but nudged Eli in passing. "Take Libby with you."

Libby's eyebrows fell. "Do I have to —"

"Follow your brothers," he demanded, his gaze suddenly finding Cassie. Anger sparked in his eyes for the briefest of moments. Though he tempered it well, she could see his frustration rising. This was taking its toll on him. Made clearer in the lines of his face, the hunch of his shoulders. She glanced away before guilt could taint her conscience.

Cassie patted Libby's hand, and the girl stepped toward the door. Gideon's father moved aside, and she timidly squeezed past him. One by one, each of her siblings disappeared into the black night. As much as she longed to follow them, Cassie was too eager to hear what news Mr. O'Riley may have brought. She might have sat in the barn loft, watching the moon as the kittens frolicked in her lap, but as much as she would like it to, that wouldn't whisk her back to her childhood. No, she was a child no longer, and she was about to pay the consequences for her actions.

Her heart beat away the seconds. Her pa closed the door.

He waved toward the fire and the empty chairs. "Have a seat."

Nodding once, Mr. O'Riley crossed the floor and sat without a sound. Cassie's parents locked gazes, and her ma hurried toward the unexpected guest. "Can I get you a cup of coffee?" She waved a hand toward the kitchen. "Or some cider?"

He rubbed his palms together. "No thank you, ma'am."

Her ma sat quietly, stained apron piled on her knees. She patted the chair beside her, and hesitantly Cassie sat. Her pa tugged a chair away from the table and sat at the head. He ran weathered hands over his face. Cassie shifted in her seat. He'd been so angry with her. And for good reason. Yet even through it all, she'd known the love of her father.

"I spoke briefly to Joel Sawyer several days ago." Mr. O'Riley glanced at each face around the table. "And he sent word to Gideon just as you asked."

Her pa nodded slowly and loosened his top button, his neck flushed and ruddy. He palmed the table, clearly hesitant. "I just wish we'd seen. Just wish we'd known." His gaze, filled with disappointment, met hers. A father's broken heart glistened in his eyes.

Cassie touched her locket, twisting it between trembling fingers.

THREE

Lonnie sat on the edge of the blanket, a pair of books tucked in her skirt. Jacob slept on his tummy beneath the broad maple where green leaves played with shades of orange and gold. His pudgy feet poked out from beneath the quilt, and his puckered lips and drooping cheeks told her he would not be waking anytime soon. Her finger skimmed the page of her book, then she flipped back several more.

Gideon sat beside her, their arms nearly touching as he tuned the eight strings of his mandolin. He shifted one leg out and pulled the other toward his chest. He played a nameless tune, a melody that changed with his mood. Though it always retained a beautiful sameness that she had come to love.

"What is that one called?"

"Called?" His hand slid up the fret board, fingers still plucking slowly.

"You've always played that song."

His eyebrows pinched together, and he glanced down at the instrument pressed to his chest. "I dunno."

She couldn't help but smile. "I'd say it's the other part of you." She nodded toward his mandolin. "The sound of that song is as much a piece of you as your voice."

He ducked his head, smile deepening. Green eyes glanced back up to her. "Wanna know a secret?"

She wrapped her hands around her ankles, watching him.

"I never played this song before you."

"No?"

He shook his head. "It's yours and yours alone." When she glanced away, he let out a laugh. "You're blushing, Lonnie O'Riley."

She slapped his leg with the back of her hand. "Well, when you tell a girl something like that, what do you think is supposed to happen?" She pressed her palms to her warm cheeks.

His chuckle deepened, and he tossed back his head. "I need to write you more songs, I see."

After closing her book, she hit it against his arm. The other slipped from her lap.

"What is it that you're doing over there, exactly?"

She held the book, spine out. *"The Art of Soap Making."*

"Don't you already know?"

She tipped her head to the side and nodded, then smoothed her fingers over the tattered binding. "Elsie lent it to me a few weeks ago. There is so much I didn't know. Different ways." She cleared her throat as if she were a teacher in a schoolroom. "See this here?" She held up the page she had been reading. "It talks about makin' soap out of goat's milk. My aunt Sarah had planned on teaching me but never got the chance."

"Ma used to have that on hand now and again."

Lonnie nodded. "Yes. I want to try it next."

"Sounds like you're gonna need a goat."

"What do I need a goat for? I have you —"

He snatched her behind the waist and, setting his mandolin aside, pulled her onto his lap. "Now, now. Here I write you a song and all you can do is make fun of me." He kissed her. Jacob stirred, rubbing his little nose against the blanket before settling his head to the other side.

Lonnie wrapped an arm around Gideon's shoulder and settled her forehead in the

38

crook of his neck.

She heard his whispered "I don't deserve you." She started to speak, but when his sigh likened to contentment, filling her heart to overflowing, she simply kissed his temple. They sat that way until Jacob stirred again, nearly rolling off the blanket. Leaves clung to the folds of his small wool sweater.

Lonnie rose and plucked him up. She lifted her gaze to the distance. "Did you hear something?"

Gideon glanced up the well-worn path. "No" — he blinked — "wait, I do now."

A harness jingled.

Rising on her tiptoes, Lonnie lifted her chin. "Think it's Jebediah?"

Before Gideon could respond, Sugar's brown head bobbed into view. Jebediah waved his walking stick overhead in greeting.

"Any news?" Lonnie asked.

Jacob squirmed in her arms.

"Plenty!" Jebediah called. Mule and cart drew closer. "Enough to keep you busy all evenin'."

Gideon rose, brushed dust from his pants, and followed Lonnie toward the path. The older man dug in the top sack. Paper crinkled as he lifted a thick bundle, puckered with a knot of gray string.

39

"How was your trip?" Lonnie asked.

A tug on the knot and a dozen envelopes filled his hand. He offered the stack to Lonnie. "Good. Real good." He reached for Jacob, kissing the boy's forehead. Jacob tugged on Jebediah's beard as they walked on. "The nights were cold. Colder than I would expect for September."

Lonnie clutched the mass of letters to her chest, shuffling through them as she listened to Jebediah. Her shoulder bumped Gideon's, and he caught a few envelopes that slipped from her grasp.

"So what do we have?" Jebediah asked.

She straightened the pile. "Several for Elsie, one for Gideon." Lonnie held out a crisp envelope. "And two" — she squinted as she read the script on the final letter — "make that *three* for me." Her voice fell at the end, and she rubbed her thumb over a man's scratchy, tangled scrawl.

Four

Lonnie tiptoed up the stairs, Gideon on her heels. She nudged the squeaky door open, holding it so Gideon could duck inside. A sleeping Jacob was pressed to his chest. He laid the boy gently in his cradle, and Lonnie tucked his quilt around him. Used and well loved, the quilt had grown thin and faded from frequent washes and hours spent drying beneath the summer sun.

The sun glinted orange beyond the treetops, forcing Lonnie to light the lamp. She crawled onto the bed. Gideon shoved up the arms of his plaid shirt before following her lead. They lay on their stomachs, pillows tucked between elbows. Two pairs of boots crossed, ankle over ankle, and the dirt-caked soles bumped against the brass footboard.

"Elsie'd have a fit if she saw us like this," Gideon whispered with a wink.

Lonnie lifted a finger to her sly smile.

Without ceremony, she passed Gideon his letter and broke the seal on her own. "We'll read our own first, then we can switch." She nearly buried her nose in the page.

Gideon ripped the end off the envelope, all but tearing his letter. He shook the envelope, and a handful of pages fell free. Lonnie peeked over his hand and saw his ma's writing.

She turned back to her own letter, but when Gideon paused and held his pages out, sliding a callused finger next to a word, Lonnie read it for him. *"Hopefully."*

"Thank you." Gideon continued reading but within a few heartbeats held his letter out again.

Lonnie scrunched up her nose and stared at the crooked scrawl. *"Difficult."*

"Difficult," Gideon repeated, then kissed her shoulder. More than once, either he or Lonnie laughed only to be quieted by the other. One by one, pages fell like autumn leaves to the floor.

"And this one?" Gideon pointed to another line.

"Certain," Lonnie read for him. She pressed her thumb to her lips.

"What's the matter?"

She set down the last page. "I miss them. My ma. My brothers and sisters. They're all growing up. And this is all I have of them." She folded the paper. "It's over so soon."

"Yes, but" — Gideon reached over and tapped a rain-stained envelope — "you have another."

"I do." She accepted the wrinkled envelope. The dry, discolored paper crinkled between her fingertips. The light flickered, the room so quiet she could hear the sizzle of the oil lamp. Slowly, Lonnie unfolded the paper. She felt Gideon, his own letter discarded, watching her scan the one and only page. Scratchy, uneven writing rambled along the top of the yellowed paper. Lonnie's eyebrows pulled together, and her lips sped along silently. She sat up; her hand flew to her mouth.

The bed creaked when Gideon sat up. "What is it?"

She thrust the letter into his hand. "It's from my pa. I've never seen him write a letter a day in his life."

Gideon skimmed the words.

"It's Ma." Shifting to the side, Lonnie gripped the quilt. "She's ill. Who knows how old this is?" She flipped the letter over as if the answer were written on the back. "He doesn't even say what's wrong with her. It could already be too late."

Despite everything that had happened

over the years — the hurt and the heartache — Lonnie's heart flooded with grief and sorrow for her ma.

Lonnie took the letter. "He said she doesn't have much time. What could that mean?" She rose, her mind and heart racing as one. She saw her ma, standing at the stove, red hair coiled into a wiry bun. The same way she'd always been — sad eyes, hopeful words. A woman never fully loved. Lonnie's heart broke anew for her mother even as she thought of her siblings all but fending for themselves. "He said that I should come as soon as I can." The words shook on her lips.

Lonnie handed Gideon the letter again, eager to be rid of it. It took him a minute to read it. He set it on the faded quilt. Her pa's misspelled words leaped off the paper: *Your ma ain't got much time. I feer the worst. Better get yourself home. Don't doddle, Lonnie. She's in a bad way.*

"It may already be too late."

"We'll leave as soon as we can." Gideon squeezed her arm.

She stood motionless, the weight of it all crashing about her shoulders. Gideon knelt, pulled the dusty pack from beneath the bed, and lifted it onto the heap of rumpled bedding.

44

"Lonnie." Her name on his lips pulled her back. "We'll leave at first light. You start packing our things; I'll go ask Jeb if we can take the mule."

"Thank you, Gideon."

He clutched her face in his hands and kissed the top of her head before striding from the room.

FIVE

Sugar stood stone still and blinked in the early morning light while Gideon added the last pack to her burden. He moved around to the other side of the beast, his boots scraping across near-frozen ground. His breath was a white fog. He eyed the rising sun, pleased that no clouds covered the sky. The days would be warm enough. Yet it was the nights that worried him.

Traveling with a baby stirred in him a desire to bind two more blankets atop Sugar's matted rump. Gideon slipped the leather strap through the buckle and yanked it with all his might. The mule nearly stumbled beneath his strength, and he patted her side in apology. Under any other circumstances he would have hesitated to set out this time of year, but not now, not when Lonnie so desperately needed to get home.

As if his thoughts had drawn her, Lonnie

stepped behind him.

"That's the last of it," he said. "Is Jacob ready?"

"He's dressed and fed. Elsie's got him inside."

Gideon pulled his frozen fingers from the final strap and thrust them into his coat pocket. He turned and looked at Lonnie. Her cried-out eyes spoke testament of last night's restless slumber. "All's left is to say good-bye, and we'll be off."

Lonnie led the way back to the house, and he followed close on her heels. The lingering smells of fried bacon and warm syrup greeted them, and Gideon knew he would miss Elsie's cooking. More than that, he would miss everything about this place. This was his home now — his and Lonnie's. It felt strange to be leaving it all behind with Rocky Knob as their destination.

Gideon looked around the snug kitchen and soaked in the familiar sight one last time. Lonnie's quivering sigh hinted that her heart was on the same path. He squeezed her hand. They would return soon. *A few weeks at most.*

Lonnie wished Elsie and Jebediah well, her voice laced with a tremor.

It was a bad time of year to travel back to Rocky Knob, and as much as Gideon

47

wished they could delay their journey until spring, he knew he could never ask it of his wife. He only hoped they were still in time for Lonnie to see her ma. *If not . . .* Gideon shook away the thought as he slid his hat over uncombed hair.

Elsie clutched his cold fingers in her warm hand. "You keep them safe."

Gideon tried to chase away his unease with a smile. "I will." Elsie tucked a small sack that steamed with warm biscuits in the crook of his elbow, and Gideon ducked his head in appreciation. "We'll be home before you know it."

Lonnie's face was flushed and her eyes wide as they stepped toward the door. Gideon wished she had slept better, but her quiet cries hadn't ceased until long after the last bag had been packed. By the time he collapsed into bed after readying their supplies, her face was toward the wall, faint sniffles breaking the late-night silence. He was certain she cried not only for her ma, but also for the lost childhood and the memories that lingered beneath the storm cloud of her pa's roof.

Jebediah threw a chunk of wood in the stove, drawing Gideon back to the present. The older man closed the heavy door with a *clang*.

When silence filled the kitchen, Elsie threw her palms up in the air. "No sense standin' 'round here with long faces." She flapped her hands at them. "Off with you two. The sooner you get on your way, the sooner you'll be comin' home."

The door opened, spiriting in the cool morning air. Gideon took Jacob. With the boy's favorite quilt tucked around him, the red-haired babe blinked sleepily. He was a bundle of warmth with his wool sweater buttoned snugly over two flannel shirts. As Gideon led the way out into the morning, he straightened his son's cap. The brown wool, knit by Elsie's loving hands, covered his downy soft curls, and Gideon watched Lonnie stuff into the pack a small deerskin hat that Jebediah had fashioned for the boy.

Gideon cleared his throat, wishing he could calm his jumpy nerves. *Jacob will be warm enough,* he assured himself. Lifting his eyes to the horizon, he watched the once-orange sky fade to blue as the sun lifted its sleepy head over the clouds. With the mule's rope in hand, Gideon tugged the old animal along. A pile of leaves blew across their trail. Shades of gold, red, and green glittered in the brightening sunshine as their feet found the trail.

Leaving the familiar farmyard, Gideon

only hoped their trip to Rocky Knob would be a short one. "Git on up!" he called and tugged the lead rope. Sugar quickened her pace, and Gideon glanced behind him to make certain Lonnie was close. Turning his attention back to the trail ahead, he eyed the changing landscape. They had yet to travel their first mile, and already the longing for home left him feeling empty.

Having caught up, Lonnie kicked at a pile of leaves, only to have them spray back on her in the breeze. Gideon's smirk widened, and she nearly smiled back. They walked on in comfortable silence. The life that called the forest home provided the song that set their feet in motion: birds chirped as they fluttered about, sending down a chorus of jumbled melodies, and the breeze in the dried leaves overhead whispered faintly as it rippled through the branches. With the forest providing the music, Gideon lifted his face, wishing he knew the words to the mysterious song.

Six

They'd hardly gone an hour when Lonnie froze and stared at the steep ravine. Even though the morning sun hit her back, warming away autumn's chill, her legs went cold.

Gideon shuffled to a standstill, and he exhaled. "Well, I'll be."

Her heart a sudden jumble of emotions, Lonnie glanced away and into her son's sleeping face. He was snuggled in the sling she had fashioned for the journey. Though his nose was red and runny from cold, he seemed peaceful enough. A blue-winged warbler called out, breaking the stillness. Gideon's hand captured hers, and he offered a firm squeeze.

Still, Lonnie shivered. "I don't like this place."

Gideon scanned the trail in front of them, and his gaze met hers. "I don't blame you. It's not my favorite place either."

They stood in silence. The rugged hillside

sloped sharply. Trees that had fallen in years past had tumbled down, only to land in a silent graveyard of rotting bark and limbs at the base of the steep ravine. Their rough edges resurrected the painful memory, but before it could form in her mind, she noticed that, with no rain falling, the place looked different. The man beside her more different still.

Gideon pointed to a stagnant puddle, an emotion pulling his voice tight. "Right there."

Lonnie nodded as the horrid images made their way back to her heart. *The cold. The rain.*

His anger.

"That's where I fell," she whispered.

She had been so tired, so weak. Nothing she could have done or said would have dispelled the anger in Gideon's eyes. Lonnie turned away, yet the grim images were not easily pushed aside. There had been pain. There had been fear. All of it hers.

She heard his words as clearly now as she did that day. "Get up!" he had hollered.

Lonnie shuddered. Even with the passing of time, she could still feel the rain beating against her hair. Feel the slick mud as she crawled toward him, praying for a deliverance. For days he had set a grueling pace, and for days she had tried to keep up. But it had been impossible, and she'd paid the consequences. The memories turned her feet to ice.

When she glanced at Gideon, his eyes were glassy with remembrance, his face pale as if carved from stone. "I'm so sorry that I hurt you. I'm sorry I let myself go that far."

"I know." Lonnie caught hold of his hand and lifted it to her lips. The man who stood before her was nothing like the man from that day.

His fingers slipped from hers.

Undeterred, Lonnie slid her arm in the crook of his elbow. Her husband. Her beloved. She peered up into a pair of eyes the color of a meadow in spring and felt the oppression of that moment slip away.

This was a new day, and her husband, a new man. She patted his forearm. "I can think of one good thing," Lonnie said, crinkling her nose. "That's where Jebediah almost shot you." She leaned her head against Gideon's shoulder. "Now there's a memory that brings a smile to my face."

His deep laugh awakened a spring inside him, and she felt her cold chills chased away.

"Thanks!" He gave her that grin. "I'm glad at least somethin' about this place makes you smile."

"Oh, I assure you it does. Though" — Lonnie tilted her head to the side and stared up at Gideon — "I don't remember it well. Remind me. What was that look on your face again?"

"Uh . . . utter terror. And now you're just hurtin' my feelings." He stifled another laugh. "I deserved that one."

Lonnie glanced from side to side but knew there was no other way around. "Well," she began. "In the name of reconciliation, Mr. O'Riley" — she nodded toward the trail they were bound to walk — "would you mind helping me downhill this time?"

Gideon held his arm out for Lonnie to take once more. "It would be my pleasure, Mrs. O'Riley."

Cassie peeled a chunk of bark from a red oak and flicked it toward the water. Her thoughts, having strayed from her chores, had carried her bare feet to the edge of the creek. The water was low this time of year, but enough flowed through the narrow gully to carry the piece of bark over a moss-coated rock and away. She sank to her knees, draped an arm across her lap, and grazed fingertips through the icy water.

Jack called her name from the house, his voice distant. Cassie knew supper was on, but she ignored him. She wasn't hungry. Her soaked hem swirled in the water, and she stumbled back. "For heaven's sake." She bent over and wrung out the blue and white calico that, like most things she owned, had more frays than trimmings.

"Cassie!" Jack hollered again. "Supper's ready. Ma wants you *now*!"

"Comin'!" she hollered back. Her voice startled a red-breasted woodpecker, and it rushed from tree to tree.

She watched Jack return to the house. At sixteen, he was her younger brother by six years. As if the age difference mattered not, he stood a head taller than she was. His shoulders, though wiry, were nearly as broad as Eli's.

Her feet clung to the damp hillside as she staggered up the creek bank, trying to keep her wet hem from dragging in the dirt. Despite her efforts, her ma would wonder what she got herself into. Cassie should have been setting the table, but she had slipped out, leaving the task to her younger sister, Libby. It was the third time that week.

A dozen brown hens swarmed around her ankles, and she gently kicked at them. "Off you go, now. I ain't got nothin' for you."

The ornery chickens followed her toward the house in a chorus of clucking, and Cassie stumbled around them as she tried to keep from stepping on feathers and wings.

Weathered boards creaked underfoot as she climbed the three porch steps. Hattie, the old basset hound, lifted her droopy face. Knowing she had but a moment to spare, Cassie quickly scratched the dog between the ears. Her ma peeked through the window and waved her inside. Cassie slipped into the warm house.

"Where have you been?" Libby groaned as she took her place at the table beside Jack. She glared at Cassie and tucked a strand of hair behind her mouselike ear.

"I wasn't gone that long." Cassie stepped toward the oven. She took the heavy pot her mother offered her and set it in the center of the table.

"Is something burning?" Samuel asked, tipping his chair back lazily.

Cassie hurried back to the oven and, with a crumpled dishtowel in one hand, lifted a pan of hot biscuits from the oven.

"Cassie's baking again." Samuel elbowed Eli and the two chuckled. "This should be good."

She fought the urge to fling a biscuit at them. They'd probably just eat it anyway. The faint burnt smell tickled her nose. She quickly moved the hard biscuits to a bowl, scalding her fingertips.

Her pa cast her a warning glance before he took his seat. "Now that we're all assembled," he said solemnly.

"Sorry, Pa." Supper had been stalled, and it was her fault.

"Must you really try his patience time and time again?" her ma whispered in passing. Her blue eyes seemed weary. "Not to mention my own."

Cassie slid into her seat on the long bench. Seeing there wasn't much cider, she quickly filled her cup and set the drained pot aside. The tin warmed her hand.

Beside her, Jack turned his empty cup in his hand. "Thanks a lot," he said for her ears alone.

She threw him a sharp look that kept him from saying more. She clasped her sister's hand and bowed her head lower than normal as if to draw some goodness from the deed.

Her pa blessed the meal, finishing with an amen and a twist of the kerosene lamp. The room brightened. Cassie's mind wandered to where she had left it at the creek. Gideon.

The same warmth puddled in her chest. Might he truly return to Rocky Knob? She'd heard it from Mr. O'Riley that Mr.

Sawyer had sent his daughter word, bidding both Lonnie and Gideon home. A shiver coursed through her at the thought of Gideon's broad frame darkening their steps. Her heart suddenly demanded her attention. She pressed her hand there, pulse quickening.

Her father spoke in hushed tones, but she heard not a word.

Cassie chewed the inside of her cheek. She lifted her cup and her eyes as one, glancing at the doorway as if Gideon would fill it at any moment. Her heart misbehaved again. She took a few sips of cider, nearly scalding her tongue. She was certain he wouldn't come. Certain.

"Cassie," her ma said. "Would you please pass the biscuits to the rest of us?" Mary dropped a scoop of creamed spinach on her plate and slid the pot toward Eli.

Cassie mindlessly lifted the bowl to her pa. Dropping her hands in her lap, she fiddled with her napkin. Gideon had once said he loved her. Not once. Many times. She smeared honey butter over a biscuit half and licked her finger clean before setting her knife across her plate. If he were to return, there would be many questions about their past. Questions that would need answers. Cassie felt her father's heavy gaze.

She wondered if his thoughts mirrored her own.

Her heart somersaulted. When Libby arched an eyebrow, Cassie pressed fingertips to her warming cheeks, glad her innocent sister did not know the worst of it.

SEVEN

"Guess we've run out of luck," Gideon yelled as he scrambled for his coat. They'd traveled for three days without a drop of rain. But now the clouds had broken loose.

Lonnie tugged her shawl over her head and tried to cover both herself and the baby. The rain fell in sheets. Sugar stumbled sideways. Gideon held the mule's harness with one hand while thrusting his other arm through the sleeve of his coat.

"Easy, girl," he said, trying to keep his voice low enough to avoid startling the beast, yet loud enough to carry over the downpour.

"What do we do?" Lonnie pulled her shawl tighter, but water dripped down her arm. A wide-eyed Jacob clung to her. His tiny face was scrunched with concern.

"I don't know," Gideon admitted. He'd never traveled with a baby before.

When a gust of wind swept through the

pass, he clutched his hat to his head. "What do you want to do?" he hollered as the rain whipped past them. Droplets stung his face, and he shielded Jacob's eyes.

Tugging the sling to make sure it was tight, Lonnie held Jacob close. Her expression was torn.

Gideon released his hat and used his free hand to help her wrap the drenched wool over the baby. His eyes met Lonnie's, and his voice rose over the rain. "Do you want to stop?"

When she shook her head, a ribbon of damp hair swung from side to side, only to cling to her cheek when she stilled. Her gaze narrowed. "I want to get home to my mother."

Nodding, Gideon surveyed their surroundings. The woods were thin, and with the oaks having lost most of their leaves, there wasn't much brush or bramble — no shelter.

Frustrated, he lifted his shoulders. "We'll keep moving and keep a lookout for cover in case this gets worse."

Lonnie peeled her soaked shawl away from her wet skin and draped the matted mess over Sugar's back. Kicking himself for not having offered it sooner, Gideon tore off his coat and handed it to her.

She shook her head, but he held up a hand. "Take it. It's oilcloth. It will keep you both dry. I'm already soaked."

If Lonnie could keep Jacob quiet and comfortable, they would survive the day. The trail, though not steep, was slick. Gideon's boots squished in the mud, and more than once, he clutched Sugar's harness.

"Watch your step," he called over his shoulder.

Turning around, he held his breath as Lonnie stumbled forward. Jacob jostled in her grasp, but she held him fast and did her best to keep Gideon's coat over the child's damp curls.

"I'm all right." She staggered toward him. "Keep going."

Lonnie ran her hand beneath her nose and sniffed. Her stockings hung loose around her ankles, and the hem of her dress was caked in mud.

Jacob's nose and cheeks were raw from cold. He was soaked through.

"I think I see something. Let me take Jacob." They traded one tired mule for a crying, wet baby, and Gideon ducked through an opening in the trees.

The ground, once firm beneath his heavy boots, suddenly gave way in a shower of wet leaves. Gideon gritted his teeth and clutched his son to his chest. He was falling, and one thought raced through his mind: Jacob was in his arms.

Time seemed to pass slowly. Somewhere in the distance, Lonnie screamed.

Then, with a *crack,* he struck the ground and rolled. Pain shot like a hot bullet through his shoulder. Air left his lungs. Jacob's shrill wails echoed in his ears. Gideon held the boy as tight as he could, doing all in his might to keep from crushing the baby beneath his own weight as he rolled down the muddy embankment. Finally, his body stilled. Jacob's cries faded until Gideon heard nothing at all.

"Gideon." Lonnie's voice was faint and far away.

Pain ripped through his arm as he rolled onto his back.

"Gideon!" she called again. His name, now louder, rang in his ears.

He opened one eye, then the other. He blinked against the rain that fell on his face and saw Lonnie leaning over him, her wet braid dangling toward him. "Gid," she cried, shaking him. "Are you all right?"

Struggling to sit up, he felt Lonnie's arm slip behind him and hoist him forward. Gideon shook his head and tried to fit the pieces together in his mind. "Where's Jacob?"

"He's here. He's fine." Lonnie lifted the boy from her lap. "He might get a few bruises, but he's fine."

Gideon stared at his son. He could not tell the tears from the rain, but under the circumstances, at least the boy could offer him that. Gideon felt a wave of relief wash over him.

"How long was I out?"

"Just a few moments." Still on her knees, Lonnie inched her way closer.

"I'm just glad Jacob's not hurt." Gideon leaned forward and gasped. He grabbed his shoulder as pain thundered through his back and down into his hand.

"But you are." Lonnie lifted his arm into her lap. "How bad does it hurt?"

Gideon grimaced and she pursed her lips. Lonnie passed her hands over the bones of his wrist, and he winced.

"I think it's just a sprain." Gideon pulled his wrist into his lap. "My shoulder's what really hurts. I think it might be out of the socket."

Lonnie held a hand to her mouth. "What do we do?"

He peered down at his mud-soaked shirt and let his breath out in a gush. "Pop it back in." He looked at his young wife but knew the answer before he spoke. "Do you know how?"

Her face seemed to pale, and she shook her head. Scooting Jacob onto his leg, Lonnie rose to her feet. "Let me see what I have."

Gideon heard fabric tear, and she sank back at his side, a remnant of ivory cloth in her grasp. Gently lifting his elbow, she slipped the portion of fabric beneath his arm.

He winced but opened one eye long enough to survey the makeshift sling. "That looks like my work shirt."

"It was." She yanked the ends in a snug knot and slipped it over his head where it draped securely around his neck. "How's that?"

"It helps," Gideon lied as he gritted his teeth.

Lonnie pursed her mouth. "I don't know what else to do until we can get some help."

When she looked up at him, worry and grief seemed to stretch in the silence between them.

The rain was slowing. Lonnie's voice was soft but strong. "We need to get you out of here."

As the rain fell in a weak drizzle, she

helped him stand. He tried to put as little of his weight as possible on her. Finally finding his feet, he rose and looked down on her damp hair. She was soaked to the skin. Jacob too. And with no prospect of shelter or a fire. He touched the small of her back, wishing with all that was in him that he could wrap them in warmth and safety.

EIGHT

Gideon paused and wiped sweat from his brow. He studied the trail ahead. The impossible trail ahead. In too much pain to get comfortable on the hard ground, he had spent the night keeping a watchful eye on Lonnie and Jacob. They'd risen with the sun and worked their way out of a shallow meadow. Now the trail rose. It narrowed.

Lonnie turned, concern etched in her face. "You're in pain." It wasn't a question.

Gideon forced himself to walk on. "We're almost there. Another day at most." If they made good time, he and Lonnie would be knocking on Joel's door by nightfall. Another bead of sweat dripped down his forehead.

As if it had a life of its own, a gnarled root tangled against his boot, and Gideon stumbled forward. He sank to his knees. His good arm flew forward, and his palm pressed into the dirt. Before Lonnie could turn, he struggled to his feet. A sharp pain seized his shoulder. Gideon gasped, unable to go another step.

Glancing around, he wiped his filthy palm on his pants. The terrain looked more familiar with each hour that passed. He scanned both sides of the damp road, hoping to see a cabin behind the trees. Wasn't there someone who could help them?

"There." Lonnie pointed. She turned, her face bright.

Gideon glanced through the trees and spotted a two-story building in the distance. He quickened his pace and waved for her to follow. As he burst through the trees, a small pond came into view, and the forest opened. Gideon tilted his head back and sent up a quick prayer of thanks. Cover Mill. As sure as he knew the familiar lines of his pa's farm, he knew that mill, and as he caught sight of the large water-wheel turning, knew there were workers inside. Workers who could help him.

Slowing, Gideon turned to Lonnie. "Wait here."

"Here?"

"Please." He winced and tugged on the edge of his coat. "I don't want you to have to see this."

A moment's hesitation hung on her parted

lips, then she smoothed them into a line. "I'll wait here." But her voice was unsteady.

He slid his hand into the base of her hair, pulling her close and kissing her forehead. "I'll be right back."

A silent prayer in her eyes, she nodded. He strode off, the water-wheel gushing louder with each step that drew him closer. The large door was sealed shut. He tugged on the handle. Pain shot down his spine, so severe that in an instant his back was damp. With a grunt and a pain that soured his gut, he pulled on the door. It rolled open, yawning a gap just large enough to duck through.

"Hello?" he called. The air was so thick with ground corn, he could taste it. A fine powder glistened in a stream of light from an overhead window. A dozen kerosene lamps lined the walls, their glass dusty. The gears squeaked and thudded — a massive groan, as if he stood inside the belly of a beast.

Two men stepped from a back room, and Gideon nodded in their direction.

"Can we help you, son?" The nearest man tugged on his gray beard, burly arms thick and threaded until they vanished beneath the rolled-back cuffs of his shirt.

Gideon touched his shoulder and, in the space of a few words, explained his request.

The older man nodded, eying his shoulder as if he could see through the soiled fabric.

"Let's see what we can do." He nodded toward a dark-haired man with caterpillars for eyebrows, who turned up the light of the nearest lantern. "I've seen it done a time or two before."

Gideon drew in a controlled breath. *All right, then.* His shirt clung like a second skin.

The dark-haired man spoke up. "I've got a bottle of brandy. Lemme grab it." Crouching, he lunged an arm into a low cupboard.

"No."

"You're gonna want something to help." He pulled out a bottle, turning it in his broad palm. The amber liquid sloshed inside the glass. He seemed to size Gideon up in one blink. His dark eyes were sober. "Trust me."

The memory of the taste flooded Gideon. His mouth grew moist. Lusty. The temptation lured him. This was going to hurt, and he knew it. When he was a boy, his pa had helped a neighbor after a horse accident. Trace Dale had downed half a quart of moonshine an hour before, and even then, his pa had walked away with a black eye. Swallowing hard, Gideon shook his head. Before he could change his mind, he motioned toward the door. "If it's all the same, my wife's out there waitin'. I'd be happy just to get this over with."

Lonnie sat in the dry grass. With her back to the sun and Jacob in her lap, she glanced at the mill door, certain she'd heard voices. One man called out to another; their words puddled beneath the water rushing over the great wheel. Jacob sat motionless in her lap, and Lonnie was certain he could feel her heart thundering against his small back.

Suddenly, Gideon shouted. Another man cursed. A shudder galloped along her spine, her heart racing. Someone hollered back — his tone as taut as a clothesline. Silence fell.

Water rushed over the wheel.

Her heart pounded faster than the seconds passed, and then the door slid open. Gideon stumbled forward. He paused long enough to look at her, then shuffled out. Two men emerged, faces drawn.

She rose.

Sweat glistened on Gideon's pale face.

"Gid?"

"He'll be fine, ma'am," one man interjected. "We set the shoulder." He exchanged glances with his partner. "If he takes it easy, it should heal up."

Gideon slowly bobbed his head. "You boys better get back to work. I've taken up enough of your day."

The men tipped their hats and wished them well. Circling back to the open door, they disappeared inside the shadowy building.

Lonnie touched Gideon's arm. "Are you all right?"

He grimaced. "You heard that, didn't you?"

She placed an unsteady hand against his back and hoped her voice was lighter than her heart. "They wrapped it well for you. And the one man said it should heal."

When Gideon moved, he winced. He moistened dry lips and reached for her hand with his other arm. Lonnie held tight.

Rocky Knob unfolded around them as they walked, the sights returning like long-forgotten memories. Still, Lonnie did not feel at ease. They were so close, yet so far from the place she felt safest. In summer, the meadow to the east would be thick with green foliage and crowned with yellow wildflowers. As if from a distant dream, their surroundings became more and more familiar.

Houses poked out through the trees. Their stout log frames were simply fashioned but strongly built. Though she could not see all the weathered shanties from the pathway, she knew the turns and the moss-laced rocks and trees that marked each property. She knew them each by name. Cole. Miller. She knew their horses. Their children.

Soon they would have a roof over their heads. As if their thoughts were born of the same desire, Gideon quickened his pace and tugged Sugar's rope. The mule followed close behind as if she too were eager for their journey to draw to an end.

When Gideon glanced back and pointed to the distance, Lonnie knew they shared the same thought. *Tom Baker's cabin.* They had reached the hollow she'd grown up in.

Almost there.

Thin logs, grayed by years of sun and snow, sat atop one another, forming the humble cabin. Smoke rose from the chimney, and the breeze carried the smell of frying bacon. The path rose. Their steps rose with it. With a sleeping Jacob in her grasp, Lonnie strained with the steep incline. It seemed to take all Gideon's strength to tug the mule along.

"Git on up!" he urged, but the creature kept her own pace. She would not be rushed, and after a few steps, Gideon gave up. Night was nearing, and by the time they had scaled the hill and stood at the base of Sawyer land, all that welcomed them was a lone candle flickering in a distant window.

Lonnie's chest heaved, and she glanced back as Gideon struggled to catch up. She switched Jacob to her other side and straightened his knit cap. "See," she whispered. "That's your grandma and grandpa's cabin."

Jacob leaned his head on her shoulder.

Finally reaching them, Gideon stopped. She looked up at him and wondered if the fading light cloaked the unshed tears in her eyes. "I'm frightened."

Gideon kissed the top of her head. He spoke softly against her hair. "I know."

"I don't want to see my pa."

Gideon nodded. "You'll be able to see Addie." He squeezed her hand. "Sid and Oliver too. And I'll be with you."

Lonnie slowly bobbed her head and swiped at her eyes. "You can settle Sugar over there." She pointed to the barn.

Gideon led the mule where she pointed, and with nothing more than moonlight shining through a pair of small windows, he ducked beneath the low doorway. Lonnie followed. He urged Sugar inside, made quick work of filling a feed bag with oats, and slid it over Sugar's long face. As quick as he could, he unstrapped the bedroll and set it aside. Lonnie helped him drape his mandolin in its sack over his good shoulder. He gripped their packs in his free hand and followed her toward the house. The voices drew Lonnie up the steps. She strained to listen. Addie's high chatter rose among the others, then Oliver's laugh. Lonnie would know that guffaw anywhere — the hearty laugh deeper than she remembered.

Her pa's slow drawl drowned them out. Her back stiffened. She heard Gideon's feet slow. Chills crept down her spine. Then the night air carried the sound of her ma's gentle voice, and the joy drew her forward.

"Ma," Lonnie breathed. Her feet flitted across the dark ground. She bounded up the steps, and before Gideon could catch up with her, she caught hold of the latch and tugged the door open.

NINE

Lonnie panted breathlessly in the doorway. Wide eyes stared at her. She scanned each face but landed on one in particular.

"Ma," she breathed. She dashed toward the rocking chair and, before the woman could stand, sank at her side. Lonnie's weather-beaten skirts billowed around her.

With Jacob pressed between them, Lonnie dropped her head into her mother's lap and cried. "Ma, I thought I might have been too late."

A trembling hand touched her hair.

"When I got Pa's letter that you were ill . . ."

Her mother lifted her face and searched her eyes. A secret seemed to fold itself into the lines around her mouth. "I . . . I ain't hardly been sick a day in my life." But her voice shook strangely, eyes wide.

Lonnie knew that look. Something was wrong.

Her ma worried a few strands of her auburn bun back into place with knobby fingers. Tears glistened in the woman's small eyes. "I sure . . . sure am glad to see you." Her voice wavered with heartache. She glanced at Jacob, and her expression was torn between yearning and worry. She breathed the boy's name, though the word was no more than a whisper. As if it were forbidden.

Lonnie squeezed Jacob tighter, chills covering her skin. "Would you . . . would you like to hold him?"

Maggie reached out and touched Jacob's hand with unsteady fingers. She pulled back quickly, her eyes darting past Lonnie. "I . . . I . . ."

Boots sounded on the steps, and Lonnie glanced back to see Gideon fill the doorway, keeping his wrapped arm clear of the jamb. His rosy cheeks were a welcome change from the pale demeanor he'd had when they left the mill only a few hours ago. Gideon dropped his pack.

She turned back to her ma. "Where's Pa?" Lonnie blurted, unease settling about her shoulders like an unwanted blanket. "Why did he send me that letter? He said you were ill." She rose, heat covering her cheeks. "It was all a lie, wasn't it?"

Eyes wide, her ma started to speak.

"Keep your mouth shut, Maggie." Joel's voice was as cool as ever.

The room fell silent. Gazes shifted to the corner of the room. It was then that she turned and faced him. He sat motionless in the shadows. Smoke rose in a curl from his smoldering pipe. He shook out the match.

"Lonnie," he murmured flatly. His boots were propped up on a stool, and his chair, balanced on two legs, tilted back and forth. "Glad you're home." His chair tipped forward. His feet hit the floor with a hollow *thud,* bringing his face into the firelight.

Gideon stepped forward. "Someone wanna tell us what's going on?"

Her pa's brows dipped. "Didn't your ma ever teach you not to speak until spoken to?" A puff of smoke escaped his thin lips.

Gideon tipped his chin, eyes hard.

Lonnie stared at her pa — his chicken-scratch scrawl as fresh in her mind as the day she had read it. *Your ma ain't got much time. Better get yourself home.*

"I wondered how long it would take you two to show up." His voice was eerily calm.

The blood that pulsed through Lonnie's veins thinned like a widow's web.

Using his good arm, Gideon pulled the door closed with a soft *click.* "You look well,

Maggie."

A small hand brushed Lonnie's hip, and she turned to see Addie standing behind her. The little girl's coffee-colored hair had grown longer, and two thin pigtails landed in curls atop her shoulders. Lonnie squeezed her sister, her heart warming. "I thought this day would never come," she whispered. Then Lonnie looked up at her ma — as healthy as she'd ever seen her.

Her pa's chair creaked as he rose. "What happened to you?" he asked Gideon flatly.

Without responding, Gideon touched his arm still wrapped in the sling.

Her pa snorted and drug his chair across the floor, shoving it against the table. "That's a shame." He reached for his hat, forcing Gideon to take a step sideways. Gideon lifted his chin, eying the man. Joel returned the stare as he slid his hat over graying hair.

"Where are you going?" Maggie asked.

"I've got some business to attend to. I won't be long."

Her ma's eyebrows rose. "Now? At this hour?"

"It ain't half-past six." Her pa tossed his pipe on the mantel next to the clock. "I won't be gone but a little while."

Her ma shook her head, but before she

could say more, he grabbed his coat and paused only long enough for Gideon to step out of his way. Throwing on his coat, his boots scuffed over the threshold, and he disappeared into the night.

Gideon glanced at Lonnie, then he forced a smile in Maggie's direction. "I see you've met our Jacob."

"Yes." Her ma made no move toward the baby. The single word hung in the balance, the silence deafening. When the sound of Joel's steps faded, Maggie reached for the child, squeezing his hand with a muted tenderness. A smile lifted one side of her mouth. She brushed her finger down his round little cheek. A noise made her jump, and she pulled away.

Lonnie held Jacob tighter. The clock on the mantel chimed, reminding Lonnie just how long the day had been. Knowing that all eyes were on her, she forced a smile as she removed his cap. "He'll be happy to sleep in a real bed tonight."

Her ma shook out her apron. "Yes." She glanced around the tiny space. "Now to make up some beds for the night."

"Please don't go to any trouble for us. Gid and I don't mind stayin' in the lean-to. Oh, but Sid and Oliver are in there."

"Take it." Oliver quipped. "We'll sleep in

the barn." He elbowed his brother mischievously. "We promise not to try and burn it down this time."

Their ma shook her head, but she smiled.

"Thanks, you two." Lonnie looked back at her ma. "It's all settled, then? Gid and I will sleep in the lean-to."

Maggie touched her own cheek, pressing pale fingertips into her aging skin. All humor faded away. "Your pa won't like that."

"What are you talking about?"

Maggie pursed her lips, a thousand unspoken words in her brown eyes. "He just won't like it."

Lonnie straightened her shoulders. "Well, he's just gonna have to live with it."

TEN

Water dripped from the eaves, and Gideon stared up at the soggy lean-to boards. No sunrise slipped through the cracks of the faded gray wood that was dark with moisture. Not this morning. He ran a hand over his face, trying to drive away the sleepiness, but it was no use. He was exhausted. And sleep had been scarce the night before.

As much as Gideon had wanted to collapse onto the cornhusk mattress and lay aside the weariness of the journey, Joel Sawyer's abrupt departure had wedged a splinter of worry in his gut. But why, he didn't know. All he knew was that Joel would scarcely look him in the eye. *That* he expected. But what he didn't expect was the way Maggie looked at Jacob. With hesitation. Fear almost.

He inhaled slowly, the musty damp air filling his lungs. Lonnie lay curled on her side beside him, her hand tucked beneath her cheek. Jacob slept between them, his ginger curls askew.

Not wanting to get up, Gideon lay back down on the cornhusk mattress and stared at the roof. His eyes landed on a small crack. Droplets of water pooled and then ran down the angle of the slanted ceiling to drip into a bucket on the floor. The sound reminded him of his childhood.

He pulled the quilt closer to his face and shivered against the cold.

Lonnie's quaint voice murmured through the blankets. "You asleep?"

"No. Did I wake you?"

"Sort of." She rolled over to face him. Her ears were red with cold, and she pulled the blanket up to her chin. "But that's all right. I should get up anyway and help Ma with breakfast."

Rain flicked off the tin roof. Another sound that reminded him of home.

Gideon realized just how long it had been since he'd last seen his folks. Perhaps he'd be able to pay them a visit. He was certain they would be pleased to see Jacob. Somebody had to be.

As Lonnie lay there watching him, Gideon voiced his idea.

"I'd be happy to," she said, truly sounding glad. "We can leave as soon as breakfast is over and —"

Gideon pressed a finger to her lips. Her eyes widened.

"Do you hear that?" He moved his hand away, curling the end of her braid around his finger.

She glanced over, then shrugged. "I don't hear anything."

He sat up, inviting a waft of cool air beneath the blankets. "There it is again. I hear horses."

Lonnie rolled her eyes playfully. "Well, there's something out of the ordinary."

"No." Gideon's feet fell to the floor. "Sounds like a wagon."

"Pa doesn't have a wagon. Maybe someone's come to visit. Maybe it's your folks." She sat up.

He doubted it.

Gideon jumped out of bed and struggled into his pants. "You always assume the best about people." He winked at her, liking the way her freckled blush scattered his worry.

Using his good arm, he carelessly stuffed his shirt into his pants and yanked his belt tight, wincing when pain ripped through his shoulder. He struggled to smooth the collar, and when he fumbled with his cuffs, Lonnie hopped up and buttoned them.

"I better hurry." With her nightgown

twisted around her torso, she was a jumble of knobby arms and legs as she scrambled to get dressed herself.

Giving her a wedge of space, Gideon pushed past the lean-to door. It fell closed behind him. Maggie emerged from the bedroom. She was dressed and combed, her striped apron already dusted with flour. She peered out the window, then studied him for several breaths. Her eyes softened. Her expression, so different from the night before, was almost apologetic.

"Mornin'." Gideon tipped an imaginary hat. "Is it my folks?" He pulled the door open.

"No . . . it's Reverend Gardner." She studied him with an unveiled sorrow so intense that a cold fog settled in his chest.

From the open doorway, Gideon watched Joel greet the stout reverend with a two-handed shake.

Joel's voice carried up the stairs. "They're here."

Gideon stepped back, but the rickety porch squeaked, and both men glanced up at him.

Joel motioned to the man beside him. "You remember Reverend Gardner."

The man had married him and Lonnie. "Yessir."

The reverend followed Joel toward the house.

"Nice to see you again, Gideon." His smile seemed forced.

They scaled the steps, and Gideon made room for them to enter. The reverend closed the door with a soft *thud.* He turned his black hat, fingers twitching as they traced around the rim.

"And the others?" Joel blurted.

Reverend Gardner glanced at Gideon. "On . . . on their way." His eyes fell to the floor. "Paid them a visit early this morning." Bushy eyebrows fell to slants. "A little too early if you ask me, but as you know, the matter is most" — he glanced at Gideon again — "urgent."

Gideon's jaw flexed. "Someone wanna tell me what's goin' on?"

Lonnie emerged from the lean-to, eyes bright. "What's the matter?"

Joel slapped his hands together. "Now that we're all assembled" — his palms swished as he smoothed them back and forth — "perhaps you'd like to begin?" He waved a hand toward Reverend Gardner, who shook his head so fast, his insipid cheeks bobbled back and forth.

"Though I don't wish to be difficult, my colleague, uh, made the discovery, and I feel it might be best to leave it up to him to" — the reverend gulped and moistened pasty lips — "break the news."

A tight smile lifted Joel's mouth. "Suit yourself. Coffee?" He pulled a chair out.

The reverend settled himself at the table. "Please."

Gideon felt Lonnie step beside him.

"Pa?" she asked. "What's the matter? What news?"

"By and by, Lonnie. See to the reverend's coffee, please."

Lonnie moved to the coffeepot, then held it close. She made no move to serve them, and Joel made no move to reach for it. "I don't know what you're up to, but I will not stand here another moment and let you play your game." Her voice, though soft, was strong. "I'm not afraid of you anymore."

His expression hardened.

Gideon shifted. He rolled his bad shoulder, and a burn shot through his back. Still, he'd use it if it came to that. If Joel even lifted one finger to her . . .

Joel stared at Lonnie. Neither moved. Finally he flicked his head toward the table as if she hadn't spoken. "The reverend's ready for his coffee."

He sat in his chair. He smiled at the reverend. A sickening rose in Gideon's throat. As if she hadn't noticed the exchange, Maggie followed behind with a plate of biscuits.

"Help yourselves, gentlemen." She stepped toward the lean-to. "Lonnie, I think Jacob might be stirring. You stay. I'll see to him."

The reverend sipped his coffee. Then, at the sound of a wagon approaching, his cup rattled to a halt on the table in front of him. His eyes darted toward the ceiling as if sending up a silent prayer. "Must be them now."

"Must be who?" Gideon slammed his palm on the table. The reverend jumped.

Joel opened the front door and smiled toward Gideon. "Reverend Brown. From the church in Tuggle Gap. You might know him."

Gideon felt air leave his chest.

"And Henry Allan." Joel's gruff voice turned smooth and cool. "Surely you remember him. He has a daughter about your age. Cassie." His tone curdled. "Pretty thing."

When Lonnie's gaze flashed to him, Gideon dry swallowed. Heat covered his skin. He stepped away from the fire but found no relief. Cassie. Each noise from outside echoed in his ears, pounding inside his mind. The horses stilled. Voices murmured. Footsteps sounded on the stairs. His world shrank to a pinhole as his heart pounded out a terrifying cadence.

Lonnie's shoulder pressed his as she whispered, "Gideon, what's going on?"

His mouth too dry to speak, he merely shook his head. The door swung open, and a waft of cool air filled the room, seeming to seep into his bones.

Reverend Brown loomed in the doorway as dark and uninviting as a nightmare. Cassie slipped into the room and lowered her shawl from her shoulders and damp hair.

Her eyes found his. The vibrant blue snapping with that familiar mischief he knew well. Too well. Regret collided into his chest, nearly choking off his air.

Lonnie stared as the visitors filled the tiny room. She recognized Mr. Allan and his daughter Cassie. But she had never seen the new reverend before. He was taller than any man she'd ever seen. Dark bushy eyebrows framed deeply sunken eyes as brown as the mud on his massive boots. Rain dripped from his black hat. He removed it, creating a small puddle on the rough boards beneath him.

Her ma handed Jacob to Addie, who carried him over to a basket of toys. Quickly, she took the reverend's wet things and laid them over a chair near the fire along with all the others. He gave her a curt nod, then glanced at Gideon, eyes piercing.

Lonnie absorbed the exchange.

She slipped her palm inside her husband's and was surprised to feel that his hands were colder than the air outside. She studied him, frightened by what she saw. His eyes glanced from one guest to another before landing on Cassie. Lonnie stared in disbelief when their gazes locked and held. His chest heaved, his breathing heavy. The room fell silent. Gideon simply stared at the bright-eyed girl.

Lonnie squeezed his hand. *Gid?*

Reverend Gardner cleared his throat. "As I was saying earlier, it's time we came to the matter at hand."

No one moved. No one sat. Each person loomed in a crooked circle inside the four walls of the small house. She shifted uncomfortably.

The stout man continued. "Reverend Brown, would you care to explain the, uh, situation?"

Reverend Brown cleared his throat, and then his voice boomed over his fellow clergyman's. "Yes, I'd be happy to."

His eyebrows dropped, and he frowned at Gideon.

The reverend pressed his hands together, interlocked his fingers, and tucked them beneath his chin. "It has come to my attention by Reverend Gardner that you" — he nodded in Lonnie's direction — "are married to this man here" — he turned to Gideon, his voice sharp — "Mr. O'Riley."

Lonnie fought the tremor in her voice. "Yessir."

The reverend's glare narrowed. "And you believe your marriage to be legal and binding in the eyes of the church . . . and of God?"

Her mouth was so dry, Lonnie could scarcely swallow. "Yes, of course." Her voice came out weak.

He grunted, clearly not surprised by her response. "Well," he said flatly. "Therein lies the problem."

Problem? Lonnie stepped closer to Gideon, afraid of what the man would say next. Fingers that had been so cold now smothered her hand in heat. Startled, she pulled away.

Reverend Gardner pressed his palms together and pointed two fingers at Gideon. He spoke up, his voice stronger than before. "Because, as Mr. O'Riley very well knows, this young woman, here" — his hands opened, palms turned toward Cassie — "Miss Allan, believes *herself* to be legally bound to Gideon O'Riley in the eyes of the church and of God."

Lonnie's jaw dropped. "How so?" she breathed, not intending to speak aloud.

The reverend seemed to grow taller as he gripped the back of a chair. "Bound by marriage."

Lonnie gasped. Gideon's chin fell to his chest. An ache fanned through her. She looked at Cassie. The young woman avoided her gaze, looking instead on Gideon. The eagerness in her eyes was a declaration that she longed for his response.

It cannot be. Lonnie shook her head. "What proof do you —"

Reverend Brown's voice boomed above hers. "We have more than what proof we need, Miss *Sawyer.*"

Sawyer. The name stung worse than a slap in the face.

"I have the marriage contract signed by myself, Mr. O'Riley, Cassie Allan, and the two witnesses. I can read you *their* names as well if you like, Miss Sawyer." Reverend Brown patted his coat pocket, and the sound of crinkled paper stunned her into silence.

When Gideon glanced at her, regret flooded his eyes. He directed his words at Reverend Brown. "Cassie wanted to end it. It was all done away with." He glanced at Cassie. "Right?"

Reverend Brown's face colored. " 'Done away with' it most certainly was not!" Each word exploded like a rifle shot from his thick lips. His cheeks shuddered as he shook his head. "You were unwise to have made such assumptions. If such proof exists, it never made its way to the court."

Shadows darkened Gideon's eyes. "Cassie, you saw to it. You told me you —"

"Don't you raise your voice to my daughter." Mr. Allan stepped forward. "She's done nothing wrong."

Cassie ran a hand up her arm, her expression brave. Bold. She stared at Gideon without blinking.

Lonnie feared her knees would buckle.

With the back of her hand, Cassie brushed damp tendrils away from her forehead, her pale cheeks flushed and rosy. Cassie Allan had meant nothing to Lonnie in the past, but now, staring at the girl with her spine as straight as a ship's mast and rosebud lips pinker than wild roses, Lonnie felt sick.

"Sirs," Maggie interjected as she stepped forward. She bounced a wide-eyed Jacob.

Charlotte clung to her skirt. "Perhaps there might be a better place to discuss all this." Her soft voice spread over the room like a soothing balm.

Joel seemed to study her a moment, his eyes shifting over the children who watched with curious stares. "We'll gather this evening, at the home of Mr. Allan. Or at the church. Anyone have any objections to that?"

"The church would be best." Reverend Gardner motioned toward the door. "We have many matters to discuss, and I fear it will take some time to come to a satisfying . . . conclusion."

Joel nodded and glared at Henry. "Any objections to that?"

Lonnie's heart lurched. *Objections? Yes!* Her marriage had been reduced to a problem in need of a "satisfying conclusion." She clutched the chair beside her, certain her knees could hold her no longer.

"If I may." Reverend Gardner stepped forward. "I feel it would be best if we head over there now. Mr. O'Riley, I would prefer if you rode with me to keep the stories straight."

"Stories?" Gideon snapped. He gripped the back of his head, his face agonized.

Reverend Brown spoke. "We both feel the

only way to resolve the matter would be to question those involved. Miss Sawyer, Miss Allan, and yourself."

Reverend Gardner slipped his hat over his head and waved with a chubby hand for Gideon to follow. "Come along, Mr. O'Riley. Let's be on our way." The quaver was gone from his voice. "The sooner the better. I'd like to visit your folks' place so that they may be present as well."

"I don't think so."

"It would be best —"

"I said no," Gideon barked. "This isn't their business!"

The room fell so silent that Lonnie heard droplets strike the roof.

Reverend Gardner nodded slowly. "The choice there is yours."

Lonnie glanced at Cassie, her pale face too calm. As if the victory were already hers. The thought of losing Gideon struck Lonnie's heart like a stone.

ELEVEN

The wagon jolted to a halt in front of the church, but Gideon sat motionless. The ride had been brief. Too brief for him to even gather his thoughts. As the wagon had jostled and jolted over the muddy road, Reverend Gardner had made small talk.

Small talk.

Gideon could hardly breathe, let alone speak of the weather or the condition of the newly improved road.

A few pellets of rain struck his arm, and Gideon looked up at the darkening space overhead. A blanket of gray haze. Heavy droplets fell, and he tugged on the cuffs of his coat. *Fine day.*

The sound of the second wagon approaching pulled him from his thoughts. *Lonnie. Cassie.* They both sat huddled in the back of Henry's rickety wagon. They both looked miserable. When the wagon jerked, each woman grabbed an edge to hold herself steady as if neither wanted to touch the other. Gideon stared at Lonnie, willing her to look at him. *Please, Lonnie.* He needed her to know he was sorry. That he hadn't known. In the depths of his heart, he had believed himself to be a free man.

Instead, a pair of blue eyes met his. A hundred memories flooded him. Gideon looked away, but it was too late.

What had he done?

He had once thought that nothing mattered in life but his own happiness. And there had been but two things that made him happy. One came in a glass jar. The other was soft to the touch.

Reverend Gardner yanked the church doors open and rolled a stone in front of each whitewashed door to keep it from slamming closed in the rising wind. "Follow me, Gideon." His jacket whipped behind him.

Lonnie climbed down from the wagon, her dark eyes as wide as a doe's. Reverend Brown scooted out of his seat, and with a flick of the reins, Cassie's pa drove away. Good. It was none of the man's business anyway.

Reverend Gardner's voice was thin when he called Gideon a second time. "Come along."

Jumping from the wagon, Gideon bumped his bad arm against the box frame on his way down. He bit his tongue to keep from cursing and stepped into the small church.

The building was chilly and dank, the potbelly stove that stood in the far corner of the church cold and untouched. Gideon shuffled forward and sank into the first hard pew where the reverend directed. No fire would be lit today. This was no Sunday service.

Cassie seated herself in the pew across from him, and though Gideon could feel her eyes on him, he could not look her way.

"May I sit by my husband?" Lonnie whispered.

Glancing up, Gideon saw her standing behind him. Her hand rested on the back of the pew. He was overcome with the urge to reach out and hold it, but when Reverend Brown stepped forward, heavy boots thudding loudly over hollow floorboards, his large frame filled the aisle beside her. "You may sit by *Gideon.*"

Slowly sinking down, Lonnie searched for his hand across the cold boards. Her fingers slipped inside his. She offered a quick squeeze. For the briefest of moments, Gideon let his eyes fall closed.

Reverend Gardner heaved two oak chairs

to the front of the church. The chairs scraped into place, filling the quiet room with the grating sound of wood on wood. After an annoyed glance from his fellow clergyman, he sat facing the pews. Reverend Brown sat beside him.

The setting seemed too informal for a trial, but that was what it felt like. Gideon feared what they might ask him. How deep would they probe into his heart and mind? How many details would he be forced to recall? Gideon shifted uncomfortably. He would answer as truthfully as he could. He had nothing to hide. He had done nothing wrong. It was Cassie's mistake. Her error. His heart quickened with nervous anticipation. This would be remedied soon.

Reverend Brown slid a pair of crooked spectacles up his nose. He cleared his throat. "I'd like to hear each of your testimonies. But first, we'll start with the church documents."

He opened a heavy book across his lap and skimmed his hand down the page. Tossing a black satin ribbon out of his way, he tapped the paper with the tip of a thick finger. "Ah. Here it is. On the thirteenth of May, 1900. A ceremony of marriage was performed, by myself, between Gideon O'Riley and Cassie Allan." He glanced at

Gideon over his spectacles. "I recall — with excellent clarity — performing that ceremony. Do you, Gideon, recall being present?"

Gideon swallowed. "Yessir. I was there."

Lonnie's hand loosened inside his.

"And" — Reverend Brown directed his gaze at Cassie — "you were present as well?"

"Yessir." Her voice was fearless. "I was present."

The reverend turned his attention back to the book in his lap. "Now that wasn't so hard," he murmured under his breath as he continued to skim the page. "But what I find interesting is that you came to me, to my small church in Tuggle Gap. Why not simply marry here, with Reverend Gardner?" The smirk on his face made Gideon think that he had arrived at his own interpretation of the truth.

Gideon pressed fists to his knees.

"Cassie, can you answer my question?" Though the reverend's voice held a hint of agitation, he kept his words slow and cool.

"Yessir, Reverend Brown." Cassie drew in a breath. "It was Gideon's idea. He thought my family wouldn't approve."

"That's not entirely the truth," Gideon muttered.

She glanced at him, blue eyes ablaze.

100

Reverend Brown snorted. He removed his spectacles and poked an earpiece between pursed lips. "Would you like to tell me what that means, Mr. O'Riley?"

Cassie shifted in her seat, and for the first time that day, her confidence visibly crumbled. At least he had one trump card in his hand.

"Mr. O'Riley."

Gideon cleared his throat. "All I'm saying is that I wasn't the only one who wanted to be discreet."

"Discreet."

He nodded once, suddenly wishing he hadn't spoken. His pulse shot through his veins like hot lead. "We both thought it best if her . . . if her parents weren't involved."

Lonnie drew in a shaky breath.

The reverend tapped the heel of his boot. "We need to get to the bottom of this. I suggest we start now. So far, what we know is that you were married. In my church. And then you married someone else under Reverend Gardner's approval? Is that correct? Did you really think no one would notice that you had two wives?" He eyed the page, then lifted his face to Gideon, taking no care to hide his exasperation. "Two wives within a few months' time."

"I married Lonnie, sir, because I was no

longer married to Cassie."

"Huh." Reverend Brown slid his spectacles up his rutted nose and searched his ledgers. He flipped forward a few pages, then back a few more. "And you have a copy of this document? Some tangible proof? From the county or the state?"

"No." Gideon leaned forward. "Cassie has it. She spoke to the circuit rider when he came through —"

"*I* spoke to the circuit rider." Reverend Brown nearly growled the words. "And he *never* received anything from the pair of you to deliver to the court."

"But he should have. I signed my part." Gideon turned to the woman he had avoided all morning. "You took care of it, right?" His voice was low as he struggled to control his anger, his words intended for her ears alone. "You said you would take care of it."

Cassie turned to Gideon. "I was going to . . ." Her mouth opened wide, but the words she spoke came out small. "I was uncertain. I wasn't ready."

Even as the heat rose in his neck, Gideon fought to keep his voice even. "Not ready for what?"

"For my pa to find out." She hissed a whisper, and Gideon knew she didn't have to say more.

Gideon hung his head, running fingers through his hair. He would never forget that moment. The moment she came to him demanding he make good on what he started, fool that he was. The truth had been clear. Unless he married her, the tattered frays of her reputation were irreparable. He had refused, telling her he didn't care what her pa knew. What her brothers knew. And with that glint in her eye, she went to find her father.

Calling his bluff.

Gideon remembered the day like it was yesterday. He'd grabbed her, halting her. And gave in.

The next day they had married in front of Reverend Brown. The day had been stiflingly hot. Gideon shoved up his shirtsleeves, remembering the heat in Reverend Brown's stuffy church.

"I didn't want my pa to find out." Cassie's voice drew him back to the present. She had the reverend's rapt attention. She always did well with an audience. "Not like that. I didn't want him to know" — her slender neck curved and her face paralleled the floor — "that I had been abandoned."

Abandoned? *The little vixen.* The tendons in Gideon's wrist worked as he pressed his hands together. She had come to him, a promise on her lips to tell her father that he had seduced her. But it took two to play that game. And Cassie Allan was no Lonnie.

Cassie glared at him from the corner of her eye as if reading his thoughts.

Gideon wanted to shake her. Instead, he slipped from the pew and sank to his knee. With Cassie only a few feet across the aisle, he faced her. "You said it was a mistake. You said you didn't want this." He motioned with his hand between them.

The words slipped from her tongue in a fiery whisper. "Don't twist the story."

"I'm *not*."

It hadn't taken more than a few weeks before Cassie had learned what kind of man she'd married. It had taken Gideon less time to realize that he wasn't the marrying type. The magic quickly faded, and they fought like two cats in a basket.

Cassie's chin trembled. So convincingly. "I thought I wanted to end it as well." A tear slipped down her ivory cheek. She quick-wiped it away. "But I didn't know . . . I was torn."

Reverend Brown waved Gideon to stand. "Please return to your seat, Mr. O'Riley. Displays of chivalry won't get you out of this mess." He closed the book with a *thud* and cleared his throat. "It's apparent we have a situation on our hands." He laced his fingers together and laid the mass of knuckles on the book. "Gideon. You have two wives."

Two wives. You fool.

Gideon jumped to his feet. "But we can fix that. We can change the ledgers. I'll sign it. Cassie'll sign it. We'll fix it. Forget the circuit rider. I'll go straight to the courthouse right now —" When the reverend looked about to reprimand him again, he sank into his seat and captured Lonnie's hand, hoping her familiar touch would calm his nerves. "This can be fixed."

"Seems simple enough." Reverend Brown directed his words to the stout man beside him who was yet to speak. "Except for one problem. Cassie has made it clear that she no longer wishes to dissolve your marriage. She —"

Boots sounded on the stairs. Every head turned to the back of the church. Henry Allan walked toward them, followed by Cassie's brothers. Jack. Samuel. Eli. Gideon noticed the shotgun in each man's hand as they strode up the aisle.

"Cassie does not want to go through with a divorce." Henry squeezed his daughter's shoulder.

Gideon's heart iced over. "Why now? Why didn't you speak up sooner?" he growled.

"I did." Her eyes snapped. "I tried to speak to you several times. You always managed to duck away. I even wrote you a letter. Months ago."

Gideon groaned, dropping his head in his hands. The letter he'd never read. The one he'd torn to pieces. To prove his love for Lonnie. And look what it had done to her.

He turned to Cassie and spoke her name. "We'll do what we need to do to end this."

Lonnie shifted beside him. Gideon wanted to comfort her. She was the woman he needed. Yet he stared at Cassie. *You'll end this. You'll give me my freedom.*

A gruff voice interjected. "My sister ain't gonna sign nothin' she don't want to."

Gideon chewed his cheek. He did not need to turn around to know who had spoken. He'd always recognize the voice of his childhood friend. Eli.

Reverend Brown leaned back in his chair and tipped his face to the unwelcome guests. "Gentlemen, if you want to be present, I must ask you to keep your peace. Please be seated." He lowered his shoulders with a heavy sigh. "There are three points that need to be clarified today. I feel the first has been done. Cassie Allan wishes to keep this marriage intact."

Reverend Gardner shifted forward in his seat. His voice was kind. "Gideon, she's made that fact clear. I'm afraid we have our hands tied." His eyes took on a sorrowful glisten. "Your marriage with Lonnie is putative." His throat worked. "That means it is . . . *invalid.*"

Invalid.

Gideon forced his lungs to fill with air. "But I have a son with Lonnie." His voice faltered as he stretched one arm out wide. "Shouldn't that carry more weight? I have a marriage certificate with her as well. Doesn't that mean anything? Shouldn't I be able to choose?" Yet the word *invalid* clouded his mind, darkening the hope in his heart.

Reverend Brown raised a hand. "If it were only that simple. That certificate may be as worthless as the paper it was written on." He used the satin ribbon to open the church ledger back to the page that recorded Gideon's past.

His mistakes.

"Reverend Gardner has shared the documents with me explaining your marriage to Lonnie on the" — his finger tapped the date — "nineteenth of August. Barely three months later. Did you not think to verify with Miss Allan that she had indeed handled things, as you say? Or that you were free to marry someone else?" He looked at Gideon, his gaze no longer sharp. "You overlooked a very important detail, Mr. O'Riley. Did you not think?"

He'd let his passions rule him the night he'd pulled Lonnie close on the hillside. Gideon glanced at her, wishing with all his might that he hadn't been that monster. When he spoke, his voice was as lifeless as his hope. "No sir, I did not."

The reverend closed the book and steadied it on his lap. He cleared his throat. "As it sits, the state of Virginia still sees Cassie Allan as your legal wife. We've been in contact with the courthouse, and they are awaiting a decision. One that may easily be made." He eyed them all. "We can settle this now. Between the lot of us. I fear that if this goes further, if this goes to the law, the results will not sit well with you, Mr. O'Riley." His face shadowed. "They will not be as merciful."

Gideon shifted his boots. They felt like lead weights against the floorboards. He glanced around the room, struggling for something. Anything. "Wait. You said there were three things to figure out. What else is there?"

"Oh." The reverend drew in a weary breath. "I take it there are no children from the union with Miss Allan?"

"No. Not that I know of." Gideon glared at Cassie. "Anything else you want to tell me?"

Cassie made a face.

The reverend rolled his eyes. "I'll take that as a no." Picking up a pencil, he made a note.

"And the third?" Gideon asked.

"From what's been discussed, I don't think the third point will be to your advantage."

"Why? What is it?" It had to be worth a try.

Reverend Brown shook his head slowly. "With all due respect to your son and his mother, there is a possibility this can be altered. But I doubt that possibility rings true."

Gideon leaned forward.

"All right then." The reverend cleared his throat and folded thick arms across his chest. "It has to do with the manner of the relationship between you and your first wife."

Gideon felt his face flush.

"Regardless of how things . . . began . . . it's more important how they ended. You've made it clear that neither of you favored the union, but was it always that way? Was the marriage between yourself and Miss Allan —"

Gideon nearly stood. "I don't see what this will solve —"

"Silence!"

He straightened against the pew. His heart banged against the wood behind him.

"Was the marriage between yourself and Miss Allan . . . consummated?"

Air left Gideon's lungs.

The reverend arched an eyebrow. "I need an answer."

Gideon's throat tightened.

Lonnie tensed.

The reverend shifted his attention to the opposite pew. Gideon looked at Cassie, but she did not meet his gaze. Her cheeks reddened, and she tilted her face away.

"Yes? Or no?" Reverend Brown demanded.

Cassie's voice was meek when she finally spoke what Gideon would not. "Yessir. It was."

Lonnie yanked her hand from his.

Like a demon that could not be cast away, his past had come back to haunt him. Gideon tried to swallow, but his mouth was dry. His two greatest fears rivaled each other for the throne of his mind. He had broken Lonnie's heart. Yes, that was bad, but the other was worse. When Gideon saw the shadow of condemnation that passed from Reverend Gardner's face to Reverend Brown's, his other fear had no rival — he was about to lose her forever.

TWELVE

It can't be. The reverends spoke to each other, their faces grave. Lonnie's stomach knotted. The room spun. Her hand was cold without Gideon's to hold, but she could not touch him. She could not look at him.

Gideon rose.

A man spoke. "Please stay where you are."

Lonnie glanced at the stern faces seated in the pews behind her, but she could not guess who had spoken. Her soul seemed to float away toward the rafters of the church.

Ignoring the warning, Gideon reached for Lonnie's hand, and his fingers grazed hers. She winced. "Lonnie, please. I love only you."

Cassie's brothers rushed to the front of the church. With fire in his eyes, Eli grabbed Gideon by the shirt collar and, in one strong motion, shoved him down against the seat with every bit of force that could have filled the man. Gideon's face struck the wood, and when Eli released him, Gideon crouched to the floor.

Lonnie shrieked. Reverend Brown shot to his feet.

Cassie jumped up. "Eli, stop!"

Gideon touched a hand to his face. Blood trickled from his nose, landing in dark, red spots on the floor.

"Don't hurt him!" Cassie cried.

Clutching Gideon by the shoulder, Samuel yanked him to his knees and grabbed a fistful of hair, pulling his head back until his face tilted toward the rafters. The shirt across Samuel's shoulders strained against his flesh. Eli lifted his shotgun and pressed the tip of the barrel to the exposed skin of Gideon's throat. Cassie shrieked. Lonnie screamed.

"You gonna run?" Eli sneered. "Huh?" The gun pressed deeper. He cocked it. Samuel's grip tightened on Gideon's injured shoulder.

Reverend Brown hurtled forward. His chair crashed to the floor. "Boys! Stop!" He tried to shove Samuel aside. "Eli!"

Eli did not budge. When Gideon tried to move, Eli shoved him down and smashed his shoulder to the floor with the heel of his boot. Gideon grimaced.

His face blurred behind Lonnie's tears.

"Release him!" Reverend Brown's voice boomed through the hollow chapel. "Now!"

"Please, Eli," Cassie cried. "Let him go."

Lonnie sank back. *Please, Lord.* She prayed it over and over, unable to put her fear into more words.

The fury in Eli's face tempered, and he pulled his shotgun away. Still panting, he stepped back and released the hammer.

Lonnie's stomach churned, and she pressed her fingertips to her mouth when the room spun.

With a groan, Gideon rolled to his side and spat out a mouthful of blood.

His face scarlet, the reverend pointed toward the door. His eyes darkened. "Outside! All of you — now!"

Still breathless, Eli stumbled as he took several more steps backward and ran curled fingers through his hair. He kept his gaze locked on Gideon, his other hand wrapped around his gun, knuckles still white. Casting a sorrowful glance at the scene, Jack turned away and followed them toward the door.

Reverend Brown strode a step behind. "I said, outside!"

Cassie crumpled to Gideon's side, and Lonnie stared in disbelief as her fingers landed on his arm. "Gideon, I'm so sorry."

114

He cocked his head in her direction and blinked up at her for several moments. He then turned to Lonnie, and their eyes met.

Gideon. Lonnie's gut wrenched. "Are we finished?" she asked, and glared up at the reverend.

Pale, Reverend Gardner clung to his chair as if it would protect him from suffering the same fate as Gideon.

Lonnie wanted to go home, but she suddenly didn't know where home was. The air around her felt stale, empty. She realized how alone she was.

"Lonnie, take him to your father's house." Reverend Gardner reached for his hat. "Reverend Brown and I need to discuss the issues."

Lonnie shook her head in disbelief and rose. Gideon slowly stood. She wished at that moment they could be as sparrows and fly from the whitewashed building, gather up Jacob, and wing their way out of this nightmare. Yet as she shadowed Gideon toward the door, she knew a peaceful ending was impossible. He had betrayed her.

Outside, Eli's gun glistened beneath a noon sun as he lowered it into his wagon.

They could not flee. They could do nothing but wait. Lonnie looked up into his face. Gideon. Her Gideon. "Why did you do this?" she breathed.

His gaze fell to her, eyes crushed with a sorrow that could never be enough. It would never be sufficient. It would never undo what he had done to her. To Jacob. She had trusted him. She had loved him.

And he had deceived her.

Every kiss. Every smile. All a betrayal. Lonnie pressed a hand to her stomach. She blinked back tears and sent a silent plea heavenward.

Cassie brushed past her and clutched Gideon's elbow. "Are you all right, Gid?"

Lonnie's throat burned. "He's fine," she blurted.

Cassie's hand fell.

Though she did not owe the woman a reason, Lonnie gave one anyway. "He just needs to get home."

Cassie bobbed her head, her eyes apologetic. Lonnie wanted to slap the look off her face. She led Gideon through the church door. Mr. Allan and Cassie shuffled out behind, but Lonnie paid them no mind. All she wanted to do was get out of this place. She wanted Jacob. She wanted Elsie.

"Gideon."

They both turned to see Reverend Gardner standing behind them. His voice steadied. "Don't try and run away. I know you're thinking it, and I don't blame you." He cast a wary glance over his shoulder. "I've met with the Allans several times over the last few months, and they assured me that they would not take it well if you were to abandon their sister a second time."

Lonnie forced herself to make sense of the man's words, rearranging them to be different — but each time the meaning was the same.

When Gideon started to protest, the gray-haired man held up a hand. "I know, I know. We have not even resolved the matter. I am just warning you. We will by this evening." With a sigh, he lowered his voice. "I'll do what I can to help you two. If this is what you want, I will try to persuade Reverend Brown."

Gideon nearly smiled — the corners of his mouth turned up, and his green eyes sparkled with hope. "I would appreciate that." He blinked slowly. "More than you know."

Lonnie didn't share his comfort. For cobwebs had stitched themselves in the path from her mind to her heart.

"Yes. Yes. Well, don't count your eggs just yet. But I'll see what I can do." He tipped his hat and cleared his throat. "Besides" — he glanced at Lonnie's face, and she knew what fire he saw there — "it looks like you have bigger problems to worry about."

You think so? Her anger bubbled, nearly sending the words to her tongue.

The reverend motioned toward the wagon.

"Just give us a moment," Gideon said.

With a curt nod, Reverend Gardner strode toward his wagon.

They stood there alone. Lonnie watched Gideon's chest slowly rise and fall beneath his white shirt. She couldn't bring her eyes to his face.

"How could you do this?" she whispered.

His hand found hers.

She pulled it away.

As if moved by an urgency, he held the back of her head, pulling her to his chest. Lonnie could hold back the tears no longer. She clutched his shirt in her hands. Wanting to shake him. Wanting to hold on and never let go. Her Gideon. He kissed her hair, lingering, and her shoulders shook with sobs. She slid free. She couldn't be that close to him.

Something had broken inside her, and she didn't know if it would ever be repaired.

How would she wait until evening? She wrapped her arms around herself, digging her fingers into whatever flesh they found. Her knees threatened to buckle. Run away.

Like a caged bird, the possibility had flitted about her mind all morning. But it was no solution. Gideon cupped her elbow, and she stepped away, lest she forget that he hadn't truly changed. At least not enough.

THIRTEEN

Lonnie hopped down from the wagon and strode off. Gideon called her name. She quickened her pace to a run. Her boots squished in the slick mud, but she managed to keep from falling. He caught her wrist, slowing her gently. She struck his arm and yanked free.

"Lonnie." He ran in front of her, halting her steps.

She shoved against his shoulders, not caring when he grunted in pain.

"Lonnie, please." He held his hands aloft, making no move to stop her.

She searched defeated eyes. "Do you have any idea what you've done?"

He tugged off his hat. Ruddy hair stood out in all directions. "I don't expect you to forgive me."

She made an incredulous sound.

"I should have told you. I thought it was all settled; I thought there was no reason to bring it up. Lonnie, I —"

"No reason to bring it up?" Her jaw went slack. "No reason to bring it up? How about the fact that I was your wife? Is that not reason enough to tell me that you were married?"

He palmed the back of his head, fingers digging into his skin. "I was wrong. So wrong. If I could do it all over —"

"Gideon, don't you know what's happening?" Her voice cracked. "They're going to take you away from me." She let out an infuriated groan and crouched down, fists pressed to her eyes. What was she saying? Why oh why did she have to love Gideon O'Riley?

"No, don't say that." His voice shook, drawing her eyes to his face. "Please." The last word came out broken.

Slowly, she stood. "Why? Because you love me?"

"Yes." He gripped her arms, lowering his face until they were eye level. "With everything that's in me."

She pulled from his grasp. "Then tell me. Exactly what happened."

As if her words had punched his chest, his chin tipped back. "You don't want to —"

"Tell. Me."

Their gazes locked and held. She refused

to glance away. The breeze swirled her hair, and she clutched it away from her face. He ran a hand over his unshaven jaw.

He took a deep sigh. Then another, his eyes on the ground. Remembering. "I was so stupid . . . I've known Cassie since I was a kid. Her brother and I were best friends."

Lonnie stepped closer, so soft was his voice.

Ever so slowly, Gideon shook his head from side to side. "I . . . I . . ."

Lonnie rolled her eyes. "You liked her. Just spit it out."

Clearing his throat, he blinked rapidly, his eyes finding hers. "I did. We started spending a lot of time together. First it was all just fun. Then it just . . . changed." He cleared his throat as if the truth tasted bitter. He shifted his feet, then straightened his shoulders. His resolve. "There's a cabin on her pa's farm. An old shack, really." Guilt tipped his eyes to the ground. "We went there so we could be alone."

A sickening rose in her stomach. "Alone."

"Yes."

"What do you mean?" But her chest collapsed because she already knew.

"Lonnie." His voice was dry, eyes filled with a self-loathing. "We weren't playing checkers."

Her head grew light. "And then what?" The words were pitifully small.

"She got scared."

Lonnie nearly scoffed.

"She came to me, saying it had all been a mistake. Which of course it was." He pinched the bridge of his nose. "She didn't know what to do. She felt trapped." He hesitated.

"And . . ."

"She said she wanted to get married. I told her no." He tugged at his hair. "She said she'd go to her father. In the end, I had no choice."

"You poor, poor thing." Wind rustled the trees on the edge of the clearing. Her skirt swirled around her legs.

"Lonnie, I don't have anything to say that will be enough. I don't blame you if you hate me. I should never have done this to you." His fingertips touched her hip. "I don't wish away a single moment with you. I don't regret marrying you. I can't." He clutched a fistful of his hair, frustration thicker than the moss of his green eyes. "If I should, I'm sorry, but I can't." He stepped closer.

She pressed fists to her eyes, everything inside her conflicting. "How could you do this?" Her voice muffled against her arms.

It was the only thing she could say. And she would say it over and over until it made sense.

"I don't want to lose you. But it doesn't matter what I want. I just want to take care of you. I want to make this right for you, Lonnie."

"I don't know what to do."

"We could leave. We could go where they can't find us."

"What makes you think I would go with you?"

Gideon lowered himself to his knees. "Lonnie. If it takes the rest of my life for you to trust me again, I'll spend every day doing just that. I love you and Jacob more than you know." His lips parted, eyes wide. "You don't deserve this, not one bit of it. Please, let me make it up to you."

"Don't you understand?" A single tear slipped and fell. She brushed it away, determined not to cry. "It's not about what I want." She waved toward the road they had just traveled. "It's what *they* want." Chilled, she pulled her sweater tighter, curling her hands inside the sleeves. "I don't even know who you are anymore."

He moistened his lips and nodded soberly. "That's fair. Very fair." A broken heart confessed itself in his eyes. "Please let me show you that I'm the same man I was yesterday. All this . . . all this is who I used to be."

Yet it had come back to haunt him.

Turning, Lonnie walked away. He made no move to follow. Good. It was better this way. She couldn't think clearly when he was so near. Lonnie wished she were a child. She wished she could curl up in her aunt Sarah's lap, open her heavy Bible to a favorite psalm, and let Sarah's calming voice lull her toward peace. But she wasn't a child and — Lord forgive her unbelief — she had just lost all hope of peace.

FOURTEEN

Lonnie lifted her glass to her lips but tasted nothing as she swallowed. Her ma exchanged glances with her from across the table, and Lonnie lowered her eyes. Her family ate with nothing but the sound of forks on plates breaking the silence. Beside her, Gideon had hardly touched his food. Yet her pa spooned stew into his mouth with gluttonous delight.

Why, Pa? Lonnie could hardly look at the man. He had done this. He had dragged them home. All she had wanted to do was see her ma. And that had led them both into the smoothly concealed trap.

Oliver's voice pulled her from her thoughts. "Lonnie, please pass the squash."

She lifted the heavy bowl and let him take a scoop before lowering the dish to the table. The silence continued. Lonnie cut a piece of her meat and forced herself to take a bite. An owl hooted. Night had fallen but still no sign of the visitors who were certain to come. Her heart quickened at a noise. She set her fork down and peered out the window but saw only inky blackness.

"Addie, get your elbows off the table," their ma said softly.

Addie did as she was told, and Lonnie flashed her little sister a weak smile. She remembered being that age. If only she could turn back time. If only she could do it all over again. She would never have set foot beside Gideon O'Riley.

His arm moved against her, the scent of cedar and smoke lifting from his white shirt. His hand rested on the bench beside hers, fingers all but touching. Tears stung the backs of her eyes. She was lying to herself. If she had the chance to do it all over again, she would have married Gideon O'Riley before any other girl got the notion. Stuffing her hands in her lap, she stared at her plate and contemplated picking up her fork. She could not turn back time. She didn't know how to unlove him.

A knock sounded at the door. Every hand stilled and every eye stared at the closed entry.

Slowly, Joel scooted back his chair. "Don't everyone jump up at once." He tossed his napkin next to his plate and stood.

The curtains danced in the cold air when he pushed the door open. The candle in the center of the table trembled. Reverend Gardner and Henry Allan entered. Eli stepped in behind them, his gaze sharp. Yet no shotgun filled his palm.

"Come in, come in." Joel hurried to close out the wet night air. "We were just finishin' up."

Cassie strode in last. Her dark hair swept to the side, a scarlet ribbon tying the unruly tendrils. She blew a strand of hair from her face, and eyes the color of an icy creek glanced around the room before landing on Gideon.

The clergyman shifted his feet, his face colorless. Lonnie pressed her hands together, willing them to stop trembling. After lifting a heavy shawl from her shoulders, Cassie smoothed the lines of her airy white blouse.

Joel waved an arm toward the already crowded room. "Come have a seat. Children, off with you."

Sid and Oliver exchanged glances. They threw down their napkins and pushed back chairs, then headed outdoors. Addie went toward the bedroom, baby Charlotte filling her arms.

"Try and keep her quiet. I'll be in in just

a moment," her ma said. "And try not to wake Jacob."

Maggie closed the door softly behind them. She moved to the stove and handed Joel a steaming cup. She wiped her hands on her apron. "Can I get anybody anything?"

Her pa shook his head. "That'll be fine, Maggie. We'll just get on with our business. Lonnie. Gideon." He motioned them forward.

They sat in a half circle around the fireplace. With Gideon to her left and her pa to her right, all Lonnie had to do was look across to see the Allans and Reverend Gardner staring back at her.

Reverend Gardner cleared his throat. "I apologize for Reverend Brown's absence. He had some last-minute business to attend to, and since we, uh, came to a mutual resolution, he" — the clergyman cleared his throat a second time — "felt satisfied if I deliver the news."

Lonnie swallowed and blinked back tears.

"And what conclusion have you come to?" Joel demanded. "Is my daughter's reputation ruined? Or will you spare us all the embarrassment?"

Reverend Gardner's mouth drew into a thin line. "With all due respect, the matter is not about Lonnie. It's about Gideon — the man with two wives."

"So let me rephrase my question." Her pa leaned forward. "Which wife must Gideon set aside?"

The stout man cleared his throat. "If only it were that easy."

Henry Allan straightened. "It is that easy. Or have you not come to a decision?"

Reverend Gardner stiffened. "Gentlemen. Would you mind giving us a moment? I'd appreciate the opportunity to speak alone to the three involved." He turned from one father to the other. "They're adults, and I feel that'll be the best way to settle this. Please." He waved a hand toward the door. "Give us some privacy."

Lonnie knew her pa would not be pleased being thrown from his home, but to her surprise, he slapped a hand on his leg. "Come along, Henry. Eli. It sounds like it's rainin', but we'll be dry enough in the barn. Come and fetch us when you're done, Lonnie."

Numb, she didn't acknowledge his words.

The mantel clock ticked away the seconds until the door closed behind them. Lonnie looked at Gideon, then at Cassie. Taking her first deep breath of the evening, she braced herself for what was to come.

Bending over, the reverend pulled the ledger from beside his chair and plopped it on his lap. Stifling a cough, he opened to the correct page. The black satin ribbon swayed when he dropped it over the edge. It glimmered in the firelight. Lonnie never wanted to see that ribbon again. How she hated that page. She pressed her hands together and squeezed them between her knees. Rubbing her palms back and forth did little to calm her nerves.

"Well." Reverend Gardner offered each person a flat smile. "I'll preface by saying this: the conclusion we've come to is a reflection of the church and its beliefs and traditions, coupled with the laws of the state of Virginia. Both Reverend Brown and I have tried to remain neutral in our opinions on the matter, and only uphold the facts and rules set forth by the documents at hand." He sighed. "That being said, I'm sorry to say" — his eyes darted around the floor as if looking to land on something that did not breathe, that did not feel — "Miss Sawyer, that your marriage to Mr. O'Riley must be annulled."

Lonnie's hands stilled. Her knees no longer trembled. She felt Gideon's gaze on her. She lifted her chest, trying to draw in air.

Reverend Gardner's voice steadied. "We ask that this be done as soon as possible so we may proceed in repairing the union that Mr. O'Riley had decided not to uphold between himself and Miss Allan. Which" — he added, staring at Gideon — "must be upheld."

Lonnie blinked up at Gideon. Firelight danced across his face. His gaze met hers, green eyes broken. She found it impossible to look away. Impossible to fold the love she had for him and tuck it away in the drawer of broken promises. Despite all that had been revealed, she didn't know how to seal her heart closed to him. Instead, the raw pieces were still his and his alone.

They sat staring at one another for several moments. The reverend cleared his throat.

Ignoring the clergyman, Lonnie swallowed. She longed to hear the cries of Gideon's heart, knowing they mirrored her own. She wished they were alone in the room. Only then could she crawl inside his embrace and cry. Instead, she sat motionless, unable to move. Gideon's gaze narrowed, nearly piercing her with urgency. And Lonnie no longer had to wonder what filled his heart. They could run. They could flee.

Then she remembered the men in the

barn and those who had not come.
They would follow.

FIFTEEN

A warbler called overhead, but Gideon hardly heard its lonesome song. Reverend Gardner had paid them one more visit. It was as unwelcome as the last. The first of October. Three days. That was all they'd given him. That was all the time he had to convince Lonnie that every fiber of his being loved her and her alone. When weighed in moments and hours, it was nothing compared to spending the rest of his life away from Lonnie. From Jacob. Unable to dwell on the realities that crushed his very soul, Gideon lifted his ax high above his head and brought it down with unapologetic force, executing the chunk of white pine into two ragged pieces.

He winced when his shoulder warned him to stop. But he didn't care. He imagined the faces of his adversaries as steel struck wood once more and a single piece shattered into two. Physical pain meant nothing. It was nonexistent compared to the ache inside. Using the back of his hand, Gideon wiped sweat from his temple.

Despite their efforts, he would never love Cassie. Anguish would be the only sensation to penetrate his heart, and grief would be his constant companion. It would stay with him for the rest of his life.

Gideon tightened his grip on the handle and steadied his gaze on the target. With a grunt, he splintered the last piece of wood. He stumbled back, and unable to hold it any longer, he let the head of his ax sink into the dirt as he surveyed the fruits of his rage. Freshly split wood littered the grass — a hundred graves. Gideon squinted into an unwelcome sun. They asked too much of him.

He would sign no annulment papers.

The wind shifted, sending a swirl of dried leaves around him. He closed his eyes but felt pieces of grit in his mouth. When the leaves settled on the dewy ground, he spat and wiped his lips in the nook of his shoulder. Looking around once more, he studied the mess he had made.

He picked up the scattered pine and stacked the pieces as neatly as his frustration allowed. When the last chunk graced the top of the pile, he straightened, struck with the sensation of being watched. Looking over his shoulder, he glanced up at the front porch. Lonnie stood at the top of the steep steps. Her unbound hair fluttered and slapped in the breeze.

Gideon stilled, unable to look away from her defeated face. He had so much to say to her. So much he needed her to understand. He loved her and her alone. Yes, he had made a mistake in marrying Cassie behind his family's back, but Lonnie needed to know that in his heart of hearts, he truly believed himself to be free of Cassie when he married Lonnie that autumn day. He had believed himself to be free when he had loved Lonnie. Taken everything she had to give and given all of himself in return.

Taking a single step forward, Gideon rolled his shoulder, stretching the abused muscle. He had to make her see. Had to stow the passion of his heart inside hers. And she alone would hold the key.

He leaned the ax against the woodpile.

Lonnie disappeared inside and returned a moment later carrying her brother's coat. She flung the faded garment over her shoulders and tucked her hair beneath the raised collar. As she descended the steps, her skirts bounced over her knees, showing stockings that had seen too many winters. Her pace quickened. His heart followed the rhythm of her feet as they moved faster. *Hurry, Lonnie.* His blood rushed as a river. He prayed she would listen to his plea. Prayed she would flee with him.

Lonnie caught up to him, her cheeks flushed. Breathless. He covered her hand with his, and they whisked away from the open yard, heading for the creek bed where curious eyes could not find them. Neither one spoke. Gideon's heart pounded with expectancy; he needed to know what she would say. His untamed spirit told him she would come, allow him to risk it to keep her. The years ahead could be full of joy. Though they would be stolen in the eyes of the law, Gideon only hoped that God would bless their faithfulness to each other.

Yet when they slowed and Lonnie pulled her hand free, tucking it safely in the coat pocket, Gideon feared he was too late.

"Why didn't you tell me?" she asked. Her eyes were shadowed as if she hadn't slept in days.

He rubbed his forehead. "I don't know. I honestly don't know." He shifted his feet, scuffing a loose shoelace through the dirt. "I should have. I absolutely should have. It honestly wasn't at the front of my mind." He dropped his face and shoved up his shirtsleeves, the cuffs unbuttoned. "When you and I were married, it all happened so fast. It was unexpected. I thought my past was my past. I thought there would be time for us to sort things out . . . I haven't exactly been there for you in this marriage."

She wrapped her arms around herself.

"Each day I wanted to be one step closer to being the man you deserved. That meant learning so many things. I just wanted to do it right. I didn't know how to dig up the troubles of my past yet." He shook his head. "I see how wrong I was."

She tilted her face to the canopy of trees overhead. He watched her swallow. "I don't know you as well as I thought."

He fought the ache, knowing he deserved every bit of it. "We can mend that. I'll tell you anything."

She scoffed.

"I mean it, Lonnie. Anything about me. I don't want to keep a single thing from you."

"It's a little late for that."

"Give me this chance. Please."

"Fine." She squared to face him. "Just tell me one thing."

He heard her sharp intake of breath.

"She wasn't the first, was she?"

His throat worked. "No."

"Was she the last?" Her eyes widened

138

slightly. "Before me."

"Yes. Absolutely yes." His stomach clenched at the fear in her eyes.

"And after me." Her voice shook, but she tipped up her chin, her resolve clear.

"Never. Not ever again. You were it. You still are." He pressed a hand to his chest where his heart thundered. "I love you with everything I have. The only thing inside here is you and Jacob."

She didn't blink.

"Do you believe me?"

"I don't know."

"That's fair." He stepped toward her, bridging the gap. "I know it hasn't always been this way. I'd be lying if I said it was. But you've become a part of me. You're pure goodness, Lonnie. I don't for one moment deserve you." Hand still pressed to his chest, he drew in a breath, knowing he was fumbling the words. "I still don't always know what I'm doing, and this God of yours who's somehow given me a second chance isn't always easy to figure out. But I want to. I want to so bad."

Her chin trembled.

He took another step closer, fighting with every fiber in his being to keep from holding her. "I can't stay, Lonnie. Not without you."

"You say that like there's a choice."

"There is a choice."

Her eyes narrowed. "Gideon. You know what they'll do." Her words were difficult to hear with the rushing water beside them. "They'll find us. We won't be a day's walk away before my pa sends them after us. The Allans will be on our trail quicker than you think."

And they would. He hadn't missed the determination in their eyes. "Then we'll outrun them."

A shadow crossed Lonnie's face. "Gid, we have Jacob. We can't." Her words crushed his.

"Lonnie, we have to try." He hung his head, struggling to get the words out, wishing there was a way to make her understand. "Let it come. I'll take it. For you and Jacob. I'll take every bit of it. Let me shoulder this."

But he quaked at the thought of danger befalling his son.

Lonnie looked away, staring at the rushing creek. When she turned her face back to him, her eyes were filled with defeat. She opened her mouth. No words came out.

He spoke before she could. "I just need to know one thing."

She hesitated. "What's that?"

"If you were free. Right now. If we were

free to walk away from here, take Jacob and go home. Would you? Would you do that . . . with me?"

Moistening her lips, she spoke evenly, slowly. "There's no point talking like that."

Gideon wished the rushing of the creek had carried her words away, but it hadn't. "You don't mean that."

Squaring her shoulders, Lonnie lifted her head. "I do."

"No. I know you. I know your heart." His throat burned.

"I'm going to sign the annulment."

He blinked once. "You what?" He stepped back as if she'd struck him. But he'd heard her.

Lonnie looked away. She pressed her palms together. "Gid, I'm not goin' any- where with you."

If she'd wanted to break his heart, she'd succeeded. Gideon ran his sleeve across his eyes, and the creek nearly drowned his voice out. "Please don't do this."

Her resolve visibly crumbled. Before he could say another word, she turned and ran down the path.

SIXTEEN

Lonnie ran as if the simple act could sever the threads that tied her heart to his. If only it were that simple. She slowed, glancing over her shoulder as if she half expected Gideon to follow. She knew deep down he wouldn't. She needed space and he knew it. She needed to clear the cobwebs from her head and make some shred of sense of the mess her life had become.

Her chest heaved. The path ' curved through the grove, and the familiar shape of her aunt Sarah's cabin stood out in the distance. A tangle of crooked aspens shaded the porch, where her aunt sat.

Sarah stood and shielded her eyes. "Well, I'll be." She hurried down the porch and in an instant surrounded Lonnie in a rosemary-scented embrace. "You've come home to me."

Lonnie nodded furiously. "So it seems." Her vision blurred. The softness of her aunt's shoulder made her feel like she was six years old again and the troubles of mind could be eased by a kiss and a cup of tea.

Pulling back, Sarah studied her.

There was no way to muster a smile.

"What's happened?" Her eyes searched Lonnie's face. "Where's Gideon?"

Lonnie pressed her palms to her eyes, forcing herself to take slow, deep breaths. "At my pa's." Despite her efforts, Lonnie's chin trembled.

Sarah's grip on her shoulders tightened. "What has happened?" She wrapped an arm around Lonnie, gently urging her up the steps and into the cabin. She sat Lonnie at the table and shoved a pile of yellowed papers onto an empty seat before sinking by her side. She took her hand, engulfing it in warmth and worry.

"It's over."

"Over?"

"I never should have married him."

Sarah's grip tightened. "*You* didn't have a choice." She scooted closer, hovering on the edge of her seat. "Lonnie, tell me what's happened."

"He was already married."

"What?"

"To Cassie. Henry Allan's daughter."

Sarah's jaw went slack. She blinked once,

then again.

Lonnie glanced away, unable to bear her aunt's shock. Fearing she would see disgrace in her sky-blue eyes.

"Oh, my girl," Sarah breathed. She wrapped her arms around Lonnie, holding her close.

When the burning in Lonnie's throat became too much to bear, she gave in to the sobs. As they racked her body, Sarah stroked her hair. "How could this have happened?"

Lonnie stared over her aunt's shoulder into the fire. A clothesline, heavy with undergarments, hung from one end of the mantel to the other. Damp stockings dangled limp, lifeless.

"I love him," Lonnie whispered, unable to pull her gaze away from the *drip, drop.* "And they're going to take him away from me." She straightened and wiped tears away. "How can I be so stupid? How can I love him after what he's done? I want to kill him and hold him all at the same time."

"Oh, my dear girl." From the fire, the kettle billowed and steamed, but Sarah didn't move. "How did this come about?"

Lonnie pulled her knees into her chest, wrapping her arms around her legs. Her boots balanced on the edge of the chair.

"Gideon . . ." She dug her fingernails into the fabric, struggling to gain control over her resolve. "Gideon put little stock in controlling his passions." She blurted the words out quickly, hoping they wouldn't sting. But it was no use. A sickening rose in her stomach at the thought of what he had done. The thought of who he had been. She'd always known the scoundrel he'd been back then. But never had she imagined the price it would cost her. Lonnie drew in a slow, shaky breath, knowing she would have to say it eventually. "He loved Cassie before me. He loved her in ways he never should have." Lonnie moistened her lips. "She wasn't the first, either." A shiver tiptoed up her spine.

Gideon had always gotten what he wanted from a girl, and Cassie had been no different. Except Cassie expected more than a ruined reputation. She had expected his ring. And his ring she had gotten. Lonnie turned her own cold band around her finger, trying with all her might to recall what she had seen in those eyes of his. She'd seen hope. The promise of better days. She buried her face in her skirt. Eventually, that had turned into love. She pressed her eyes closed, unable to wipe Gideon's face from her mind. The closeness of him quickened her heart as if she could reach out and touch him. "He's a changed man. I know it." She lifted her face. "He loves me. He's proved it over and over. The Allans have insisted he return to Cassie. They have the law and the church on their side. I can't lose him." She pressed a palm to her forehead. "Oh, Lonnie, you're so stupid." She shook her head from side to side. "Why couldn't he have been honest with me? Why couldn't he have just come out and said it? been honest about his past?"

Sarah studied her.

Lonnie wondered what truths she would discover.

"You're thinkin' of runnin', aren't you?"

Ever so slowly, Lonnie nodded.

Sarah drew in a slow breath. "Is that what Gideon wants too?"

Fingers tangled together, Lonnie pressed them to her chest. "Very much." Her hand in his. And in time, the pain in her heart at what he had done would lessen. Because he would spend the rest of their days proving his love. Of that she was certain.

Would God but grant her those days. For she had only one left.

"And?"

"And I told him I wouldn't go."

Slowly, Sarah bobbed her head. "Did you

mean it?"

A quick breath, and Lonnie glanced away. Did she?

"The Allans, you said."

"Yes."

Sarah stared at the kettle. The steam filled the room with warmth and moisture. Sarah's chest lifted, then dropped in a shaky sigh. "Do you know what Samuel and Eli Allan can do?"

"Yes."

"Gideon's crazy." Sarah pursed her lips. Slowly, one side lifted. "But I can already tell he loves you." She pressed fingertips to her heart. "To risk it."

Lonnie gritted her teeth when emotion overwhelmed her. "That's what I believe too."

"But you're not going to let him."

Her heart lurched at the thought of any other outcome. But no matter how she tried to rewrite the story, she couldn't. Gideon had married Cassie first. And with her he must stay. "I don't know what to do."

Sarah fiddled with the edge of a napkin. She rose, and her stockinged feet made nary a sound as she crossed the room. She swung the kettle away from the flames, then lifted a small, wooden bird from atop her Bible and pulled the big black book down. Licking her thumb, she moved forward several pages, finally pressing her hand to the words. She set the book in front of Lonnie.

Lonnie read the first few lines. She lifted her eyes. "The judgment of Solomon." Floorboards squeaked underfoot as Lonnie shifted.

Sarah nodded and sat. "Two women claimed to be the mother of the same child. So the king tested them, putting the child's life at stake."

She knew what happened next, and she wished there was another way.

"The child's mother — the one who truly loved him — offered to give him up so that he might live." Slowly, Sarah set about putting together two cups of tea.

It wasn't until Lonnie had taken a sip and then another, that she finally spoke.

Putting voice to her answer.

Seventeen

When sunlight finally streamed through the cracks of the lean-to, Lonnie rolled away from the light only to find the place beside her cold. It came as no surprise. She knew Gideon was gone. Her pa had refused to let him back in the house. She'd seen the fire in her father's eyes and knew it was hate she saw there.

Standing on the porch, Lonnie had watched Gideon go. Felt her heart lurch as if to sneak from her body and follow.

Jacob stirred beside her, and Lonnie closed her eyes to shut out the morning light but could not turn back the clock. Another day had gone. Another day with Gideon was lost to her forever — reduced to a memory.

She smoothed her palm over the cold sheet. The mattress was rough beneath the threadbare covering. Lonnie imagined Gideon lying there. What would she say?

Rolling onto her stomach, she reached for her pack, which she caught by the strap and dragged across the floor. It fell still when her hand went limp. Unable to move, Lonnie stared at it. The paper Reverend Gardner had given her had been carefully folded and tucked in the bottom beneath her few belongings. It was safely out of sight, but not out of mind. Lonnie wished she never had to retrieve it. But as she carefully unfolded the ivory paper, words leaped off the page as if they were written in blood and not Reverend Gardner's shaky penmanship.

She ran her fingertips down the lines until the tip of her pinkie smoothed over the letters of her name. She traced her way across until her finger stilled where her husband's pen was meant to fall. She would ask Gideon today. If he refused, which she knew he would, she would beg him. With an uncontrolled gasp, Lonnie let the page slip from her grasp and float to the bed. She would fall to her knees if she had to.

Her pain was raw. Fresh. But entwined with the ragged pieces of her hope lay a love she feared would never die. She would be the one to let go. And he would marry another.

It had to be this way.

Slinking from beneath the sheets, she wasted no time. She unbuttoned her night-gown until it fell around her ankles. She kicked it free and shivered as she reached for her dress. Her motions were stiff but quick as she buttoned the collar and tugged the sleeves over her wrists. Even so, she could not stop shivering. The cold cotton clung to her skin. Tossing an apron across her lap, Lonnie tied it securely, then eyed the paper lying limp among the rumpled blankets. She hesitated and then, in one quick motion, folded the page and slipped it into her apron pocket.

After scooping up her sleepy-eyed son, she stepped from the lean-to. Her pa glanced up from the table, eyes bloodshot. His hand shook as he reached for his coffee. Lonnie wondered what he had added to the dark brew to help him get through another day. She didn't care to stick around to find out.

She strode past her ma and grabbed a biscuit for Jacob and herself, ignoring the breakfast that steamed from the table.

"Where are you going?" her pa demanded.

Lonnie shut the door behind her, certain he wouldn't follow. He probably couldn't even get out of his chair in the state he was in.

She held Jacob to her chest and kissed his

downy curls. He smelled of straw and milk, and she held him tighter. The O'Riley farm was a few good miles, so she settled into a comfortable pace, knowing she wouldn't reach it for a while. She made slow progress, taking care not to stumble on the mountain path with Jacob in her arms.

The baby was fast asleep, his head limp against her shoulder, by the time the cabin loomed in the distance. She glanced around, hesitating as she wondered where to begin. She decided to try the workshop.

She tugged the latch, but the door was too heavy and, with Jacob in her other arm, impossible to budge. In an instant, the door creaked open and Gideon stepped out.

He breathed her name.

"Gideon."

"What are you doing here?"

"I — I have a few more questions."

"All right." He nodded earnestly. His fingers brushed her elbow. "I'll answer anything you ask." He ushered her into the workshop and shut the door behind them. He lifted Jacob from her arms and, with his head, motioned for her to sit. Exhausted, Lonnie sank onto a bench against the wall. Gideon sat beside her. Their sleeping son resting against his broad chest. His shirt was unkempt, his collar crooked, and frayed cuffs rolled back haphazardly. Shadows circled beneath his eyes. Lonnie bounced her foot nervously before speaking.

"So my pa . . ."

Gideon nodded slowly. "Your pa wasn't too pleased, was he?" He crossed his ankles. His long legs nearly touched the workbench. "Can't say that I blame him." When he diverted his gaze, she sensed defeat in his eyes. The paper weighed her pocket as if it were a stone.

It's what you want, she reminded herself. The good outweighed the bad. He would no longer be hers, but he would not be hunted down like an animal. His heart would continue to beat.

He would still know his son, watch him grow up.

In time, Gideon would smile, though it would not be at her. Lonnie knew she had to focus on that truth. It was as cold a comfort as a threadbare quilt in the wee hours of the night.

She shifted and their shoulders pressed together. She felt his warmth through his wrinkled shirt and sensed the shape of his flesh that could only be formed by years of wielding a heavy ax. He was so close. How she wished she could turn back the clock. But Lonnie folded her hands in her lap.

There was no use.

What had been was gone. She glanced at Jacob. He would be her constant reminder of Gideon. Lonnie stared at the boy who mirrored his father. She wondered if the resemblance would be a blessed reminder of the man they loved or a curse to make her long for Gideon when he was no longer hers.

Gideon cleared his throat, his voice soft against Jacob's hair. "You said you had questions."

Questions. Yes. But they flitted like butterflies around her mind. He was too near. Lonnie scooted away ever so slightly and pressed her hands between her knees. "I guess I don't know where to begin. I feel like I don't know you anymore."

Grief folded itself into his brow.

"What's going to happen with Jacob?"

The little boy sighed in his sleep. Gideon's eyelids fluttered closed. "He'll stay with you. He needs his mama."

"He needs his papa too."

Gideon's nostrils flared, and he cleared his throat as if to contain his emotions. "How I wish that were possible," he said softly.

"And you no longer think it is?"

He glanced at her, his expression earnest.

"Is it?" He lifted his head from the wall. "Tell me now if it is." His eyes were hungry as they flooded with hope.

The word *yes* slid to the tip of her tongue. But she tucked it back. He was too close. She needed air. "How about a walk?" she blurted.

"That would be nice."

She rose and handed Jacob to Gideon.

Without speaking, he slipped his free hand against her back. Her eyes shifted to the house, but only for a moment. With Gideon's hand warm against her apron strings, he guided her forward. They crossed the footbridge over the creek and worked their way through the small meadow, their footsteps but a whisper on the path.

The land rose and Gideon held Jacob fast. The little boy woke, rubbing his sleepy face against his pa's shoulder. Together they climbed. Gideon's heart beat faster. The farther they drew from the farm, the more his hope grew. She hadn't said yes to his question . . . but she hadn't said no.

"How 'bout here?" Lonnie pointed to a soft spot where the noon sun feathered through the trees.

The leaves crunched beneath their boots as they circled the small opening. Lonnie sank to the ground. Her skirts billowed around her. Gideon placed Jacob in the soft fabric of her lap and settled beside his wife and son.

He played with a dry leaf in his hand. She voiced her heartache. Her questions. He answered with every shred of honesty that was in him. She spoke of days gone by, and he felt himself smile. She shared her fears. Each one pierced him. He wanted to throw them to the wind. Blow each one to smithereens with a shotgun. But he couldn't. He could only listen and nod, give what little comfort he could form into words. His fingers grazed hers. How he wished it were more.

And more than once she reached for his hand, only to tuck her own beneath her skirt.

The afternoon moved quickly. Too quickly. The sun danced across Lonnie's chestnut hair, making it shine — making Gideon wish he could run his fingers through the silky strands. Jacob crawled around, picked up leaves and twigs, then stuck them in his eager mouth. As they watched their son's explorations, they laughed and exchanged smiles. More than once, Gideon found himself lost in such delight, he almost forgot the purpose of this outing. Almost forgot what sat waiting for him come sunrise.

The sun made a slow arc. Their time was drawing to an end.

"We should probably head back. It's gonna get dark soon."

Gideon knew he could delay his plea no longer.

Lonnie brushed dried grass from her skirt. She scooped Jacob in her arms. "Look at you, my wee thing." Her words were light, but her voice held a thousand sorrows.

Gideon took hold of her hand, and with surprise in her face, Lonnie watched the action. "Please," he whispered. "Let me say this. I —"

A twig snapped. A gritty voice followed.

Gideon scrambled up and crouched in front of Lonnie. In the distance, leaves rustled beneath heavy boots.

Eighteen

"Step back," Gideon whispered. He pressed her behind himself. When Jacob fussed, Lonnie shushed him. Another twig snapped and then another. Gideon peered in the direction of the noise. Figures approached. Men by the looks of it — but he could not see their faces. As they moved between stands of trees, patches of russet flannel and faded green cotton, hand dyed and home-spun, came toward them. Familiar colors worn by the men whom Gideon had come to consider his enemies.

Narrow brown eyes locked with his. *Eli Allan.* Gideon's hand instinctively twitched as he remembered his rifle that he'd left back home.

Eli used the tip of his gun to point in Gideon's direction. He closed one eye in mock aim. "Whatcha doin' all the way out in the woods like this?"

The men drew closer, and Gideon made

out each face. Henry. Samuel. Jack. Then he spotted a face that made his stomach sour. *Joel Sawyer.* They circled quickly, and Gideon counted the faces. Five against one. His eyes dropped to the guns that each man held, and all he could think about was his family behind him.

"Lonnie, what are you doing?" Joel asked, the barrel of his gun a shiny reminder of whose side he was on.

"This isn't necessary," Lonnie said coolly.

"It's necessary if I say it is."

Gideon's pulse quickened.

Lonnie squared her shoulders and set Jacob down for the briefest of moments. She rose, and a waterfall of leaves slid from her skirt. She picked up Jacob and held him close.

"Reverend Gardner asked that the two of you meet him at the church tomorrow morning. He would like to resolve the situation as soon as possible. And frankly," Joel added, "I would too. Get back to the house."

Lonnie stepped around him, gingerly taking each stride on the uneven hillside. "I'll head back when I'm good and ready."

Joel grabbed her arm, yanking her toward him. Jacob's head lurched.

Lunging forward, Gideon shoved the man, using his shoulder to barrel him to the ground. Joel's head slammed against the forest floor, and scrambling to his knees, Gideon struck his stomach as hard as he could. He grabbed Joel's collar and, forgetting his bad shoulder, pulled his arm back — but his fist never came back down.

Pain seared through the back of his head, and Gideon fell forward — the crack of steel against his skull echoed in his ears.

Somewhere in the distance, Lonnie screamed.

Rolling onto his side, Gideon grabbed his head. His fingers felt something warm and wet. He blinked, but the world blurred. Before he could bring his eyes into focus, someone yanked him to his feet.

Strong arms held him. The angry fingers that clamped around his arms dug into his flesh. Eli grabbed Gideon by the hair and lifted his head. Their eyes met. Gideon stared into the face of Cassie's brother. Her defender. His childhood friend.

The cold end of Eli's sawed off shotgun pressed against Gideon's temple.

His heart thundered, but he locked gazes with his oldest friend.

Eli's eyes, once soft with kindness, were now brown slits beneath uneven brows. Gideon gulped. They had grown up together, fishing in the summer months and hunting

160

all winter long. Now those days were nothing but a blur.

"You've ruined my sister." Eli spat out the words. "You used her!" he shouted. His eyes narrowed, and the rough-edged gun dug into Gideon's skin. "I should shoot you like the dog you are."

Gideon had no words to deny what he'd done. The grip on his hair tightened.

Cassie's brother glared at him in disgust.

"Eli," Jack murmured, laying a hand on his brother's thick arm. "Ease up, will ya?"

Eli shook his head, tightened his grip on Gideon's hair, and cocked the gun with a *click.* Gideon closed his eyes and heard nothing other than Lonnie's crying.

Jack's voice was sharp. "Eli, stop. This isn't the way to settle this."

Gideon opened his eyes in time to see Jack reach for the shotgun.

"He'll do right by Cassie." Jack's eyes met Gideon's, and the severity of his words struck Gideon like a blow to the chest. "Won't you?"

Gideon swallowed as the steel warmed to his skin. A bullet still lurked inside the barrel. Eli's words tore through him. *"You've ruined my sister."* Gideon knew what his reply would cost him.

But when Eli's trigger finger twitched,

161

Jacob's face flashed through his mind.

"I'll do right by Cassie," Gideon blurted. "You have my word." He slammed his eyes closed.

With that simple phrase, he gave up everything.

And what had he gained? *Cassie.* His first bride. She had given herself to him completely. Gideon cringed, wishing it had all been a bad dream. *You fool.*

Eli did not release him. Jack laid his other hand on the barrel of the gun. "You heard him, Eli. He'll make good on his word."

Furious eyes blinked, then softened with a brother's sorrow. Eli lowered his gun.

Gideon did not care about Eli. He did not care about the gun. Turning to look at Lonnie, he saw the despair in her ashen face. *I'm sorry.* He wanted to wrap his hands around her heart — fend off the pain. Take it. Bear it.

Yet her chin trembled. And he was the cause.

Seemingly satisfied, Eli turned away. He paced back down the hillside without another word. Jack followed close on his brother's heels. Gideon stood motionless as one by one the men started away.

Lonnie stood there, waiting. Neither one spoke.

162

Finally, Gideon nodded toward the east. "Let's get you home."

She shook her head. "I'm not leaving you like this."

He started to protest, but she flashed him a look that kept him silent. "Very well then."

The candle burned low and did little to light the chilly workshop. Gideon sat on the edge of the bench. He tried to keep still as Lonnie dabbed at the back of his head with a damp rag.

"Does this sting?" She rinsed the tattered cloth in the wooden bowl on her lap.

"A little."

"Good."

He grinned, then winced. "You're welcome to take a swing. I promise I won't move."

She dabbed at his skin, her touch gentle. "That's actually quite tempting." She pressed her fingertips to his collar, which was unbuttoned and folded back to his shoulders. Blood splatters stained the left side. "I just wish I understood why," she whispered.

"I do too." He caught her small hand still pressed to his shoulder, engulfing it in his own. "I have no excuses for not telling you. I wish I could say that it was the farthest

163

thing from my mind, that all I wanted to do was win your heart, not break it. But I know those reasons are not enough. Lonnie, I would do anything to earn your forgiveness."

Murky water sloshed onto her ticking-striped apron. Lonnie pursed her lips and dropped the rag in the bowl.

"You'll agree to the annulment then." It was not a question.

The answer came out of his numb heart. "In the morning."

Her words hinted at uncertainty. "The morning." She looked more grown than she ever had to him.

But she was too young for such heartache.

Lonnie lifted the rag, and water trickled from the twisted fabric. Several droplets slid down her pale wrist. Unable to look her in the face, Gideon suddenly found himself entranced with the thin frame of her hands.

Somehow he had to let her go.

"I'll stay here with my pa," she whispered, her voice tight.

Gideon lifted his gaze. He saw the lines in her weary face, the wideness of her uncertain eyes. She was putting up a wall. The pieces had formed block by block since Reverend Gardner had broken the vile news.

He looked away and shook his head. "No,

you won't. You'll go home."

Lonnie's voice filled with surprise. "To Jebediah's?"

Staring at his lap, Gideon nodded.

"But what about Jacob? You won't see him —" His fingers on her lips silenced her. Lowering his hand, he let it rest in the soft folds of her skirt.

"And I will love him forever. Just as I'll love you." He did not have much time to make her see his heart.

Lonnie dropped her forehead in her hand. "Gideon, you can't promise that."

He turned on the bench, facing her. "I can and I will."

"I can't be that far away," she choked. "Jacob needs his —"

"You have to go. This is no place for you, and it's no place for him. I need to know that you're safe . . . that you're loved. The Bennetts will take care of you and Jacob."

With tender movements, Lonnie wrung out the rag. After a moment, she spoke slowly. "He'll always remind me of you." She laid her damp hand in his palm.

The candle flickered, sending shadows across the shop. Gideon tipped his chin to better look at her. He swallowed, surprised by the quickening of his pulse. His other hand moved to her hair and loosened the ribbon that bound it. The yellow fabric slipped free, and he slid it into his pocket. "I'm keeping this," he whispered as he began to unravel the twist at the nape of her neck. Loosening the strands, he felt her chestnut hair fill his hand. Silk on his fingers. When Lonnie closed her eyes, he kissed one eyelid and then the other.

"My wife." The word rumbled low in his chest. Even if only for a few more hours. He was satisfied at the sound of it, yet heartbroken that a word was so important.

"How can it be over?" she whispered, the ache in her voice as thick as the fog outside the window.

Gideon shook his head as he released her hair, letting it cascade down her shoulder. It would never be over. There was nothing they could do to change the course of his heart. Though they might bar him from her life, she would be in him and through him. In every way.

NINETEEN

Her sleep had been restless. The hours too few. Because the night before, Gideon had led her home beneath the lantern of a full moon. They had walked mostly in silence as if neither wanted to break the spell. It would have been easier to walk upstream on a stormy day than take the steps she made in the dark hours of night. The steps that took her further from the life that had once been.

And by the time her head hit the pillow, sleep eluded her. When she finally drifted off, her breathing had been rough. Her sighs many. There was no comfort even in the absence of mind. No dream sweet enough to keep her from the harsh reality that would come with daybreak.

Weak morning light filtered through the cracks in the roof. Lonnie rose and, taking care not to wake Jacob, pulled on her brown calico dress, sliding it over her shoulders with jerky, careless movements. She dragged stockings the color of coal up her calves, tugging them tight.

Her chin quivered, and she fought to steady it. But it was no use.

She slid her worn shoes silently into place and laced them over her ankles. After unraveling her braid, she pinned the twists and curls at the base of her neck with weak, shaky hands. The motions were slow, drawn out. As if to delay the inevitable.

But it was time to go. Lonnie glanced around the small space, wishing Gideon were here with her. Jacob still slept peacefully. Her mother had promised to listen in on him. With that, Lonnie stepped from the lean-to, glad it had its own door to the outside. She did not want any lingering stares, any pitiful words of encouragement.

Lonnie started down the trail toward the church, but her ankles nearly collided as she glanced up and froze.

Gideon stood stone still looking more handsome than she'd ever seen him. His hair was slicked back and combed to one side. His crisp white shirt stood out in the foggy, misty morning. Despite the cold, he held his jacket draped over his shoulder.

"Gideon."

"I just couldn't waste this hour."

She nearly smiled.

When he stepped closer, he slid his jacket over her shoulders. His earthy scent engulfed her. He fiddled with the cuffs of his freshly pressed shirt. His crisp collar lay folded into place, tempting her fingers to trace the line that ran above the fabric where his hair curled at the nape of his neck.

He cleared his throat, but his voice still came out gruff. "We better be off."

As they walked, their eyes never met, although she felt him watching her when he thought she wasn't looking. It was better that way. It was better they didn't touch. It would only make saying good-bye harder.

The breeze scurried along in its haste. Lonnie held the jacket close as they were surrounded by the cold mist. The walk to the chapel would not take long. Their boots fell into a slow rhythm as they headed away from the small farm. One more hour. It could never take long enough.

His hand found hers, his fingers so soft and warm she didn't know how she would let go. Fog devoured the trail ahead, forcing them to take each step by memory. They walked in silence, but there was so much Lonnie yearned to say. He seemed to escort her, his shoulders nearly protective beside hers. Ahead lay the church. She'd never forget the hour they exchanged vows that soggy afternoon. Now, they were returning to undo what had been done. But the deep places of her heart were rooted and tangled — a love like that could never be undone.

Clearing his throat, he voiced her name. It fell from his lips like sweet honey. Would he ever have a reason to say her name again? Perhaps he would have to whisper it in the silent places of his heart to keep himself from losing his mind. They continued walking, and Gideon waited until he had her attention. He longed for her forgiveness, but that seemed selfish. He focused instead on bringing her peace.

"I'm sorry for what I've done," he finally managed to say. "I never wanted to hurt you. I never meant to lose you." He hoped she would hear the truth in his words. "I only loved you. I should have told you my past. I should have let you decide."

Lonnie looked at him. "How I wish we could begin again."

He stopped walking. "I should never have kept such a secret from you. But truly, Lonnie" — he paused long enough for her to turn toward him — "I thought myself a free man when I married you. I would never have done what I did had I known that Cassie —"

170

The shadow that crossed over Lonnie's face made him wish he had never spoken the name. When she squinted, he knew she was trying not to cry.

After a long pause, Lonnie spoke. "This is the way it should be." When she peered up at him, Gideon knew she was being brave for him.

"I don't love Cassie." Would she believe him?

"But you did. And" — glassy eyes focused on the fog-shrouded path ahead — "you will love her again."

Gideon caught her arm, forcing her to halt. "No. I won't. Please don't say that."

Lonnie allowed him to pull her forward. "What else is there to say? You have to. We had our time. But it was stolen time that never should have been." Her eyelashes fluttered as she blinked away tears. "It's time to let it go."

The ache burned deeper. "Do you mean that, Lonnie? Is it that simple for you?"

She walked on, ignoring his question. Her hand slipped from his, and the distance between them grew as Gideon stared after her.

"Answer me, Lonnie." He darted toward her and stepped in her path. She stopped. "Will it really be that easy for you? Because

171

if it will, tell me now, and I will do every-thing in my power to accept this."

Lonnie's chin trembled. "Gid . . . I . . ."

He pulled her close. Lonnie coughed and choked on her tears. He held her face against his shoulder and closed his eyes. Their breathing melted into one as her chest rose and fell against his. His eyes burned. With fog hiding them from the world, he wished they could stay that way forever. When Lonnie's body shook with sobs, he slammed his eyes shut, sending two tears plunging.

He kissed the top of her head. "I love you," he whispered.

TWENTY

Reverend Gardner was waiting for them when they stepped through the church doors. A fire crackled in the potbellied stove, making the church surprisingly warm. Lonnie slid out of Gideon's jacket and handed it back to him. Gideon loosened his tie. His pa had loaned it to him. He'd tried to refuse, then in the end gave in.

Not for Cassie. For Lonnie.

He grazed her sleeve with the back of his hand. Reverend Gardner eyed the action, and his eyebrows lifted. Gideon stared at him, daring him to speak. The silence was broken only by droplets that fell from the ceiling into a bucket in the corner.

The reverend was somber. He accepted the paper, and an unexpected look of surprise passed over his features. Carefully unfolding the wrinkled document, he scanned the page and grunted. Gideon began to speak, but the reverend silenced him by lifting a weathered hand.

"I must admit," the gray-haired man began, "I am surprised to hold this right now." His voice dropped to a low murmur. "I could never imagine what this has cost you both."

Gideon tipped back his chin, surprised by the man's blunt sentiment. Had this been the will of the church or simply the personal ambition of Reverend Brown? If so, perhaps it was not too late. "Do you mean to say —"

"What I mean is, had there been another way, I would have fought for it. But" — Reverend Gardner dipped his pen in the inkwell on his desk and held it aloft — "there was nothing that could be done." A droplet of ink dripped onto the paper. The reverend quickly scribbled his name. Lonnie looked at Gideon, her eyes filled with unshed tears. She pulled her hand slowly from his. The ink pen fell to the desk with a soft *clang.*

It was finished.

When Reverend Gardner cleared his throat, Lonnie looked at him. "Your ring." He said it so softly Gideon scarcely heard.

Lonnie tugged the tin from her finger and slid it into Gideon's palm. Her head shook from side to side, but she said nothing. She sank onto the pew. Not wanting to let her go, Gideon sat beside her.

His gaze soft, Reverend Gardner peered at them. "You're doing the right thing. God has many blessings in store for you both."

As much as Gideon wanted to believe him, he couldn't. How could God have any role in this? It was Gideon's mistakes and his alone that had placed him here. Was God even watching? Did He know what was about to happen? Obviously not or He would put a stop to this. Not for his sake — of that he was certain. But surely God cared about Lonnie and Jacob. His frustrations mounting, Gideon glared at the reverend.

The man in black rose. He pulled his chair from behind the desk and set it with a *thud* in front of them. "Take Lonnie's hand."

When Gideon hesitated, Reverend Gardner tipped his head, a silent signal that it was all right. Gideon slid his hand over Lonnie's, and their fingers interlocked.

"There has been something missing in all this, and I don't blame Reverend Brown . . . I blame myself." The stout man placed a cool hand over theirs and gave a firm squeeze. "Will you bow your heads with me?" He removed his glasses and set them on his knee. Closing his eyes, he bowed his head.

Lonnie and Gideon exchanged glances, and when she bowed her head, Gideon followed suit. The reverend closed his eyes. With quick fingers, Gideon slid the ring in Lonnie's apron pocket. He heard her breath catch.

"We come before You, Heavenly Father . . ." The reverend paused.

Gideon glanced up.

Reverend Gardner wiped a bead of sweat from his wrinkled brow and ran his palm across his leg. Then Gideon saw an emotion he did not expect. The man looked dismayed. After clearing his throat, he began again. "We come before You, Heavenly Father, to ask forgiveness for our sins. Our transgressions have been many."

Rain plopped into the bucket. *Drip. Drop.*

"I pray their hearts will be comforted as they go their separate ways. Keep Lonnie safe in her travels, and may Jacob grow up to be healthy and strong. Heal Gideon's hurt as he takes the hand of his new wife, his other . . ." Reverend Gardner stumbled.

A slight gasp escaped Lonnie's lips as she choked back her tears.

The reverend paused, and when she righted herself, he continued. "There is no pretending that deep sorrow does not lie ahead for both of these young people.

176

Remind their hearts that time on earth is fleeting and it is not this life that will keep them, but their faith in Your Son that will hold them fast for eternity. Finally" — Reverend Gardner sighed and shifted his feet — "restore their joy. The joy that comes only from You. May You fill their hearts with Your love and peace as they heal." His voice grew faint. "For it is the only way . . . there is no other way."

With his whispered "Amen," Gideon lifted his eyes. Lonnie was weeping. It took everything he had to keep his own tears in check. He lifted her hand and pressed his lips to the inside of her fingers.

"I would like to drive Lonnie back home. Gideon, will you please wait here for my return? We have much to discuss."

Gideon had not realized he'd nodded until Lonnie tugged her hand from his. He started to stand.

"Please don't," she whispered as she rose, her eyes like wet river stones. "Please."

He wanted to shout for her to stop, but bit his tongue as hard as he could. She stepped away and, with her back to him, squared her slender shoulders and bravely strode down the aisle. Gideon watched in dismay as she slid through the doors. With a dip of her head, she stepped from the church.

- - - - -

TWENTY-ONE

As the wagon swayed and the seat creaked, Lonnie wiped her eyes and looked at the reverend as he climbed up beside her. His face was somber. "I'm sorry it must end this way." He let out a heavy sigh and flicked the reins. The wagon jolted forward, seat bouncing on its springs. Lonnie clung to the weathered wood.

She longed to glance over her shoulder to see if Gideon had followed them outside. Unable to resist the urge, she looked back at the open church door. She saw nothing other than the peeling paint of the empty doorframe.

"Like you said," she whispered. Fresh tears made their way to her eyes. "There is no other way."

Reverend Gardner nodded. Reaching into his coat pocket, he pulled out a folded letter and handed it to Lonnie. "A copy of the annulment." When she hesitated, he contin-

ued. "Since you have a child, I felt it necessary for you to have proper documentation
of your marriage to Gideon." He shook his
head from side to side, indicating that the
matter hung heavy on his heart. "You have
done nothing wrong, Lonnie. I don't want
you to suffer for —" He fell silent, but she
heard his unspoken words.

Gideon's mistakes. Lonnie slowly took the
paper. "Thank you."

"I will take you home to collect your
things. Gideon mentioned that you will be
returning to the home of Jebediah Bennett.
Is that so?"

Keeping her gaze on the folded paper, she
nodded. "I can't stay here." She would go
home to Jebediah and Elsie. That was where
she belonged.

With a sigh, the reverend continued.
"That is what I suspected. This morning, I
spoke to your aunt Sarah, and she will drive
you as far as the pass. There, Mr. Bennett
will meet you and escort you home."

Lonnie's mouth fell open. "Jebediah?
Meet me . . . but how?"

The reverend's small eyes found hers.
"Gideon planned it. He wrote a letter to
Mr. Bennett, day before yesterday —"

"Two days ago?"

Somberly, Reverend Gardner nodded.

"Though Gideon was clearly clinging to hope, there must have been a part of him that wanted to take precautions."

She had always been the sensible one. Gideon, so unruly and untamed. Yet even in these last moments, he surprised her. Lonnie gripped her apron so tight, her knuckles whitened. Though he'd tried to persuade her, deep down he must have known that she would refuse. Her heart broke afresh.

"I commissioned a young man who has recently devoted his life to the church. He — that is, Reverend McKee — has hopefully delivered the letter by now. If not this very moment. Do you feel confident that Mr. Bennett will respond?"

"Oh," Lonnie sighed, eyes burning. "Jebediah will." He would be there. Of that she was certain. Come rain or snowstorm, he would be waiting. She wrapped her arms around herself. Homesick.

Reverend Gardner tipped his head to the side. "Gideon said as much. He was most insistent that a familiar face and safe escort were in order. We all wanted to do whatever we could to help ease your journey home." Kind eyes landed on Lonnie. "You have enough to worry about."

Overwhelmed, Lonnie could hardly speak. The reverend drove on in silence. When a lone sunbeam broke through grim clouds, he lifted his face to the light. Lonnie followed his lead. She closed her eyes and savored the warmth on her skin.

When the sun disappeared back behind the gray mass of clouds, she instantly felt the chill of loneliness. Glancing sideways at the reverend, she knew she had to ask him the question that hung heavy around her heart. If she didn't, she would always wonder. Doubting she could form the words, Lonnie moistened her lips. There was no going back. She needed to know.

"For Gideon," she began. "And Cassie, I mean. When will he . . . When will they . . ."

The reverend slowly nodded, the understanding in his round face genuine. "I'll bring Cassie to the church today. Though their marriage is still valid, we thought it best to verify and renew those vows. I feel it's best to finalize what must be done and bring this to an end. It is the only way for healing to begin."

Lonnie's chin quivered, but she forced a nod. *It is the only way.* Like bark being torn from a young sapling, she would be separated from the only man she loved. When drawing breath became a struggle, she tilted her face to the tempest above.

Gideon will marry Cassie. And I will go home.

The pain of her loss throbbed through her core. Grief stretched itself into every limb of her body. It bound its powerful hands around her throat and draped an unwelcome weight over her lungs. Lonnie blinked, hoping the fall breeze would dry her eyes. Gideon was gone. He was no longer hers. *Oh, God,* she cried out as the black cloak of sorrow covered her heart. *Will You see me through this?*

"I'll be right back," Lonnie told the reverend when the wagon came to a halt. "Please wait for me."

Her movements were swift. She crossed the floor of her pa's cabin with silent resolve. She pressed open the lean-to door and paused. Her bag, which she had packed that morning, sat like a lone soldier on the freshly made bed as if it were awaiting her orders. Lonnie moaned and stifled a fresh wave of tears. She could smell him. Looking around the crooked, worn boards of the tiny room, she could see him. She could hear him. *God, be my strength.* Lonnie slipped her wrist through the strap of her pack and tugged it toward her. Her eyes landed on Gideon's plaid coat. Without

183

thinking if he would need it, she stuffed it in her bag. Then, without a sound, she left the lean-to.

Every eye followed her movements, but Lonnie took no notice. All she needed was her son. All she wanted was to be free of this place. Jacob clung to her ma's arm. Maggie kissed the top of his head as if she no longer cared what it might cost her. The little boy who mirrored his pa in nearly every way was Lonnie's sole concern. When she reached for him, her pa stepped in her path, and Lonnie deliberately moved around him.

Her ma's compassion-filled eyes met hers, and Lonnie forced her voice to remain steady. "I'll take him now," she whispered.

With a quick nod, Maggie held Jacob out. The warm, soft form of her child filled the void in Lonnie's arm, and she held him close. Maggie kissed Lonnie's hair, and Lonnie clutched a handful of her ma's apron before stepping away. This was good-bye. She looked around at the faces — each one tightening her chest until she could bear it no longer. She did not scan the walls or wish farewell to the home of her childhood. Not this time. She could bear no more good-byes. Without a word, she left.

Before Reverend Gardner could help her

into the wagon, she flung her pack in the back and climbed up. After she'd settled, he drove away. Sarah's home was not far. All her life, Lonnie had walked the curving path that led to her aunt's door, and when the small cottage came into view, Sarah's broad smile greeted them from the doorway. A shawl the color of a robin's breast draped her aunt's shoulders, and Lonnie instantly felt the reassuring warmth of her loving presence.

With a pale hand, Sarah shielded her eyes as the sun broke through the clouds. Her smile was wide, but her blue eyes filled with sorrow. "Come in, come in. I've got a fresh pot of tea. Will you join us, Reverend Gardner?"

He shook his head. "Thank you, but I have business to attend to." He glanced at Lonnie. "You'll take care of that son of yours? Raise him up right?"

She bobbed her head. "I will, sir." *And will you watch over Gideon for me?*

With a tip of his black hat, Reverend Gardner flicked the reins, and his wagon jolted from its spot in the mud. The wheels turned, and the rickety wooden box swayed, bumping slowly out of sight.

Gideon sat alone in the church. Closing his

eyes, he succumbed to his thoughts and the memory of the life that had brought him here.

It had been spring when he had held Cassie in a way a husband holds a wife. Spring when she had wept over the tatters of her innocence. Like the wretch he was, marrying her had been the furthest thing from his mind that reckless night beneath the stars. Yet it rushed to the front of his awareness when she demanded he make good on what he started. Or else. And the last thing Gideon had wanted was her father and brothers hunting him down.

So they had hurried off to the small church in Tuggle Gap. Reverend Brown had placed their hands together, and they swore their devotion. For weeks they had kept their marriage a secret. They knew they should tell someone, but they were both so deep in trouble, they didn't know where to begin. With Cassie only his come nightfall, and suddenly distant at that, Gideon struggled to understand what a husband truly was.

It wasn't a perfect situation, made clear the day Cassie threw up her hands, insisting it wasn't working. With that fire in her eyes, she demanded her freedom. He put up no fight. She was miserable and he knew it.

Together, they spoke to the circuit rider, the man who tended to court business for those who couldn't make the journey, when he passed through. He explained what would need to be done. Caring little for his conscience, Gideon did his part. So did Cassie. Or so he'd thought. But clearly he had been wrong. For the proof never made its way into the rider's satchel.

Gideon's eyelids threatened to flutter open.

Like a fool, he had thought himself to be a free man. Free to smile at the other girls in the holler. Whisper sweet nothings in their ears. Free to walk Lonnie Sawyer home one moonlit night. He'd vowed he'd never marry again. But he never expected Joel's shotgun aimed at his back.

Eli's words haunted him. *"I should shoot you like the dog you are."*

Footsteps sounded on the church stairs, but Gideon did not turn around. Voices passed over the threshold and fell soft as feet shuffled in. Still Gideon did not lift his face. He wiped his eyes, then dried his wrist on his pants, wishing this day had never come.

A hand patted his shoulder.

The reverend looked down at him. "The Allans are here. So is your family. We are ready to proceed."

Straightening, Gideon pressed his back against the hard pew. He glanced sideways but saw no one. Turning in his seat, he stared toward the back of the church. Henry Allan slipped his hat from his head. His wife, Mary, untied the laces of her bonnet, and when she caught Gideon's gaze, she looked away. Libby, Cassie's younger sister, stared at the floor, large ears poking through her hair.

Some celebration.

They were getting what they wanted from him. Soon he would owe them nothing but time. The rest of his life.

He glanced at the final person. The pale-faced girl stared back with eyes wider than he'd ever seen. *Cassie*. What? Was she nervous? She had no reason to be. It wasn't like she was wearing white.

His family strode in, his ma's face as grim as ever. She sat in a nearby pew, and his brothers and sisters filed in beside her. His pa followed behind, hat in his hands. He gave Gideon a curt nod.

Gideon turned to Reverend Gardner, and his eyes locked with the old man's. So this was it.

"Where's Lonnie?" Gideon blurted, not caring if it were rude to speak of her in front of the Allans. He had to know she was safe.

"She's in good hands."

Jacob? Gideon knew the answer. He was with his mother. He would grow to be a strong lad. Gideon searched the reverend's pudgy face, though in his mind's eye, he saw only the image of his lost son. *Jacob.* The joy of his life.

The words that fell from the reverend's lips drew him back to the present. "Are you ready to proceed?"

Gideon stood. He would never be ready, but what did it matter?

"The Allans will serve as witnesses. Hopefully you have no objections to that?"

He shrugged. Henry snorted.

Gideon stared at the man. Henry Allan simply glared back.

A muscle flexed in Gideon's jaw. If the man didn't want to give up his daughter, then why was he? Henry could keep Cassie for all Gideon cared. Gideon loosened his tie, tugging it free. He tossed it on the pew beside him. Cassie's eyes followed the movement. What did she care for? She'd seen him in his tie. They'd been here before.

She stepped forward at the reverend's bidding, and Gideon's feet turned to lead.

Reverend Gardner placed a hand on Cassie's shoulder. "Stand here. And you, Gideon." He pointed to the floor. "Stand here."

Gideon did as he was told. His muddy boots shuffled forward until his toes nearly touched her black shoes. Freshly polished. He forced himself to lift his gaze. He ran fingers through his hair, beyond caring what he looked like.

Gideon fought the anger that rose in his chest. His actions had been such a mistake, and they would cost him the rest of his life.

"Please join hands."

Cassie hesitated. Gideon had no desire to prolong the painful event. Grabbing her hand, he held it in his. Her fingers were cool, her skin soft. Memories flooded him, and he shook off the thoughts. He needed only Lonnie. He wanted no more of Cassie. The less they touched the better.

Reverend Gardner began. His words seemed to float toward the rafters, for Gideon heard none of them. When prompted, he spoke the vows he was required to say. In his mind, he saw the glimmer of Eli's rifle and the hatred in the man's eyes. Gideon was finally doing right by Cassie. Their hatred had no more fuel.

Cassie's soft voice drew his attention. "I will," she whispered.

"And will you, Gideon, take Cassie to be your lawful wife, love her, honor and keep

190

her in sickness and in health" — he cleared his throat — "forsaking all others, keep only unto her so long as you both shall live?"

Silent seconds passed. The seconds grew into a lengthy span until Gideon finally iced his heart over, glanced past Cassie, and spoke into the empty deep.

"I will."

Twenty-Two

Cassie felt the heat of Gideon's words, but not in comfort. She looked up at him and saw the truth in his eyes — he did not love her. Worse. He despised her. He was simply doing his duty. Typical Gideon. She touched her boots together as demurely as possible and blinked up at him, glad she'd pinched her cheeks to the point of pain before arriving. She had her work cut out for her. But she was more than ready for the challenge.

The reverend cleared his throat and hesitated. The darkness beneath his eyes and the silver stubble on his round face hinted that this incident was taking its toll on him.

He looked from her to Gideon. "You may kiss . . . the bride." The last words fell from his lips with sorrow and tumbled down.

Stones to her heart.

Cassie held her breath, but before another moment passed, Gideon released her hand and wiped his palm on his pants as if needing to be rid of her touch. She looked at her ma, who offered her a soft smile.

"So we're finished here?" Henry asked.

The reverend nodded.

"I need some air," Gideon murmured. "I'll wait outside."

He grabbed his jacket from the pew, ignoring the tie. Cassie watched him leave. Every footfall stomped harder on her heart than on the floorboards below.

So this is what she had to look forward to. A husband who did not love her.

Why would he? She was not Lonnie. She couldn't begin to guess what was so great about the woman. Lonnie was so . . . plain. Cassie fiddled with her locket, running it up one side of its chain. She knew a thing or two about getting Gideon's attention. If Lonnie Sawyer could do it, for heaven's sake, she could too.

Though the sun still held its ground, spreading rays of light across the land, tiny droplets of rain began to fall. Lonnie looked up at the thickening clouds and realized the sun fought a battle it could not win.

"Take this," Sarah called. She propped the door open with one hand and held a basket out with the other. "Just pulled this bread from the oven." Suddenly alarmed, she looked around her. "Where's Jacob?"

"He fell asleep, so I bundled him in the cart."

Sarah nodded and disappeared back into the house. Lonnie took the basket and carried it to her aunt's cart. The snug box sat on a single axle and could hold only two people on the narrow seat. What space was not taken up with feet and provisions offered a tiny corner for Jacob to sleep in. Sugar's lead rope was tied to the back. The old mule's eyes hung at half-mast, as if she were about to fall asleep any moment.

"That seems to be the last of it." Sarah sighed and stepped out of the doorway. She secured the latch behind her. Lifting her face to the sky, she shook her head. "Fine weather to be traveling. Won't you consider staying for a few days at least? A week? A month, even?"

"No. I need to be free of this place."

Another month? Lonnie's eyebrows pulled together. She couldn't imagine staying around another moment and was grateful her aunt had been at the ready. Lonnie dropped another blanket in the back of the cart, not caring that it came unfolded.

Determined not to cry, she put one foot in front of the other and climbed onto the small seat. She slid over as far as she could

194

to make room for her aunt.

Sarah took the reins in one hand and slipped her other arm through the crook of Lonnie's elbow. "Cozy, ain't it?" Her smile faded when Lonnie did not respond, and she gave her hand a reassuring squeeze.

With a click of Sarah's tongue, Elliot, the old farm horse, was off at a slow trot. When the cart lurched into motion, Lonnie clung to her aunt. Sugar lumbered along, matching the pace.

"Wait!"

Lonnie knew that voice. She spun around on the seat to see her ma running toward them. Addie struggled alongside her, moving as fast as her short legs would allow. When the cart stilled, her ma slowed her pace and pressed a hand to her chest.

"I'm so glad I caught you," she panted.

Lonnie jumped down and ran to her ma. When she drew closer, she noticed a fresh red mark, high up on her ma's cheek. The makings of a bruise. Lonnie gasped. Maggie waved away her concern.

"I'm all right." She covered her cheek with her hand. "Just a little argument." Lonnie stared in disbelief as her ma fell to her knees in front of Addie. "Take your sister," she pleaded. Lifting her face, her forced smile faded. Her cheek caught the sunlight, and her chin trembled. "I don't want her to have this fate."

Lonnie swallowed. "Of course I'll take her. But what will you do without her?"

Maggie shook her head. "Don't you worry none about me. I just want to know that my girls are safe. I've heard nothing but good things about the Bennetts. Please." She tugged a thin wad of bills from her blouse and stuffed the paper in Lonnie's hand.

Lonnie started to protest.

"I don't want to take advantage of anyone."

"But, Pa'll know —"

Ignoring Lonnie's words, her ma pulled her into a tearful embrace. "Give her a better life."

"Oh, Ma, I will pray for you."

Maggie sniffed and wiped her eyes. She cast a wary glance over her shoulder, then forced another smile. "Now off with you. You want to get a good start before dark."

Lonnie knew what her ma meant. Hurry.

Within moments, space was made for Addie. She huddled in the back with her knees to her chin. Their ma pressed a kiss to the girl's head and dropped a gunnysack of Addie's belongings inside the already bulging cart. Before Lonnie could whisper another good-bye, Maggie darted around the front of the cart and slapped the horse on the rump. The horse jolted forward. Lonnie gripped the seat. She glanced over her shoulder and watched her ma's figure grow smaller. Maggie waved overhead, and Lonnie lifted a hand in farewell.

Addie's tiny voice stole her attention. "Am I gonna see Ma again?"

Lonnie exchanged glances with her aunt before replying. "Hopefully." It was the only truth she could think of. "We're gonna be together now. You, me, and Jacob. How does that sound?"

Addie nodded happily, then rested her chin on her knees and closed her eyes. Lonnie doubted if her sister understood the weight of her ma's plea. The little girl would not be returning home. Lonnie thought of her own fate and the time that had passed since she'd finally returned to Rocky Knob.

When the cart jolted, she turned forward.

"So this is it," Sarah said cheerfully.

The landscape changed as they started downhill, yet Lonnie saw no cheer in any of it. "This is it."

Sarah nudged Lonnie in the side. "I'll look after your ma. She's gonna be fine."

Words could not be found, so Lonnie nodded her head.

"You're gonna be all right too."

Looking off into the distance, Lonnie shrugged and Sarah fell silent. Her aunt's words were meant as encouragement, but watching the sky ahead darken, Lonnie wondered if they were true.

TWENTY-THREE

Using his boot, Gideon kicked his thin sack to the other side of the wagon bed. He'd stuffed what little he owned into a gunnysack.

"Where we goin'?" he asked without looking at Cassie, who sat beside him.

A sweet smell lifted from the fabric of her dress.

"The cabin. Ma and I fixed it up."

Gideon tugged at the patch of hair beneath his lip.

Huddled in the back of Henry's wagon, he was careful not to bump into her as wheels jolted over ruts. The rain had started up again, and Gideon pulled his hat over his ears. Cassie drew her coat collar tighter beneath her chin. An old army coat, from what he'd seen of it. He tried to ignore her movements.

The minutes passed while Cassie fiddled with the sleeves that were too long.

Gideon turned his attention to the road behind them. The Sawyers' farm had long since disappeared from view, and judging from his surroundings, it would not be long before they pulled onto the Allan farm. He knew the place well. He had spent countless afternoons fishing and swimming with Cassie's brothers.

How long ago that seemed now. Cassie had first caught his eye when she started acting shy around him. No longer Eli's kid sister, she had a braid that fell past her hips, and her laugh was that of a woman. She'd avoided Gideon's gaze and blushed when he tried to speak to her. And that left him mesmerized.

Gideon glanced at Cassie from the corner of his eye. He let out a slow breath.

Mary clutched her bonnet when the wagon bumped. Beside her, Henry sat with his back hunched. His spine poked through his thin shirt. His hat, faded by the sun, was pulled low. Gideon turned his attention back to the road behind them. Cassie's pa had yet to speak to him. When a wheel struck a rock, both Gideon and Cassie bounced and clutched the splintered sides of the wagon to keep from bumping into each other. Henry flicked the reins, and the horses leaned into their load.

After another mile of silence, Gideon spoke. He was careful to keep his voice low. "I guess we'll be stayin' with your pa?" He kept his eyes on the road but caught Cassie shaking her head.

"The old cabin on the north side of Pa's farm. Like I just told you."

That's right. He hadn't really been listening.

Cassie rested her elbow on the wagon box and pressed her cheek to her forearm. Her eyes fell closed. Gideon peered at her. Her skin was pale. More so than Lonnie's and not a single freckle appeared.

He quickly looked away when she opened her eyes. As if she'd expected him to watch her. He'd have to be on his best guard with Cassie. She knew exactly what she was doing. She could seem very sweet when she wanted to.

"It's a little run down, but Ma and I fixed it up a bit inside."

"What?"

She sighed and rolled her eyes. "Never mind."

He shrugged and glanced away. He surveyed the landscape and knew one thing — no matter where they stayed, it would not be home. When the farm came into view, he scanned it for signs of Cassie's brothers.

They were nowhere in sight. Gideon exhaled. The horses paused in front of the main house, but before they could lower their weary heads, Henry slapped the reins, and the wagon jolted forward.

Gideon strained to see what was ahead. His heart dipped into his stomach at the sight of the cabin. He'd been there many a time. How he wished he could forget. Gideon scanned the weathered boards of the old building. Those memories were buried deep within him, and he had no desire to revisit them.

The old cabin was small. Smaller than Gideon remembered. "Hmm," he grunted as he surveyed the sorry house. It would be a long winter cooped up in such a place with no one but Cassie. And he was trying not to think about Lonnie at this moment. Trying and failing. Emotions bottlenecked in his throat, and he swallowed hard.

The wagon came to a stop in front of the porch where a basset hound lifted her head. Gideon did not know what sagged worse, the dog's long ears or the porch floor. He climbed out of the wagon and, after a moment's hesitation, reluctantly lifted his hand to help Cassie down. He released her as quickly as he could.

While Cassie wished her ma and pa farewell, he climbed the rickety steps and paused long enough to scratch the dog on her wrinkled head. As his fingers grazed her velvet fur, he looked into large brown eyes and searched his memory for her name. Her droopy eyelids lifted, and she cast him a pitiful stare. *Hattie.* That was it.

"Good girl," he murmured when she rolled away to start another nap.

The boards creaked behind him, and Gideon turned. Cassie stood on the bottom step, hands clasped. Her shiny boots just touched beneath her hem. Gideon forced a wave when Henry lifted a stiff hand in parting. The wagon jolted and headed back the way it had come. Gideon passed his gaze over Cassie before turning to open the door. As she hovered behind him, he suddenly realized that they were alone. Completely alone.

He tested the doorknob and, when he found it unlocked, nudged the door open and made his way over the threshold. It took a moment for his eyes to adjust to the darkness. Cassie strode in and hesitated before moving to the window, where she pulled back blue-checked curtains. The patched fabric hung crooked.

As if reading his mind, Cassie tried to tug them straight. "This is it." She waved her hand as if to dismiss the place. A piano stood against the far wall, the wood freshly polished. He remembered watching her sit there. They used to play for hours. For a moment he let his gaze wander over her face.

"Are you hungry?" she asked flatly.

"Not really."

"Good." She fiddled with her hands as if she needed to busy them with something. She reached for his hat.

"Leave it." He didn't need any favors. Especially not from her.

She moved to the bedroom, then halted. "Why are you doing this to me?"

"What am I doing?"

Her eyes sparked. "This." She waved a hand. "Punishing me."

He needed air. Gideon unbuttoned the stiff collar of his shirt. "What do you want?" When Cassie shook her head, he lifted his shoulders in a shrug and held out his palms. "I have nothing to give you."

She turned away and ran a hand over her face.

They stood silent for several moments. Her shoulders rose and fell. Finally, Gideon spoke. "You wanted me gone. You asked me to leave. Do you not remember that?"

Staring at the floor, she said nothing.

"And you assured me we had ended things. Do you remember *that*?"

"It didn't make it right," she snapped.

"I'm not saying it was right. But it's what *was*. It was a lie, Cassie. You lied to me."

"Well, if you hadn't have ran off and married —"

"I didn't *run off* and marry her." His gaze captured hers. Cassie could have spoken up. She could have told the reverend. She could have done *something* to let them know that she still had his last name. And yet she watched from the shadows as they placed Lonnie's hand in his. Gideon rubbed the bridge of his nose.

This had been the longest day of his life.

When Cassie faced him, her voice was barely audible. "I know you didn't want this, but we have to make the best of it."

"You have no idea what I want," Gideon said softly. "What I want is my wife and son back. They're gone, and I don't know that I'll ever see them again." His voice wavered. "I might never see Jacob again. You have no *idea* what it's like."

"Yes I do!" She threw her hands up. "I know exactly what it feels like."

"Don't try and make me feel sorry for you."

"I don't want you to feel sorry for me."

205

She moved into the bedroom and shut the door.

Alone, Gideon sat at the table. He did not have to follow to know that the door squeaked or that the bed was pressed up against the wall beneath a tiny, four-pane window. He already knew. He'd been there before. He hated everything about this house. About his life.

Thrusting his hand into his pocket, he touched a fold of wool. He pulled it out and held it in his palm. Fingering it lightly, he stared at the tiny knit cap. The late afternoon light danced across the room. Gideon traced the tip of his finger over the soft wool. And thought of his son. The heart that raced with fury inside his chest began to ache.

Cassie picked up a pillow and threw it at the door. She sank onto the bed. Exhausted, she cradled her head in her palms. *Gideon.* The man had more heat under his collar than a steaming kettle.

She didn't want this.

The room was graying. She stared at the candle on the nightstand. The new wick was pale; it had never been lit. Fresh. Pure. She wondered what that would be like. Cassie hung her head. If only she had been different. If only she had been smarter. Better. Like Lonnie.

But she wasn't Lonnie, and she never would be. Cassie rubbed her arms, feeling more alone than ever.

What was it her ma had said? *"Give him time."* No time would be enough for that man. She would never be what he needed. Wanted. Yet here she was. She looked out the window and tried to remember the rest of her ma's words from just that morning when, once again, Cassie had voiced her reservations.

"The Lord will be your strength."

Yeah, well, the Lord and her weren't exactly on speaking terms of late. Cassie unlaced a boot, the leather shinier than it'd been in a year. She unlaced the other and set them on the floor, then sat cross-legged in the center of the bed, her back straight. She stared at the closed door, and it seemed to stare back. For several minutes, she didn't move. Then a fresh tear stung her raw cheek, and she smeared it away. Yet she did not ache for herself.

She ached for the man whose muffled sobs swept past the pine boards.

Twenty-Four

"You haven't hardly touched your food." Sarah set down her napkin and raised an eyebrow.

Lonnie stared down at her cold corn cake. She wiped crumbs from her skirt and shrugged. "I guess I'm just not hungry." She folded the tiny meal into her napkin and tucked it safely in the food basket that sat beside her on the forest floor. She pulled her hand away and let it fall in her lap. Perhaps she would eat it later . . . perhaps not.

Sarah sat across from Lonnie with her legs folded in. A mound of colorful skirts had been pulled up around her knees, and her plump, pale calves caught the light of the sun. The blanket of dried leaves beneath them served as their humble table. The sky, the color of blue-eyed grass, shimmered through the canopy of autumn-hued trees. Deciding her aunt had the right idea, Lonnie stuck out her legs and hoisted up her skirt until the folds of brown calico draped around her own pale knees. Her winter stockings caught the afternoon sunlight, and she instantly felt its warmth through the black wool.

She drew in a deep sigh and let it out slowly as she savored the woody fragrance around her. There seemed to be a peace about these woods. About this day. Lonnie wrapped her arms across her stomach and hoped some of that peace would seep through her skin. Even as her eyelids grew heavy, Jacob's joyous laughter stole her attention. It took little effort to keep him occupied with Addie around. The little girl entertained Jacob by stacking a pile of acorns and letting the little one scatter them with a carefree shriek. While Addie gathered the acorns in her hands, Jacob looked up at his mother and smiled.

"Look at you," Lonnie said. "You're quite the little destroyer."

Jacob lowered his head and searched the ground in front of him for things that crinkled and crackled between his tiny hands. Lonnie smiled. Her son was content, and Sarah still had another corn cake to eat. She knew they would not be leaving anytime soon. Her lower back ached, and her knees were stiff from sitting in such cramped quarters. She was in no hurry to climb aboard the rickety cart.

Lonnie rested her chin on her shoulder. The road, once new and untried, had become well traveled by her and Gideon. The road that led home. Lonnie wanted to put as much distance between them and Rocky Knob as possible. She knew it was useless, but she hoped the farther she got from Gideon, the easier it would be to breathe. Lonnie pressed a hand to her chest. There was just one problem with her plan — he was everywhere inside her. He was in and through her son. She sighed and closed her eyes. Distance would do nothing.

When a chickadee landed nearby, Addie jumped up and chased it. Jacob lifted his little head and watched as his young aunt ran in circles. More than once, Addie slipped on the layer of dried leaves, and though she was quick, she was no match for the spry chickadee.

Sarah's voice was soft and low when she broke the silence. "A penny for your thoughts."

Lonnie eyed her aunt and felt her brow unfold.

When Jacob tried to stick a dried leaf in his mouth, Sarah pulled it from his chubby fingers and threw it to the wind. Turning her attention back to Lonnie, her face gentled. "You all right?"

Knowing her chin would tremble, Lonnie dared not answer.

Sarah pulled Jacob into her lap and stroked his curls. The breeze rustled through the trees. A flurry of scarlet and gold leaves glistened toward the ground. Sarah hummed quietly. The lows of her voice blended with the highs of Jacob's babble. She tilted her face to the sunshine, and the pair swayed. The song ended, and Jacob flapped his arms.

"We've made good time." Sarah smoothed her hem and fingered a loose thread. "Very good time." She yanked the thread free. It floated to the bracken below.

"We would have never made it this far so quickly on foot. We'll be to the pass in no time."

Sarah stood and hoisted the food basket onto the crook of her arm. "How far is the pass, would you say?"

Lonnie tilted her head to the side. "Maybe another day. At least not much farther than that." She squinted up at her aunt. "I hope Jebediah will be there."

Lifting a piece of sun-bleached canvas, Sarah set the basket into the cart. "From what you've told me of the Bennetts, those two would move mountains to get to you." She turned and smiled down at Lonnie. "I'm sure Jebediah'll be there."

"Addie," Lonnie called as she scooped Jacob into her arms. "Time to get goin'."

A tiny fist patted against her neck, and Lonnie looked down into Jacob's face. She smoothed his hair and kissed his brow, fanning the tiny flame of fear in her heart. The day would soon come when he would ask about his pa.

Her heart nearly stilled in her chest. *Is he even old enough to remember him?*

Addie gave Sugar a gentle pat, then climbed into the cart. Lonnie lifted Jacob onto her little sister's lap. She vowed that Jacob would know his father. Even if he never saw him again, she would keep Gideon alive for her son. She would tell him stories and share all the good memories she had made with her husband. She slipped a hand in front of her mouth. He was not her husband anymore.

He was Cassie's.

When the cart's wheels rolled forward, they left the warmth of the sun, and the shadows of the forest engulfed them. Reaching behind her, Lonnie pulled a blanket free and handed it to Addie. "If Jacob seems cold."

Addie took the blanket and, with all the care of a young mother, carefully tucked it around the sleepy child.

Lonnie started to pull the canvas back over her things when something caught her eye. She grabbed the plaid sleeve and tugged the jacket free. Sliding it onto her lap, she fingered the collar and ran her hands across the chest pocket that was still missing a button. How many times had she reminded herself to fix it?

She slipped her arms through the sleeves and draped the jacket over her shoulders. What did it matter now? It was hers. Her instincts directed her hands as Lonnie folded the collar up. The action made Gideon flash through her mind. Would she forget his face someday? Would his sweet woodsy smell fade from the plaid flannel? She pressed her hands between her knees when they began to shake. It was impossible to hope.

Twenty-Five

Gideon scratched the rake across the dry yard, leaves tumbling toward his boots. He looked up into his pa's face. "That's the whole of it."

His pa shook his head, thin face filled with sorrow. "I'm so sorry, son."

Gritting his teeth, Gideon simply nodded.

"It pains me that it's come to this. The Allans . . . Cassie." His eyebrows lifted. "How did we never know?"

"Nobody did. I made sure of it." And look what it had cost him.

"And what of Lonnie?"

With his eye on the rake and its slow, measured movements, Gideon relayed the story.

When he finished, his pa let out a puff of breath, his exasperation clear. "I'm so sorry." His pa lifted his face toward the cabin.

Gideon followed his gaze to where Cassie

sat on the porch, snapping beans.

"Stay for supper," Gideon blurted, hope leaking into his voice. He could use the company.

"I'd love to. But your ma's expectin' me. She wanted me to tell you she'll visit as soon as she can. Lil'uns are under the weather, and she's got her hands full."

"I'm glad you came by. It was good to see you."

His pa flicked his head toward his farm. "Come with me. Get some of your things."

Gideon tapped the rake in the dirt. "I don't know . . ."

"Come on." His pa waved him forward. "The leaves will still be there."

It would be nice to have his tools. Some small piece of normal. Gideon bobbed his head in a nod and followed his pa. He leaned his rake against the chicken coop, and together, they strode from the farm. A fierce autumn wind rippled through the treetops, but as they sank deeper within the forest, the air was nearly still.

His pa chatted calmly, asking questions, answering the few that Gideon sent his way. Their boots crossed onto O'Riley land, and they headed straight for Gideon's shop.

Gideon opened the familiar door and inhaled the scent of wood and grease. He froze, unable to move. This had been his life.

A squeeze on his shoulder and his pa spoke. "I'll give you some time to sort through all this. I'll go get the wagon ready to drive it back."

After flinging off his jacket, Gideon stepped into the dark building. He didn't bother lighting the oil lamp that hung over the workbench. He didn't need to. The faint light that spilled through the grimy window was enough to trace the outlines of his things. His work. He knew it all by heart. Gideon dragged his hand along the edge of the workbench. The same place where Lonnie had. He remembered her small hands as she'd studied the surface. Her eyes wondering, innocent. She had trusted him. Not because she was a fool. But because he knew how to capture that trust. Knew all the right words. It was an art, and he'd been the master of it.

"You idiot." He kicked a crate and tools rattled. He kicked it again. Picking up a hammer, he flung it across the shop where it clattered against the far wall, nearly shattering the board. He let out a growl and wanted to punch something, anything. But he forced himself to press his hands back to the bench. They shook as anger pulsed through his arms like venom.

He'd taken advantage of all that Lonnie had. To what? Prove to his friends that his luck with women hadn't truly changed with Lonnie Sawyer. Gideon let his head hang low. His sweet, sweet Lonnie.

She was nothing like Cassie. Cassie was nothing like Lonnie.

There wasn't an innocent bone in Cassie Allan's body. She and Gideon were cut from the same cloth. A convenience, he had once thought. An advantage to his desires in the dark hours of night.

"Everything all right?" His pa's eyes flitted around the dark room. "I heard a ruckus."

Despite the ache in his chest, Gideon forced himself to collect his tools. "Everything's fine." He filled a wooden crate with saws and chisels.

His pa lowered a pair of hammers into another. "I remember this one," his pa said fondly. He turned the small hammer around in his hand. "It was one of the first. You were just a little tyke — couldn't even fasten your own overalls yet. Always wanting to pound nails and use a saw. Your ma thought you were going to cut off a hand, so I decided it was time to teach you."

Gideon felt a half smile form. "I remember that."

His pa set the hammer in the crate and reached for another, followed by a large mallet.

His files were in a rusty tin can, which Gideon clutched to his chest as he moved to the door, then stacked them haphazardly on the stoop. Sun hit his shoulders, but the wind, here in the clearing, blew strong, tousling his shirt. The cold seeped all the way through to his bones.

"What about these?" His pa's voice drew him back.

Gideon watched him lower a small rocking chair from a hook overhead and then pulled down a stool. He motioned to the body of a mandolin that dangled. "That looks mighty fine, son."

Gideon pulled down the half-formed instrument.

"Don't you want to take it with you?"

What he *wanted* to do was beat it over Eli Allan's head, but he just nodded. "Sure. I'll take this and a few others." He motioned toward a stack of candleholders and other odds and ends. "Give those to ma."

"You can sell these." His pa moved a copper milk can filled with walking sticks

218

toward the door. "They'll catch a pretty penny."

He doubted it.

Gideon snatched up a dust broom, a pair of leather work gloves, and a dozen rusty clamps; he tossed them into a crate and straightened. "That's the last of it. I'll fetch that wood there. And we can be off."

"Won't you come up to the house, have supper with us?"

He thought of Cassie alone. He pressed his tongue to his sharpest tooth and glanced up at the house. That wasn't home anymore. The wind stirred his hair, making him feel small against the vast clearing. He didn't know where home was.

TWENTY-SIX

As the wind picked up, Gideon and his pa unloaded his things into a small, rickety shed that accompanied the little cabin. It wasn't much, but it would keep him out of the snow through the winter months.

Gideon set down the last crate. His pa squeezed his shoulder.

"I'll leave you now. Stop by soon, will ya?"

"I'll try," Gideon said halfheartedly.

He watched his pa drive away.

All day, he'd managed to stay busy, but now as the sun sank behind a black line of trees, he could delay no more. Shrugging deeper into his coat, he left the mess to be organized tomorrow.

Seeing the trickle of smoke from the stovepipe, he grabbed an armload of wood. "Hmm," he murmured. "Not enough."

Since no dried logs sat waiting to be split, he would have to go into the woods to collect more firewood. He glanced at the house where light poured through the small kitchen window. Cassie walked past, a pair of plates in her hand. She was angry with him now, but Gideon knew better. As mad as Cassie was, deep down she still cared for him. He saw it in the way she looked at him. The realization stood his senses on alert. He knew what she was capable of.

The porch steps groaned beneath his boots. When he swung the door open, it scarcely missed hitting her.

With a grunt, Gideon dropped the armful next to the tiny stove.

"Thank you." Her tone was reined in.

Brushing dirt and splinters from his shirt, he felt her gaze on him. He sniffed and wiped his sleeve across his forehead. The house smelled good — very good.

"You missed dinner this afternoon." Cassie said, still working. "Supper's almost ready."

His eyes didn't meet hers. "Then I'll wash up."

She pointed to the water bucket warming near the stove. "There's soap next to the washbasin."

Gideon dipped his head and stepped around her. "I'll just be a minute." The bedroom was dark, and not wanting to fetch a candle, he waited for his eyes to adjust.

He washed slowly, working the soap through his hands and up his forearms. The warm water felt good as he rinsed his skin.

When he returned to the kitchen, Cassie motioned toward the table. "Sit." She tugged out a chair for herself. Her hair was pulled back into a soft bun, tied with the same scarlet ribbon. It grazed her pale skin. Gideon glanced away, wishing he hadn't noticed.

A wise man kept his eyes on his food when Cassie Allan was in the room.

His boots thudded forward and he sat. The table was small, too small. When their knees touched, he pushed his chair back with a disturbing scrape. Letting his attention fall on the spread before him, he surveyed all she had done. Warm cornbread steamed inside a cast-iron skillet, and a dutch oven sat in the center of the table. The succulent smells hung heavy in the air.

She lifted her hand to her chin, pausing slightly, before placing it on the table, palm up. Gideon fought an eye roll. Since when was Cassie the praying type? Setting his jaw, he placed his hand over hers. Her skin was warm. Soft. He fought the urge to pull away.

Cassie closed her eyes, and he followed her lead. Silence continued.

He gulped and cleared his throat. "Thank

You, Lord, for this food . . . and for the hands that have prepared it."

The words were stiff, forced. *Forgive me, Lord, it's all I have.*

Her hand lingered inside his, relaxed beneath his rigid palm. But it was the wrong hand. Without saying *amen,* he gently unfolded his fingers from hers.

Cassie lifted the lid of the dutch oven, and a cloud of steam, thick with the smell of onions and broth, greeted him.

He hoped not much conversation would be required of him.

"I hope it tastes all right." She filled their bowls. "It's just vegetables."

"I'll try to get some meat tomorrow." He knew of a good spot up the way. At least it used to be good.

Cassie sipped from her spoon. "Sure." Her voice was gentle, but not eager.

Careful to keep his eyes on his bowl, Gideon lifted broth to his lips.

They ate in silence. The only sound was the clanging of their spoons against black enamel. He swallowed another bite but could not swallow the sinking feeling in his stomach.

She seemed to study him, and he braved a glance. Her eyes danced as she searched his. She set her spoon down and folded her hands in her lap.

"Joel tricked you, didn't he?"

The man's name made his feet grow cold. Gideon smoothed a hand over his unshaven jaw and nodded.

Cassie fiddled with the edge of her ribbon. "That wasn't what I had in mind."

Sure it wasn't.

"When my ma found the papers, the ones I hadn't turned in, she was furious with me." Her eyebrows lifted. "Furious." Cassie set her spoon down. "She told my pa right away. He and my brothers got so stirred up. It all went out of hand from there."

Gideon was glad he hadn't been around. "So this wasn't your idea?"

"Not really."

"But it's awful convenient, isn't it?"

"I didn't exactly have a lot of options." Sass leaked into her tone. "Once they found out, they took the matter straight to Reverend Gardner, furious at the mix-up. It was all over then. Word spreads quickly among listening ears."

How he knew it. He was certain her reputation had been destroyed within the week.

The way she studied him, eyes filled with sorrow, confirmed it. But he wouldn't feel sorry for Cassie. She didn't deserve it.

"Why didn't you go through with it?" He hated how weak his voice was. "You wanted to put an end to this." He motioned between them. "Why couldn't you have meant it? Why did you have to let me —"

She tugged on her earlobe, and the shrug she offered fueled the fire in him.

"Are you saying you have no good reason for why those documents didn't make it to the courthouse?"

"That's not what I said."

"Then I'm all ears, Cassie. Tell me one thing. Did you know that I was going to marry Lonnie?"

She didn't move.

He waited.

Finally, she nodded.

"And yet you said nothing? Why didn't you come to me? Why didn't you speak up?"

"I was scared."

"I keep hearing that! Scared of what?"

Silence crushed the air between them.

After a long breath, he spoke. "You didn't know what you wanted, did you?"

She looked away.

"Well, thanks so very much for pulling me down with you."

She straightened, leaning forward so quickly she nearly bumped her bowl. "I didn't mean for this to happen. I didn't know what I wanted, and I thought I could figure it out."

"I *married* her, Cassie. I married her." His voice hitched. "Did you not see what a big deal that was?"

Her eyes fell.

He gripped his cup so tight he was glad it wasn't glass.

"I don't know what to say to make this better," she said softly.

"That's because nothing you could say will make this better."

Small boots brushed his, and Gideon pulled his feet back. She studied him, a glassy look in her eyes. Regret clear in her face. A tornado raged inside his chest as he watched her.

"So here we sit," he said.

"Here we sit." Her spoon hovered motionless above her bowl.

"I'm not going to love you."

"I didn't ask you to."

"Then good."

TWENTY-SEVEN

"There's the pass." Lonnie pointed to a cluster of trees. They did not look out of the ordinary. Still, she recognized the curve in the road and the slope of the mountain, and she knew that just past those russet oaks, one could cross only on foot. To get a cart and horse around would mean more than a day's journey. Lonnie eyed the narrow path, rutted and sloped by rain storms. Elliot's arthritic legs could not carry them through. She would go on alone. *Lord, be my strength.* Never in her life had she been alone.

Sarah stared in the same direction, and when Lonnie glanced at her dear aunt, the older woman's eyes were tender. Lonnie's chest tightened. She stared at the small path ahead, studied the mass of scraggly oaks, and prayed Jebediah would be waiting on the other side.

Sarah flicked the reins. "Git on up!"

Elliot lumbered toward where the path

narrowed, then the cart stilled. Sarah lowered the reins. Lonnie glanced over her shoulder and saw that both Addie and Jacob were fast asleep. Curled beneath a tattered afghan, neither stirred when the cart settled back on its rickety wheels.

"Might as well let them rest." She turned forward and sighed. Lonnie trusted that if Jebediah were truly at the bottom of the hill, he would not mind waiting another hour.

"So I suppose this is it," Sarah said. The breeze played with a loose strand of her ginger hair, sending it dancing across her lightly freckled forehead. She tucked the lock behind her ear. "You know . . . it was hard enough having you leave me once. But twice." She shook her head and fell silent. A tear crawled down her ruddy cheek. Lonnie rarely saw her aunt cry. The confession made her love the woman even more.

Lonnie squeezed Sarah's hand. "I'm gonna miss you more than ever."

Sarah's soft bun shook when she bobbed her head. "Look at me. A silly woman." She wiped her eyes with the hem of her apron and chuckled. "Guess I'm not as good at good-byes as I thought I was."

"I hope you'll visit someday. It would be nice to have family around." Since Gideon could not love her, anyone who could would be welcome company.

Drawing in a deep breath, Sarah's eyes narrowed beneath the weight of her words. "That man of yours —"

Lonnie raised her hand. "Aunt Sarah. Gideon isn't my —"

Sarah caught hold of Lonnie's wrist and pressed it down. "I don't care what you say or what *they* say, but if I must, I'll just call him Gideon." Her voice softened, and she picked up Lonnie's hand, folding it inside her silky palm. "You two have gone through what no couple should ever be forced to do." Sarah, a woman who had never married, who had never found her own true love, closed her eyes, and the lines in her face drew sharp. "It *angers* me to see it happen. I know it's what should be and what *must* be . . . but that don't make it any less wrong in my heart." Her voice trailed off, and she turned away.

Wishing her aunt did not have to water the small bud of desire for a man she could not have, Lonnie pulled her hand free. "Yes," she stated. "But I'm afraid it's too late. Now *Cassie* is Gideon's wife."

The reins fell from Sarah's grasp. She chucked her skirt up to her calves and spun toward Lonnie. She waved a fist in the air. "You've got fight in you. I know it —"

"No!" Lonnie snapped. "There's no use." Her voice cracked. "Perhaps he's made her his wife by now."

A sorrowful shadow crossed over her aunt's face, and Lonnie looked away.

She eyed the pass that separated her from more than her aunt Sarah. Soon, it would separate her from Gideon. She took a deep breath. *If there had been any other way.*

A cool breeze stirred their skirts, and Lonnie felt the chill of the late afternoon on her arms. After a long silence, Sarah put her hand over her niece's. "Lonnie, I'm sorry. I shouldn't have waited until now to voice my opinions. I don't know what came over me." She touched Lonnie's cheek. "I admire your courage."

Lonnie fiddled with the tin wedding ring in her apron pocket. "I'm just doing what has to be done. There's nothing courageous about that."

Sarah wrapped an arm around her. She formed her words slowly, and they seemed to hang in the quiet stillness around them. "Sometimes duty takes courage. Often-times, more than we think we have."

Lonnie scaled the narrow path with Jacob snug in his sling. A gentle tug on Sugar's line and the old mule plodded along, their two sacks draped over her sloped back. Addie clung to Lonnie's skirt. Lonnie glanced over her shoulder to where Sarah stood at the edge of the ravine. She heard not a sound as she listened for Jebediah's presence. *Lord, let him be here.*

Then she saw him.

Smoke swirled around the man in the plaid coat. Having been busy tending his fire, he rose to a stand. Even from a distance, his smile was broad. Lonnie glanced back, and Sarah waved from the top of the hill. Her patchwork skirt flapped in the breeze, and she wiped her hands across her eyes.

"Good-bye," Lonnie whispered. She waved. The late afternoon shadows blocked out the sun, and even though she'd slipped into Gideon's flannel coat, she shivered. When Sarah disappeared from the ledge, Lonnie strained to listen until she heard her aunt holler out a command to Elliot. Lonnie prayed that some of her aunt's strength had been planted like a seed inside her.

"Who's that?" Addie interrupted Lonnie's thoughts.

Lonnie squeezed the small hand inside hers. "That's Jebediah. He's a kind man. You will like him." When Jacob saw Jebediah, she could hardly hold the boy, who nearly squirmed from her grasp. She lifted him from the sling.

With the gait of a man half his age, Jebediah rushed forward and engulfed both Lonnie and Jacob in a tobacco-scented hug. The bristles of his beard tickled her cheek. Crushed beneath his strength, she instantly felt at home. Pulling back, Jebediah caught Jacob as he dove toward him.

"There's my boy," he said with a wide grin.

Jacob patted Jebediah's cheek and bounced up and down.

"We missed you," Lonnie sighed.

"And I missed both of you." Jebediah looked down at Addie, who huddled at Lonnie's side. "And who's this?"

Lonnie stepped back. "This is Addie. My little sister." Lonnie watched Jebediah's face for a reaction as she continued. "Would you and Elsie mind if she stayed with us for a while?"

"You kiddin'? Elsie'll be thrilled." Jebediah's eyes softened when he looked down at Addie. "She always wanted a full house." Jebediah pinched Addie's cheek, and the little girl stepped behind her sister.

Undeterred, Jebediah winked. "That's all right. An old grizzly like me . . . well, I don't blame the girl." He knelt and his grin widened. "Would you like to come sit by the fire? You look like you could use a molasses cookie. Elsie made them fresh."

Like a child on Christmas morning, Addie's eyes widened with surprise. She nodded eagerly and her dark curls bobbed. She darted toward the campsite without her host. Jebediah followed, Jacob pressed to his chest. Addie sank onto a blanket, and Jebediah lowered Jacob next to her. After pulling two cookies from a dented tin, he handed one to each of them. Addie immediately took a bite, but Jacob rolled his cookie around on the blanket before taking a small taste.

Lonnie watched the joyful trio, but what little peace had tried to spread its wings in her heart was shattered when her torment returned. Unable to move, she stood frozen. The air pressed on her.

Jebediah turned. "Lonnie? You all right?"

She'd held her tears at bay as long as she could. She was tired of trying to be strong. "No."

"Oh, Lonnie." He strode back, and his hands cupped her arms.

She pressed her forehead to his shoulder. Her throat burned. "I'm so frustrated."

Jebediah placed a hand against her head,

and his voice was low. "I know. I know. I'm sorry."

Her head slid against his coat as she shook her head. "He's gone, Jebediah. He's really gone. Why did this happen?"

Standing in the presence of Jebediah — the one man who truly loved and shaped her husband, helped mold him into the man she loved — Lonnie felt the loss of Gideon afresh. Sobs overtook her. "It's gotta be a bad dream." She clutched the fabric of Jebediah's coat.

Jebediah's voice remained soft. "You did what you had to do."

She pulled back. "I keep hearing that! Why did he do this? Why couldn't things just have turned out well?" She shook her head so fiercely, curls tumbled from her bun. "I didn't ask for this."

"No." He gripped her shoulders, ducking his head until they were eye level. "You didn't ask for this, Lonnie. Not for one moment do you deserve this." Jebediah glanced to the children who cuddled on the blanket, the tin of cookies at Addie's side. "But sometimes God puts us into the hot water. And when we're in the middle of it, it's almost impossible to bear." He shook his head slowly, face grave. "Why He does that, I'm not sure. But you're gonna be stronger for it." His eyes bore into hers, and he shook her shoulders with a gentle strength. "You're gonna get through this."

"How do you know?" Apron clutched, she wadded it beneath the weight of broken hopes. "Was I a fool, Jebediah? Was I wrong to trust him?"

"No, Lonnie. You're anything but a fool. He loved you." Jebediah spoke the last words slowly, each one deliberate. Coupled with the honesty in his eyes, the words brought a fresh wave of emotion bubbling up inside Lonnie. "That man still does. He loves you with everything he has. I know it. God was working in that man's life."

"He was." The words seemed to break as they fell from her tongue, but she believed them. "I saw it every day. He was changing." Gideon O'Riley, the man who had once cared about no one but himself, was changing every day for her and for Jacob. She knew it in her heart of hearts to be true. But now he was gone. Lonnie locked her trembling hands together and sent up a prayer — no, a plea — that God would fill the void inside her with His strength.

Twenty-Eight

Gideon knew that sleep was fooling him, but he clung with all his might to the world he saw. Plaid skirts billowed around her form as Lonnie set down a shallow pan. Icy water sloshed over the edge. A crow flew overhead, and she arched her neck, lifting her face to the thick row of river birch at the edge of the water. Morning dew glistened all around as Lonnie rolled the cuffs of her blouse past cream-colored wrists.

Gideon's hand twitched as if to trace his fingers there.

The crow called again.

Startled, Gideon opened his eyes.

It took him a moment, searching the ceiling, to recognize the dark wood, the narrow walls. Lonnie faded. The nightmare of the situation made his heart sink.

He rolled onto his side and stared at the dark window. The gray sky hinted that the sun was not long from rising. Gideon closed his eyes and tried to bring Lonnie's image back. The light brightened. He reached over and, from the pocket of his shirt that he'd tossed to the floor, pulled out her ribbon. He fingered the tattered fabric.

That was all he had left of her. Yellow calico. As it always did, it struck him like a blow to the gut. It was not the first time the realization had come to him, but this time it was final. There was no way around it. It was all he would ever have. She would not change to him. She would not grow with the seasons as he would. Forever in his heart and mind she would be the wife of his youth. Eighteen-year-old Lonnie. Jacob too. The boy would never seem to age beyond the baby who crawled about, causing mischief for his ma and pa. He would grow older in Gideon's mind, but never in his memories.

Though it pained him, he tucked his hand beneath his pillow, fighting the urge to lift the ribbon to his nose. It was no use. Her scent was gone. It had already faded away. Sitting up, he forced himself to face the day. With a soft groan, he left the comfort of the mattress and stood before the window. The sky was lighter now, the sun just peeking through the trees.

He turned and leaned against the windowsill. The room was bright enough now that he could make out the figure lying in the bed. When Cassie rolled onto her side, he held his breath. What would she think if she found him watching her? Her eyelids fluttered but remained closed. Her hand slid across the white sheet and rested beneath her cheek. The messy hair draped over her shoulder lay dark against the pale sheets, dark against skin the color of cream.

As if sleep had chased away her boldness, her peaceful expression kept his eyes on her face. How many times had he watched her sleep? Gideon blinked. His heart twisted in his chest. She was beautiful. Only a blind man could disagree. Needing to be free of the cramped room, he dressed quickly and left without a sound.

He grabbed his oilcloth coat and hat. The trees were still and quiet, the sky a mind-numbing blue. A trio of birds darted overhead. Their black wings glinted in the bright sun. It brought him no peace. None of it did. Nothing made sense but the cold that bit at his bare hands. Gideon stuffed his arms through his coat and pressed his hat over his hair. He needed space.

His boots carried him toward the barn, and without checking to see if he was being watched, he flung the door open. With not so much as a glance over his shoulder, he moved to the farthest stall where the second of the Allans' horses stood, black tail swishing. The horse glanced at him, large eyes almost curious. Knowing.

Gideon reached up and yanked a bridle from its peg. He flung a saddle blanket over the stall and reached for the latch. Time to put some distance between him and his troubles, and the sooner the better. Whether he owned the beast or not. He unlatched the stall, moved toward the gelding, and slid his palm up the horse's muscular neck. He slid the bridle over the long, chestnut nose and gently pressed the bit between two rows of broad white teeth. "Thatta boy." His hands moved to the buckle, the permanence of his reality driving a wedge into his gut.

"Come to steal a horse?"

Gideon jerked his head up to see Jack standing in the doorway.

"Or are you just tired of female company?" Jack grunted out a laugh. He moved to the edge of the stall, hitched his boot on the lowest rail, and draped his wrist on the top.

Gideon moved his eyes back to the beast and gave the brown coat one final stroke. "Little bit of both," he admitted.

"You weren't going to ask, were you?"

"I was thinking about it."

"Liar."

Gideon chuckled, the sensation foreign of late. "Don't worry." He pulled the bridle off and hung it up. He moved back for the blanket. "Your horse is safe."

"You know what they'd think." Jack studied him. His eyes were serious, but his posture still dangled slack on the stall as if he couldn't have cared less.

"That I'm running away," Gideon said flatly.

Jack screwed his mouth to the side and lifted his eyebrows. He stepped into the stall, picked up a bristle brush, and worked long strokes down the horse's sleek back.

"Well, don't worry. I'm not going anywhere." Gideon pulled his hat off, sifted through his hair, then slid it back on.

"Of course you're not." Jack grabbed the bridle from its peg. He thumbed the smooth leather, eyes down. Finally, with a slow lift of his chest, he stepped around the animal. With quiet movements, he slid it over the horse's face.

"What are you doing?" Gideon tapped his knuckles on the stall.

"Gettin' 'im ready."

Gideon's hand stilled. "But your brothers. Your pa."

Jack draped the saddle blanket over the

horse's broad back. "It's not their horse." He settled the burgundy mat squarely, followed by a quilted pad. "Besides. Someone around here needs to show you that there's a sane one among this lot. We're not all ogres with shotguns." The saddle creaked when he lifted it from the stand, and with a grunt Jack hefted it onto the horse's back.

"What about Cassie?" Gideon stepped in to help.

"Cassie's made her own choices in life. She's a big girl." Jack gripped the pommel, straightening the saddle while Gideon buckled the girth beneath the horse's belly.

"How do you know I won't steal it?"

Jack chuckled. "Because then I'll have my own reason to shoot you." He patted the gelding's rump. "His name's Abel and he's mine. Bring him back in one piece, all right?"

Gideon nodded once, sobered by the man's faith in him. "I promise." For the first time in weeks, Gideon took a deep, thorough breath. The cool air lifted his lungs, an invisible weight shifting. "I'll be back in a few hours." His voice nearly hitched, so desperate was he to be free of this place.

Jack moved to a trunk. The heavy lid groaned when he lifted it, and he pulled out an armful of riding gear. "Might as well make a day of it."

"Git on up!" Abel scaled the steep slope. The *clop, clop* of his shod hoofs and the creaking of leather were the only sounds to be heard. They scaled the hill, and the land leveled out into a broad, flat valley. Gideon glanced around. Nothing but open land for miles. He pulled his hat off and used it to shove his hair back before settling it into place. He moved the mount along a stand of trees, the road beneath him unfamiliar. Untested.

And the urge to run hit him like a blow to the chest.

His eyelids nearly fluttered closed. A handful of days and he could be at the Bennetts' door. Lonnie's familiar form in his arms. Her scent. Her tears. His hand gripped the reins tighter when a burn threatened to clamp his throat shut. His son.

Gideon gently tapped his worn-out boots into Abel's side, and the horse broke into a trot. A tumble of clouds shifted in front of the sun. The air cooled. Gideon tugged his coat tighter, the oilcloth smooth in his fingers. Moments passed as light danced with shadow before the sun broke free. It hit Gideon's face in a burst of warmth, and he tilted his chin up, wishing he could ride toward it.

Ride toward it and never stop.

Not until he reached his bride. And in her hands he could place the tattered remains of his heart. For she was the only one who could mend it.

TWENTY-NINE

Though Gideon kept his eyes down when Cassie pushed a small plate of biscuits in front of him, he couldn't help but notice the scent of lilac she left in her wake. He'd bet everything he owned that she'd dabbed the fragrant water along her collarbone while dressing. A memory of her he wished away with every fiber in his being.

He pressed his tongue in his cheek when her hip bumped the table in passing, apron strings bouncing. He caught his coffee cup before it tumbled from the table and into his lap. Hot droplets scalded his hand. That woman.

Finally sitting, she flashed him a smile. "Ham?" She tipped the pan toward him.

He lifted his plate without speaking. He knew what game she was playing at, and he wasn't about to take part.

A biscuit steamed when he broke it in half. A knifeful of blackberry jam and he folded it back over itself. He licked the tip of his thumb before sliding the jar in Cassie's direction.

"Thank you."

He gave her a halfhearted nod.

"I was thinking that maybe we'd get some chickens. It would be so nice to have eggs."

He stuck out his bottom lip.

Blue eyes shot heavenward for the briefest of moments. "Are you really not talking to me?"

He chewed and swallowed, then reached for his coffee. "It doesn't really seem like there's a whole lot to say."

"Well, when our conversation consists of you grunting and making faces, then no, there's not a whole lot to say."

"Fine." He straightened, folded his hands, and rested his forearms on the table in front of him. With nothing but the small surface between them, he nearly towered over her. Her eyes widened slightly.

"Good morning, Cassie. How did you sleep?"

"Now you're just mocking me."

"No. I'm making conversation."

"You can be really annoying when you want to be."

"Well then, I suppose I'll just keep silent."

She nibbled her bottom lip until it pinked.

Finally, she rose and turned toward the bedroom. She brushed past the piano so quickly that her music toppled and floated to the floor. With a flush in her cheeks, she bent and gathered the pages. Gideon rose.

"*Don't* help me."

Slowly, he sank back down.

With a surprising tenderness, she stacked the pages, tucked them in the rickety piano bench, and without so much as a word, disappeared into the bedroom.

The quilt caught the morning light as Cassie flung it over the bed. After folding it down, she fluffed both pillows and stuffed them in their places. She fought the urge to smooth her hand over the white linens. He was so close, yet so far. She'd spent the day yesterday scanning the horizon, wondering if he would return. Jack had spoken to her not long after sunrise, promising that Gideon hadn't flitted, but her spirit struggled to believe it.

Cassie worked her way around the bed. She paused and stared at her reflection in the small wall mirror. *A bride.* What joy should accompany the title, she did not know. Cherished, loved. She was none of those things.

Cassie turned away.

Had he truly sworn his love and devotion once? At least he had pretended to mean it. She closed her eyes and pressed her palm to her forehead. Images of the past came back to haunt her. She remembered Gideon's smile when he looked at her. The confident way he reached for her hand. She had been desired. Longed for.

Those days are gone. Reaching down, she picked up her discarded nightgown and tossed it onto the bed. Maybe she was going about this all wrong. Clearly that life was no more. Only a fool would continue to hope. Fine then. No more glances. No more trying to get his attention. He obviously didn't want her around. Besides . . . playing hard to get had its own advantages.

Cassie folded the nightgown carefully, slipped it in the top drawer of the dresser, and shut the drawer quietly. The front door opened. Her hand stilled on the cold wood. The front door closed. There was no need to look out the window to know that Gideon was gone. He had no reason to hang around. Cassie knew the way of his heart; the farther he was from the tiny cabin, the better. He wanted nothing to do with her.

Well, two could play at that game.

Making her way around the bed, she stumbled into the dresser and, with a stifled yelp, crouched down. She rubbed a hand across her toes, but the sting remained. After a few deep breaths, she fought the urge to cry, then sank to her knees in a defeated heap. She leaned her forehead against the side of the bed and stared at the floor. Then something caught her eye. She ran her hand beneath the bed and caught hold of a piece of fabric. She pulled it into the light. A yellow ribbon streaked with dust filled her palm. Cassie turned it over and gently wiped it clean. She sat back on her heels and stared at it. It wasn't hers. Her heart sank even as she let her hand fall to the floor. She'd seen Lonnie wear it that day at the church.

Her cheeks flushed with heat, and she jumped up to open the window. She loosened the rusty latch, and it took both hands to wiggle the window open. A breeze that whispered of coming snow breathed into the room.

But what Cassie heard were her mother's soft words. *A little fresh air never hurt anything.*

Sinking onto the bed, Cassie tilted her face to the cold air that floated past the curtains. She remembered the day well. When Reverend Gardner had sealed their fates, she and her ma had come to the cabin to give it a final cleaning.

"Ma, he doesn't love me."

Her ma had nodded understandingly. *"He did once. Just give him some time."* With a mother's skilled hands, her ma flung the freshly ironed sheet in the air, and it slowly floated to the bed. She looked at Cassie and smiled softly. *"If he's angry, it's because his heart is broken."* They folded the top of the sheet down in unison, and her ma smoothed the fold. *"God will do His work."*

The memory faded away. Cassie looked around the tiny room, feeling more alone than ever. She studied the token in her hand. *How much time, Ma?* As much as it pained her, she folded it carefully, walked to the dresser, and slid open Gideon's drawer. She did not know where the ribbon belonged. Perhaps it had fallen out of his pocket. She laid it on top of his shirts.

Seeing the yellow fabric lying among Gideon's things pained her, and Cassie heaved in a shaky breath. There was nothing she could do to sever the unbreakable bond. The ribbon silently taunted her — it had more of Gideon's heart than she ever would.

THIRTY

Gideon stared at the coop. The structure leaned to the side, and with a puff of his cheeks, he shook his head. A can of grease and a pry bar sat at his feet. As he continued to stare at the miserable coop that needed a new roof and a new door, he shook his head and turned the old hammer around in his palm. *This should be interesting.*

After working in a fingerful of grease, he tugged on the metal handle of the small door. It didn't move. He pulled harder, using all of his weight to pry the door free. The sharp-edged handle dug into his fingers. Still nothing budged. He jerked away. Trying to brush off the sting, he wiped his fingers on the hem of his shirt. Hattie, who slept against the side of the coop facing the sun, lifted her head at the racket. She sniffed the air and eyed him before dropping her head into the dirt with an unladylike snort.

Gideon picked up the pry bar and jammed

it between the door and the frame and tried to force the door open that way. It refused to budge. He pushed harder. His boots dug into the mud, and he grunted against the resistance. The bar slipped, and Gideon's hand smashed into the splintery wood of the coop. His shoulders heaved as he stared down at his scraped knuckle.

He picked up the pry bar with two fists and with a growl struck the door as hard as he could. The weatherworn boards shattered. All he had to show for his effort was a giant hole large enough for a chicken-hungry critter to crawl through.

"Well, that's *one* way to do it."

Still panting, Gideon stumbled back and turned to see Jack Allan watching him. The kid's arms were crossed over his chest, and his smile seemed one of satisfaction. Squinting into the sun, Jack scratched his jaw and smiled. "Looks like you could use a hand." He stepped closer.

Before Gideon could respond, Jack reached out, and his eyes trailed the length of the weathered wood before giving the stubborn door a tug. He braced the toe of a patched-up boot against the coop wall and yanked. The door did not move.

Gideon grunted. What did the man think was going to happen? "The hinges are rusted over solid."

Jack ran a hand up one side of the door and fingered the freshly made hole. "This ol' coop probably ain't been opened in twenty years."

Rotating the pry bar in his palm, Gideon shrugged. "Then I guess I've got my work cut out for me."

"Mind if I lend you a hand?"

Gideon did not want anyone's help — he already had a cabin that wasn't his on land that wasn't his. Even the butter in his crock, dwindling as it was, came from a cow that wasn't his. But fixing this coop was the first step in changing that. "Thanks, but I've got it covered."

"Clearly." Jack studied Gideon. "I'd like to help you if that's all right. Don't know nearly enough about working wood as I should. Not really Pa's specialty." Then his head bobbed dramatically with each word. "I ain't got nothin' else to do today."

"Fine." Gideon grumbled as he strode off.

Jack jogged ahead of him. He turned and grinned. His overall buckles glistened in the early morning light, and the torn pocket across his chest flapped with each backward step. "Try to curb your enthusiasm, all right? Good grief. Cassie told me you could be grumpy. She wasn't kidding."

Gideon gave in to a low laugh.

They stepped into the shed where Gideon had organized his things in a haphazard fashion. The wood he had brought from his shop lay stacked against the far wall.

"Where do we start?"

Gideon lifted a pair of boards. "Considering that I just smashed through the old door, we need to make a new one."

Jack lifted a saw and held it at the ready.

Gideon lowered it. "At ease, soldier." He eyed Cassie's brother. At sixteen, Jack was seven years his junior. Most of Gideon's boyhood had been spent with Eli and Samuel. He'd never paid much attention to the youngest son. Not until the day Jack kept Eli's rifle from putting a hole in Gideon's skull.

"First we need to measure the opening for the door."

"I can do that."

Gideon held out a yardstick, something he rarely used, but he didn't trust Jack's ability to gauge measurements on his own. While the young man was gone, Gideon moved several more boards to the workbench he had rigged up.

Jack returned and gave him the measurements.

Using a pencil, Gideon scratched the

numbers on the wood. "Very good." As Jack watched, he measured and marked where each piece would be cut.

"Do you need this?" Jack held the saw up again.

Gideon slipped the pencil between his lips. "Just about," he mumbled. He marked the rest of the wood, stumbling more than once over the figures. It's what made his work slow. Jack didn't seem to notice his hesitation as he added the sums again for good measure.

"How things been goin' with you and Cassie?" Jack's even voice scarcely hinted interest.

Surprised, Gideon did not know how to respond. "Fine enough." He motioned toward the saw, and Jack moved into position. He hoped the kid wouldn't pry further. Jack sliced the metal teeth through the pale lumber.

"Cassie's a good girl once you get past all her annoying ways. Then she's easy enough to get along with, I suppose."

"Sure."

Jack let the matter fall and cut the rest of the boards without speaking. Gideon poked through his can of hinges, finding two that would do the job well. He laid the boards together on the workbench and eyeballed the length he would need for the cross-pieces.

Did Jack hold no grudge against him? Did he not hate Gideon as his older brothers did? Jack helped keep the work surface clear with a broad smile. There didn't seem to be an angry bone in the young man's body.

"Now what?" Jack asked.

"Fetch that can of nails there." Gideon pointed. He pressed the saw through the pair of boards, and the ends fell to the growing pile of sawdust around his boots. They worked as the hour passed on. Gideon tried to explain the process as best he could, but he'd never been the teaching type. His brothers had taken no interest in wood. It had always been him and the quiet. Jack was a quick learner, though, and before long, they had the new door ready to hang.

"We should probably seal it, but I don't have any on hand."

"Pa does. I'll see about borrowing it."

"That's all right." Gideon ran a hand over the finished door. He grabbed his pry bar and hammer and motioned for Jack to follow him back outside. "I'll figure out another way." He had no interest in taking from the Allans, and he doubted they had any interest in him. Why Jack was hanging around was beyond him.

Jack cast him a sideways glance. "If you say so."

Together, they carried the new door out into the sunshine, propping it up against the side of the chicken coop.

"So where are the hens gonna come from?" Jack asked.

"Is there a sign on my back that says I have all the answers?"

Jack chuckled. "No. There's a sign on your back, but you don't want to know what it says. Trust me."

"That bad, huh?"

Jack nodded. "Pretty bad."

THIRTY-ONE

Lonnie's boots squished in the mud as she hurried forward. "Hang on, Jacob," she said breathlessly over the thrum of rain and pulled the blanket over his tiny head. "We're almost home." Her feet slid, but she righted herself. Home called to her.

At her side, Jebediah rushed along. With Addie's hand in his, he helped the little girl over the slick path. A screech made Lonnie turn. Each of Addie's small shoes was sliding in a different direction, but Jebediah held her fast.

"Easy," he said.

Addie pushed a clump of wet hair away from her forehead. She looked up at the old man with fright-filled eyes. Lonnie knew her poor sister, with only a thin knit sweater, had to be terribly cold.

"Here" — Jebediah crouched down, and his knee sank into the mud — "climb up on my back."

The little girl hesitated and blinked wet lashes up at Lonnie. When Lonnie nodded, Addie climbed onto Jebediah's back. She wrapped her thin arms around his neck and sank her ashen face into his shoulder.

Rain pelted down in thick sheets, its deafening pulse washing away every other sound. Lonnie wiped her eyes but could scarcely see the path ahead of her. With Jacob nestled beneath the thick blanket, it was a miracle he was so quiet. Every so often, Lonnie lifted a flap to see his tiny face peek up at her with an expression of uncertainty. His cheeks were as rosy as sun-ripened apples, and his nose ran. "That's my sweet boy." Lonnie tugged the wilted blanket in place and continued onward.

When Addie started to cry, Jebediah patted her mud-caked boot. "Look. Do you see that light in the distance?" He pointed.

Addie wiped her nose with her wet sleeve and nodded.

Jebediah grinned, sending his damp mustache skyward. A small waterfall trickled from his broad hat when he tipped his head forward. "That's home."

Lonnie stared. She hadn't recognized their surroundings. She smiled when she spotted the weatherworn rails that lined the Bennett farm. Grayed with age, the ghost of a fence curved this way and that in the fog. With Jacob pressed to her chest, Lonnie stepped over a fallen board. Her skirt snagged, and she yanked it free of a nail. The fabric ripped, but she was too determined to care. Jebediah tugged on the line, and Sugar lumbered into the yard. Lonnie broke into a run.

"Elsie!" she cried.

Her own breath sounded loud in her ears as she flitted across the muddy yard. She called the woman's name again, not caring if it was proper. Jacob bobbed in her grasp, but Lonnie held him fast.

The back door opened, and Elsie's soft build filled the frame. "That you, Lonnie?" She left the shelter of the porch and hurried into the rain.

Tears stung Lonnie's eyes. They met in the middle of the yard where Elsie pulled Jacob from Lonnie's weary arms. The older woman wrapped a hand around Lonnie's, and they darted toward the house. Safely under the porch eaves, Elsie pulled her into a wet embrace.

"My child," she whispered.

Lonnie pinched her eyes closed and breathed in Elsie's scent of cinnamon and sugar. Jebediah bounded up the squeaky steps and lowered Addie to the porch. When

Elsie pulled away, she smeared Lonnie's wet hair away from her cheek. Elsie's sorrow-filled eyes followed the line of the fence.

Lonnie's chin trembled, and she nodded. "It's just me."

Elsie squeezed her hand. She glanced down at the girl beside them.

"Who's this little one?" She crouched and took Addie's small hand. "Why, she's plumb frozen! Come in, come in!" She pulled the child through the doorway. Elsie paused and turned to Jebediah. "You too." She planted a quick kiss on his cheek, and the wet crowd stumbled into the kitchen.

Lonnie took Jacob and sat him on the floor in front of the stove. She stripped him of his wet clothes. Elsie handed her a towel, and Lonnie wrapped him up. Jebediah excused himself to see to the mule, and Elsie padded up the stairs, singing to the rosy-cheeked boy. Lonnie helped Addie out of her wet shoes and tugged drenched stockings from her icy legs. As she ran a towel over her sister's feet, Elsie returned.

"This'll do for now." She handed Lonnie a tattered sweater. "I found it in the bottom of your drawer."

Lonnie peeled away Addie's wet coat and unbuttoned her soaked dress. Addie held onto Lonnie's shoulder as she stepped out of her clothes, and by the time Lonnie had buttoned her sister up in the old sweater, the redness in Addie's cheeks had faded, and the little girl smiled.

"Is that better?" Lonnie gathered up the pile of drenched clothing.

Addie nodded.

A soft hand landed on Lonnie's shoulder. "Now what about you?" Elsie asked.

Lonnie unlaced her filthy shoes and tucked them out of the way. She stood with a weary groan. "I'll be right back." As she strode off, the lid to Elsie's cookie jar clanged out of place. Lonnie knew she would return to find both Jacob and Addie covered in crumbs.

She tiptoed through the parlor, trying her best not to leave wet marks on Elsie's clean floor. Stealing the oil lamp from the mantel, she tarried long enough to light the cotton wick. The dark parlor came to life. All was as she remembered — the house, the smells, everything. Sliding her hand up the railing, she climbed the stairs two at a time and shuffled down the hall. The door to her bedroom was closed, and with a turn of the squeaky knob, Lonnie pushed it open.

As if awakened from a dream, the lantern light flickered across the small room. Her heart caught in her throat, and she froze.

Forgotten images rose up to haunt her. Elsie had made the rumpled bed and pressed drawers snugly into place. Products of her and Gideon's haste. Lonnie placed a hand to her mouth and felt her heart break anew. Gideon's favorite shirt lay draped over the brass headboard. He'd talked about packing it but at the last moment decided to leave it behind. When his words of indecision echoed in her mind, she stepped forward.

She touched the cold collar that would never again feel the warmth of his skin. *Gideon.* He was all around. Not daring to disturb the shirt from its spot, she let her hand slip away. He was gone.

With slow, shaky movements, she peeled off her stockings and dropped them in a pile on the floor. She shrugged out of her damp dress and kicked it aside. After opening her drawer, Lonnie dug through what she had left behind. Her black gingham dress caught her eye. It desperately needed to be ironed, but with long sleeves, it would keep her warm. Lonnie slid the wrinkled gown over her head, then pressed the silver buttons into place and straightened the skewed collar.

She closed the drawer softly and turned to face the empty bedroom. Stepping in a slow circle, she did not know what to do next. Just the sight of the bedroom made her feel Gideon's presence, and Lonnie could not bear to lose that. After lifting a corner of the quilt, she slid between the cold sheets and huddled against her pillow. She crossed her bare ankles and closed her eyes.

Coveted images filled her. She smoothed her hand across the empty side of the bed. Gideon's rumpled hair in the morning. The sight of him standing in front of the moonlit window when sleep was not his friend. His touch. His voice. Reaching out, she gently fingered the fabric of his pillow, his scent more than a memory.

THIRTY-TWO

The outdoors called to her. Cassie left the warm bed and dressed in the dark. She snatched a rag from the dresser, then tied it over her hair and slid the knot out of sight. She tiptoed across the bedroom and hurried out. When she opened the front door, a cold gust greeted her.

She'd forgotten her army coat in the bedroom. She knew just where she left it — draped across the back of the rocking chair. Dare she slip back into the bedroom? Reaching around the door, her hand fumbled along the wall until she felt Gideon's coat. Cassie yanked it free and tossed it over her shoulders. She smiled when his earthy scent rose from the dark oilcloth. It was not the same as the real thing, but it was as close to the man as she'd gotten in a long time.

The sun was yet to rise, but the night sky had warmed to a soft glow. Cassie crossed the yard and hurried through a thin layer of fog to the chicken coop. Gideon had bought three hens the day before, and she was eager to search for eggs. After opening the stout door, she tiptoed into the cozy coop. "Mornin'," she whispered to the caramel-colored hens, still huddled on their perch.

It took a moment for her eyes to adjust to the darkness. Her hands shuffled through the straw until her fingers grazed something hard. Cassie smiled to herself. She tucked the treasure in her apron pocket and offered her quick thanks to the three hens, wishing she knew which feathered creature had provided it.

She slipped out as quietly as she had come and, when the latch clicked into place, hurried back to the house. A misty fog shrouded the farm, hiding the cabin from sight.

The dawn of a new day. Of a new life.

She let the cold air fill her chest. She wondered what the weeks and months ahead would hold, trying to shrug off the knowledge that those that had passed had been anything but easy. Today was a new day, and Gideon O'Riley was her husband. She still wasn't sure what to make of that, but it would be enough to temper the whispers. Enough to open up a lifetime of possibilities. Gideon would change. She knew him. Knew his heart. Deep down, there was a yearning for something greater. Perhaps that's what he'd seen in Lonnie. She fought a surge of jealousy.

That would get her nowhere. Could it not be something he saw in her as well?

Cassie pushed her unruly hair from her face, the resolve sinking in that she would no longer pursue him. Let the man come to her. *Oh, that it may be one day.*

Gideon crouched and pressed his head to the floor. He scanned the dark oak planks beneath the bed. He smoothed his hand out but felt nothing other than dusty wood. A muscle in his jaw twitched, and he sat back on his heels. He crammed his fingers beneath the mattress.

His blood thinned. He yanked his pillow away and tossed the quilt aside. After ripping the sheet free, he saw only the faded ticking stripe of the mattress cover. Gideon thrust the blankets back over the bed. He turned, and his gaze flicked over the room. There was only one possible answer.

Gideon stomped across the bedroom and scanned the front room. Empty. He stepped to the window and yanked the curtains aside. The sunrise nearly blinded him. Reaching behind the door, he grasped for his coat, but his hand landed on an empty peg. He slammed the door, and the walls shook. Biting back a curse, he jerked it open and trudged into the cold.

The air stung his skin as he started toward the woodpile. A low fog skittered across the farm on a gust of wind, moistening his shirt. The icy fabric clung to his back. Gideon grabbed an armload, bounded up the steps, and hurried inside. With a flick of his boot, he snagged the door, and it slammed behind him.

As if it had a life of its own, the door creaked open. Gideon spun around. Cassie stilled beneath his pointed stare.

When she held up an egg, he noticed her smile was hesitant. "I found breakfast."

"Come in and shut the door." He dropped the wood next to the stove, and oak clanged against the floor. With his boot, he jammed the wood into a muddled pile.

Cassie stepped forward, brows knit together. She pressed the door closed with a soft *click*. She pushed up the oversized sleeves, a reminder that the coat was not hers.

Still shivering, he glared at her. "Why did you take my jacket?"

Cassie blushed and hurried to take it off. She folded it over her arm and carried it to its place behind the door. "I'm sorry. I thought you were asleep." She slid the coat on its peg. "I didn't think you would mind."

Irritated, he shook his head. "Did you go through my things?"

Her features sharpened. "No. Why?"

"Because I lost something." His voice wavered, and he cleared his throat. "Did you take it?"

Mouth pursed, Cassie stepped forward and placed the egg on the table. "Gideon, I did not take anything of yours." She pulled open the cupboard and, rising on her tiptoes, fumbled around on the top shelf. She set the frying pan on the stove and spoke without turning around. "If you'll tell me what it was you lost, I might be able to help."

He ran his hand along his forehead, suddenly warm. "I . . . I lost a ribbon," he began. "It was yellow."

A shadow crossed over Cassie's face. She released the handle of her frying pan, and it tipped back. She brushed past him and disappeared into the bedroom. Gritting his teeth, he followed.

She opened the top drawer of the dresser and pushed aside his things. A rumpled shirt toppled over the edge and fell to the ground. Snatching it up, Cassie jammed it back into the drawer and continued her search. When her hand stilled, she looked at Gideon.

"Here." She lifted the ribbon. "I did find it, and I put it where it wouldn't get lost." Her fingers opened. The ribbon spiraled down to the dresser. She slammed the drawer. "I did not go through your things, and I would never take something that was yours." Without meeting his gaze, she stepped around him.

"Cassie."

She turned, and her name hung in the silence between them.

"This isn't going to end well."

"What?" Her voice was heavy with a weariness he understood all too well.

He motioned between them. "This. No good will come of it."

"So you've said."

"Just don't get your hopes up, all right?"

"Don't think so highly of yourself." She strode out, leaving him alone in the bedroom.

Thunder crashed. The walls seemed to shake. Gideon looked up and stared at the ceiling, half expecting it to come crashing down on him. The clock on the mantel chimed eleven. He had tried to sleep, but the rain that beat down on the roof seemed bent on keeping him awake. Not wanting to disturb Cassie, he had gone to the kitchen table and set about the arduous task of cleaning and greasing his traps.

He wiped his fingers on a rag, then laid the greasy cloth on his thigh. Two days ago, he had set snares behind the house, and already he'd caught a pair of rabbits. That night, Cassie had spooned stew over their biscuits.

Another crash made him jump. The deafening *crack* lifted his gaze to the window. He set his trap down and looked at the closed bedroom door. When the thunder faded, he listened to the symphony of raindrops build. Wind blew the rain against one side of the house; moments later, it dashed off the roof with nary a sound. The gust built and sank.

After picking up the rickety contraption again, Gideon worked grease through the joints. He tilted his head and tried to fight a glance at the bedroom. It was useless. The wind shifted, softened. Rain tapped against the glass, then faded as if the earth were drawing a slow, deep breath. Gideon's fingers stilled. His ears pricked to a new sound. His chair scraped across the floor, and he hesitated before standing.

He stepped toward the bedroom as quietly as possible and paused at the door. He held his breath and listened to muffled sobs. His hand twitched, but he kept it at his side. Pressing his forehead to the door, he stared at his feet. He grazed the metal knob.

Gideon stepped into the dark bedroom. The candle on the dresser had long since burned out. The curtains were drawn open, but the moon provided no light through the rain. Cassie lay on her side facing the window. After moistening his lips, he spoke her name. He stepped closer, leaving the door ajar so weak light could filter in.

Cassie sniffed. Her hand lifted to her face. Tucking her sleeve over her wrist, she wiped at her cheek. The floorboards creaked as he made his way around the bed. Gideon crouched in front of her, but he had no words.

He owed her an apology, yet he couldn't seem to make it form.

"Are you all right?" he finally asked.

She blinked up at him.

Gideon's eyes widened at the sight of the yellow ribbon between her fingers.

Thunder cracked. Cassie jumped.

After smoothing his palms over his pants, he unbuttoned the top of his collar and folded his sleeves past his wrists. "Can I sit down?"

Cassie scooted back.

He sat beside her and leaned against the bumpy logs of the cabin. "Some storm," he whispered.

Still lying on her side, she looked up at him, the spark in her eyes long gone. In its place was a heavy sorrow.

"I keep thinking the window is gonna break," she murmured.

Gideon felt his mouth lift in a half smile. "Let's hope not." He reached for the ribbon, and her hand trembled against his. He set it aside.

Cassie sniffed. She swiped at more tears.

Her voice was nearly inaudible over the rain. "Are we really married?"

He crossed one foot over the other. "Last time I checked."

"It feels strange."

He couldn't disagree.

"Do you miss her? Lonnie?"

Thunder crashed, and they startled in unison. When it faded, he left her question unanswered. He couldn't lie. His heart had been put aside — it was no longer his to give.

He folded his arms over his chest to keep from touching her. Still curled on her side, she lay quietly for several minutes. He nearly drifted off, so heavy were his eyelids. Finally, she spoke.

"Can't say that I blame you." The words were soft. "I'm sure it's hard for you not to think about them . . ." Her voice trailed off as if sheer exhaustion had carried her words away.

She had to bring them up.

The only way he got through the day was by icing over the fire in his heart. Numbing the pain. Her words threw kindling on the coals, igniting a yearning in him that clamped his chest closed. He waited until he was certain she was asleep. When her breathing slowed, her lips slightly parted, Gideon rose soundlessly and made his way to the front room. Pulling the rocking chair beneath the window, he settled down. He folded his arm up and tucked a hand behind his head. Closing his eyes, he tried to let the crackle of the fire lull him to sleep.

THIRTY-THREE

Lonnie stood on the porch, Gideon's plaid coat and her small Bible in hand. The clouds that had loomed all day finally sent down a dusting of snow. She flung the coat over her shoulders and, in one swift motion, stepped out from beneath the porch. Her shoes pressed down into the thin layer of light snow that covered the frozen ground like sugar sprinkled over a cake.

She crossed the yard, her feet leading where they would. As unwavering as the roots that held it in place, the chopping block stood steady and quiet near the barn. The one spot she could still see Gideon.

Jebediah's words had been unmistakable that evening at supper. *"We need more firewood. Ain't touched the ax since Gideon last chopped some."*

Now, with the meal long since over, Lonnie drew closer. As she did, she could feel the air leaving her lungs. She walked along

274

the dwindling woodpile. Her eyes grazed the last of the tidy rows, each log split by Gideon's strength and determination. She swept her hand along the bumps and grooves of the stack, not caring if a splinter caught her skin. All she cared about was that she saw Gideon. His memory was in everything. He was everywhere. Faint snowflakes melted on her neck. Guiding her fingers along the rough collar of his coat, Lonnie tipped the plaid forward. His warmth surrounded her.

And it was time to say good-bye.

Not caring that snow would soak her dress and dampen her petticoats, she sank onto the chopping block. She rested her palms on the frosty wood beneath her. Lonnie lowered her head and stared down at the small Bible in her lap.

She sucked in a deep breath of cold mountain air, and when her lungs began to burn, she let it out slowly. How was she going to do this?

When saying good-bye would not ease her pain?

A cold wind picked up and swept through the yard. Snow lifted and swirled, spinning wherever the wind willed it. It tapped icy kisses on her cheeks. Looking around the sleeping farmyard, she saw Gideon's smile.

She heard his laugh. Saw the pensive determination in his face as he split wood beneath the summer sun. Lonnie wrapped her arms around herself and let the unforgettable images warm her through. Closing her eyes she watched him toss his shirt aside and imagined grazing her hand across his sun-warmed back.

"Good-bye, Gideon." She pressed her fingertips to her lips. "Good-bye."

He was gone, and he wasn't coming back. The life she had come to love was built on sand. On dust. It had crumbled beneath them. She lifted her face to the sky. It was time to begin anew. She had no idea what that looked like, but she knew she had to put one foot in front of the other. Today. Tomorrow. And on. Pulling her legs into her chest, Lonnie let her heels rest on the edge of the block. She pressed her face to her knees and sighed. It was time to stow the memories in the deepest places of her heart and turn the lock behind her.

"Lonnie," Elsie whispered. A soft hand touched her shoulder. "Jacob's fussin' for his mama. Why don't you come in out of the cold?" Elsie helped her to her feet.

Elsie's voice was gentle in Lonnie's ear as they slowly worked their way back to the house. "You seem near frozen."

If only it would sink deep, hardening the places soft with hurt.

Lonnie put one stiff leg in front of the other, and by the time they reached the porch, she felt blood in her limbs again, and the stinging in her feet told her that they really were still down there.

"How 'bout a hot bath?" Concern etched its way across Elsie's face as she pulled the door open.

Lonnie followed her dearest friend into the house. The heat from the stove stung her cheeks. "Really, Elsie. I'm all right."

Copper eyes searched hers. "Do you mean that?"

She heard Jacob babble from the other room, followed by Jebediah's smooth voice. "I have to figure out how to go on from here. For me and for Jacob." Lonnie shivered.

"Look at you, frozen through."

Lonnie moved the kettle to the hottest part of the stove. "I may take that bath."

"That sounds like a right good idea."

"I'll see to Jacob first."

"I don't mind —"

"No." Lonnie patted Elsie's arm. "I want to." She moved about, putting together a bowl of oats sweetened with the juice of Elsie's canned peaches while Elsie put another pot of water on the stove. Lonnie fed Jacob his supper, wiped his chin and hands, and kissed his downy head as she set him back on the parlor rug. Addie sat beside him, a box of dominoes in her hand. She dumped them out with a clatter. Immediately Jacob picked one up, turned it in his small hand, and tasted a corner of the black playing piece.

Elsie bustled in. "You go on now. I'll keep watch."

"Thank you, Elsie." Lonnie moved to the kitchen to fetch the kettle. It took several trips, but she soon had the tub filled halfway.

Lonnie undressed slowly. Her red, chapped fingers fumbled with the buttons, but finally, she kicked her dress away, and it landed beneath the dresser. Her petticoats and stockings fell in a pile by the bed. Wriggling free of her shimmy, she tossed it on the bed, then froze. Sinking to her knees, she pulled the shimmy into her lap and stared at what she saw. Her heart plummeted like stones in a brook. The worn-out fabric fell from her lifeless fingers, and Lonnie crawled toward the tub. After climbing in, she sank into the hot water and closed her eyes.

Her hope severed as if it had been cut by a hunter's blade. There would be no more children. She would have no more of her and Gideon. Too tired to cry, she covered her face with her hands and simply fought to breathe. If she could breathe, she could outlast the pain — outlast the heartache — and maybe someday, it would lessen.

Lonnie did not move. The water did not stir. She closed her eyes. Snow continued to fall outside the bedroom window, and as time passed by, the water grew cold. Her arms began to tremble, and chills covered her skin.

She would not cry. She would not cry.

She would not. Gideon was gone and she would move on. One step at a time. She would be brave. She didn't know what that looked like, but she made a resolution to find out. She would not cry.

Lonnie repeated the words over and over, fighting the sting in her eyes.

THIRTY-FOUR

"Who's Jeb out there talkin' to?" Lonnie squinted out the window and pulled the curtains back farther for Elsie to peek out.

Elsie wiped a flour-covered hand across her forehead and studied the man in the yard. "Oh!" She smiled. "That's the new reverend. Nice young man. He's the fella who delivered your letter from Rocky Knob. I told him to come around for supper sometime." She placed her hands on her waist and leaned in closer. Her voice muffled against the glass. "I hope Jebediah remembers to ask him again."

Stepping away, Elsie returned to kneading her bread dough.

Lonnie watched Addie run from one end of the yard to the other. Lonnie's nose bumped the glass. "I think he did 'cause they're headed this way." Her voice fell soft. "Doesn't look much like a reverend," she mumbled.

Dressed in a striped shirt and dark pants, he looked nothing like Reverend Gardner or Reverend Brown. No black hat, no serious expression. He shook Jebediah's hand. With a slap on the man's broad back, Jebediah led him toward the house. She dropped the curtain and stepped back.

Heavy feet pounded up the back steps. Jacob crawled toward her and tugged at her skirt. Spinning around, Lonnie lifted him into her arms just as the door opened and Jebediah stuck his head inside.

"Ladies," he said with a smile, "Reverend McKee is here."

The door opened wider, and the young man followed Jebediah into the kitchen. He pulled a hat from dark hair.

"Well, I'm glad you remembered to come visit us!" Elsie waved him forward. "Come in, come in. Don't be shy."

The young reverend tipped his head. "Aye. Thanks."

At the sound of his Scottish accent, Lonnie lifted her eyebrows.

His gaze bounced from Elsie to Lonnie and back again. With Jebediah standing so near, Jacob squirmed, and Lonnie feared he would jump out of her grasp. She quickly returned the reverend's nod with a smile and set her son down. Finally free of her arms, he lifted himself up on his belly and looked at the tall stranger before trying to scoot toward him. With a loaf of freshly risen bread in her hand, Elsie paused and waited for him to pass by her before opening the hot oven door.

The reverend smiled. "An' who's this wee thing?" His voice was deeper than the murky pond Lonnie swam in as a girl.

The oven door closed, and Elsie placed a round fist on each hip. She grinned down at the baby. "This is our Jacob."

Jebediah politely excused himself to finish his afternoon chores, bidding the reverend to make himself at home.

The young man ducked down long enough to place a large hand on top of Jacob's head. "Well, hello there, Jacob." He stood and turned his hat in his hands.

Elsie hurried to take it from him. "I'll take your coat too."

The reverend placed it in Elsie's waiting hands. "No need of this, I s'pose. It's plenty warm in here."

"Reverend McKee comes from Scotland," Elsie declared with a broad grin.

Lonnie smiled. "So I noticed."

He held up his hand. "But please" — the simple phrase resonated with a rich cadence not liken to the hills of Virginia — "call me by my first name."

Elsie spoke. "Tobias? Was it?"

He grinned even as his cheeks colored. "Just my mother calls me that. Most folk call me Toby. And no more of that rev'rend nonsense. I only just finished my studies and hardly deserve the title."

"Toby here preaches at the church to help out Reverend Gardner. Ever since Reverend Finch passed, poor Reverend Gardner has journeyed from Rocky Knob to Fancy Gap every other month." She pulled a tin of cinnamon from her spice rack and sprinkled it into a bowl of whipped cream. "Now that Toby's here, he will be able to settle in one spot."

"That's my hope." He grinned at Elsie, then when his smile fell on Lonnie, it seemed to soften.

Lonnie tried to join in the conversation. "And in the meantime?"

"Well," Toby sighed. "In the meantime, I've got a little place up the way. A nice set of folks have lent me a wee shanty on their property. It's not much. It's wet in the winter and hot in the summer, but it's home for now." He paused, and Lonnie watched his eyes move over the planes of her face. "I s'pose that doesn't answer your question." His voice came out weak, distracted. "In the meantime, I've been going 'round and visiting with the folks in the area. Making friends and seeing where I can be used. I've done everything from fixing fences to helping a few learn to read. My time is the Lord's, and that's how I'll use it."

Elsie placed a hand on Toby's sturdy arm and pointed him toward the table. "Like delivering our letter."

He gingerly stepped over Jacob and made his way to the table. "Aye, like that." After pulling out the nearest chair, he sat and propped heavy fists on the table.

Lonnie stared. Another man was sitting in Gideon's chair.

"Well, that was a lucky chance, I'd say." Toby smoothed his hands across the table, and they made a swishing sound on the dry wood. "I had gone back to Rocky Knob with Rev'rend Gardner to help him tie up a few loose ends."

The room fell silent, and Lonnie looked at Elsie.

As if remembering why the reverend had come, Elsie jumped. "Why don't we eat? I'll go holler for Jebediah."

Elsie disappeared, leaving the door open. Lonnie scanned the room, hoping for a topic of conversation to come to her. "Let me fetch you a plate," she blurted.

Toby chuckled. "Thank you."

Lonnie stacked a fork and knife on top of the plate. "So what part of Scotland do you come from?"

"Crovie." When she shook her head, he continued. " 'Tis a wee fishing village on the north Banffshire coast. Beautiful place." His smile widened, and a dimple dented each cheek. "I can almost smell the sea . . . just talking about it."

Lonnie slipped his dinnerware into place, and the passion in his voice drew her gaze to his face. "Bet you miss it somethin' awful."

In the middle of the kitchen, Jacob tipped over a basket of rolling pins and laughed as he twirled them about.

Toby's dimples deepened and his eyes sparkled. "I do at times."

She sank into the chair across from him. Their knees collided, and Lonnie quickly slid her chair backward. Toby cleared his throat and did the same. Sitting so close, she noticed the musky scent of soap that lingered on his skin. When Jacob scooted toward her, she pulled him into her lap.

Elsie rushed inside. "Jebediah's gonna be awhile. Thinks a storm's comin' in the morning, and he wants to bring in a few armfuls of wood. Supper's not quite ready anyway, so we have no need to hurry."

"I'll lend him a hand." Toby offered Lonnie a polite nod, then stood and trudged across the floor. Elsie closed the door for him.

Lonnie fiddled with a hole in the faded lace tablecloth. She rose, and with Jacob in her arms, stepped to the window. How many times had she peeked through the glass only to wave at Gideon? He'd flash her that grin of his, the one that brought a smile to her own lips. If only she'd noticed his brow knotted with half-truths. Secrets left untold.

The *clang* of the stove lids pulled her attention back. Elsie stirred hot coals until they crackled and popped. She lowered a heavy cast-iron circle into place with a *bang* before stepping behind Lonnie. "Well, he's a nice fella. Always eager to lend a hand wherever there's a need."

Lonnie watched Toby and Jebediah carry armfuls of firewood toward the porch, chatting happily. "So I see." The young reverend grinned at something Jebediah said. Just as Gideon had once done. She let the curtain fall, brushed her hand over Jacob's russet curls, and turned to help Elsie with supper.

Thirty-Five

Gideon strode toward the Allan home, and though his breath was white before his face, a cool noon sun shone down on his shoulders. He scaled the steps and hesitated a single moment before rapping his knuckles on the door. The cold made his hand sting.

A burst of warmth hit his face when Libby opened the door. She blinked up at Gideon with wide-set eyes, paler than Cassie's. Before she could speak, a broad shadow moved in behind her.

"What do you want?" Eli said, his voice low, gruff.

Annoyed, Gideon shifted his feet. "I came to ask your father if he has a handcart I can borrow."

"What for?"

"The question's for your pa."

"Now see here —"

"Eli, don't be such a bully," Libby cut in. "I'll go get Pa." She strode off.

They stood there, neither one blinking. Gideon stuffed his hands in his pockets and tipped his chin up. So it had come to this.

Small footsteps drew near. "He has one, and he said you could borrow it." She spoke to Gideon, then glanced up at her brother who towered over her. "He wants you to show him where it is, Eli."

"I don't think so."

She waved a hand behind her. "Then you speak to him."

Setting his jaw, Eli brushed past Gideon and stalked into the yard.

"Guess that means I'm supposed to follow him." Gideon nodded a thanks to Libby and went after the man who had once been his best friend. Eli's long strides barreled him toward the barn. Gideon matched his pace. Neither one spoke. Eli strode around the barn and quickly scanned a pile of rubble. He lumbered through weeds, followed by Gideon, the near-frozen grasses clinging to their pants. A half barrel sat almost buried in the dirt, and a rusted plow leaned up against the barn. Still no cart.

Gideon snorted. "Lose something?"

"Shut up."

Gideon held up his hands.

"You." Eli growled out the single word and thrust a thick finger in Gideon's face.

"Watch. Yourself."

"Or what?" Gideon nearly laughed it. "You'll finish what you started?" He held his arms out wide. "Go ahead. I'm gettin' awful tired of this. Tell you what: I'll let you have the first swing."

They stood eye to eye, but Eli had once been taller than Gideon. Those days they'd spent their summers swinging from the knotted rope into Saddler's pond just on the other side of the holler. They had water fights, ate apples beneath the shade of the great maple, and whittled wooden swords when the weather turned too cold to shed their overalls on the grassy banks. And with Gideon's mandolin and Eli's harmonica, they'd spent many an evening serenading the stars with the anthem of summer and boyhood.

Those days were long gone.

Eli glared at him. "You're lucky I didn't shoot you."

Gideon twisted his mouth to the side, neither denying nor confirming the man's words. He could still feel the barrel of Eli's rifle pressed to his throat. The memory forced down a swallow.

"She deserved better than you."

It was the truth and nothing less. "She did."

Frustration burned through Eli's brown eyes. "Why did you have to . . . my kid sister?"

Something in Gideon's chest began to ache. "I never should have."

Eli shoved past him. He took but a few steps, and Gideon followed. Gideon trailed him toward the wood crib that sat slanted on the hillside. Eli walked the perimeter, finally pointing to the cart that sat against the west side. "There it is. Try and return it in one piece."

"I'll do my best."

Eli strode off, shoulders hunched. Gideon watched him go. Turning back to his task, he hitched the cart free of the weeds and yanked it from the brambles and brush, finally shoving it onto the hard-packed path. The wheel creaked as he worked his way toward the small cabin, where he parked the cart in front of his workshop. His stomach rumbled, and not wanting to set out without a bite of food, he ducked into the cabin.

Cassie stood at the kitchen table, clearing away scraps of pumpkin skin. The tiny space smelled good. Really good.

"Where have you been?" she asked, not unkindly, as he poked around inside the cupboard.

"Borrowed your pa's handcart."

She stared at him as if he'd just sprouted antlers.

"Yes. If you're wondering if it went badly, I assure you it did."

Her mouth tipped up on one side.

At least someone found it amusing. "I'm going to make the rounds. I have a few things I'd like to try and sell." He grabbed an apple from the basket.

Wiping her hands on her apron, Cassie moved the scrap bucket toward the door. "I'd like to go with you. I need to get out of this house. If you can wait just a few minutes, I'll have this pie out of the oven."

He wanted to tell her no, but for some reason he didn't. "I'll wait." Not liking the smile that crept into her eyes, he added, "I need to load the cart anyway."

"I'll be out in a few minutes."

"If you say so." He turned and stepped from the crowded cabin, wishing with all his might that his life could have turned out differently.

Thirty-Six

Gideon lowered the cart and stretched his hands. Cassie stopped a few paces off. She pulled a pin from her hair, tucked it between her lips, and loosened the coils at the nape of her neck, plaiting it quickly. The November sun glistened on the dark strands. Gideon watched her. Then in an instant, he peeled his gaze away and quickly shook his head. What was he thinking? Shaking out his sore wrist, he looked around and took a quick inventory of his surroundings and the fork in the road.

He'd already sold a walking stick and a pair of buckets, and now a few dollars lined his pocket. It sent a surge of satisfaction through him. Cold, he wanted to keep moving and started up the trail.

"Why are you going that way?" Cassie loosened her amber scarf, straightening the knobby folds.

"Because I want to."

"But there are a dozen more homes up this way." She studied him a moment, her hand propped up on her waist. A trait he'd forgotten about. "Your folks are up this way, you know."

He set the cart down. "I know."

"And?" She hitched her thumb in that direction, flashing a pair of gray, fingerless mittens. Her skin was paler than usual on this cold morning, making her eyes as vivid as ever. Reaching up, she fiddled with another pin. "Oh come on. Don't be such a baby."

He tugged at the patch of hair beneath his lip. Had she always been this annoying? "Fine."

They walked in silence for several minutes. Cassie hummed a tune, and though Gideon knew the words well, he kept silent.

What he wouldn't give to hear Lonnie singing beside him. Have her steps lead his through the frostbitten leaves. Cassie walked slowly just a touch ahead, matching his pace. They passed through a chestnut grove, and she bent, plucked a burr from the ground, and let the nut fall into her hand. Dropping the burr, she rolled the chestnut between her wool-covered palms as they walked.

"Tell me about Jacob," she finally said.

He lifted an eyebrow. "You want to hear about my son?"

"I do. He's a part of you, isn't he?" She stepped gingerly over a root that stuck boldly out of the ground.

He struggled to push the cart over it. "I don't really know what to say."

"He's very young, no?"

"Jacob was born this spring, a month and a half early."

"Oh?"

"He probably shouldn't have made it. But by some miracle he did." Gideon shifted his grip on the cart handle, and though the splintery wood scratched his palm, all he could think of was the downy feel of his son's head. A swell filled his chest. How many times had he kissed that little head? Watched Lonnie press her lips there? His wife. His son. His family.

"Gideon?"

For some reason he'd stopped walking altogether. Cassie stared at him.

"Did you hear me?"

"No."

Her expression was soft. "I said you must have been so nervous. Terrified that he wasn't going to make it."

"I wasn't there."

"You weren't there?"

Gideon leaned into the weight of the cart, wishing Cassie wouldn't pry. "It's a long story."

She swung her hands back and forth. Her petticoats, a mismatch of colors and textures, bounced beneath her skirt. "It's a long walk."

They turned the corner, and he was glad to see their first stop. He spotted Old Man Tate in his garden, squatted down among a patch of greens. Gideon showed him the goods in the cart, while Cassie gleaned sprigs of thyme poking through the garden gate. In the end, the man chose a walking stick and paid Gideon with a pair of coins. The sum was small, but the stick would be put to good use by the eighty-year-old.

They bade farewell, and Cassie sidled up beside him.

"So where were we?" Her brown braid bounced on her shoulder, and she fiddled with the ends playfully.

Gideon tried not to notice.

"Jacob."

He slowed.

Cassie followed suit.

"Look. If it's all the same, I'd rather not talk about it."

"Sorry. I thought it might make you feel better."

"No, Cassie. It doesn't make me feel better." He motioned with his hands toward the south. "They're gone. Gone." His voice hitched. "And there's nothing I can do to get them back. Talking about it does not make it easier."

She pursed her lips. The breeze blew her bangs across her face, and she tucked them into place. "How long are you going to hold on to her?"

"You don't want me to answer that question."

"Yes, I do."

He stopped. This was a bad, bad idea. He should be in his shop. Alone. Not standing here on the hillside with Cassie Allan peppering him for answers that were best left buried. Deep. "Fine . . . forever. I'm not going to stop. Happy?"

Her eyes sparked. When she stopped walking, he glanced up and realized they were in front of his parents' farm.

"Perfect." Grabbing her arm, Gideon tugged her into a stand of trees. "Just what are you trying to do? Bringing me here. I don't want to go back there." Didn't want to relive the memories of the life that had brought him here. He'd tried to make a clean break. He and Lonnie.

Cassie worked to pry his fingers loose, and

he let go. "I'm not trying to do anything. Will you stop acting like I'm ruining your life?"

"But you are."

"No. *You* are. You, Gideon O'Riley, have been ruining your own life since I've known you. Every choice — every *mistake* — was yours. Stop putting it on me . . . or anyone else for that matter." She pressed her hands together soundlessly. "I know you see this as a mistake." She motioned between them. "But I don't."

"You think this is all right? You think it's going to work out? Do you honestly think that God is going to bless this after what we've done?"

"You never cared before."

"I care now!" He nearly shouted it and forced himself to lower his voice. He ran both hands through his hair, keeping them there. "I care now." Because Lonnie had gotten under his skin. In the best of ways. And the remnants of the faith he'd tried to borrow from her remained. He didn't want to lose that. Didn't want to slip back into the darkness. Cassie would never understand that. Yet here they stood. His ring on her finger.

God, why?

When she finally spoke, Cassie's voice was

small. "We have a chance to make this right, Gideon. If this faith you speak of is real, then surely there's a way to redeem what was lost." Sunlight laced through the trees, dancing along her face.

No. It was impossible. God didn't work that way. He and Cassie were too far gone. Their choices too selfish, too sinful. Yet something inside him — memories of what God could build out of nothing — told him he was wrong.

THIRTY-SEVEN

Lonnie sat on the back steps, Jacob in her lap, as she laced her boots. Addie sat beside her, doing the same. A letter to Gideon seemed to weigh her pocket. She'd written it late in the night. For weeks she'd put it off, uncertain if she was strong enough to pen her heart. But then, as she watched Jacob sleep by the light of a single candle, she couldn't bear the thought of Gideon's missing every single moment. What little she managed to express in her words would have to suffice. Lonnie fingered the envelope, wishing she could blot out the tear stains that betrayed her.

Jebediah worked at the edge of the yard, tossing vines from the garden into a smoldering heap. The scent of smoke and the herby aroma of the spent summer garden filled the air. Jacob rubbed his nose with his pudgy hand.

When Addie was finished, they strode

toward the gate.

"Where ya headed?" Jebediah tossed a squash vine onto the heap and straightened, his pants stained with soot and soil.

"To get a goat." Lonnie blinked up, and Jebediah was outlined in the glint of the morning sun. "Elsie and I spoke to Gus the other day, and he's gonna trade me for one."

"A goat."

It felt strange to smile, but with Jebediah looking at her like that, she couldn't help it. "Yes. A whole goat. Addie's gonna come with me. We won't be long."

Jebediah motioned toward the neighboring farm. "Well, I leave you to it, ladies. Try not to get into too much trouble." He winked at Addie.

Addie's round cheeks dimpled in a smile.

Bitter air nipped at her nose, and Lonnie tugged Jacob's wool sweater down over his round belly. He flapped his arm, eager to be on an adventure. The forest was quiet as if all the creatures were still snug in bed. Lonnie was glad she tucked an extra petticoat beneath her brown dress and insisted Addie wear two pairs of stockings. Lonnie slowed when, somewhere in the distance, she heard a fiddle. The long, lone sound drew her eyes toward a cabin just beyond the nearest trees.

Addie tugged gently on her sleeve. "It's

that man," she whispered and pointed up the trail. "The one who talks funny. The nice one."

So it was. Lonnie brushed at a strand of hair tickling her cheek.

He was dressed in the same dark garb Reverend Gardner always wore. The man clutched a Bible to his chest with a thick hand, his features drawn. Dawn broke in his troubled face when he glanced up and spotted them.

"Morning," he breathed.

"Morning."

One of his dimples appeared. "You're out early."

"As are you."

He squinted down at her, a shadow of a beard along his jaw. "Aye. It's been a bit of a night." A slow glance over his shoulder to the cabin, then his attention fell on her. "Mrs. Bennick passed, and I've been sitting with the family."

"Oh, I'm so sorry to hear that."

" 'Twas an easy passing. And her spirit was at peace."

The words soothed. "A blessing to the family that you were there for comfort."

He ducked his head humbly, then glanced down at Addie. "And where might you be going? I see you're keeping an eye on your older sister here."

Lonnie caught his disguised wink.

"We're going to get a goat," the little girl declared.

"Oh. A goat."

"For myself," Lonnie blurted.

"Oh."

She hitched her foot off to the side. "Why does everybody look at me like I'm crazy when I say that?"

"Am I looking at you like you're crazy?"

"Yes."

His face quickly broke into a wide, awkward grin. After several heartbeats, he spoke through his teeth. "I'm frightening you, aren't I?"

"A little."

He chuckled and his smile turned natural.

The side of her mouth lifted. "Better."

"May I . . . may I walk with you a ways? I'm headed in that direction."

She studied him a moment. "If you'd like."

Autumn hues — nearly a memory — burned gold in patches overhead as they strode down the path. The early sun illuminated the still forest, and Addie skipped ahead. Lonnie and Toby walked a whisper apart, Jacob between them.

"So tell me about this goat of yours. What

are you going to use it for? Meat, cheese, soap?"

"How did you know?"

"Meat?"

She chuckled. "No, soap." She fiddled with the cuff of Jacob's pants, her fingers stiff from the cold. "I've been experimenting with a few new varieties. My aunt taught me, but I've never made it with goat's milk before." She drew in a full breath, holding it briefly. She let it out in a gush. "You could say it's time for a little change." She glanced up at him. "Honestly, I just need something to keep me busy."

His face softened as if he had absorbed more than her words. "Aye, I ken the feeling." He lifted the Bible. "Part of the reason I'm always working with folks 'round here. Can't just wait on Sundays or a sickness."

Her braid slid off her shoulder and bounced against her back. "No, I suppose you can't." They approached Gus's barn, and Lonnie thought about trying him at his house first, when he appeared in the great doorway and waved overhead.

"I've been expecting you!" He waved them forward, his smile broad.

"Want to see them?" she asked Toby.

He dipped his head. "Love to."

The vast space was a far cry from Jebediah's cozy barn. The front portion was set up as a workshop, and beyond that half a dozen stalls lined each side. Gus led them down the narrow aisle, the essence of animals and feed thick and swampy.

With a hitch of his thumb, Gus alerted them to a stall near the rear. "This is the lot of 'em." He motioned for Lonnie to take a closer look, and she led Addie in front of her as they crowded around the narrow space. Gus's raspy voice, as kind as Jebediah's, fell soft beside her. "Four all together, though only two are nannies." Tattered boots carried him into the pen. "This one" — he rubbed the back of a pure white goat — "and that'n." A speckled kid trotted across the pen. "You may have your pick, Lonnie. Just let me know which one you choose."

Something warmed in her heart as she watched the pair. "When will they be ready?"

"Too young to breed this year, so come the spring after next, I'm hoping they'll both deliver a pair of kids. After the babes are weaned, she's all yours. As long as you don't mind waiting."

Lonnie rested her chin on the gatepost. She rather fancied the white one, but something about the way the speckled one moseyed about kept stealing her attention.

"Do they have names?" she asked.

"No." Gus ran his hands up and down his overall straps. "Don't fancy myself as sentimental as you women folk. Though it's high time I got around to calling them something."

Lonnie watched the speckled one, wondering what she might call it.

"That one's a bit of a handful," Toby said, pointing to a brown goat in the corner who was rubbing its head against the post. The kid turned and rammed the other male in the side, sending it trotting out of the way.

"That little billy gives me more trouble than the lot of them put together. Unruly. Stubborn as they come. A spirit about that one." Gus's mouth tipped up in a smile despite his complaint.

Lonnie had the perfect name for it come to mind. Gideon's memory sent a shard of pain through her chest, and she pressed her hand to her blouse.

"You all right?"

She glanced up to see Toby watching her and realized she was frowning. "Yes, fine." She cleared her throat, folding the sadness in a hidden place, and held Jacob tighter to chase away the yearning. She struggled for words. "I . . . I'm thinking of that one

305

there." She squinted one eye and pointed at the speckled one. He looked where she pointed.

"Aye. Good choice." Toby lifted Addie onto the railing for a better view. "And what do you think?"

"I like that one the best too." Addie bounced her heels, pigtails dancing. Toby grinned down at her as if she were his own. The action called Lonnie's heart from its hiding place.

"Then that one it is." She winked at her sister and fought the urge to tell Gus she'd take the brown male too. *Pull yourself together, Lonnie.* "I'll bring you all the soap you need."

"It's a deal." He reached out to shake her hand, and she took it. "A fine deal for an old bachelor like me."

And she would have a way to make a little income. For the first time in her life, she would be able to stand on her own two feet. She couldn't rely on Jebediah and Elsie's kindness forever. She had to see to Jacob's needs. Addie's too. She wouldn't have much, but it would be a start. Suddenly, she remembered the letter in her apron pocket. She pulled it out. "Jebediah said you're making a trip into Mount Airy."

"That I am. Day after tomorrow."

"Would you take this to the post office for me?"

"Be happy to." He took the letter and slid it inside his coat.

She bid farewell to Gus and led the way back into the fresh air. The sky had clouded over, blanketing the morning in cool, gray light. The air was damp with a coming rain. Lonnie held Jacob close.

"May I walk you home?" Toby asked.

"I don't want to take any more of your day." She motioned to the road. "It's a short walk."

"To the end of the drive then? What say you, Addie?" He winked down at the girl. "Will you walk with me, lass?"

The little girl nodded heartily and held his hand with both of hers. They strode a step ahead, Addie skipping. Lonnie watched them for several minutes, a thousand thoughts colliding in her mind and heart. Finally, Toby stopped and turned.

"This is where we part ways." The breeze tousled his dark brown locks. His dimples deepened in a smile. "I thank you lassies for letting me accomp'ny you this fine morning." He pressed a broad hand to his chest. "I was feeling a bit melancholy before and spending the hour with the pair o' you chased that away." His large, brown eyes

307

held Lonnie's gaze.

The feeling was mutual.

THIRTY-EIGHT

Feet propped up on the porch railing, Gideon tipped his chair back and watched a tumble of clouds move boldly toward the farm. With his mandolin to his chest, he picked a slow song — a harmony of fragments as if the indecisiveness of his spirit had found its way to his hands. His unlaced boots bounced, the tempo increasing, as emotions that were best laid to rest stirred things inside him. The scent of something colder than rain carried on the wind.

He thought of Lonnie. He thought of Cassie. And no song would form. From the eight strings, he merely plucked a jumble of melodies, a tangle of notes. A dance between melancholy and yearning — all that was in him and through him. All that he had become. He sang here and there, but pain rubbed sand through his voice.

Hymns danced on the outskirts of his mind, beckoning him to partake, but he wouldn't let himself go there. His soul wrestled too fiercely to allow himself that kind of reprieve. He needed to get this out. Needed to make sense of the mess his life had become. If only for an hour. If only for a night, he needed to give in to the madness.

A glance over his shoulder confirmed that the kettle steamed. He let it billow several minutes more, exhausting his senses. Finally he rose, set his mandolin aside, and using the edge of his shirt, carried the kettle into the bedroom.

Cassie was at her parents, so for a few blessed moments, he had peace and quiet. He filled the washbasin and tested the water, shaking scalded fingers like an imbecile. He hadn't shaved in two weeks, and staring at the small, square mirror, he could see that a pass with the razor was long overdue. He peeled his shirt off and tossed it on the bed. His long underwear clung to his skin, and with quick hands, he shoved the dingy sleeves past his forearms. He flicked the top buttons loose and pulled the fabric away from his collarbone to keep it dry.

With a rag, he dampened his whiskers. The hot water stung, but only for a moment. He lathered his skin. Without having anything to sharpen his razor with, he ran the straight razor up his throat in slow, steady strokes. He rinsed the blade clean and worked his way up his jaw.

Lonnie used to sit on the bed, watching him. The side of his mouth tipped up. He'd never known if she'd meant to keep him company or if she was keeping watch to make sure he actually committed to a clean shave, so sparse they were. He dragged a long breath in through his nose, remembering the sight of her lying on her stomach on the bed, feet crossed behind her. She would talk and talk, and he would listen. He glanced at the rumpled bed. How he wished she sat there now.

And what would you say?

He wouldn't have to say anything. He would simply listen. Listen to how his son was growing. Listen to how she made it through the day without him. For he had yet to understand the secret to making it through the day without her.

Hands braced on each side of the wash-basin, he stared at the murky water, his shaving forgotten. Lonnie. His hands itched to hold her. To cup her face between his palms. The coals in his chest that he tried to smother bloomed, fanned by longing. His sweet, sweet Lonnie. His Jacob. He glanced in the mirror and saw Cassie in the doorway.

"You're back." With the damp rag, he wiped the rest of the cream from his face and rinsed his hands.

Sinking onto the edge of the bed, Cassie pulled a knee up and began unlacing her boots. She set one aside and then the other. Blue eyes found his in the glass. "I thought there might be a handsome man under all those whiskers." She pulled her skirt up past her knees and slid her stockings down.

Letting her words hang, Gideon rinsed the blade. He stifled a cough.

"My folks invited us over for supper. I thought it might be nice to visit." Reaching behind her, she worked on the buttons of her dress.

"If you say so." Lifting the rag, Gideon wiped his neck clean. He glanced at her in the mirror.

She freed one shoulder, the strap of her shimmy poking through.

"What are you doing?"

Her hands stilled. "Changing. I've been peeling apples, and my dress is damp."

Their gazes locked, and he could tell she was trying to read him. He had no words. No words to prevent her from being his wife in every sense of the title. She wiggled free of her dress and stepped out of it. Averting his gaze, Gideon cleared his throat, knotting the rag in his hands. It was all too familiar. The cramped room. The woman. What it was doing to him.

Without even bothering to fetch a clean shirt, he strode from the bedroom and embraced the cold outside.

"Help yourself to seconds please, Gideon."

Gideon glanced down at his empty plate and licked his fingers. "Thank you, ma'am. This is the best fried chicken I've ever had."

"Eat as much as you want. And potatoes . . . another scoop?" Cassie's ma reached for the wooden spoon before he could respond.

He held out his plate, and Mary piled a heaping spoonful next to his chicken. He sank his fork in, then licked butter from his thumb.

Henry Allan accepted another serving of potatoes but did not lift his eyes as he stirred his food around on his plate. Gideon cleared his throat.

"Thank you for lending me that cart of yours."

A curt nod was Henry's only reply.

"Jack told me you taught him how to build a few things in your wood shop, Gideon." Mary smiled kindly. "That was awful nice.

He's spoken very highly of you."

Henry nearly choked. He reached for his cider.

Gideon stuck his tongue in his cheek.

Beside him, Cassie pushed food across her plate and listened to a story Libby was telling about school.

"Where are the boys?" Cassie set her fork down, eyes fixed on her pa.

Gideon lifted his head, trying to appear curious. But he knew the answer. Her brothers wanted nothing to do with him. He was an outcast to his own friends. At least to Samuel and Eli, but considering that Jack was outnumbered, Gideon could not blame the youngest Allan boy for tagging along with his older brothers.

Mary waved her checked napkin in the air. "Oh, they're off on some jaunt. Guess they think they're too old to tell their ma where they're goin' anymore."

A sip of cider and Gideon cleared his throat. He had a hunch that the Allan boys had decided to skip dinner when he had been invited.

"Probably off on a coon trail or some such nonsense." Cassie elbowed Gideon in the ribs. "Remember the time you all went out huntin' for squirrels and got lost? By the time supper was on the table, Pa had to go look for you boys. You couldn't have been much more than ten."

Gideon took another sip. "Who'da thought your brothers could get lost in their own backyard? Guess that's what happens when the sun goes down."

Mary smiled.

"All I remember was the four of you up to your knees in mud and not a squirrel to be seen." Still laughing, Cassie reached for her cider. She bumped the glass, and it crashed against Gideon's plate.

Cold cider trickled into his lap, and he jumped. "Oh, Lonnie!"

The room fell silent. Panting, Gideon glanced at Cassie. Her face paled.

"Gid, I . . ." Her chin trembled. She dropped her napkin to the table. Her chair skidded back. Before he could stop her, she flitted from the kitchen.

He felt heavy gazes as he swiped at the spill with his napkin and brushed the cider from his pants. "I . . ." His neck burned, and he glanced to the door. The auburn liquid trickled to the floor.

Lonnie? You idiot.

"I . . . excuse me." He jogged through the kitchen and pushed past the back door.

Cool night air hit his face. "Cassie?" he called into the darkness.

With a full moon out, it did not take long for him to spot her running for the cabin. In a few short moments, his long strides overtook hers, and he caught her by the wrist.

"Cassie," he breathed.

She wriggled her arm and yanked away.

He caught up to her, circling her small wrist gently with his hand. "Cassie, wait. Stop." He dug his heels into the rain-soaked ground. She kicked at him. "Cassie," he panted.

She tugged once more, then stilled. Her other hand brushed across her eyes before turning around.

"I'm sorry." Gideon wished he could say it less plainly. "I really am." Reaching out, he grabbed hold of her other hand so she faced him. Dipping his head, he tried to catch her gaze. "It slipped out." Cold air bit through his shirt, and he suddenly wished he had a coat to offer her.

Cassie sniffed. She would not look at him. "I don't believe you. It meant everything." Her voice wavered. "She means everything."

His eyes slammed closed, and he breathed away the seconds. "She's not my wife anymore," he said flatly. "You are."

Pulling her hand free, Cassie wiped her sleeve beneath her nose. Her hair whipped in the wind, and she collected the unruly strands before twisting it over her shoulder. Moonlight played with her features, taunting him. "That means nothing, and you know it." In the dusky light, her eyes searched his. They searched his soul, and Gideon hoped that the truth, hidden in the depths, would not be seen.

"It . . . it will," he lied.

"Then say you don't love her."

That he couldn't do.

She was shaking.

"It's too cold for you out here without a coat." He tilted his face to the tar-black sky and stared at the glitter of stars, wishing it were in him to say more.

"I better go help Ma clean up," Cassie murmured. She ran her fists over her eyes. Her rosebud mouth trembled from cold, and Gideon forced his gaze away. She was too pretty to linger on. He gently touched her elbow, helping her back toward the house.

She seemed to relax beneath his touch. Taken aback, Gideon pulled his hand away.

THIRTY-NINE

Wind howled against the side of the house, and Cassie folded her arms in front of her, convinced the cold was seeping through the cracks in the cabin walls. Knowing there was nothing she could do to help, she paced the floor. At the sound of splintering wood, she lifted her eyes to the ceiling and imagined Gideon on the roof.

When the wind changed directions, icy sleet pounded against the window, and Cassie peered out, hoping to catch a glimpse of Gideon. Instead, she watched in dismay as another shingle flew past. Sleet slapped against the glass, and Cassie jumped back. *Poor Gideon.* He could not do this alone.

Shuddering, she turned to face the empty room. How long had he been out there? What little light worked its way through the storm would soon be gone, and he was surely far from finished. Cassie couldn't wait any longer. She darted into the bedroom and slipped another petticoat beneath her striped dress, then grabbed a second pair of wool stockings. She dressed near the fire and made certain to set another piece of oak onto the coals before heading toward the door.

Throwing on her coat, she made quick work of the army buttons before grabbing her shawl. The wind rattled the door. She eyed the latch, half expecting it to break open. She draped her shawl over her hair and tucked the loose ends inside her coat. Something banged against the roof, and even as her hand fell on the doorknob, she prayed her husband was being careful.

An icy gust enveloped her, and it took all her strength to keep the door from flinging out of her grasp. Cassie hurried outside and used the weight of her body to push the door shut. Her shawl caught, and she wrenched it free. After tucking it back into place, she tightened the collar of her coat. Sleet swirled around her. For a moment, she hesitated, then stepped away from the safety of the porch.

Tilting her face to the gray sky, Cassie searched the roofline. "Gideon!"

She shut her eyes when the wind blew a gust of wet snow into her face. Cassie ran her hand over her eyes, certain her voice had been lost on the wind.

"What are you doing out here?" Gideon hollered from the edge of the roof. Crawling on his knees, he slid a nail from his lips and pounded a shingle into place. Another snapped, and the pieces darted away on the wind. Gideon lowered his head and tossed his hammer to the side.

"I'll get it!" Cassie called.

He waved her down. "It's no use," he shouted. "Broke clear in two." He paused and stared at the land below him. Another blast of snow pounded them, and he threw his arm up to block his face. When the snow settled, Gideon pointed. "There."

Cassie turned to look.

"Two shingles are over there. See if you can get them."

Her boots slid in the wet snow as she struggled to run. When she slipped, Cassie yanked her hands free from her warm pockets and used her arms for balance. The cold stung her bare skin. Her gloves were in the house. She imagined them on top of her dresser where she had left them.

Cassie spotted the first shingle wedged in the snow. She grabbed it and clutched it to her chest as she searched for the other. With a life of its own, the wind blew a fresh layer of white powder across the land. The piece of wood vanished from sight, and Cassie knew it was hopeless to search.

She ran back to the cabin and braved the first two rungs of the ladder before another gust struck the side of the house. "Gideon!" she shrieked. Sleet stung her neck and ears. She closed her eyes as her frozen fingers clung to the ladder.

A sure voice called to her. "I'm here."

She looked up to see him staring down at her. The snow seemed to settle and the wind softened. For the first time that day, the land quieted enough for Cassie to hear her frantic breathing.

"I'm here," he said again.

She wanted to cry, but Cassie lifted a stiff arm and held the shingle out for Gideon to take.

His fingers barely grazed the wood. "Can't quite reach it."

A gust crashed against the house, rocking the ladder. Swallowing her fear, she urged her feet to move up one more rung. She prayed it would be enough for Gideon to reach. His gloved hand grabbed the wood, and it left her grasp.

"Got it!"

She let out the breath she'd been holding and scrambled down. She scanned the yard. Shingles littered the ground. Time seemed lost to her as she tried to gather what she could. With several in her grasp, she rushed back to the cabin. As if she had awakened a sleeping bear, the wind that had mellowed engulfed her in an icy whirl. She lifted a shingle to protect her face, but the wind's angry fingers snatched it from her grasp.

Cassie yelped and grabbed her stinging hand in time to see blood surface on her palm. Looking away, she stared at Gideon, who stumbled along the roof. The wind tore at his coat, but he bent and pounded another nail in a single blow. Clambering back up the ladder, she lifted the three shingles she'd managed to hang on to.

When one flew from his grasp, he thanked her for the two he was able to grab hold of. Her legs shook as she stepped back down. They fought a battle they could not win. Jumping from the last rung, she crouched against the house and studied her injury. A shard had embedded itself into her hand, leaving drops of blood smeared across her palm. With frozen fingers, she tried to pull it free, but it was too deep. She winced.

Suddenly, Gideon was kneeling behind her, his face close. "It's no use," he murmured and wrapped a broad hand around her arm. "Let's get inside." The words fell warm against her ear when he helped her to stand. "I'll deal with the damage after this storm has passed." Unable to argue, she leaned into the shelter of his chest and allowed him to lead her around to the porch.

He held the door open long enough for her to slip inside, and the wind slammed it shut behind them. Still shaking, Cassie sank into the kitchen chair. The fire crackled in the small stove, and as her hands thawed, the pain of her injury intensified.

"Gideon," she mumbled.

He yanked his coat from his shoulders and hung it up. His damp hair curled around his ears, and he tugged at the unruly locks with a weary sigh. When his attention fell on her, Cassie held up her hand.

"I'm gonna need your help."

He sank to his knees in front of her and gently took her hand. "Your fingers are frozen." His concerned gaze pinned her motionless. "You should have had gloves."

Her lips parted, but nothing intelligent came to mind — he was too close. "I was in a hurry," she finally managed.

Gideon searched her face. "You shouldn't have even been out there. Not in this weather." When he smoothed his finger across her palm, she squirmed slightly. His fingertip stilled beside her wound. "This shard is *deep.*"

Cassie looked up at him. "Can you get it out?"

He rose and crossed the floor, yanking his shirttail free from beneath his belt. The damp wrinkles hung around his waist as he stood over the stove. "I have to." He slid a small pot to the hottest part of the stove and filled it with steaming water from the kettle.

Searching through a jar of knives and utensils, he finally retrieved a small paring knife and held it up for Cassie to see. "This should do." He dropped it into the pot that had already begun to bubble. He stared at the water. Cassie watched him. He snatched a clean towel from the basket and moved the pot to the table, where he sank in the chair across from her. He pulled himself closer until their knees touched.

"Here," he said, his voice soft. He pulled her hand into his lap. "Hold your palm open." Cassie uncurled her fingers. "Yes, like that." Then he grunted. "I can't see anything. Hold on." He jumped from his chair and grabbed candles from around the kitchen. Bringing them to the table, he lit the wicks with sure fingers. Cassie watched his face illuminate. In one quick motion, he nabbed the knife from the water and set it on the towel. He shook his arm as if to cool his fingers.

Sinking into his chair, he hesitated before taking her hand. His brows furrowed, and he moistened his lips as he grazed his fingertip over the wound. Cassie winced but tried to keep her hand steady.

"Sorry," he mumbled, then shook his head.

He dipped the towel into the hot water. Droplets trickled from the drenched cloth as he wrung it out. With slow movements, he dabbed at her palm with the warm rag. When a smile tugged at her lips, Cassie struggled to keep it hidden.

"Don't worry," she reassured him. It took all her restraint to keep her eyes from savoring the familiar shapes of his face. "You can't hurt me."

He tipped his head to the side. "I'm not so sure about that." His voice was low and as smooth as velvet.

Green eyes met hers, and he seemed to be waiting for her final consent. When Cassie gave a slight nod, he reached for the knife. His hand now steady, he squinted against the failing light. The knife blade broke her skin, but Cassie felt no pain.

Gideon's eyes lifted. "Did that hurt?"

A quick shake of her head. "Not really."

The second pass with the knife made her

grimace. She glanced away when Gideon assured her he was almost done. His breath was faint in her ears, and Cassie closed her eyes. She willed herself to keep still, yet all the while her head spun.

"There." He held up the thick shard and leaned back. "Got it."

Cassie slunk down in her chair. "Thank you."

Gideon did not release her hand. Instead, he held the warm rag against her wound and gently squeezed her wrist. He spoke of needing a bandage, asking her where he might find one.

"Um . . . ," she blurted, suddenly unable to put two words together. Not with him so close, holding her hand so.

As if he sensed it, his eyes danced between them. Quickly, he released her. "Sorry." He wiped his palms on his pants as if to be rid of her touch.

Cheeks warming, Cassie glanced away. He didn't need to apologize. He had every right. If he would but see it.

FORTY

Lonnie sat on the parlor sofa, her feet tucked under her, and lifted Jacob to her shoulder for a burp. "That's my boy." She rubbed a slow circle on his back. With a belly full of milk, he would soon be fast asleep.

She heard Elsie's footsteps before she saw her. The gray-haired woman appeared, a paper-wrapped bundle in her arms.

"Had this tucked away. Nearly forgot all about it." With a twinkle in her eye, Elsie set it at Lonnie's side.

"What is it?" Her brow furrowed.

"Open it and find out." Elsie's voice was bright. She held out her arms for the baby. Rising, Lonnie slowly transferred the sleeping boy. He let out a soft sigh. "Now." Elsie nodded to the parcel.

A tug on the string and it unraveled. The paper crinkled under her hand as Lonnie turned it over. "Oh, Elsie." Soft folds of pink eyelet fabric tumbled free. "Is this for me?"

The woman's bun bobbed in a nod. "Yes, and you must make yourself something very fine with it."

"Are you sure? How did you . . . *when* did you?"

"On Jebediah's last trip to Mount Airy. Weeks and weeks ago. Remember that fabric you asked for to make a new skirt? Gideon wanted you to have a blouse to go with it."

"Did he?" Her voice was pensive, soft with yearning. Her throat suddenly felt tight.

"I believe it was going to be a gift." Elsie's eyes held a sweet sadness. "He had asked me to hide it away. I'd nearly forgotten about it. I know he'd want you to have it."

"Oh, Elsie." Lonnie pressed a hand to her mouth when her chin trembled. She closed her eyes to fight the sting of tears. She would not cry. She would not.

But her heart was tired of listening.

Her shoulders shook once. Twice. Elsie wrapped an arm around her, pulling her close. Lonnie's cheek pressed against Jacob's soft back, shattering the last of her resolve. She clutched the package close, wishing with all her might that it was the man himself.

"Whatever am I going to do? I miss him something fierce." She sniffed, tucked her thumb inside her sleeve, and ran it over her wet eyes. "I don't know how to make it stop."

Elsie's soft hand traced comfort along her back. "Not so much about making it stop" — she gave a gentle squeeze — "but about putting one foot in front of the other." She ducked her head until Lonnie's gaze met hers. "I see you taking those strides. I see it in you every day."

"I'm trying." Lonnie's voice was thin. "It doesn't seem to be enough. It doesn't make it easier."

"Nothing but time will make the hurting stop. And" — Elsie kissed the top of Jacob's head, lingering — "not so much stop but lessen. The bitter will become smaller, and the sweet will grow."

Lonnie felt the delicate fabric, wishing with all that was within her that Gideon was standing there this moment. She wanted to thank him. She wanted to hold him. She wanted to hear from his lips that it had all been a bad dream. *Oh, Gideon.* Impatient, unruly Gideon. Who always ran headfirst into life without weighing the consequences. The green-eyed man who'd spent months and months changing, growing, learning. All to deserve his family. Was he really lost to her? She had stitched her heart inside his chest pocket and didn't know how to break that thread.

"Elsie, thank you. I'm so glad you found this." She clutched it to her belly, and her vision blurred. "Thank you, thank you."

Water sloshed over the edge of the bathtub when Cassie rose. Her teeth chattered as she hurried to dry off. Then she dropped her towel and, using her foot, blotted up the wet mess on the floor. A knock on the door made her heart leap. "Almost done." She snatched a clean shimmy from the dresser. When she slammed the drawer shut, she nearly caught her finger.

Gideon's low voice came muffled through the door. "No hurry. I just wanted to tell you that we're nearly out of wood, and it looks like another storm's comin'." He fell silent before continuing. "Might be worse than the one we had last week. I'm gonna go out into the woods and see what I can gather to get us through."

Cassie flung her dress over her head and jammed the buttons into place. "Wait for me," she called. Stuffing her feet into a pair of clean stockings, she pulled the gray wool up and over her knees. "I want to come."

"It's pretty cold out there," he said. His

voice grew clearer when Cassie opened the door.

He stepped back. "That was quick."

She tossed a sweater over her shoulders. "I hurried." Her stockinged feet crossed the floor without a sound.

"It's gonna be boring work."

Cassie slipped a foot inside her boot and tugged the frayed laces into place with unladylike force. "All the more reason to have company." She reached for her other boot.

Doubt betrayed his eyes when she looked up at him.

Perhaps only certain company. Without waiting for him to respond, she jumped up and snatched her things from the hook behind the door.

Gideon held the door open with the toe of his boot, and she stepped out. Before her spirits could fall, her ma's words echoed in her ears and were as real as the moment she'd spoken them the morning of the wedding. Cassie knew Gideon would never love her but couldn't overlook the bead of hope in her mother's eye. *"What that boy wants and what he needs are two different things."*

Let it be so.

Gideon seemed focused on the path ahead, but Cassie knew him well enough to understand his thoughts were far from the snowy trail before him. *Oh, Gideon. What happened to you?* What anguish did he suffer? That moment, Cassie wondered if she would *ever* be enough to mend his grief. She had once been the delight of his eye. The name spoken on his lips with affection — with passion.

Her steps fell in sync behind his, and Cassie studied the man before her. What sorrow tormented his heart? She wished she did not understand, but she did. She knew the anguish of being separated. Her pa's words from long ago echoed fresh in her mind. *"Gideon's going to marry the Sawyer girl."* Alone with her own secret, she had run off to the barn and wept for hours.

Her husband had found another. And that life had changed him.

The Gideon she had once known was no more. In his place was a sober, almost pensive man. Gone were his rowdy ways. She hadn't seen him take so much as a drop of moonshine. He was so different from the man she had once known. In more ways than one.

Gideon slowed, letting Cassie catch up. He couldn't help but notice that the tight bun at the nape of her neck smelled like rosemary soap — the heady scent inescapable — and he found himself unable to look away.

Dark lashes flicked up, and she studied him, her round cheeks smooth.

Time goes by better with company. As much as he wanted to, he couldn't disagree. Gideon watched as she took the lead. She looked so petite beneath the coat draped loosely across her thin frame — so small beneath the sinister spans of swollen clouds overhead.

Cassie spun around and smiled. "I've seen hogs walk faster than you."

It wasn't the first time he'd been teased about being slow. But that only made his chest ache and his mind race toward his treasured memories. Trying to keep his mind in the moment, he quickened his pace to match hers. "Would *you* like to pull the sled?"

She waited for him to catch up. With nothing else around the snow-covered farm to distract him, Gideon's full attention fell on her. He looked down at her silken hair, still shiny from her bath. Like he was being awakened slowly from a long dream, everything about her was becoming familiar once again — the round shape of her mouth, the pinch at the tips of her ears, and the way her nose wrinkled impishly when she smiled at him. Gideon cleared his throat as different memories from the past reminded him how he had adored her once. Intensely. He wished the sweet fragrance of her bath didn't linger on her skin and was relieved when she wandered off. He rubbed the back of his neck. The muscles there were stiff, complaining. A roll of his shoulders did little to loosen the tension.

It wasn't easy sleeping in the hard rocking chair every night. Rarely did he give in to the luxury of a soft mattress, a warm blanket. Because he wasn't as good as any of them gave him credit for. Sure, he was trying to change, but some habits were hard to break. Sleeping beside Cassie Allan was a habit best left untouched.

"Here's one." She knelt and plucked a thin branch from the ground. Without ceremony, Gideon followed her, and in no time, frozen sticks of all sizes cluttered the inside of the sled. Cassie struggled with a heavy branch.

"Let me help you." With a tug, Gideon freed it from the frozen ground and hoisted it into the sled.

Cassie chatted as they worked. Gideon did his best to respond in complete sentences. She was cheerier than he ever remembered, and after a while, he found himself enjoying the morning — the company. Perhaps this could work. Perhaps he could take pleasure in Cassie's presence as the companion she was becoming. Gideon freed a chunk of wood from the frozen ground and wiped away powdery snow. But would that be enough for her? for him?

It has to be. He knew of no other way. Gideon tossed the wood into the sled, and it banged against the side. He chewed his lip and cast a wary glance in Cassie's direction, glad she could not read his thoughts. The thoughts that hovered around the woman who held every happy desire in the palm of her small hand. Lonnie.

The name seemed to bore a hole through his lungs, making it impossible to breathe. His love. How he longed to touch her. Hear her voice, her laughter. Feel the curve of her silken cheek on the back of his hand. If only she were here with him now. He would bury his face in her hair and inhale the warm scent of cinnamon that always seemed a part of her. She was forever in the kitchen, endlessly covered in flour and sugar . . . with Jacob at her feet.

"Cat got your tongue?"

"Sorry?"

"I asked if you think that's enough." Cas-

335

sie dropped a pair of heavy sticks into the sled. "Or should we head deeper into the woods?"

Gideon blinked into the sun and forced his mind back to the present. His new wife bent to yank a heavy branch from beneath a tree. She tugged with all her strength, then gave up, tilted her face to the sky, and laughed.

"Maybe we should call it a day before you hurt something."

She flung a stick in his direction.

"Or someone."

Cassie laughed, and the fondness in her face when she looked up turned something inside his heart, humbling him.

FORTY-ONE

"Are you sure you wanna go?" Elsie whispered as Lonnie set Jacob on the kitchen floor.

Before pulling her hands away, Lonnie swiped her palm over the baby's rumpled hair. "I'm certain. Some fresh air'll do me good."

Elsie pursed her lips, but her eyes softened.

"I need to get out and stretch my legs." Lonnie rolled the cuffs of Gideon's plaid coat past her wrists so she could tuck in her bulky wool gloves. She tugged the thick plaid back in place and clapped her hands together with a muffled sound. "Jeb's probably waitin' for me." Squatting, she pressed a kiss to Jacob's warm forehead, then rose and squeezed Elsie's hand in a silent thank-you. "Jebediah said we shouldn't be gone long."

Before her son could fuss about her hasty

departure, Lonnie slipped from the cozy kitchen. Just as an icy gust of wind took her breath away, the sun peeked through thinning clouds. As expected, Jebediah stepped from the barn and waved.

"Chores are done. Ready to head out?" he called.

Lonnie left the porch and stepped through thick mounds of snow. "I'm ready."

She fell in step behind him and used his large footprints as her pathway. Even so, the snow rose to her kneecaps, and the warmth of her legs melted what clung to her wool stockings.

They walked in silence. The December sun made the white landscape glisten, making it hard to believe that only a few days before, the sky had been an angry shade of gray. Lonnie savored the warmth and knew it could fade by tomorrow. She glanced over her shoulder but could no longer see the house behind them. Only the northeastern corner of the fence poked out of the snow. They followed the trail as it wound around a cluster of red oaks.

Jebediah switched his shotgun from one hand to the other and peered behind him. "You all right back there?"

Breathless, Lonnie merely nodded. Jebediah's footsteps were farther apart than hers, and she struggled to keep up with his steady pace. When he called back to her again, his breath blew white in short puffs.

"First snare's not far from the farm," he panted. "Just a little ways more."

They walked in silence, chests heaving. Lonnie's calves began to burn, and with a grunt, she lifted her boot out of the snow only to have it sink down again on the next step. Finally, Jebediah paused and raised his arm. Lonnie's gaze followed the length of his plaid sleeve.

"Looks empty, but I'll check it just the same. You can wait here." He veered off to the right and sank in the drifts beneath the trees. Chilled through, Lonnie crossed her arms over her chest and shivered. The tiny rabbit tracks that littered the freshly fallen snow wove this way and that in a delicate lace pattern she found strangely beautiful.

Jebediah slowed as he approached the snare. "Yep, empty." He looked back at Lonnie. Even from the distance, she could see the disappointment on his face.

"You still got a few to check, though, right?"

He waved her forward. "Yeah. We'll keep goin'." They walked toward each other until their trails united, and Lonnie fell in step behind his heavy boots once more. They'd hardly gone a dozen paces when he motioned to another snare.

"Would you look at that!" Jebediah handed his shotgun to Lonnie and hurried off toward the trap. "Got one. Come see." Wrinkling her nose, she followed his bidding.

"See how it sprung?" He clamped his gloves together in a swift motion. Jebediah sank back on his haunches and smiled. "Gid chose this spot. I remember 'cause I didn't think it was a good place. Told him so several times, in fact, but that boy wouldn't listen." He shook his head, a smile forming beneath his mustache. "He was right."

Her insides hollowed. Lonnie stuffed her hands into the pockets of Gideon's coat. She closed her eyes. Feeling nothing but the cold in her toes and the bitter air on her face, she could almost imagine Gideon standing in the exact same spot only weeks prior.

Jebediah yanked off his gloves and struggled to loosen the frozen snare. When the critter had been freed and placed in a burlap sack, he reset the coils. They moved on to check the final location. It was as empty as the first.

"This one's yet to bring me luck. Ain't touched it since . . ." Jebediah's voice trailed off to a mumble, and he scratched his jaw before stuffing red fingers inside his glove.

Staring at the lone trap, Lonnie felt a secret thrill knowing it was empty — exactly the way Gideon had left it. Even now, she could almost see his rough, steady fingers as he cautiously prepared the dangerous metal spring. Lonnie clasped her cold hands between her knees. *Come on, Lonnie. You've got to do better than this.*

They trudged along in silence, this time side by side. They were in no hurry now. Her stockings were wet, her toes stiff, but there was nothing she could do other than continue on. Her hem trailed along the snow, the worn flannel frozen and caked with white powder.

"I know it's gotta be hard to talk about him," Jebediah began, breaking the unstated agreement of reverence — the silence that had settled between them. "But I sure miss that boy." His voice trailed off, and he scanned the quiet land around them. "More than I ever thought I would." He chuckled. "I still remember the day we met." Jebediah lowered his eyes and draped his gun over his shoulder, the same gun he'd used to protect Lonnie that fateful day on the hillside. A shiny reminder of Gideon's past offenses. "Who would have thought I'd miss that boy as if he were my own son?"

Lonnie stuffed her hands into her coat pockets. Gideon had touched them all in ways none of them had expected. She changed the subject. "I want to thank you for everything you and Elsie have done for us. Addie and Jacob and myself."

"It's our pleasure." His voice was so sincere she could have hugged him. She could hardly express her gratitude to Jebediah and Elsie for offering them a safe shelter when they needed it most. It humbled her further when he had later refused her ma's money. *"Save it for a rainy day."* Jebediah had winked and folded Lonnie's hands back over the bills.

A trio of golden sparrows darted from the safety of a small fir, their tiny feet hardly denting the soft snow as they hopped to and fro. They flapped tiny wings and returned to their hiding places. Lonnie peered through the velvety branches where the birds settled and watched them shake frosty feathers.

The air was strangely still. The breeze that had carried them out like wind in their sails ceased to blow, and now their feet crunching in the snow was the only sound breaking the stillness of the forest. The sun that had offered down its warmth had slipped behind the highest peak. The snow, once golden white, softened to gray blue, lost its shimmer, and seemed to cool the air. Lonnie walked slowly — the rhythm of her steps lulling her into a sweet trance — and she nearly forgot all about her frozen toes.

A horse nickered in the distance. Stumbling to a halt, Jebediah turned. Startled, Lonnie froze in place.

An accent as rich as Scotch whisky broke the silence. "Well, if it isn't two familiar faces."

Lonnie turned. Glancing between the trees, she saw a horse and rider approaching.

Jebediah chuckled. "Toby!"

The dark-haired man tugged the reins, and the brown mare pranced sideways. Snow sprayed from beneath the horse's hoofs when her muscular legs stomped to a halt.

Toby's smile was warmer than any fire. "I thought I'd take Elsie up on her offer for supper." He was breathless, eyes bright. "Didn't think I'd run into two frostbitten trav'lers on my way." He pulled his hat from his head in a brief salute, and his ebony hair stood on end. Smiling at Lonnie, he replaced the hat.

Jebediah held up the burlap sack. "Care

for some rabbit stew?"

Those darn dimples appeared.

"Sounds wonderful, but only if Elsie'll let me do the dishes." He winked at Lonnie. "It's good to see you again." His kind eyes danced over her face.

"You, as well." The words held an honesty that surprised her.

FORTY-TWO

Lonnie smiled at Elsie. Toby's eyes twinkled as he indulged Elsie's plea for one more joke. "The young housewife gave the tramp a large piece o' pie on condition that he should saw some wood. The tramp retired to the woodshed, but presently he reappeared at the back door of the house with the piece o' pie still intact save for one mouthful bitten from the end."

Elsie was already chuckling, and Toby paused long enough for his audience to lean forward in their chairs.

" 'Madam,' the tramp said respectfully to the wondering woman, 'if 'tis all the same to ye, I'll eat the wood an' saw the pie.' "

Elsie turned red with laughter. Her cheeks bobbed and her eyes watered. She swiped the back of her hand along her silver hairline. Jebediah chuckled too, and Toby sat back with a grin.

Jebediah lifted his cup in Toby's direction.

"You do have a way with words." He nodded a salute.

"As we say back home, slàinte!" Toby lifted his cup of sweet cider and waited for the others to follow suit. Lonnie's tin mug clanged against the others, and she took a sip. A soft head of dark curls grazed her arm as Addie leaned forward, her mug barely reaching.

With Jacob on her lap, Lonnie tipped a spoonful of broth to his mouth, and he took it vigorously. "You like that, don't you?" she whispered into his velvet ear.

At eight months old, Jacob had taken to his first weeks of solid food with ease. She dabbed at his mouth with her napkin, and he clapped his hands, an unbridled declaration that he wanted more.

"Well, you can have all you want." Lonnie retrieved a chunk of carrot and nibbled it smaller before poking the sweet orange flesh into Jacob's open mouth. "Chew on that until it's all gone, and I'll give you more." Pinching off a chunk of cornbread, she took a bite and licked the honey from her sticky fingers.

She felt Toby watching her.

"He's a braw eater," he said.

Lonnie nodded and ran her hand across Jacob's delicate hair. *Just like his pa.*

When Toby's spoon finally clanged inside his empty bowl, he sank against the chair and tossed his napkin on the table. "That was a fine stew, Elsie." He stretched back and rubbed both his hands across his abdomen with a sigh.

Elsie dabbed at her mouth. "Thanks to Jebediah for the fine rabbit."

Jebediah shook his head. "Like I told Lonnie earlier, the credit is Gideon's."

After taking a long gulp of cider, Toby lowered his cup to the table. "Gideon?" His Adam's apple dipped.

Elsie and Jebediah exchanged slow glances before directing their gazes at Lonnie.

She had never spoken of it aloud to anyone other than Jebediah and Elsie. Lonnie cleared her throat and wondered what the words would sound like. "He was . . . my husband." Her voice came out smoother than she had expected.

Needing to pull her attention from Toby's face, she dipped her spoon into her stew and lifted it to Jacob's lips.

"I'm verra sorry." He stared at his plate a moment before speaking. "Had I been around longer, I might have known of his passing, and I would'na have brought it up." His eager gaze met Lonnie's. "Please, forgive me."

Her hand stilled, but Jacob lunged toward the spoon, sending several drops of broth into her skirt.

"Well . . . ," Elsie began but fell silent.

Toby glanced from one face to the next before looking at Lonnie. Setting her jaw, she forced the truth. "It's not that." She shifted. She had never said it aloud before. Glancing at Jebediah, she looked for help.

The older man propped his elbows on the table and leaned toward Toby. "Did you not read the message you brought from Rocky Knob? Did Reverend Gardner not tell you?"

Toby shook his head. "No sir."

Jebediah peeked at Lonnie from beneath bushy eyebrows. When she nodded, he continued. "Gideon didn't . . . die. He's back in Rocky Knob. Matter of fact, you may even have seen him."

"Oh," Toby's voice lifted, and he leaned back in his chair. "For a moment I thought . . ." His gentle voice sharpened, and he tilted his head. "What's he doing in Rocky Knob?"

Jebediah hesitated.

Needing the torture to end, Lonnie moistened her lips. "He lives there . . . with his new wife."

Silence.

Every eye bore into Lonnie's, and she

348

blinked, surprised at how the words had leaped from her mouth. But it had to come out sooner or later. The neighbors would want to know. She sighed. The world would want to know where Jacob's father was. Forcing her head up, she tipped her chin and stared bravely at Toby.

To her surprise, Toby's eyes darted away.

"Who would like some pumpkin pie?" Elsie shoved her chair back and stood. The pie pan clanged onto the stove, and she moved for a knife.

"That would be lovely," Toby murmured.

"And coffee, Elsie?" Jebediah hinted.

Elsie tossed her napkin to the table. "Comin' right up." Her smile seemed forced. "I'll slice the pie, Jeb, if you'll grab some clean mugs."

Jacob squirmed, and Lonnie lowered him to the floor. Addie asked to be excused and slid out of her chair. She carried Jacob into the dimly lit parlor, and Lonnie heard the basket of wooden toys being tipped onto the rug.

Finally Toby spoke, his words thick. "I'm sorry to have brought up such a difficult subject. 'Twas not my place. I apologize."

To her surprise, Lonnie found her lips curving of their own free will. She felt lighter having the news off her chest. She

349

had expected his questions — his probing. But instead, he was giving her privacy that, as far as Lonnie had thought, in the eyes of the church was not due. There was something about Toby's kind face and sincere way that made her believe him.

"It's all right." She turned and looked into the parlor at her son. His small hands fumbled with a wooden top. "I expect folks to have questions."

Toby lifted his elbows from the table as Elsie slid a slice of pie in front of him. Lonnie accepted a plate, and silence fell as she dipped her fork into the pastry.

Scooting his chair closer to the table, Toby lowered his voice. "Well, all the same, it was daft of me to question you."

Her heart beat away the seconds as his gaze lingered on her. He picked up his fork and turned it around in his oversized hand before finally, to her relief, shifting his attention to his dessert.

Arms elbow deep in hot dishwater, Lonnie strained her neck to peer out the kitchen window. The sun was nowhere in sight, but the fading glow promised another hour of daylight. Through the glass, she watched Toby toss his black coat onto the woodpile and set his hat on top. Lonnie stepped closer.

"What is he doing out there?" she mumbled.

Toby heaved the heavy ax toward the chopping block, dropped it on its head, and paused to stretch his neck from side to side.

"Jebediah got him choppin' wood?"

Elsie walked to the window. "Must be." Her voice muffled against the glass. "Though Jebediah would never ask him. He'd just as soon do it himself. I suppose the reverend must have offered."

Toby hoisted the ax over his head and brought it down with a swift blow. The wood split in two — each piece flew in opposite directions across the yard. Lonnie lifted her eyebrows as he reached for another. No, he was nothing like Reverend Gardner. Not wanting to stare, she returned her attention to the dishwater that had cooled. "I still have a hard time believing he's a preacher."

"Is that so?" Elsie laughed. "Is it his wild ways?"

Lonnie felt a smile form. "Well, he doesn't look much like a reverend. Not like Reverend Gardner or Reverend Brown."

"Well, I'd hope not." Elsie's soft cheeks bobbled when she chuckled. "That boy's a good thirty years younger than both those

351

men." Her voice fell soft. "And after what those men put you through, a lot more useful."

Elsie moved away from the window and propped her hands on her hips. "Toby's a good worker." She reached up and pulled a tin mug down from the cupboard. "Here, take some cider to the poor man." From a pan on the back of the stove, Elsie poured a cup of frothy, auburn liquid and set it near Lonnie. "As hard as that man works, he'll be plumb tuckered out in no time."

With her hands wrapped around the warm mug, Lonnie stepped onto the porch. He looked in her direction.

"Care for something to drink?" she asked.

He straightened and watched her approach. "Aye." Toby lowered the ax.

"Elsie . . . I mean, Elsie and I thought you might be thirsty."

She held it out so fast it nearly sloshed on him.

He took a step back. "Shall I just try and catch it then?" He held his hands out, his grin wide.

"Sorry." Her cheeks felt aflame. She made a show of taking slow steps toward him. He chuckled and accepted the offering, his fingers brushing hers. The dark stubble that tinted his face could not conceal his deep dimples. Lonnie wiped her hands on the sides of her skirt. Feeling strangely at ease, she settled down on the chopping block, and when he sat beside her, she was in no hurry to be anywhere but there.

FORTY-THREE

Cassie wiped the coffeepot clean and couldn't help but notice that the black enamel had seen better days. She set it with a soft *thunk* on the stove. Then she lifted a pair of plates, stacked them in the cupboard, and closed the door. The scent of roasted meat hung rich in the air, and a small square of cornbread that was left over sat beside her teacup with a spoonful of jam.

Dinner had come and gone with little conversation, and now Gideon leaned back in the rocking chair, one ankle propped on the opposite knee. His boots were unlaced haphazardly, shirt untucked and wrinkled at the hem, the cares of the day long spent. He strummed his mandolin softly and sang not so much as a word. It was the same tune he played every time he pulled out the instrument. Cassie already knew it by heart. It was hauntingly beautiful. A window into the heart he kept so heavily guarded.

She shook the damp dishtowel and hung it on the low nail beside the stove where it would dry by morning. She tasted her tea, the brew warm to her palate. Closing her eyes briefly, she let out a sigh of satisfaction. Another day was done. Another night sat waiting. She took a sip of tea, her eyes on her husband. She had no doubt that this night would be as lonely as all the others.

The fire in the stove crackled and popped, filling the little cabin with a heat that led her to prop open the far window. A blanket of stars hung overhead as if it would float down any moment. Cassie watched it for several minutes, stunned once again by the vastness of it all. Stunned . . . and feeling very small.

Gideon played on. Finally, she turned, wiped her hands on her apron, and moved a stack of books off the rickety piano bench, setting them on the floor. She sat and stared at the keys. The song continued, and she knew where it would go next. Her fingertips found the ivories. She pressed one and then another. Gideon didn't seem to notice, so fixated was he on the night sky beside him.

The melody continued, each note more haunting than the last. He played with a hunger that would never be satisfied, and as if to express the same yearning, Cassie played along. So this was what it felt like. Neither of them spoke. In fact, he played as if she weren't in the room. Weren't in his life. So this was it. This was what it was like to be so far from happiness it seemed unattainable. She on her bench. He in his chair. Both of them worlds apart. He'd fall asleep there, she was certain of it.

He slept there almost every night. If by some miracle he collapsed on the mattress, he took care that he didn't so much as brush his hand against her. Each night that passed was as lonely as the rest. Gauging them against the years of her life, Cassie wondered if joy was lost to her. Love certainly was. *Make no mistake.* She'd given up on that hope. Not in an instant, but little by little, it had faded. The spark of hope — of possibility — had been trampled on one too many times. Reviving it seemed impossible.

In an instant, she froze. Gideon had grown so silent that all she could hear were the vibrations of her last note. She felt him watching her. A glance confirmed it. Without peeling his eyes from her face, he began again, the song as soft as ever. Cassie's fingers found one key and then the next. Did he feel . . . did he hear her longings?

She wanted to be loved. She wanted to love. But Gideon O'Riley was making that impossible. Lonnie would always be the mother of his child. Always. And Cassie was beginning to fear that she would never hold a baby in her arms. Fear that a small laugh would never fill this room. She glanced at Gideon, his eyes still studying her, his foot bouncing slowly. Had she forgotten?

He was already a father. He had a son.

Cassie let her hands slip from the keys, and he followed her lead, falling silent as well. She couldn't imagine the grief she would feel if she were to finally have a child — a piece of her and the person she loved — only to have someone take that child away.

"I'm tired. I think I'll go to bed now."

He lifted his bottom lip. "I'll be along soon."

Sure he would. She closed the lid to her piano. "Good night."

"Sleep good, Cassie."

His voice was so genuine she halted. "And you too." She pressed her hand to his temple and kissed the top of his head, lingering. "Good night." She stepped into the dark bedroom, wondering if the end had come.

FORTY-FOUR

A pair of thin crows darted from her path. Their black feathers caught the morning sun and shimmered. Cassie's feet skittered across the melting snow, and it was not long before she arrived at her parents' back porch. Seeing her brothers walking toward the woods at the back of the spread, guns in tow, Cassie called out their names and waved when they turned around.

"Ma?" she called, even before her boots pounded up the porch steps. She grabbed the door latch with a gloved hand, threw it open, and nearly slid into the kitchen.

Her pa looked up from his breakfast. He grinned at her. "Well, what brings you here this beautiful morning?"

Cassie slammed the door and tugged off her coat. Her voice came out quick and breathless. "I felt like some fresh air." She scanned the large kitchen. Instead of seeing her mother, she spotted a basin full of dirty dishes and a frying pan on the stove. The lingering scent of burnt hotcakes hung in the air. "Where is she?"

Henry lowered his voice. "She's in bed with one of her headaches." Kind eyes looked out from beneath his rumpled hair.

"Is it bad today?" Cassie lifted the griddle and slid the remains of the burned cakes into the slop bucket.

Her pa lowered his voice. "Ain't had one of her headaches in a few weeks, but this one plumb knocked her off her feet."

Cassie turned to pick up the half-eaten breakfast in front of her pa when a basket on the edge of the table caught her eye. "What's this?" She lifted a checked cloth. A loaf of bread nestled against a generous round of butter.

"Your ma was gonna run that up to the Coles' place. I don't know why." Her pa downed the last of his coffee and slid his plate away. "But you know your ma and her favors."

Cassie fingered the handle of the basket. "I can take it for her."

"I don't think she'd mind doin' it herself." He patted her arm. "Maybe tomorrow she'll be up and about. Usually doesn't take her long to kick what's ailin' her."

"But this bread is fresh. Knowin' Ma,

she'll want it to get to the Coles' before tomorrow." Cassie grabbed the basket and slid it onto her arm. "Ma's done so much for me lately. Let me do her a little favor." She flashed her pa a smile, then stepped around the table. "I'll finish the dishes and start a pot of beans when I get back."

"Who are you, and where has my daughter gone?"

Swinging the basket to her other arm, Cassie laughed. "Will it set your mind at ease if I burn the beans a little?"

"I appreciate your help. Your ma will too." He opened the door. "I'm off to do the mornin' chores. I'll check on her when I'm done."

Headaches had plagued her ma for as long as Cassie could remember. It was common for her ma to be chipper one moment, then suddenly stricken with a throbbing pain that sometimes kept her off her feet for the day and more than once left streaks of blood on her white handkerchief.

Tripping, Cassie stumbled but righted herself. She yanked her hem free from beneath her heel and tossed the blue and white calico out of her way. She was even more resolute about her actions — her ma could in no way have made this walk in her condition.

It was a good two-mile trek to the Coles'. She dashed down the steps, and as she crossed the snow-covered farm, Gideon stepped around their chicken coop on the other side of the property. He pushed a wheel-barrow full of wood, leaning into the heavy weight of his load.

He lifted his head and, pausing, lowered the wheelbarrow. He held a hand over his eyes, watching her. Cassie felt her cheeks warm, and she ducked her head. When she braved a quick wave, Gideon waved back. He was tall and stark against the vast white-ness that surrounded him. His smile was nowhere in sight. And she knew the reasons. Even as he continued to watch her, she turned away and trudged forward, eager to get to the Coles' so she could return home.

Her pa's farm stretched out smooth and flat, making it an easy walk. It was one of the few pieces of acreage in the area with little or no steep grade. Now, away from the boundaries of the homestead, her path rose and her footsteps rose with it.

Cassie opened her hand, letting the sun-light hit her palm. She was glad that her relationship with her pa was better. She shuddered, remembering how deeply she'd broken his heart. The day her ma had revealed her secrets, her pa had pegged her for answers, and just like with Gideon, she had none.

At least not any good ones.

A part of her had loved Gideon's untamed ways. Loved being on the arm of the most handsome man in the hollow. In other ways it had frightened her. One moment he was all she thought she wanted, the next he was impatient, unruly. And she had been torn. She wasn't nearly as fond of the through-thick-and-thin bit as Lonnie clearly was. So Cassie had asked him to leave. There was no crime in that. Wives did it all the time. Didn't they? The basket swung gently against her hip. Once freedom was at hand, she suddenly realized that perhaps she loved him after all. Perhaps.

His handsome face filled her mind.

Cassie glanced at the vast sky overhead, so vivid a blue it nearly hurt her eyes. Was there more to this world than Rocky Knob? More waiting on the horizon? Her feet rushed her forward. The cloud of breath before her face quickened, and Cassie paused to switch the heavy basket from one arm to the other, expectancy spurring her forward.

Cassie rapped on the front door of the Coles' tiny cabin. The small sound echoed as if the house inside were hollow. When no one replied, she knocked again, forcing her knuckles to make her presence known. Expecting Caroline Cole to come to the door with her cheery smile and young face, Cassie bit her lip. Silence. She peered through the window. She saw nothing other than the sun's bright glare on the streaky glass. She knocked harder, and the force made the door creak open. Cassie pulled her hand back.

"Hello?" she called into the dark cabin. "It's Cassie Allan . . . I mean O'Riley." Her cheeks warmed. "Ma sent you a basket of bread."

No one answered.

She glanced over her shoulder but saw no one in the barnyard or nearby fields. Nothing moved other than the saplings on the south side of the run-down barn. *Where is everyone?* She'd already come this far, she might as well drop the basket on the table to be found easily. Cassie crossed the threshold and left the light of the outside world for the darkness of the Coles' cabin. The curtains were pulled closed, and her eyes struggled to adjust to the dim light as she slipped into the dark room. Her boot hit something soft, and bending, she picked

up a blanket and draped it over her arm.
Strange.

FORTY-FIVE

Cold air nipped through her sweater as Lonnie carried the pot of ash to the center of the yard, safely away from where Addie and Jacob sat playing on the porch. The book on soap making that Elsie had lent her sat on the top step, and as the memory of that day in the woods washed over her, Lonnie tried not to think of Gideon.

But when Jacob babbled from the porch steps, she watched their son play, and thoughts of what the future held for Gideon and Cassie struck her spirit. She envisioned Cassie. Wondering if her skirts mounded over his growing child. Lonnie's heart twisted as if being wrung out. Did Gideon love Cassie out of duty? Or did his affection now run deeper than that? Richer, impassioned? Her breath felt caged in her chest; she pressed a hand to her throat. It couldn't be.

It was. Cassie was his wife now. She was

stunningly beautiful. And Gideon . . . was Gideon. Passionate, reckless, heady Gideon. Lonnie's cheeks flushed as if she'd been slapped. *Lord, see me through this.*

Knees suddenly unsteady, she struggled to balance the old pot on one of the rocks that circled the fire ring for wash day. Her old work apron covered her skirts, and all the folds were tucked and pinned so as not to drag in the mud. Elsie lugged a pot of water over. Her boots were covered in muddy snow. As filthy as Lonnie's.

"Something the matter?" Elsie asked.

Everything was the matter. It was Cassie who was holding Gideon and not her. But Lonnie simply nodded. "Thank you," she said weakly. Her cold fingers complained as she gripped the pot, which she poured slowly and evenly over the bucket of ash. The first trickles of water passed through the holes Jebediah had punched in the bottom, running in an inky stream into the pan that sat waiting for what would become the lye mixture.

Here she was, clinging to a love that could never be, and it suddenly struck her — what if Gideon no longer thought of her? What if his joy had returned? His laughter reflected in another's eyes? Lonnie swallowed hard and felt Elsie watching her.

"That'll take a bit to drain through," Lonnie said, as cheerfully as she could manage. She glanced over to see that Addie held Jacob in her lap, cooing in his ear. The little boy babbled. The sight of his sweet, rosy cheeks cinched tighter the threads that bound her heart. "I'll wait for this to finish if you want to get the lard measured." Her ankle itched, and using the toe of her boot, she rubbed it.

"Good idea. Shall I take the little ones in now?"

Lonnie glanced overhead where the sky was darkening. "It's getting colder by the minute. That's probably best."

"I'll round them up something to nibble on while we wait for you."

"I won't be long."

Elsie toted off the empty jug and ushered the children into the house.

A dozen chickens clucked around, and Lonnie shooed them away. "Off with you, ladies." Her tone was sharper than she'd intended. "Don't get too close, or you'll be sorry." She held herself as she watched the liquid drain. The air was cold and damp, feathering the curls of her hair. Lifting her gaze, she stared at the point hovering between north and east. Her stomach soured at the thought of Gideon and Cassie together. Anger bubbled up inside her. *Why, God? Why did this have to happen?* Why did she have to love Gideon? A man who could never love her back. Her spirit as punctured as the bucket she watched, Lonnie studied the stream of liquid that thinned, slowing to a *drip, drop.* With it nearly finished, she knelt.

It wasn't the first time she'd made lye, but it was the first time she'd done it for soap she aimed to sell. The act brought her aunt Sarah to mind. How she missed that woman. How many years had she spent dreaming of living under her aunt's roof, making soap and whiling away the days, just the two of them? Happy as could be.

How different her life had turned out. Her heart had been broken, time and time again, then in one last act, shattered completely. Lonnie glanced around the yard as the chickens pecked and scratched at the mess of soil and ice. Here she stood, slowly, piece by piece, trying to put it back together. What was this great plan of God's? And how did it include her?

Lonnie tilted her face to the darkening sky. *God, why? What's to come of this?* The wind twirled her hair, lifting her apron with its cool fingers. She listened, waiting. And in her heart of hearts knew the Lord had a purpose. He had to. Nothing was in vain.

Not even this heartache.

Her spirit clung to the hope that somehow, some way, Gideon might hang on to the faith she'd seen bloom in him. That one day they might stand face to face again, though not in this lifetime.

Lonnie rubbed her collarbone when the loss of him struck afresh.

"Gideon." She dared to breathe his name. Just once. A deep inhale and she tried to chase away all that could never be again. She would be brave. She would be strong. She glanced northeast, where somewhere out there, she was certain, he worked beneath the same sky. Her eyes fell closed, and she tilted her face to the breeze that blew like a stormy kiss over the farm. She could see him now. See his collar pulled up to his jaw, and she was certain he hadn't shaved in a week. Maybe two.

Her fingers opened as if to trace the lines of the face she knew and loved so well. Sweet Gideon. Her longing burned as strong as ever. But she braced it against the reality that he would never come back. Forcing the ache into the deepest places of her heart, hoping the depths were enough to contain such sorrow.

Opening her eyes, she turned back to the

task and knew she'd wasted enough time with her daydreams. A gust rustled through the jagged and leafless limbs that towered overhead. The cold seeped beneath her scarf, chilling her to the bone. It was high time she hurried into the kitchen before she froze through.

With a grunt, Lonnie lifted the pan. It was now filled with the dark, pungent water. The beginning of soap. She dared not let it splash her clothes or skin, and with slow, careful steps worked her way into the house. She nudged the door open with her boot, and instantly the heat of the kitchen stung the tips of her frozen fingers and ears.

She shuffled in. "Will you get the door, Addie?"

The little girl hopped up and pressed it closed. Elsie pulled a tray of dried-berry scones from the oven. Even in the failing light, the dusting of sugar and egg wash tempted. "I just brewed some tea," Elsie said, sliding the kettle to the edge of the stove so Lonnie could set down the pan.

"The lye will need to thicken over the next few hours." Lonnie held her stiff hands over the hot stove, and her palms tingled back to life. She washed up, taking care that her hands were very clean before scooping Jacob up in her arms. She squeezed him tight, savoring his warmth, and tried to nuzzle away his fussiness. A patch of skin showed beneath his wool sweater, and she kissed it. She held him close, and his green eyes searched hers. "My sweet boy," she whispered into his hair. With a hymn on her heart, she turned him in a slow circle, delighting in the way he pressed his head sleepily to her shoulder. His small back rose and fell in a soft sigh.

She brushed crumbs from his hair. "I see you've had your snack." He flapped his arm, and she caught a sticky hand, kissing it once. Twice. Wishing with all her might that she could bottle this moment, seal it with her love, and send it to Gideon.

FORTY-SIX

She had run home without stopping. Finally halting in front of her pa's well, Cassie pressed a hand to her cheek. Her fingers trembled against her skin. *What have I done?*

She had wandered into the Coles' cabin when no one answered the door. A bleary-eyed Caroline Cole had struggled to sit, her nightgown falling off one shoulder to reveal the rash that dotted her throat and chest. *"Scarlet fever,"* she murmured through gray, chapped lips. She coughed and pressed a wrinkled handkerchief to her mouth.

Adam Cole had ushered Cassie from the cabin as quickly as he could. *"You shouldn't be in here! You must get out! Hurry, Cassie."* His broad hand pressed against her back to move her along. *"It isn't safe for anyone."*

Stricken with fear, she had rushed toward the door.

Now as she struggled to catch her breath, she fought back the lump in her throat.

Needing a distraction, she decided to pour herself a nice bath. After filling a bucket at the pump, she heaved it closer and, with a grunt, hoisted it off the ground. Her other hand grasped a second, and she turned toward the house.

The buckets were so heavy she had to take very slow steps.

Water sloshed over the edge, dampening her already-frozen boots. Her arms shook. Cassie looked down at her fingers wrapped around the bucket handles, the taut skin nearly as pale as the snow. She looked away, not liking the reminder it brought of Caroline Cole's own hands as she clutched her bed sheets.

Hasty footsteps crunched behind her. Cassie turned in time to see Gideon dart past the well. In a few long strides, he was at her side.

"Let me help you with that." His hand brushed hers, and although it was brief, the touch left a warmth that lingered. "Just ask next time, and I'll be happy to do this." Without another word, he took each bucket from her.

"I didn't know I needed water." She slid her hand inside his elbow.

Gideon's brow furrowed.

Her footsteps were slow.

"Are you all right?"

Cassie kept her gaze straight ahead. Her body felt fine — it was her spirit that quaked. Dare she confess her foolish actions? "Just tired. That's all." She hoped her hidden fear did not echo in her voice. "Thought a hot bath might soothe me." She lifted her eyes to Gideon's. "That's why I came to fetch water."

"Just holler next time, all right?"

Wishing she could turn back time, Cassie forced a smile. "Where did you go, anyway?"

Gideon glanced over his shoulder. "Jack invited me to head out with him scoutin' deer. He said there's been a few bucks 'round lately. We hoped we might get us one."

Cassie pulled herself closer to him. "See anything?"

"Not a thing. But while we were out, I helped him reset some small game traps with fresh bait. I'll go back out in the morning. Tomorrow's another day."

So it is.

"And where were you? I saw you take off this morning."

Cassie did not want to lie, but she wasn't ready to put words to her mistake. "I went for a long walk."

Gideon did not question her. They strolled

the rest of the way, and he filled in the silence with small talk about his morning with Jack. His voice was mahogany, deeply rich and smooth. It lulled Cassie to a slow cadence, and she had to fight the urge to press her head against his shoulder. Less than willing, she released his arm when they reached the steps.

Gideon lowered his buckets. "If you start the kettle, I'll go fetch the washtub."

"Thank you." She filled the kettle and plopped it on the stove. She thought about making herself a cup of tea.

By the time Gideon lugged the washtub into the bedroom, she had poured water into several more pots and set them to heat. Before long, the tub was full and steaming. Gideon left and shut the door behind him.

Stripping herself of her cold clothes, Cassie shivered as she sank into the tub at the foot of the bed. The water warmed her toes and fingers, and she sighed. When she tugged the ribbon from her hair, the brown kinks fell around her shoulders, and before the tips could hit the water, she caught hold of the mass of hair and twisted it into a low bun, securing it by looping it through itself.

Gideon called to her. "How ya doin'?"

She stared at the closed door. She should tell him the truth. She was frightened. Sinking as low into the water as the cramped tub allowed, she stuck her chin beneath the warm water. She knew Gideon was waiting for a response.

"Cassie?"

"Yes," she called at last. "I'm just fine."

Something wasn't right. Sinking to the floor, Gideon sat and pressed the back of his head against the door and listened to the muffled sound of churning water and the soft drips and drizzles that sang out like tiny chimes whenever Cassie moved. She wasn't herself — and he knew the reason.

He was hurting her.

She knew the truth. Surely she saw it in his face when he looked at her, heard it in his voice when he spoke. He'd finally gone to visit his family. Never once had he considered bringing Cassie with him. Cassie knew the truth as much as he did.

He did not love her.

Gideon banged the back of his head against the door, inflicting a small amount of pain. He was miserable. And he made her miserable with him. Gideon groaned. He was trapped. He had no choice. The chains that held him here were invisible yet unbreakable. *What chains?* Gideon silently scoffed when he made himself sound like the victim. This was the life he had chosen when he'd married Cassie before Lonnie. This was his sentence. He cringed at the callous word that should never be used to describe a marriage. No wonder Cassie was miserable. No woman deserved to be that to her husband.

Gideon rubbed his finger and thumb together as the thoughts built on one another. Was it in him to change? His fingers stilled. He could try — he could pretend. Gideon swallowed. He knew what that would entail, and he didn't know if he had it in him to fool Cassie that way.

He banged his head again, this time inflicting as much pain as he could muster.

"Gideon?" Cassie called, her voice hesitant. "What are you doing?"

"Oh, sorry." He stood.

Water trickled from behind the door. Pressing his forehead to the wood, Gideon closed his eyes and wondered if he had the courage to move forward with this.

FORTY-SEVEN

After her news poured forth, Mary fell silent. Gideon struggled for a coherent response. Three facts moved around in his mind. The first — there was talk of scarlet fever in the Cole cabin. The second — Cassie had been in their home a week ago.

Gideon ran his hands into his hair, tugging at the strands.

And the third — Caroline Cole had died in the night.

"I wonder why Cassie didn't tell me she'd been there." He breathed out the words as best he could.

Mary shook her head, then lifted her face to the horizon and the setting sun. Although the day was nearly done, a cock crowed. The familiar cry sounded melancholy as it echoed through the evening air, finally fading into silence.

Elbows on knees, Gideon folded his hands together. "I wish I'd have known. She may be frightened."

Sitting on the back steps of her house, Mary stuck her shoes together and tapped her worn heels repeatedly.

Gideon's mouth felt strangely dry. "Do you think she has a . . . reason to be frightened?" He pressed his palms against the porch step. When Mary hesitated, Gideon's grip tightened, and the coarse wood scraped his fingertips.

"I hope not." Her shawl slid from her shoulders, and she made no move to retrieve it. "They say scarlet fever occurs more often in children." Hugging herself, she stared into the distance before finally facing him.

"And Caroline was younger than Cassie, right?"

"Not by much." She said it as a sigh.

Gideon saw a mother's love traced inside the thin lines of her aging face. He ran a hand down his face and struggled to put his frustration into words.

"Surely she couldn't catch the fever so quickly. You said she was in there but a minute."

A shadow crossed Mary's features, and she did not respond. Needing answers, Gideon stared at his mother-in-law. Lifting her hands to her face, Mary cupped them over her mouth and closed her eyes.

His heart felt as heavy as a stone. *Please answer me.*

Mary turned to him, her mouth drawn in a thin line. Her eyes searched his as if hunting for answers of her own. Gideon wondered what question she could have for him. Then, when it struck him, he turned away, unable to watch the pain in Mary's features. He could not give them what they wanted.

For in the deep blue eyes, he'd seen more than a mother's pain. He saw a mother's heart for her daughter's happiness. Her hope for something greater.

Cassie stared out the window and watched Gideon cross the yard toward her. His gait was slow. His head hung down. Cassie moistened her lips. She touched the pane and wished for more than cold glass beneath her fingertips. When Gideon covered his face with his hand and smeared fingers over his eyes, her heart plummeted.

He missed his son. He missed Lonnie.

Like a bad dream that would not free her, she knew it to be true. The possibility of waking from the trance they were in felt slimmer than ever before. Then Cassie tipped her chin up, clinging to the tattered frays of wisdom she'd gained from her mother, wishing with all her might that she'd been smarter, more apt to listen with a humble heart. Cassie searched within for all she knew to be true. Truths she'd pressed down for far too long. Wasn't the sun's warm promise on the horizon? Perhaps someday — though it may be a long way off — they would each find joy.

Stepping from the window, she lumbered toward the bedroom. Her body was weary. Supper still needed to be started, but she needed to stoke the fire first. The bedroom circled her in darkness. The gray shadows that had grown long across the floor had finally chased away any last traces of sunlight, engulfing the room in evening's cool cover.

Her cheeks tingled, and Cassie pressed her palms there. She licked her lips again, the flesh warm. *Please, God. Don't let it be.*

Gideon scanned the front room, but she was nowhere in sight. With the bedroom door cracked open, he slipped in as quietly as possible and halted. Cassie's hair was pulled off to one side. Her cheeks were flushed and rosy. The dress she was unbuttoning draped over her small shoulders in a silhouette of blue and white.

His breathing slowed, and Gideon struggled to speak. "How ya doing?"

She shrugged. "Fine, why?" Her dress fell to the floor, and she kicked it aside into a muddled heap beneath the dresser.

Gideon stared at her. "No reason."

Sinking onto the bed, Cassie sighed and let her head hang forward. The sharp curve of her slender neck arched gracefully, and she closed her eyes. After rubbing her hands together, she stared at her palms. "With all this cold weather, my skin is so chapped." Her voice was muffled against her chest.

Gideon eyed his own rough palms. "Mine too."

She lifted her head long enough to point toward the dresser. "There's a can of salve in that drawer. Would you fetch it for me?"

His movements were slow as Gideon slid the drawer open. He pushed aside a hairbrush and comb and found the jar in the back.

As he stepped toward the bed, the wide eyes peering up at him were rimmed in red. Knowing of nothing else to say, Gideon touched his chin to his chest and stared at the jar. "Here." He sank down beside her and lifted her hand onto his knee. She tried to pull away, but he held her wrist. "Please."

Her face softened even as he allowed his gaze to trace the smooth forms. He dipped his finger in the thick salve and set the jar aside. Holding Cassie's hand in his, he smeared the cool balm over skin that radiated heat.

As he worked the ointment in, it seemed every nerve in his hands was wide awake. His shoulder moved against hers. The subtle sound all that broke the silence. It had been so long since he had touched her . . . since he had touched any woman.

Gideon fought back the image of Lonnie's pretty face.

As much as he wanted to linger on the memory of her, it would only make what he was about to do that much harder. He looked down at Cassie's round face and swallowed the bitter truth — it was *her,* and her alone, who would fill his future. She was his wife now, no matter how many ways he wished it weren't so.

His hand worked in slow circles over Cassie's. Lowering it to her lap, he reached for the other, his movements gentle — asking. He dipped his finger in the jar, and the warmth of her skin melted the salve, making it easy to smooth in. "Does that seem to be helping?" he whispered. Tense apprehension made his voice come out weaker than he had planned.

She nodded slowly.

Gideon squinted down at her and sent up

a quick prayer. He wasn't much of a praying man these days, but he didn't know how else to get the strength he needed. Finished, he did not lower Cassie's hand as he had the other.

He lifted it toward him.

He kept his gaze glued to her face and watched her eyes widen as he slowly lifted the inside of her wrist to his lips. He paused briefly, as he waited for the last reservations of his mind to numb over. Then, closing his eyes, he kissed the silken skin softly, letting his lips linger longer than he wanted. His head felt hot but not with desire. *Forgive me, Lonnie.* Leaning toward Cassie, he pushed her hair away from her face and then gently kissed the base of her neck.

Cassie let out a soft sound. Gideon couldn't name it, but he knew what he was doing to her, and he felt instantly ashamed. He could stop now and spare them both the heartache this would cause. But then Cassie pressed her forehead to his chest and sighed. Taken aback, Gideon found himself unable to move.

He watched her shoulders slowly rise and fall as she breathed. Finally, she turned her head from side to side. "You don't mean this." Her voice muffled against his chest.

A vise of shame tightened his throat. "I

don't?" he whispered.

She struck her fist against his knee. Her words were so faint, it was as if she didn't want to respond. "We both know the answer to that."

A long silence followed. Gideon wished he could say what Cassie needed to hear, but a weak excuse came out instead. "I'm trying my best," he murmured. "And it's not enough. I can see that. I want it to be more." He stared down at the messy array of her hair. "All I know is that I hurt you. I hurt you by leaving."

"I didn't exactly give you a choice." Her words floated softly between them.

"I should have tried to change. That's the worst part." He pinched his eyes shut. "But I didn't. I wasn't what any woman deserved. And then Lonnie . . ."

Had somehow picked up those pieces.

He swallowed hard. "I . . . love her." He choked the last words out and forced himself to look at Cassie.

Tears slipped silently down her cheeks.

Gideon groaned and took her face in his hands. He pressed his forehead to hers, closing his eyes so that all he could feel was her hair beneath his hands and her soft breath on his face. "That's not fair to you. I don't know if I can give you what you need. I want you to be happy, Cassie." He placed a firm kiss to her forehead. "I truly do. I wish more than anything that this could be different."

Her body went limp. "But you don't. Because you could never have loved Lonnie in the first place."

With their foreheads touching once more, Gideon nodded softly. "I'm so sorry. Please forgive me."

She pressed her hand to the top of his, securing it in place. She squeezed her eyes closed, forcing one more tear to plunge after the others. Releasing him, her hand slid to the mattress. "Can we forget about this tonight?"

"Of course," he said softly.

She looked exhausted — no, weak. Her frailty only fueled Gideon's guilt. He helped her lie down, then lifted the covers over her. He tossed his shirt aside, blew out the candle, and crawled in beside her. The room was dark. They faced each other. Her knees were pulled up — a barrier. Gideon wrapped his hands around hers. She did not seem to mind. He heard her sniff in the darkness, and more than once she tugged her hand from his to wipe her cheeks. And each time, she nestled her damp fingers back inside his.

Closing his eyes, Gideon hoped sleep would find them quickly.

FORTY-EIGHT

Cassie opened her eyes and found herself looking into Gideon's sleeping face. Tilting her head toward the window, she blinked into the sun's bright rays. Her throat burned, and she pressed her hand to her neck. She felt miserable. Even her cheeks seemed raw from the tears she'd cried. Feeling exhausted, and a little foolish, she nestled her head back into the cool contours of her pillow and sighed.

And then she remembered what this day was.

A smile played at the corners of her lips, and it felt strangely good. After the agony she'd endured the night before, anything above misery was welcome.

How could she have forgotten? Then again, she had been exhausted when she had decided to turn in early. But then Gideon came in and . . . no wonder today had slipped her mind.

Cassie tucked her arm beneath her cheek and watched Gideon sleep. Her gift could wait until later. She ran the side of her thumb over his arm. Her hand stilled when she waited for him to stir. As she propped her head in her palm, the strap of her shimmy slinked down around her arm, and she tugged it back into place. The air of the bedroom was frosty, and she did not need to tiptoe through the house to know that the fire in the stove had long since burned out.

In his sleep, Gideon moistened his lips. Cassie whispered his name. "Wake up." She nudged him, and when he squirmed, her smile widened, completing itself.

His eyes finally opened, and he stared at the ceiling for a few moments before turning to her.

"Morning," she whispered.

Gideon closed his eyes and groaned. "Morning." Flinging his arm over his face, he rested the crook of his elbow over his eyes and sighed. "Did you sleep?"

Slowly, Cassie sat upright and pulled the quilt to her shoulder. "I slept just fine." Her throat was dry, and she had to stifle a cough. It suddenly took all her will to keep her words light, but she blurted out the greeting, hoping the cheery distraction would ease his apprehension. "Merry Christmas."

He squinted at her, his face void of expression. "Christmas? I forgot that it was —"

"I have something for you."

"You didn't . . . have to."

She smiled and found it surprisingly effortless. "I don't have to do anything. I wanted to."

His brow furrowed.

"It's under the bed. Just a moment." Crawling from the warm sheets was not easy, and she paused once her bare feet landed on the cold floor.

She crouched, her shimmy billowing around her, and she peered beneath the dark bed. She snuggled back beneath the quilt and held up a package wrapped in wrinkled brown paper that had seen many Christmases and was sure to see many more.

She laid the package in his lap. His eyes darted from the gift to her face.

"Well," she began, but the word came out hoarse, and she had to clear her throat. "Open it."

Gideon turned the package over and loosened the ends. The wrinkled paper fell open, and a dark green scarf tumbled free. Picking up the soft folds of knitted wool, his eyes widened. "You made this for *me*?"

His surprise was her reward. Cassie sank back into her pillow. "I noticed you didn't have a scarf."

He shook his head. "I don't."

"Well, I'm glad you can use it."

The man beside her simply nodded. He stared at the gift.

She squeezed his hand. "Gid—"

"Thank you." His gaze flashed to her face before falling back. "I don't deserve this. I have nothing for you."

Pressing her forehead to his shoulder, Cassie closed her burning eyes. Nothing that he could give.

Gideon rolled back the sleeves of his flannel work shirt, letting his dingy undershirt, which pressed tight to his forearms, poke through. He set Cassie's piano bench on his work surface and let the mixture of sawdust and solitude make sense of his life. Even if only for an hour.

A touch of his hand, and the old bench wobbled. He eyed the legs, making inventory of what needed to be done. He picked up a chisel and worked one of the legs loose. Shoving aside a pair of files, Gideon turned the bench to the side to get a better angle, nearly knocking a can of nails to the floor. Crowded space.

He reached for a larger chisel, sliding it in with a *tap, tap* of his hammer. The leg loosened more.

"Knock, knock." Jack stuck his head into the shanty. He propped the door open and strode in uninvited. He glanced around the shack. "Don't you ever pick up after yourself?"

"Don't you have anything better to do?"

"Not really. Cassie's over at Ma's, and they're startin' to talk like women folk." He rolled his eyes, then pulled up a stool and sat, his boots nearly touching Gideon's.

Gideon glanced at him. Jack rose, pushed his stool farther back, and sat again. "Better?"

"Thank you." After choosing a mallet, Gideon tapped the leg, and the nail budged. He tapped again, careful not to damage the piece. He pulled the leg loose and set it carefully on his work surface.

"Whatcha doin'?"

Gideon set his mallet down. This was going to be a long morning. "How 'bout this? You can sit and watch, but I get to charge you a nickel for every stupid question."

"Whoa. Who spit in your oats this morning?"

"Now you owe me ten cents."

"I don't know how Cassie puts up with you."

Gideon lifted his eyebrows. He didn't either. With a piece of sandpaper, he smoothed the part where the leg had once rested. "Hand me that can of nails there."

Jack reached for it. "Oh, so now I'm useful."

"No. You're just in my way." But Gideon chuckled as he shuffled through the rusty can, pulling out a pair of nails that would do the trick.

"Whatcha doin' this for, anyway? That old bench has worked just fine for years."

"Guess I wanted to see if it could work better than fine." Like something else he knew. Maybe there was more to life than just getting by. He'd realized that when he was with Lonnie, something in her had brought him to that point. But when everything he'd ever loved had been stripped away, the first thing he'd done was lose sight of that.

Tipping the bench on its side, he placed the leg in position and with a few taps, hammered it on. He set it upright and shuffled through a box of sandpaper, all of which had seen better days, and found one with enough fine grit to work.

The sun made its graceful arc in the clear

blue sky, but he hardly noticed. Jack spent most of the time talking, and Gideon listened on, finding himself laughing more than once at the stories the kid told. He worked fresh oil into the bench, coating every surface.

It wasn't until shadows stretched long across the yard that he brushed dust from his work surface. Jack swept the floor as Gideon put away his tools.

"Thanks for the company," Gideon finally said. He could remember a time when it was he and Jebediah working together. Reaching out, he shook Jack's hand and, with a slap on the young man's back, led him from the shop. "Suppose I'll follow you and walk Cassie back."

"Look who's turnin' out to be quite the gentleman."

Hardly. Yet the desire to try kept growing within him.

Cassie sat on the porch with her ma, a plate of cookies between them. Upon seeing Gideon, she rose, said a good-bye to her mother, and hurried toward him.

Her breathing was heavy when she came to his side.

"You feelin' all right?"

"I think so. I'm a little tired. Ma and Pa

are headed to the church. It's been so long since we've gone, it would be nice. Especially with it being Christmas. But" — she looped her arm through his, and Gideon couldn't ignore the heat that penetrated his shirt — "I just don't feel up to it."

"Why don't we go inside, and you can take it easy."

"Sounds good, but I've got to get supper together." Her eyes seemed clouded as she looked up at him. "I thought I could fix us something special."

Gideon reached an arm around her. "Let me do it."

"You?" She peered up into his face in awe.

"Hey, I've been known to throw together a batch of hot cakes now and again." He held the door with his back and helped Cassie over the threshold. "Maybe it's been a few years, but if you sit at the table and put your feet up, you can talk me through it."

The crease in her forehead softened, and she smiled. "If you insist."

She sat, and he pulled a chair around, then helped her perch stockinged feet on the seat.

As he mixed the batter, he felt Cassie quietly watching him. Gideon cracked an egg, and the yolk landed in the bowl. When he wiped his fingers on his pants, he fought the urge to turn around and look at her. He picked up a small can.

"How much of the leavening stuff?"

She half smiled. "About a teaspoon."

Gideon shuffled through the silverware crock and held one up. "Too big?"

She nodded, and he rummaged for a smaller one. As he stirred the lumpy batter, his chest tightened. All that afternoon he'd worked in his shop. For hours he had labored away. Not for Lonnie — for Cassie. In truth, he hadn't once thought about the woman he'd sworn to love forever. Instead, his thoughts had lingered on the blue-eyed girl sitting behind him. The girl who had knit him a scarf in secret despite everything he had done and said to her.

The girl who kept helping him along when he'd struggled to even be her friend.

Gideon grimaced.

After smearing bacon grease around the pan, he lifted a spoonful of batter over the smoking skillet, and it sizzled when he formed the first round cake. It felt impossible to admit, but somehow, in her own special way, Cassie had claimed a piece of his heart. His fingers trembled as he poured another spoonful of batter into the pan. *A piece, only a piece.*

It can't be. He had sworn it over and over.

But he remembered Reverend Gardner's words: *"It must."*

When Gideon slid a plate of steaming hot cakes in front of Cassie, their eyes met.

"Thank you," she whispered.

Unable to speak, he simply nodded. Her cheeks were red, and sweat formed along her hairline. Gideon dropped his gaze. Dare he speak the words aloud? Why hadn't she come to him first? He scraped the last of the batter from the bowl, turned the cake over when it browned, then settled himself in the chair across from Cassie. He cut his hot cake in two with the edge of his fork. It was then that he noticed she had yet to touch her own supper. When she dropped her head in her hand, Gideon wiped his mouth.

"You shouldn't be up. We need to get you in bed." When she started to protest, he insisted. "You need your rest."

Cassie quickly shook her head. "I'll wait for you."

And she did. In the course of a few bites, Gideon stuffed down a single hot cake, scarcely tasting it, then walked her into the bedroom. He helped her into bed and tucked the quilt snugly around her shivering frame.

"Don't leave me," she whispered.

He hesitated for the briefest of moments before crawling on top of the quilt, where he lay down beside her. He listened to her shallow breath grow slower and slower until she drifted off to sleep. Gideon rolled onto his side so he could see her face in the moonlight. She was waiting to be loved in so many ways, and he was yet to be the husband she deserved.

And she had waited. *For so long.*

The burning in his chest seemed to get worse — as if it was trying to divide itself. But no matter how much he cared for Cassie or how much he allowed her into his life, his heart would remain whole. And as long as it was Lonnie's, it could never belong to the woman beside him.

Cassie had been so cheerful that morning. So kind when he least deserved it. *"Merry Christmas."* Her voice rang clear in his memory.

Gideon scoffed. *Some Christmas it's been for her.* He would have once thought she was simply putting on an act. The sweetness, a role she knew how to play so well. But something within her had blossomed. A goodness that he admired. For he knew the impossible road she walked. The road he himself was on. Yet did he see a change within himself? Shaking his head, Gideon wished it could be more. Much more. He shifted to his other side and stared out the darkening window where the first stars had appeared in the gray sky.

And what of another Christmas?

His eyes slid closed. He could almost see Lonnie pull Jacob out of the doorway as Jebediah lugged a frosted tree into the parlor. He imagined his son squirming to get free. Jebediah would have let out a deep belly laugh, insisting the little boy only wanted to help. He could smell the scent of fresh-cut spruce mingling with the heady aroma of Elsie's cooking. Sliding his hand beneath the mattress, Gideon pulled out Jacob's knit cap. He nearly crushed it in his grip of yearning. His son was growing. And he was missing every day of it.

Gideon's breath caught in his throat when he was struck with the memory of the boy's silken cheek beneath his palm. The sensation was as fresh as the day he last touched him. He imagined pressing his lips to the downy head and inhaling the scent of the boy's mother.

He rose, unable to stay still in this small house. The world — though large it may be — seemed to close him in. He strode out into the moonlight and glanced up at the stars overhead.

Merry Christmas, my love. My family.

Gideon covered his aching heart with his hand.

The next morning, Cassie rose from bed, and her body felt as heavy as her heart. *Please, God. Don't let me fall ill.* She knew the seriousness of scarlet fever. Having never had it as a child, she had every chance of catching it now. Cassie pushed open the bedroom door and, when it squeaked, glanced behind her at the bed. Gideon's broad frame filled more than half the mattress, his pants wrinkled. An arm hung limp and heavy over the edge; his knuckles grazed the floor beside his discarded shirt. Night was just turning into day, but her head spun with too much turmoil for her to rest.

She knew the signs well. Her ma had checked her over. Mary had forced Cassie to unbutton her collar, and with a flickering candle held so close to her skin Cassie could feel the heat, her ma had looked for signs of the rash — the reviled mark of scarlet fever. That was days ago.

Every day since, Cassie had checked herself to see if the rash had appeared. Even now as she thought of it, she pulled up her sleeves and turned her arms from side to side. She saw nothing but pale skin. Stepping to the mirror, she stuck out her tongue. It looked pink, but her vision was weak. She blinked, trying to clear the fog.

The fire had all but gone out, and it took all her breath to blow the cooling embers back into a flame. She tossed a piece of fir over the warming coals and waited for the wood to catch before sitting back on her heels. Leaving the door open allowed enough light for her to see by. *Might as well save the candle.*

Cassie went to sit at the table, intending to wait for the sun to rise. Glancing at her piano, she froze at the sight of her bench. The wood shone so richly, she could nearly see her reflection in it. With a touch of her hand, she felt how sturdy and strong it was.

"Oh my goodness," she breathed, running her hand along the silken wood. It was smoother than the river stones she collected as a girl. Tucking her nightgown around her, she sat on it, and the bench didn't so much as wobble. Her chest burned hotter than the coals awakening from their slumber. She pressed her hand to her throat and felt a soft pain — a mending. As if the broken pieces of her heart were drawing closer.

FORTY-NINE

"Easy, girl." Lonnie patted Sugar's soft, brown face. The mule eagerly accepted the gnarled carrot, and Lonnie wiped the wet remains from Sugar's rough tongue on her already dirty apron. "You like that, don't you?" She scratched the bristles on top of Sugar's head. The mule's ears twitched.

Lonnie and Elsie had spent the morning cleaning up the root cellar. Baskets of dirt-caked potatoes had to be sorted. The softer ones, those that had already sprouted little roots, were moved to the top to be used first. The firmer, sounder potatoes were left toward the bottom in hopes they would last the winter. The worst of the lot would be saved for planting. Elsie had gone off to take Gus a bushel of vegetables, and Lonnie had come up for a breather, bringing with her a stolen treat for Sugar.

The sky outside was a clear blue, but the sunless barn harbored an endless chill. Lonnie shivered beneath her shawl and thought about hurrying back into the warm house. When Sugar stomped her foot and tossed her head, Lonnie laughed.

"Don't worry, girl. I won't leave you just yet."

Rising to the toes of her boots, she reached into the pen and scratched the mule's neck, then stroked her mangled coat. Knowing Sugar always liked a good brushing, Lonnie glanced around for the bristle brush but saw none.

"Another time," she promised.

She had not visited the mule often enough, and the eager way Sugar nudged her open palm made Lonnie feel guilty. "I know. I'm sorry I have not come to see you." Sugar's long eyelashes blinked. With a rough nose, she sniffed at Lonnie's now-empty palm.

"That's all I have, girl." Lonnie leaned in closer so she could whisper. "But I promise to bring you another treat tomorrow." She knew of half a dozen bruised apples in Elsie's root cellar that were just right for such an unfussy creature.

The mule stomped her hoof again and swished her tail.

Lonnie chuckled. "That's all! I promise."

Addie's footsteps pounded into the barn,

startling Lonnie. The little girl's cheeks were rosy with cold. Her breathless words tumbled forth. "Lonnie, Lonnie! Come quick." Addie pointed toward the house, a grin on her round face. "Come see!" She spun around and darted away. Dark curls bounced above her shoulders as she ran.

With a final pat on the mule's scruffy neck, Lonnie left the quiet solitude of the barn.

She straightened her shawl and was careful to close the heavy door behind her and latch it. Spurred on by her own curiosity, Lonnie started toward the house. Before she could guess what all the fuss was about, she spotted a brown mare lowering her head to the snow. Large, fresh prints that could only be Toby's led up to the house.

Her heart thumped, sending a warmth through her.

Voices from the kitchen carried out into the yard. The cheery chatter pulled Lonnie forward. Laughter slipped through the screen door, and she quickened her footsteps. Before her hand landed on the door latch, Toby pushed it open and stood just inches from her.

"Come in." His deep voice filled the kitchen, and he made no move to step out of her way. His eyes were soft on her face, his words even softer. "I was wondering if you'd show up."

Speechless, Lonnie squeezed past him and into the kitchen.

Addie's feet did a funny jig. "Mr. McKee brought presents!"

Lonnie eyed her sister curiously.

Toby nodded toward a potato sack. "A few ladies from the church helped." He tugged the sack closer, and his broad hand disappeared inside the brown burlap. He sank to his knee and lifted his face to Lonnie. "They made some rag dolls for the lassies, and a few men whittled wooden knives for the lads."

Turning to Addie, Lonnie noticed the small doll clutched in her sister's tiny hands. A scrap of pink calico had been sewn into a humble gown, and the plain-faced doll had red hair made from several tidy rows of knotted yarn.

Like a ship mast being raised, Toby stood, towering over them.

"That's awful nice of you. I assure you Addie won't forget this."

"Not just Addie." Toby pulled a pair of small wooden blocks from his bag — the unfinished wood roughly formed into crooked cubes. "These are for Jacob. They didn't make anything for the wee ones 'round here." As if he were embarrassed, his voice fell soft. "I hope they're not too rough." He lowered the blocks into Lonnie's palm. "I tried to sand 'em down smooth."

Lonnie fingered the silky wood that was still warm from Toby's hand. She opened her mouth but again found herself unable to speak. With much noise and clattering, Toby thrust his arm back into his bag.

"And this is for you," he blurted.

He handing Lonnie a small sachet made from the same fabric as Addie's doll. Lonnie turned it over in her hand. She hesitated briefly, then lifted the sachet to her nose. "Mmm," she sighed. "That smells lovely."

Toby's dimples deepened. "I thought you might fancy it."

Lonnie looked up at the man watching her. "This is so unexpected."

"I have a few more stops to make. Perhaps" — his deep voice stumbled over the words — "if you have nothing else to do . . . perhaps you'd like to join me." Before Lonnie could respond, he quickly added, "You could ride Gael." His eyes twinkled. "I'm sure she'd appreciate a lighter rider."

"I don't know that I can."

He shook his head. "You're right. That was inappropriate of me to ask." His crisp shirt grew taut across his shoulders as he bent over to retrieve his sack. He stood and looked down on her. "It would not be seemly for us to be out without an escort."

Lonnie shook her head. "It's just that Elsie has so much to do this afternoon, and with Jacob due to wake from his nap any minute —"

"No need to explain." His smile was genuine. He looked at her with brown eyes that seemed to grow richer by the moment. Lonnie could not help but stare up at him.

She lifted the sachet to her nose once more.

Toby gestured toward the door. "I should be on my way if I'm to make all my deliveries by sundown."

She thanked him again, and with a wave toward Addie, who had already taken her doll out for a stroll, Toby mounted his horse. With a brisk tap of his heels, he was off.

Running her fingertips along her apron strings, Lonnie watched him ride away. Toby was different from any man she'd ever met. Different even from Gideon. He was mature from years of study and schooling. Cold seemed to seep through the window, and Lonnie shivered. Perhaps that's what intrigued her so. Gideon had always been wild at heart, an unpredictable force of passions. Toby was a settled man — sure of his path in life and steady in his ways.

Gael's hoofs pounded in the snow. The muscular mount carried its broad-backed rider away from the farm and into the woods. Stepping from the door, Lonnie pushed it closed. She made her way to the bedroom and checked to see if Jacob had woken.

She sat on the bed and crossed one ankle over the other. Bundled in his quilt, her son slumbered peacefully. Lonnie tried not to shift her weight. With the afternoon light fading, she knew she should start supper for Elsie. Her palm opened, and Jacob's blocks fell to the quilt. Wanting him to see his surprise the moment he awoke, she pushed them closer.

Her fingers tenderly grazed the wood. It was not the gift. It was not the outing. It was the man and the way he looked at her. The way his face softened whenever their eyes met. And she had a sense — a burning sense — that hers did the same.

FIFTY

"Nice." Gideon lifted his boot only to find it caked in cow dung. "Thanks," he murmured to the brown beast. Lifting the pail of warm milk away from the dairy cow's stall, he carried it toward home. Henry had offered Gideon and Cassie milk, and determined to make his own way, Gideon had offered to take over the morning milking.

The gloves that stuck out of his back pocket bounced with every step. The narrow milk handle dug into his already chapped hands, and more than once, he thought about putting the gloves back on. One glance at the gray sky confirmed coming snow, and a warm house lured him across the farm. Setting his sight on the little cabin, he made his way through the snow with clear determination.

He set the pail on the porch near the door. Once it settled, he would lug the galvanized pail inside for the rich cream. Chilled, he rubbed his hands together and slipped inside. The door closed softly behind him. Stepping toward the front window, he pushed the curtains aside. Dull winter light struggled to brighten the room, and he turned in search of Cassie.

In the corner, the rocking chair creaked. "Cassie?"

She blinked but did not speak. Gideon stepped toward her.

Her bare feet arched against the wood floor, and the rockers thudded forward and back. The shawl around her shoulders slipped and slid to the armrest. She made no move to retrieve it. Dark circles framed her eyes like muddy puddles. Gideon sank to her side, picked up her shawl, and was careful not to brush his cold hands against her as he draped the gray wool back over her trembling frame.

Looking up at him, her voice barely formed the words. "I couldn't make breakfast."

He slid his hand behind her and tried to help her to her feet. "I don't care about breakfast." He pressed against the small of her back, but she did not budge. "Let's get you into bed."

Cassie rolled her head against the back of the rocker until her face tilted toward him.

Her eyelids hung like heavy curtains, and the blue jewels beneath her dark lashes seemed to focus on nothing at all. "I don't think I can stand."

Gideon hesitated before breathing.

"I'll help you," he whispered. When he grasped her hand to lift it over his head, he was stunned to find it limp and lifeless. Bracing himself, he hoisted her frail body from the chair and turned toward the bedroom. "You need to rest."

"Gideon." Hollow eyes pinned him motionless. "There's . . . something I need . . . to tell you." She panted, and the words seemed to take the last of her strength.

As he lowered her to the bed, her arm slid free from his neck and fell to the mattress.

"Don't worry," he whispered. "Your ma already told me."

"I" — Cassie began between uneven breaths — "I should have done it myself."

"It doesn't matter now. We need to get you well." With one hand, Gideon slid both of her thin ankles beneath the quilt and tucked out the cold. He smoothed a hand across her warm forehead and down her cheek. "Just rest."

Cassie nodded, but before she could reply, her eyelids slid closed and her breathing slowed. Gideon watched her for what must have been minutes. When he was sure she had drifted off to sleep, he hurried from the cabin. His mind raced faster than his feet as he darted toward the Allan house. After banging on the door, his heart pounded in his ears. Knowing she could scarcely stand, he was certain he shouldn't be away from her. Without waiting for an answer, he banged again.

"Coming!"

The door swung open, and Eli loomed in the entryway. "What?" he demanded and ran a napkin across his mouth.

"I need your ma. It's Cassie."

Mary rushed toward the door. Her pitch elevated even as her eyes widened. "She's ill, isn't she?"

Grabbing her shawl, Mary flung it over her shoulders and stuffed her feet into boots without bothering to lace them up. Before Gideon could respond, she thundered down the steps. As they ran, he instinctively kept a hand out to keep her from falling in the thick slush.

Her mouth drew into a tight line, and her thin cheeks bounced with every step she took. "Where is she?"

"In bed," Gideon panted. "She's awful weak."

Mary rushed on but stopped when she

reached the porch steps. Turning to Gideon, she caught hold of his elbow. Eyes the same color as Cassie's searched his. Mary's voice was grave. "This is what I feared."

Gideon cleared his throat at a sting of emotion. Mary tiptoed through the house and disappeared into the bedroom. Gideon tore off his coat. He tossed it over the nearest chair and yanked his sweaty shirttail free from his pants. He approached the bedroom and stood outside the door.

Kneeling at her daughter's bedside, Mary fumbled with the buttons of Cassie's collar. She spread the fabric and pulled it away from her daughter's neck. Mary's head fell.

"We need to fetch a doctor!"

Gideon stepped closer. "Where? Where do I find him?"

She waved him from the room. "Hurry! Get Eli. He'll know where to go." As Gideon stumbled over his feet, Mary shouted after him. "Hurry back and get this fire goin'!"

He darted across the farm and burst past the door without knocking. The words that passed from his lips to Eli were minimal, and Cassie's brother took off toward the barn. Breathless, Gideon rushed back home.

When he tugged the front door open, Mary's cries pulled him into the bedroom.

"Help me!"

She was struggling to sit Cassie up. Slipping between them, Gideon pulled Cassie upright as Mary shoved one sleeve of Cassie's nightgown up. Then the other. "This is bad." Her chin trembled. "She should never have been at the Coles'. It's my fault. I should never have —"

Gideon's forceful words silenced her. "What will get her well?"

"I'm not sure. The doc will know what to do." Mary's fingers dented Cassie's arm, and she seemed torn to release her.

Understanding the desire, Gideon reached for her.

Mary stopped his hand. "Have you ever had scarlet fever?"

Gideon held Cassie as Mary pulled the nightgown back in place. The heat coming off Cassie's skin stung his chapped hands. "No."

"Then you shouldn't be —"

The look he gave her silenced her. He'd failed Cassie too many times already.

She sighed. "We're the only two who can watch after her. The boys are older, but still . . ."

Gideon gently lowered Cassie back down.

Mary stepped back. "I'll fetch a cool cloth for her head."

She disappeared from the bedroom. Sinking to his knees, he smoothed his hand across Cassie's forehead and pushed the moist locks away from her rosy skin. "You're gonna be just fine," he murmured. "The doc's on his way. He'll know what to do."

Her eyelids fluttered but did not open.

Cassie. His wife. Yet he had spent months punishing her. *For what?* For loving him when he was hers to love. For wanting him when he was hers by law.

Tears stung his eyes. He lowered himself and interlocked his fingers, pressing his forehead there. He listened to Cassie's quiet breathing.

And a strange yearning tugged at the key to his heart.

FIFTY-ONE

Her ascent upstairs was slow. Lonnie pressed her palm to the wall and paused. *This must be done.* She took another step and then another. At the top of the stairs, she shuffled her way into her bedroom and halted just inside the doorway. She slid free of Gideon's plaid coat and tossed it onto the bed. A few steps took her to the small wardrobe. She gave the ill-fitted door a forceful yank. It was time.

She stared into the dark wardrobe, glad the thinning light of day gave her only a hint of what was inside. Fearing she would change her mind, Lonnie pulled out a shirt. Frightened to hold it longer than necessary, she stuffed it into the sack. Before she could lose her courage, she spun around. Her knees hit the floor.

She yanked the bottom drawer open, clutched a handful of clothing, and stuffed it into the sack. An extra pair of socks, two clean undershirts — all the things Gideon had not needed on their short journey to Rocky Knob. Pressing the collar of his best shirt to her nose, she breathed in the spicy scent of his skin, which lingered like a dream she could scarcely recall. Lonnie laid a hand on the drawer and leaned her head against the wardrobe. *God be my strength.*

Her eyes fell closed. If only she hadn't fallen for her pa's malicious scheme. Although she had wished it a thousand times in the wee hours of the night, when loneliness was her only companion, Lonnie knew the truth — the past could not be undone. She slammed the drawer shut.

Turning around, she surveyed the room for anything else that did not belong to her. The bed, freshly made, reminded her of Gideon. How many nights had they huddled together beneath the warm quilt? Lonnie glanced away. Some things could not be stuffed in a burlap sack to be discarded so easily.

Turning, her gaze traveled the length of the bedroom. Her bedroom. A half-burned candle sat on top of the dresser, a dusty doily beneath it. Lonnie smoothed her hand along the brass footboard and crossed the room to the window. A wooden box, nestled behind the lace curtain, held a few coins and other odds and ends.

She lifted the lid and counted the money. It wasn't much, but it was Gideon's from the furs he'd sold. She opened her hand, and the coins jingled back in. She clamped the wooden lid and slid the box back behind the curtain. They were no longer Gideon's. They were Jacob's. Surely Gideon would want it that way. She did not want to keep anything that was not rightfully hers.

Ever so slowly, she moved to the nightstand, tugged open the single small drawer, and found her wedding ring. Lonnie balanced it in her palm. Pulling the box back out, she set the ring among Jacob's few coins. Another gift for her son. The small lid closed with a soft *thump,* and Lonnie touched the skin of her naked finger. Gideon was not coming back. And tomorrow was a new day. She would not cry.

She would not.

Lonnie swallowed hard, fighting the sting of tears. *You can do this, Lonnie.*

Determined to find her strength, Lonnie stuffed Gideon's clothes deeper into the sack with a resolute sigh. She cleared her throat and carried the small sack out the door and down the hall, then dropped it in the parlor. It would just have to wait a few days until she could get rid of it. *A few days, please, God. No more.* Lonnie released the burlap. Spent, she sank in the chair at the writing desk.

She fumbled with the slender drawer beneath the writing surface, and she gave the thin brass handle a tug. She tucked her fingers beneath old letters and notes. Lifting the drawer lining, she found three sheets of paper, safely hidden from sight. Her shaky handwriting littered the pages.

Lonnie splayed them across the desk. The name, so elegantly lettered on top of the page, made her heart leap.

Gideon.

She stared at the curving letters written by her own hand in the midst of her deepest sorrow. Her gaze ran the length of the page — weeks' worth of prayers and pleas. The words written there Lonnie would never share. Not with Gideon, not with anyone.

The pen sank into the bottle of ink, and she lightly tapped the tip on the edge of the small glass bottle. With a sigh as heavy as her heart, Lonnie smoothed a hand across the third and final page. The pen trembled as she struggled to form a good-bye. After several minutes, the pen slipped from her hand, and she let her head fall into ink-stained palms.

■ ■ ■ ■

The room had long since fallen under shadow of night. A single candle burned on the nightstand, the tiny flame illuminating Cassie's face. Propping his elbows on his knees, Gideon leaned forward. The doctor had come and gone. His words were clear. *"Do your best to keep her fever down. There's little to be done but watch and wait."*

Gideon lifted his eyes and studied Mary across from him. She was nestled in the rocking chair, but the plaid blanket that covered her drooping shoulders did little to conceal her restless slumber. Gideon did not blame her. He could never sleep. Not now.

"Only time will tell." The doctor's own words.

He lifted the rag from Cassie's burning skin and dipped it in the bowl of cool water that sat between his knees. He wrung out the cloth, and dripping water was all that broke the silence. Gideon folded the rag carefully and placed it against Cassie's cheeks with an unspoken prayer that it would draw the fever from her body.

She stirred. Her eyelids fluttered open.

Gideon leaned toward her. "Cassie," he

whispered, not wanting to wake Mary for fear their private moment would come to an abrupt end.

Her lips formed his name.

"You've been asleep all day." He fumbled for the right words, not knowing how long she would be able to steal away from her much needed sleep. "Can I get you some water?"

When she blinked, he snatched a tin mug from the nightstand and held it to her lips. He slipped a hand behind her head and tried to help her up. Her lips parted. His hand trembled. Water dripped and ran down her neck and onto the bed. Swallowing what little water she got, Cassie sank back against her pillow. Her misty eyes searched his.

Knowing this was his chance, Gideon ran a hand along his forehead and braved the words he should have spoken long ago. "I'm so sorry." His voice was hoarse. "I'm sorry for everything I've ever done to you. You deserve so much better than what I've given you."

Cassie blinked again, and the corners of her mouth turned upward in the faintest of smiles. Lowering his face to hers, Gideon kissed her hair. Her eyes closed.

Standing before the fire, Lonnie held the

letter out to the open flames. The parlor had long since fallen dark, but the glowing embers in the hearth had offered enough light to finish. The small flame licked at the open air, summoning her to do what must be done. Lonnie hesitated, then, accepting the invitation, she opened her fingers. Three pages sailed from her hand and floated down.

She dropped to her knees and stared as her words caught fire. Words of love. Words of hope. Lost hope. The ivory paper smoked, and the curving lines of black ink were devoured. What once was, was no more. When every brokenhearted word had turned to ash, she sank back.

Elsie shuffled in and stopped beside the burlap sack. "What's this?"

Lonnie moved away from the fire and laid her hands in her lap. "Just some old clothes." She tipped her chin up, hoping Elsie wouldn't notice her tears. "I don't need them anymore, and I figured I would donate them to the church."

The woman's voice was soft. "Toby could take it there for you."

"That was the idea." Lonnie held Elsie's knowing gaze. "I'll ask him next time he stops by."

Elsie folded her arms in front of her and

stared out the parlor window. She smoothed her hands up and down her arms and mentioned stoking the fire. Lonnie scarcely caught her words. Instead, it was Elsie's listless gaze that captured her attention. When Elsie turned to face her, the older woman's eyes glistened with unshed tears. Although the words never escaped her lips, Lonnie saw that Elsie's unspoken distress mirrored her own.

It wasn't supposed to turn out this way.

FIFTY-TWO

"Still no change?" The doctor leaned over Cassie's bed and studied her through thick spectacles. "What have you been doing for her?"

Gideon blinked up at him through stinging eyes. "Everything you said to do."

At Henry's insistence, Eli had gone to fetch the doctor once more. *"I don't care what it costs. Just get him!"* Henry had slapped Eli's mount on the rump, and both horse and rider tore through the fog-covered land at dawn. Gideon watched as Eli rode away, back hunched, horse's hoofs thundering away into silence.

Now, with the doctor at a loss for words, Gideon hung his head. There had to be something he could do for Cassie.

Anything.

The doctor lifted his black leather bag from the floor and set it on the edge of the bed. He pulled out a shiny stethoscope and wrapped the earpieces on each side of his neck before sliding them into his ears. Smoothing two fingers down the silk-lined tubing, he fumbled with the black chest piece before slipping it beneath the collar of Cassie's nightgown.

Lifting his eyes, he stared at the wall before him. Gideon counted his own heartbeats as the doctor listened without speaking. Finally, the old man shook his head.

"Too fast," he murmured.

The morning sun that streamed through the window glistened against shiny metal as the doctor slid the contraption back in his black bag. *Snap.* The bag closed, and the doctor turned to Gideon.

His brown eyes seemed to frown, and his brows fell. He pressed his spectacles against his face with the tip of his finger. "Time will tell." He averted his gaze. "Keep doing what I told you."

"That's it?" Gideon stepped through the bedroom doorway with the doctor close behind. Although Cassie was asleep, he lowered his voice. "Nothing more can be done for her?"

For the first time that morning, the doctor's gaze bore into Gideon's. "I'm afraid not." His words, though gently spoken, were clear.

Gideon ushered the doctor from the small cabin, and the tall, slender man climbed into the saddle of his horse. With a stiff wave, Gideon watched him depart, certain another sickbed required his services. Several others had come down with the fever across the hillsides. Gideon wasn't the only man to receive dire news.

He ducked inside and paced the short distance to the bedroom. Standing in the doorway, he watched Cassie sleep. Her ma had spent hours combing her hair, and now the unbound strands draped over her shoulders. To the doctor, she was just one of many. Gideon stuffed his fists into his pants pockets and continued to stare at the woman fighting for her life.

And to me?

He sank into the chair at the bedside and crossed his arms. Leaning forward he rested his elbows on his knees.

"Cassie?" His raspy voice broke the stillness.

Her ashen lips did not part in the smile he hungered to see.

"The doc just left. But I'm here. I'll take care of you." He took her limp hand in his and rubbed small circles across her smooth skin with his thumb. With her round mouth slightly parted, her chest rose and fell slowly beneath her nightgown. Mary came and went. Once. Twice. Gideon didn't move. He glanced to the nightstand, spotting Cassie's scarlet ribbon coiled beside the candleholder. Taking it, he rested his forearms on his knees. The ribbon was silk in his fingers.

He wished he were stronger. Wiser. A stronger man would pray. A wiser man would have the words. Not the growl of a bear in his chest. The desire to fight against whatever it was that made these things happen. Fingers interlocked, Gideon gripped the back of his neck. So here he sat. A thousand questions filling his mind. If Jebediah were here, he'd know what to do. He'd say something about the Lord's will. And that it might be done.

Gideon hung his head, not sure what to make of that. He yearned for just one minute at the man's side, sawdust scattered about their boots, Jebediah's sage advice filling the air with a husky reverence. Heart thundering, Gideon wished with all his might that the man's voice might cross the miles. For he was in desperate need of guidance.

Cassie heard him say her name, but other than the familiar word, she heard so much more. Did he love her? Could it be? Trapped

427

in a restless slumber, she wished she had the strength to wake, if only to open her eyes long enough to voice what had never been wanted or desired. *I love you, Gideon.*

Her flesh was on fire. She squirmed, but there was no escaping the prison her body had become. *Is this the end?* Was God going to take her away from this life? Cassie tried to swallow, but her burning throat was too dry. Tears stung her eyes, and her hand twitched where it lay at her side, but she had no strength to wipe them away.

She wanted to see his face one last time. She struggled to open her eyes, but it was useless. Overwhelmed by fear, she could scarcely breathe, and she forced down a cry lest it choke her. *Wake up!* She was a fool to hope, but she had to try.

"Cassie."

She knew that voice. Oh, how she loved that voice.

Gideon, I'm here.

Sorrow crushed her chest until it burned. Cassie gasped and felt a hot tear slip from the corner of her eye, only to slide toward her pillow. She felt herself drift away.

Gideon hung his head and saw Cassie not as she was, but as he remembered her.

"Gideon." Cassie laughed.

Closing his eyes, he heard her cheery voice in his heart. He could almost see her small frame cross the bedroom in the wee hours of the morning when she had thought him sleeping. He cringed. How many times had he stayed away? How many times had he avoided her touch? Gideon covered her hand with his, engulfing it in the cool embrace of his chilled palms. Was it in him to make it right?

Footsteps shuffled into the small cabin, and a voice, so similar to Cassie's, broke the silence. "Gideon. I brought you something to eat."

He did not lift his eyes from Cassie's face. "I'm not hungry."

"You must eat." Mary's voice grew thin. "She'll be there when you're done."

Gideon shook his head.

"Please, Gid. You both need your rest. Let her sleep. You'll be no use to her if you don't keep your strength up."

As much as it pained him to leave Cassie's side, he did as Mary asked. Sinking down at the small table, he watched her pull food from a basket.

"I made you a sandwich." She laid the meal in front of him, then lifted out a jar of cider. "And this." She unscrewed the lid. "You eat. I'll go sit with her."

Needing to form the words, Gideon cleared his throat and spoke her name.

Mary turned slowly.

"I'm sorry," he finally managed. Unable to eat, he lowered the sandwich to the table. "I'm so sorry."

"Oh, Gid." Mary sank into the chair across from him.

There wasn't enough moisture in his mouth to swallow his guilt. He could still see Cassie reach for his hand only to have him turn away. He could still feel her touch his shoulder only to have his muscle tense beneath her palm. *God, how do I fix this?*

There had to be a way to change. Alter the course of his heart to be the husband Cassie needed. It would require more than sacrifice. It would require more than a lie. It would require his life — his heart.

A muffled noise caught his attention, and Gideon lifted his head. Mary followed his lead. Her brow furrowed.

Crash!

"Cassie," Mary breathed.

Gideon jumped from his chair, sending it spinning across the floor. He rushed toward the bedroom and barreled past the door.

FIFTY-THREE

Hot wax spilled from the candlestick that rolled across the floorboards. The tin candleholder spun away.

"Grab that bowl!" Mary darted toward the bed, nearly knocking over a chair. She tore the quilt off Cassie's trembling body.

Gideon reached for the chipped crock, but his hand knocked it from the nightstand. The ivory stoneware hit the floor with a disturbing *thud.* Water pooled beneath the nightstand, spreading wherever it willed. Gideon dropped to his knees.

Mary tossed the quilt to the floor and waved her hand at him. "Just toss me the rag!"

Gideon snatched up the rag and wrung it out over drenched floorboards. He tossed it to Mary's outstretched hand and stared as she swept it across her daughter's glistening forehead. She folded the rag and dabbed at Cassie's lips. What pain tormented her body, Gideon would never know. All he knew was that while he had stopped for supper, she had been alone in the bedroom. Fighting for her life.

He struggled to his feet. Cassie tossed her head from side to side and arched her back. Her wrinkled nightgown, now damp, clung to her translucent skin. The illness inside her was raging now. Gideon watched in horror as she fought violently to breathe. Her lips parted. She extended her frail neck. Pressing her head deeper into the pillow, she pitched her head to the side and gasped. Gideon's mouth went dry.

Breathe, Cassie!

He found himself holding his breath, and when he finally drew air into his burning lungs, fear consumed him. There was nothing he could do to help her. Cassie gasped and her body settled. Rolling to the side, she coughed into her pillow.

"She's burnin' up," Mary said.

Cassie's hand searched the disheveled sheets. Her fingers groped at nothing. Gideon slid his hand out for her to grab. Instead of taking hold, her lost fingers blindly fumbled the rumpled bedding.

Mary swiped her sleeve across her own forehead. "I've never seen a fever this bad."

Mouth dry with fear, he rose. "I'll get

432

more water."

He needed to make himself useful some-how — someway. Snatching up the crock, he dashed into the kitchen and thrust it into the bucket of cold water. He returned in time for Mary to dip the rag and wring it out once more. She laid the cloth over Cassie's forehead. "I just don't know what else to do." She shook her head.

Gideon stared at her. It wasn't over. It couldn't be.

Finally, Cassie's body settled. The rise and fall of her chest slowed.

"There has to be something else we can do." He grabbed the rag and rinsed the tattered fabric before smoothing it down Cassie's arm. He lifted her limp wrist and pressed the cool cloth into her palm.

"There must be some way to draw this out of her." Despair wrapped its merciless hands around his heart.

Then the idea struck him. Pushing the rag off Cassie, he slid his arms beneath her frail frame and hoisted her off the bed.

Mary stood. "What are you doing?"

Swiveling through the doorway, Gideon thundered through the kitchen and out the door, Cassie's hot body clutched against his chest.

Mary followed him. "Gideon!"

433

He sank to his knees in the snow and held Cassie tight. "She's burning up." He lifted his eyes to Mary. "Please help me."

She knelt at his side, and her hands trembled in hesitation. Then she grabbed a handful of snow and ran it along her daughter's collarbone. Cassie winced and shuddered. The snow that melted against her skin dribbled beneath the lace neckline, dampening her nightgown.

With red fingers, Mary scooped up another mound of snow; this time she smeared it down Cassie's arm. Frail fingers curled around the snow. Water trickled from the creases of Cassie's hand. Turning toward Gideon, Cassie buried her face in his chest. Her body began to shake.

He held her that way for several minutes, then finally Gideon spoke, his voice faltering. "I don't know what to do."

Cassie shook harder and coughed into the sleeve at her wrist. Gideon looked at his mother-in-law.

"Get her inside," Mary gently urged.

Gideon carried Cassie back into the house and laid her on the rumpled sheets.

When her body settled, he knelt beside her and clasped her hand. "I don't know if this is right. I can't do nothin'."

Mary crumpled into the rocking chair and

dropped her head to her knees. Her silver-laced bun tumbled free, and her body shook with sobs. Kneeling against the bed, Gideon pulled Cassie's hand into his.

"Cassie. Listen to me. You hang on. Just hang on —" When his voice cracked, he dropped his head to the mattress.

He heard Mary whisper a prayer. Her plea so fervent, he closed his eyes. His own lips moved in quiet petition; he hoped the words would be enough. A hot tear puddled and fell.

The wind picked up, swirling snow in a glittering spiral across the yard. Lonnie stood on the porch steps and watched the land before her transform. What had been a sunny day was being swallowed up by the menacing storm that loomed on the horizon, threatening to drop its heavy burden on the land below.

Jacob had babbled the word *Mama* that morning. Filling her heart to overflowing. Yet she wondered if he would ever know another word — *Papa.* The sack of Gideon's things still sat in the parlor. All that they had left of him. Waiting. Waiting for her to let go. Lonnie ran her fingertips together.

Lifting her face to the trees on the other

side of the house, she watched dark-gray clouds slowly roll in. The thick mass that filled the sky promised more snow. Lonnie shivered and wrapped her arms around herself. The sun was gone, and she was certain it would be days before its light warmed the land once more.

A cold wind, colder than any she'd ever felt, crept beneath her thick layers. Her shawl flapped, but Lonnie hugged herself tighter.

The stove inside clanged closed, and Lonnie knew she should be in helping Elsie with supper. She had hardly set a plate in front of each chair before she conjured up an excuse to head outside. She glanced at the woodpile. Elsie would be suspicious if she returned empty-handed.

Though she stood alone, Lonnie heard Elsie's words spoken only moments ago.

"Reverend McKee is coming by for supper this Sunday." The older woman had searched Lonnie's face as if hunting for a reaction — some window into her heart.

Lonnie had excused herself and now stood alone against the elements, weighing the meaning of what Elsie had said.

She stepped toward the woodpile and lifted several rough logs into her arms before lumbering back up the steps. Sunday was six days away. It wasn't much time to prepare her heart, but even so, Lonnie could not wait that long to see the reverend. And that startled her. Snow began to fall, and she watched the first flakes float and flutter down.

Lonnie knew what she had to do when this storm cleared.

FIFTY-FOUR

Sun streamed through the window, stinging Cassie's eyes even from behind her lids. She felt her lips part, but she could not speak. *Water.* She needed water. Frustration overwhelmed her when she could not speak the simple word, and she turned her head to the side. That's when she felt his hand, tracing a slow pattern on the back of hers. The flesh beneath his fingers burned but not from the fever, and her skin felt amazingly alive. Cassie tried to stiffen her hand to let him know she was there, but even that was too much.

Turning her thoughts back to herself, the sweetness of victory made her current weakness minimal.

She had won.

She could feel it. The fever was retreating. How long it had raged, she didn't know, but for the first time since the fever reigned inside her, she felt her skin cooling, felt the ache in her body resigning. It would not conquer her. The sweat that covered her skin and had soaked her nightgown was now drying. She felt sticky, and her cracked lips tasted like salt, but it didn't matter. She was alive.

And all that time, all those hours — days of torment and pain — the ebb and flow of her relentless thoughts rushed around one thing: Gideon had said he was sorry. And he had meant it. The ache in his voice, the pain in his apology was unmistakable even in the dark depths Cassie had slipped to.

But she did not feel free. She did not feel joy. Something still felt unfinished.

That last thought built a lump in her throat so thick, Cassie had to struggle to force air in and out of her lungs. This sent a course of fear through her, and every muscle in her body tensed. Her throat was so parched she wanted to cry out for water. She felt her lips move but wasn't sure if the word formed. It must have, for a moment later, Gideon's hand lifted her head slightly and a cool cup pressed to her mouth. Cassie sipped. The cup clanked on the nightstand.

Gideon gently squeezed her shoulder. Cassie wanted to say thank you, but instead, she simply savored his touch. All the while, she couldn't get the sound of his prayers out of her mind. She hadn't deserved them. Not a single one. And as he spoke, sweet words falling from his lips, the same question had circled her mind: Was this life truly hers?

She didn't like the answer she came up with.

He had a wife. A son. And she had lied to him. Lied about his freedom. All for what? Because she was scared? undecided? Cassie cringed. She tried to move her legs, but they felt so heavy. She focused instead on the hand holding hers. Tears stung her eyes.

Lonnie. Jacob. They were somewhere out there. His family.

The lump in her throat grew.

FIFTY-FIVE

"Easy, girl," Lonnie patted Sugar's thick neck. She tugged her shawl tighter and slid from the broad-backed mule, sinking into ankle-deep snow. Her hands were stiff with cold and her movements slow, but Lonnie managed to tie Sugar's line to a low spruce branch. She turned and laid a gloved hand on the gentle animal's back long enough to gather what courage she had inside herself.

The small shanty sat silent before her. The thin trail of smoke that swirled from the stovepipe promised that the man she sought was home. Although the curtains were pulled open, Lonnie saw nothing but the faint flicker of candlelight coming from the small building. With the sun a mere hour from setting, the cozy hollow was already swallowed in shadow.

Lonnie tugged the burlap sack from Sugar's back. When she stepped forward, her boots crunched in the snow. She held her breath, convinced that the faint sound would give away her presence. She stared at the front door, wondering if Toby would appear. *Silly girl,* Lonnie chided herself. Of course he wouldn't. Did she expect him to be waiting for her?

He had better things to do.

She tiptoed up the single step, crossed the tiny porch, and although her conscience scolded her, peeked in the one and only window. Two stubby candles burned along a narrow mantel. And then she saw him.

Toby.

His back was to her. A shirt was draped over a chair, and standing in his pants, he ran a cloth across his chest and down his broad arm. Lonnie gasped and jumped back. Shame burned her cheeks, and she struggled to dislodge the image from her mind.

Forcing herself to turn her attention to the matter at hand, she dropped the sack at her feet. Her fist hesitated before striking the door.

When she finally knocked, she heard Toby's deep voice call out. "Coming!"

She listened as he stumbled about.

The door flew open. With his eyes down, Toby pushed the top button of his shirt through its hole. He glanced up, his eyes registered her, and he stumbled back. Turning away, he stuffed the rest of the buttons into their places. "Lonnie." His ears reddened. "What are you doing here?"

She lowered her gaze until he stepped forward. "I've come to ask you something." Her feet remained glued to the porch. Her eyes searched the tiny room behind him as if the sight of his home would give away secrets about the man who lived there.

Toby's wide eyes explored her face.

Her heart pounded in her chest, but she was fueled by her resolve. "I brought this," she blurted. "Just some clothes that I wanted to donate to the church." As Toby continued to stare at her, she felt her strength wavering. "Perhaps you know of a family . . . a man . . . who could use them."

He clutched the top of the sack and slid it toward himself. His eyebrows pulled together. "A young man?"

"Yes."

He spoke the words slowly. "These things must be dear to you."

"Maybe once . . . but not now." The half-truth sent a jolt of pain through her.

His eyes met hers, hunger clear in the brown depths. "Would you like to come in?"

"I'm sure it would be better if I didn't." Although she tried not to let her gaze linger, the damp curls at the nape of his neck stole her attention. *Perhaps this visit wasn't a good idea after all.*

Toby fiddled with the loose cuff of his shirt. "Sorry. It was inconsiderate of me to ask."

Unable to think of a response, Lonnie waved toward Sugar. "I should probably be going." What a fool she must look. Such a long journey and in the dead of winter, only to deliver a donation of clothing. She bit her lip and hoped Toby would not think her a fool.

"Well, this was kind of you." Pressing his hand against the doorjamb, he ran his thumb over the oiled wood. His casual stance did little to conceal his tortured expression. "I ken several families who have a need." His eyes softened when they landed on her face, and Lonnie saw a twinge of pain, an understanding she did not expect. " 'Specially this time of year."

She shifted from one foot to the other, growing colder by the moment.

Toby clumsily darted away from the door and returned with a black coat. "Please take this," he urged.

Too cold to do otherwise, she accepted the garment. She still had a long ride home. Without standing on ceremony, she slipped the oversized coat over her shoulders, and as the thick fabric blocked out the chill, she fought back a smile. Folding the collar up, Lonnie let the tip of her nose brush against the rough wool — a habit. *Why did I do that?* She hoped Toby hadn't noticed. Her cheeks burned, and Lonnie wanted to kick herself. "Well, I better be going." She backed away.

"Wait." The tips of his fingers brushed against hers.

The faint touch sent a bolt of heat through Lonnie's arm. It ended in her toes. Toby stepped forward and closed the door behind him. He hurried to tuck in his shirttails, but his wet hair and socks did little to change his untailored appearance. "I . . . I feel like I should say something." His brows lifted sheepishly. "But I don't know what." He gestured toward the sack of clothes. "This can't be easy for you."

"It's fine."

"Fine?"

"It's life," she blurted. She would not cry. Lonnie blinked quickly.

Toby's eyes explored hers. His warm palm wrapped around her cold fingers, and Lonnie felt her whole arm stiffen. "You should get home," he whispered. "It's getting colder by the minute."

She opened her mouth to speak, but her

mind was suddenly blank. "You're right. I really better go. Sugar'll be wantin' her oats soon." Toby released her hand, and Lonnie tucked her fists inside the pockets of his coat. "Elsie mentioned you might be comin' by for Sunday supper. I suppose I will see you then."

"Lonnie, I . . . ," he began.

She froze but her pulse quickened.

"I've been meaning to ask you . . ." Toby crossed his arms over his chest.

Lonnie could see her own breath before her face, and for a moment, she wished she had taken him up on his offer to step inside. A warm fire called to her like Eden's apple, but she knew it was better not to partake. Besides, the coat that covered her shoulders blocked out the chill, and even as she huddled beneath its warmth, she couldn't help but think of the man to whom it belonged.

"Would you mind . . . I mean, would it be all right . . ." His voice trailed off and he glanced away.

He sighed. Lifting his thick arms, he ran his hands through his hair, and a deep groan growled out of him. "Would it be all right if I came to call on you sometime? Not just to see Elsie and Jebediah, but to . . . see you." His brown eyes widened. "To be with you."

When a cool breeze crept up her stockings and ruffled her petticoats, Lonnie crossed her ankles, one over the other.

His face a jumble of emotions, Toby moistened his lips, setting his dimples even deeper as he waited for her response. For the briefest moment, she no longer noticed the man before her.

Another face came to mind, and Lonnie's breath caught. *Forgive me, Gideon.* There was nothing left for her to do but move on. Besides, she needed to be loved. She *wanted* to be loved. After drawing in a shaky breath, she relieved Toby of his doubts. "That would be all right."

FIFTY-SIX

Gideon shifted in his seat, wondering how long this would take. He glanced at a window, where the January sky glinted gray on the glass. His collar was buttoned too high, and his tie was too tight. He tugged at the knot at his throat, and when a plump woman in a bonnet arched an eyebrow, he pressed his palms to the pew seat beneath him and leaned forward into a stand. He helped Cassie to her feet, laying her small hand on his arm. At his side, Cassie held the hymnal. She sang the words as if she knew them by heart, her pretty voice soft.

He heard a rustling beside him, and his father pressed his shoulder against Gideon's. It wasn't uncommon for the O'Rileys to be tardy to church, and seeing the flush on his ma's face, he could only imagine the morning she'd had. She ushered his brothers and sisters into the row. She stood like a sober bookend, the baby in her arms.

The hymn came to an end, the vibration of a church full of singers drawing soft. Silent. Cassie sat, and Gideon settled beside her.

His father leaned toward him. "This came for you last week." He pulled a letter from his vest pocket. Gideon reached out and took it. Turning it over, he spotted Lonnie's handwriting. A cold sensation puddled in his chest.

Reverend Gardner moved to the front of the church, his movements slow, drawn out. Gideon tapped his foot anxiously, knee bouncing haphazardly. His pulse raced, the cold turning into a heat — a fever — that forced him from the bench. "Excuse me," he whispered to Cassie. She leaned back, and Gideon sidestepped from the pew, barreling toward the door as if Reverend Gardner was not in the middle of his prayer. Heads lifted, but he didn't stop.

Lonnie.

The sides of his jacket flapped open when he strode into the icy mist that surrounded the church. His boots thundered down the steps, past crooked tombstones that sank haphazardly into the moist grass. It wasn't until the reverend's voice was but a memory that he finally stopped. Crouching, he rested his forearm on his knee and studied the letter. The paper was worse for wear, but that was Lonnie's pretty writing. Make no mistake. A muscle tripped through his jaw.

He tore into the envelope, letting the ripped portion float on the breeze that tousled his tie. He shook the envelope, and a single page fell into his palm. A flip of the folds and her words were before him, sinking into the deep mire of his heart that he'd forced numb. He breathed her name. He breathed their son's name. Tears stung his eyes as he read words of Jacob's life. How the boy was growing, what trouble he managed to get into. Gideon chuckled and swiped his hand over his eyes when the page blurred. His sweet Jacob.

Lonnie's words grew smaller as if trying to squeeze more onto the page — more into her message, into his heart. *Oh, Lonnie.* He touched her soft letters, emotion bubbling up inside him. How he missed her. He read the letter once, twice. At the sound of a hymn rising from the chapel, he knew he'd been gone almost an hour. Knowing he'd be sorely missed, Gideon forced himself to stand and, carefully folding the page that had grown supple in the misty air, slid it into his pocket. He strode into the church. More heads turned. In the span of a few whispers, he was at his pew, sliding back beside Cassie. His pulse still raced. He cleared his throat, realizing how heavy he was breathing.

Cassie leaned toward him. "Are you all right?"

After a moment's hesitation, Gideon pulled out the letter and handed it to her. She studied the inscription a moment before sliding it into her apron pocket. Her face was grave. Gideon hated parting with the letter, but he didn't want to hide it from Cassie. It wouldn't be right.

The reverend stood for a final benediction. They rose, and Cassie's hand was soft beside Gideon's. Feeling more than a few eyes on him, Gideon covered her palm with his. The reverend closed his Bible and clutched it to his chest.

The reverend's eyes never found his, but Gideon felt the man's words as if they stood boot to boot. "I pray that as you go out this day, you will be reminded of God's calling in your life. Be of strong faith; be of good courage." He nodded and lifted his hymnal. "We'll close with a favorite of mine, number one hundred and three."

Licking his thumb, Gideon struggled to find the page. Reaching over, Cassie helped him, her face soft, pensive. Finally, he smoothed his hand along the page. The congregation began.

"Before the throne of God above, I have a strong and perfect plea . . ."

Yes, he had a plea.

Gideon sang the words softly, the hymn foreign, yet a memory of it stirred within him. "A great high Priest whose Name is Love who ever lives and pleads for me." Pleads for me. Gideon cleared his throat. Did God plead for him? He wanted to scoff. There was nothing in him, nothing about him, that was worthy of such an act of love. Surely God knew that.

Cassie sang beside him. "My name is graven on His hands. My name is written on His heart."

Shifting on his feet, Gideon read the words again. He couldn't imagine the name *Gideon O'Riley* written on the Lord's heart.

It was impossible.

The congregation sang on, but Gideon couldn't make the song form. Even so, he followed along, each word sinking into him like a stone into a river. Plummeting to the bottom. The stones built on one another, filling him in a way that made him glance at Cassie. Not Lonnie. Cassie. She peered up at him, a smile on her face. He loosened his tie, not because it was bothersome, but because he wanted to draw a deep breath.

Pull into his lungs whatever it was that flowed in this wooden room.

The words sank in as no words ever had. They seemed to fill him. Fill the spaces of his soul that had felt so empty. "Upward I look and see Him there who made an end of all my sin." Gideon lifted his eyes to the window behind Reverend Gardner, the small panes crisscrossing over a fog-shrouded sky. The door sat propped open behind him, and he shivered as the mist worked its way in. Cassie moved closer.

It didn't fall past him that it was the same doorway he had escorted Lonnie through. His young bride. Gideon lifted his eyes to the rafters above. A plea — no, a prayer — filling his heart. *Lord, be with them. Take care of them in the ways I cannot. Look after my son. Be with Lonnie.* A lump filled his throat, and he tried to swallow it down. *Be with Cassie and with me. Show me what to do.* Gideon hung his head. *Show me what to do.*

The wind rose, and the door shook ever so slightly. An unbound strand of Cassie's hair brushed against him. She wiped it away, but the sensation lingered.

Lead me. He could not do this on his own. Not one more step of it.

FIFTY-SEVEN

Lonnie lowered her hand mirror and patted her hair for the third time. With a sigh, she grabbed the handle once more and examined her handiwork. Freshly bathed, her hair was still damp and shiny. She had combed it smooth and shaped it into an artful bun at the nape of her neck, finally securing it in more loops and coils than seemed prudent — something she never did. As she wrapped a brown ribbon around the mass and tied it in a secure bow, she bit her lip. Was it too much?

The grandfather clock in the parlor announced the time, and she scarcely breathed as she counted all six chimes. Toby would arrive at any moment. Wringing her hands, she turned on the ball of her foot to find herself looking at Jacob. He sat in the center of her bed, the stains on his rumpled sweater a reminder of the mashed pumpkin and molasses he had eaten for supper.

He looked up at Lonnie but continued rolling his blocks around in front of him. The freshly carved wood only made Toby come to mind — dark hair, dimples. Lonnie picked up a block and turned it in her hand. Jacob peered up at her with wide green eyes. Toby's image vanished. Peering into her son's face, she saw nothing but Gideon, the man she had once thought forever hers. Jacob reached for his block, and Lonnie let it fall into his lap. Spinning away, she pressed her palms to her burning cheeks. *Why Gideon? Why now?* He was Cassie's. She was a fool to think otherwise.

A noise captured her attention, and Lonnie rushed to the window, pushed back the curtains, and tried not to be seen as she peered into the yard. Gael trotted into view. Lonnie stepped back slightly but saw Toby lift his face to her window. He was here. He had come to call . . . on her.

She smoothed her eyelet blouse and straightened the lace collar. Her hands flew to her hair, and as soon as she had tucked a silken strand in place, Lonnie forced her hands to her sides. She watched Toby dismount and lead Gael to the barn. She nibbled the tip of her thumb until he emerged a minute later, smoothing his brown jacket. He seemed to hesitate ever so slightly before approaching the back door. He disappeared beneath the porch eaves. Then Lonnie heard a knock.

"Well, Jacob," she murmured against the window. Lifting her hand, she touched the cold glass. "This is it."

The back door opened. The back door closed. Lonnie lifted Jacob from the bed and rested him on her hip. "This is it," she whispered.

She left the bedroom and walked to the stairs. As she slid her fingers down the cold banister, the freshly oiled wood felt too smooth and tranquil beneath her balmy hand.

Happy voices rang from the kitchen, but their cheer did not quicken her pace. Lonnie turned the corner, and her freshly scrubbed boots found the large rug at the base of the stairs. *Lord, grant me peace.* With a heavy sigh, she pulled Jacob close and kissed his soft cheek. "Be my comfort." Even as her heart pounded and her knees trembled, she started into the kitchen. *Direct my steps.*

FIFTY-EIGHT

Jacob was beautiful when he slept. Motionless, with only the rise and fall of his tiny chest, he was impossible not to watch. Enchanted by the boy's hair that curled around his cherub face, Gideon found himself unable to turn away. His son's mother slept at his side, her fingers curled instinctively against his cheek as if she couldn't help touching him, even in her sleep. Her pale ankles were crossed. Bare beneath her nightgown. Gideon considered waking her. But she was so peaceful — they both were.

Then someone called his name. Why did they have to bother him now? He was finally with his family. Finally close enough to scoop his son up in his arms. He'd just gotten here, and he wasn't ready to give this up. Not yet. Whoever it was would just have to wait.

"Gideon."

His name was called again. Suddenly, he couldn't see his family anymore. There was nothing but darkness. Then the darkness started to tremble, and Gideon found himself opening his eyes. He blinked at the room around him, so different from what his dreams held.

"Gideon."

He sat up with a start. Looking around, he took a moment to absorb his surroundings. The room was nearly dark except for the few candles flickering about the room.

"You were sleeping so peacefully, I didn't want to wake you."

"I can't believe I fell asleep. It feels like I just sat down." Moving closer to the bed, he straightened the quilt around Cassie's waist.

"You did just sit down. That's what was so funny." Her eyes wouldn't meet his.

"Are you —"

"I'm fine."

He pressed a hand to her forehead, smoothing unruly strands away from her face. The flush was gone from her skin, the rash nearly faded. "You look like you're feeling better." He sank onto the bed beside her.

"I feel a little stronger this morning."

"You don't know how good it sounds to hear you say that. Can I get you something?"

Eying the empty cup on the nightstand, he offered to get her more tea.

"No. Thank you."

"You didn't finish your dinner. I hope the hot cakes weren't —"

"They were wonderful. I just wasn't hungry quite yet."

"Like you weren't hungry for the stew from yesterday or the eggs from the day before?"

With a slight smile, Cassie reached for her plate and speared the last few bites onto her fork, finally stuffing the unladylike stack into her mouth. She made a funny face. "I think you used a little too much leavening."

Gideon chuckled. "Sorry about that." He shook his head. "I thought something was wrong. You're not the greatest actress; do you know that?"

She shrugged playfully, still chewing, but her eyes were sad.

"Seeing as you've been indoors so much the last week, I thought a little fresh air was in order." Without waiting to see her response, Gideon hoisted her off the bed, quilt and all. She weighed hardly anything.

"What are you doing?" The thrill in her voice was refreshing. "I can walk!"

Smiling, Gideon blew out the candle on the nightstand, then stepped carefully to the dresser where he blew out another. The room fell dark. It took a moment for his eyes to find the doorway, and he stepped toward it.

Then he heard her gasp. Felt the intake of breath through the quilt. It was the only response he needed. Suppressing a smile, Gideon carried her through the dark house, toward the glow of the fire he'd built in the yard, just off the porch. The flames licked the cold night air, dancing for their audience of two. The sun had all but set, its final efforts scattered along the horizon like tiny candles, refusing to be snuffed out. The dips and rises of the snow were painted in dark valleys of blue, shimmering mountains of orange.

"It's beautiful," she whispered.

"Thought you could use a change of scenery."

Cassie lowered her head to his shoulder and kissed it. She ran a hand over her eyes as if she were fighting something back.

He kept his voice light. "Your throne," he teased, swiveling toward the chair he'd set out for her.

He felt Cassie shake her head against his shoulder. "I like this," she whispered.

Gideon hesitated, then allowed his body to relax. Pressing his back against the porch post, he sank to the top step of the stairs and leaned back. "How's this?" he whispered into her hair.

"Perfect."

The fire crackled and popped, then seemed to grow brighter. Gideon glanced down at Cassie's face and saw the soft glow dance across her features. As if she noticed he was watching, her lashes flicked upward. Troubled blue eyes met his.

"Let me know if you get too cold, now." He shifted her against his chest. "I'll take you right back in. We need to be careful with you still . . ." He fell silent when he saw her gaze had drifted into the dark.

Her eyebrows pulled together.

"So you can get your strength back."

"I don't know if I care." The words came out soft — distant.

Gideon felt his eyes narrow. "Don't say that."

She nestled her head against him without responding. They sat that way for several minutes.

"Gideon."

"Hmm?"

"What were you dreaming about?"

"When?"

"Inside. Just now, when I woke you."

"I don't remember."

Cassie pulled back slightly in his embrace. She turned her face to his. "Yes you do."

Gideon stared at the fire for a long time before he spoke, and when he finally did, he knew it would be impossible to keep the ache he felt out of his voice. "What difference does it make?"

"It makes a world of difference."

Glancing down, he studied her, took in the taut lines etched into place by her stubborn curiosity. "Why do you ask?"

She stared into the darkness. When she spoke, each word came out slow, controlled. "Because you said, 'I love you.' "

Gideon felt his Adam's apple rise and fall. "I did?"

"Twice."

He didn't know what to say to that, so he said nothing.

After a long silence, Cassie pressed her cheek to his shoulder.

"I don't want to wear you out." He kissed the top of her head — a habit, nothing more. But if he kept doing it long enough, and the days turned into months, the months turned into years . . . Gideon ran his hand over his eyes, willing himself not to think of it.

"You are so sweet."

He grunted. "And you're generous."

"I'm horrible."

"What?"

Her voice plunged toward silence. "I'm ashamed."

"Ashamed? Cassie, what are you talking about?" He pushed her away, but only so he could see her face. "What's wrong?"

"Gideon, I —" She scooted to sit beside him, nestling in the shadows.

Chilled, Gideon folded his arms across his chest.

Her face was pure agony. "I should never have done this." She shook her head slowly. "Yesterday in church, the reverend's message felt like it was just for me."

"What was it?"

"He spoke of honesty. Letting your yes be your yes and your no be your no." She held up Lonnie's letter. He hadn't realized she'd been holding it. "This was my yes. This was me telling you that I wanted you out of my life and that I would follow through. But I didn't."

He watched her swallow.

"You thought you were free to marry another, and I did nothing to stop you. I didn't hold to my promise to see that everything was finalized between us. I didn't come to you. I didn't do anything. And you married Lonnie."

"Cassie —"

"You had Jacob."

The name silenced him.

"A child needs a father. I had no right . . ." The way she choked out the words, he knew she was going to cry.

"What are you saying?" His body warmed as if the sun were rising within him, pooling its light through his every limb. His hand captured hers, and when she groaned, face agonized, he let her tug it free.

"I should have done this long ago. I don't know what I was afraid of." Folding the sleeve of her nightgown back, she pulled out another piece of paper. "But I'm not afraid anymore."

She unfolded it slowly, and when firelight danced along the formal writing, Gideon felt his breath catch. "Cassie."

"We had both signed it. I should have sent this long ago." She turned her head; her eyes found his. "Gideon, I should have kept my promise. You trusted me. I want that to be worth something. I want my word to be worth something."

She began to tremble.

"I need to get you inside."

"Go to them." A lock of hair slipped off her forehead when she tipped her chin up, and tears filled her eyes. "Please. And when you have your son in your arms, tell him that you love him." She wiped at her wet cheeks. "Because he deserves all that and more."

Breath bated, he searched her eyes. She was shaking. Or was it him? He pulled back, needing his head to clear. A deep draw of air and life seemed to fill him.

"Why did you have to change?"

"What are you talking about?"

"Why couldn't you have just hated me until we were old and gray?"

Her words broke his heart. "I never hated you."

"But you're different now." She glanced at the fire he had built her. "If you hadn't changed, this wouldn't be so hard."

He turned to face her, gripping her arms so tight, he forced the muscles of his arms to relax. "Tell me." The words shook, breath shallow. "Cassie, what are you saying?"

She motioned to the westward skyline. "Lonnie. Why her? Why not me?"

His eyes searched her face. "I don't know." It was the only answer he had.

"That's my point. This" — she touched his chest and then hers — "this is what assures me." She stared into the distance as if she could see the Bennetts' house from where they sat. "I want more. I want to steal someone's heart the way she's stolen yours. Deeply, purely." A smile lifted her mouth. "You know I can do it."

He chuckled. How he knew it.

"More than that, I want to be *good.* I want to be trustworthy. I want this chance to do something right."

Sensing there was more, he touched her hand when she fell silent.

"Lonnie, she's —"

"She's what?" The words fell from his lips so urgently that her eyes widened.

"She's your perfect fit." Her eyes flooded with sorrow. "There's nothing to do about that." She squeezed his hand, her frailness alarming, stealing a piece of his heart. "Go home to her. You must." With a tenderness that would break his heart whenever he thought of her, she touched his cheek. "Go home to them."

AUTHOR'S NOTE

This was by far the most challenging story I've written. I've prayed over these words time and time again that they would be nothing less but honoring to God and that any piece that fell short would be trimmed away. At times it's been overwhelming to tell the story of a scoundrel, the sins of his past and the ways he and those around him were affected by it. I can't tell you how many times I saw this manuscript as crazy, and to hear from my editor that it was "brave" filled me with the courage to keep going — and as a dear friend shared with me, "Brave is not easy, but brave and courageous is the atmosphere where the Lord says He is in your midst and with you wherever you go" (see Joshua 1:9).

Though My Heart Is Torn is meant to shed light on the fact that though sin will bring us far from God, there is always a way back, and that though choices in life aren't always easy, we must look to grace: "an unearned and unmerited favor; the absolutely free expression of the loving kindness of God to men finding its only motive in the bounty and benevolence of the Giver."[*] Sometimes life lands around our feet in broken pieces, and all we can do is allow the Lord's strength to fill us as we pick up those portions, fitting them back together with His promises and mercy, our repentance and devotion. God will restore the broken. He gives grace to the humble and freedom to the captive.

As a storyteller, I constantly desired to ensure the historical quality of this book and to uphold the beauty and integrity of the Blue Ridge Mountains at the turn of the last century. One of my greatest desires is to write and research as accurately as possible. For any mistakes that appear, my absolute, sincerest apologies.

Research gems always seem to live in the most surprising places. Sometimes it's the tattered copy of the Sears, Roebuck and Co. catalog from 1900 that I found in the country store of the apple orchard in Oak

[*] This definition of *grace* came from *The Complete Word Study Dictionary: New Testament* (Word Study Series), edited by Spiros Zodhiates.

Glen, or the photograph of a winter path in the *Blue Ridge Country Magazine,* or the gem of an e-mail from the Patrick County Genealogy Society, sharing the story of their kinfolk's annulment and the circuit riders. I am indebted to the resources I've used over the years.

I have been so blessed by the amazing readers who gave this new author a chance. Your support, enthusiasm, and encouragement have meant the world to me. Your feedback gives me a peek into your hearts and how these stories touch you. I am forever grateful to you all for walking this path with me.

If you would like to stay in touch, you can sign up at www.joannebischof.com to receive my free e-newsletter, The Heartfelt Post, sent out each spring and autumn. While you're there, you'll see where I'm out and about on the web and can sneak a peek at my latest shenanigans — whether it's moonshine pecan pie or a folk music spotlight, via my blog. It's always a blessing to meet new readers. I would love to hear from you! If you like paper and stamps as much as I do, you can write to me at WaterBrook Multnomah, 12265 Oracle Boulevard, Suite 200, Colorado Springs, CO 80921.

Thank you for being a part of Lonnie and

Gideon's love story with *Be Still My Soul* and *Though My Heart Is Torn*. I hope you will join us for the final stage of their journey in *My Hope Is Found.*

READERS GUIDE

1. What does the title, *Though My Heart Is Torn,* signify to you? Who do you think it applies to — Lonnie, Gideon, or Cassie? Perhaps all three?
2. The first interactions between Lonnie and Gideon are much different in *Though My Heart Is Torn* than they were in *Be Still My Soul.* What differences do you see in Lonnie? What do you see in Gideon as a husband? a father?
3. The situation surrounding Gideon and the dual marriage is a tricky one. How has Gideon's refusal to follow God's ways affected his life? How did Cassie's behavior contribute to their situation?
4. How do you feel the reverends handled their role as overseers of the dilemma that ensnared Lonnie, Gideon, and Cassie? Did they make wise choices, or did they complicate the quandary? Considering the

culture and conventions of 1901, could they have handled the situation differently?

5. Gideon and Eli Allan were childhood friends. Yet when Eli discovers the secrets of Gideon and Cassie's relationship, a war erupts between the two men. Though Gideon is striving to be a better man, he is also a work in progress who has much to learn. In what ways did Gideon fight against his old sin nature when interacting with Eli? In what ways did Gideon give in to anger and impatience?

6. When Cassie first regretted her marriage to Gideon and wanted him out of her life, she panicked and chose to lie about the status of their marriage. How did her choices affect others? Can you think of a time when the choices, whether great or small, of another person changed your life?

7. Maggie sends Addie to live with the Bennetts. What do you feel was motivating her? What do you think that decision cost Maggie? What difference could this make in Addie's life?

8. As an act of grace, Cassie lets Gideon go. In wanting to break free of her lies, she sees an opportunity to finally let her yes be yes and her no be no. (Matthew 5:37 says, "But let your 'Yes' be 'Yes,' and your

'No,' 'No.' For whatever is more than these is from the evil one.") This is a heartrending choice for her, but it's one that brings her freedom. What do you feel this says about her character? How has she grown or changed? Can you think of a time when you relied on grace to resolve an issue?

9. How do you see the series title, The Cadence of Grace, reflected in *Though My Heart Is Torn*? The series title is based on 1 Peter 5:10, "But may the God of all grace, who called us to His eternal glory by Christ Jesus, after you have suffered a while, perfect, establish, strengthen, and settle you." Based on this verse, what do you think is on the horizon for Lonnie and Gideon in the third and final book, *My Hope Is Found*?

ACKNOWLEDGMENTS

Unending thanks to my Lord and Savior — the One who holds us up when nothing and no one else can. It is my constant prayer that these pages honor You.

To my wonderful husband and my research source for all things manly. I love following you around, notepad in hand, learning how to do everything from hunting to cooking outdoors. Thank you for swinging an ax, oh so well. And letting me watch. You are my best friend through and through. To Levi and Mabry who think it's pretty neat that Mommy's an author, and to baby Caleb who would eat my manuscript if given the chance. You three mean the world to me.

A very special thank you to my agent, Sandra Bishop. Living in this book are the first pages I ever sent you. The possibilities you saw helped bring us here today. Thank you for taking on this series and for believing in it from the start.

A huge thank you to my editor Shannon Marchese. You have a special skill for pushing writers beyond what they think they can do, and in turn, growth happens. I'm so grateful for your ability to shine light on my strengths and weaknesses so that this could be the best story possible. And a huge thanks to the entire team at WaterBrook Multnomah for all you do to put these stories into the hands of readers. Magic is created within your walls, and I can say from experience that, thanks to you, dreams really do come true.

There seem no sufficient words to express the sweetness of friends. Thank you to Amanda Dykes for your friendship and words of encouragement whenever the road felt rocky or too steep. Not to mention a good laugh and a cup of tea when nothing else would do. And thanks just doesn't seem enough to Tricia Mathys, for being a lighthouse when everything went dark and for holding my hand each step of the way until the sun began to rise. You are a blessing to the lives you touch.

A very special thank you to Beverly Nault for being the first to read this manuscript. Your critique opened up a wider world of writing for me. To Ashley Ludwig for your priceless wisdom on the synopsis. And to Dona Watson, for being the only sane one among us. Your quiet, gentle encouragement speaks volumes.

A never-ending thank you to my parents. Keep singing and praising the Lord. It's contagious.

And lastly, to all those — friends old and new — who read *Be Still My Soul* and sent an outpouring of love through reviews, letters, e-mails and hugs, I am so thankful for you.

ABOUT THE AUTHOR

Married to her first sweetheart, **Joanne Bischof** lives in the mountains of Southern California where she keeps busy making messes with their homeschooled children. When she's not weaving Appalachian romance, she's blogging about faith, writing, and the adventures of country living that bring her stories to life.

The employees of Thorndike Press hope you have enjoyed this Large Print book. All our Thorndike, Wheeler, and Kennebec Large Print titles are designed for easy reading, and all our books are made to last. Other Thorndike Press Large Print books are available at your library, through selected bookstores, or directly from us.

For information about titles, please call:
   (800) 223-1244

or visit our Web site at:
   http://gale.cengage.com/thorndike

To share your comments, please write:
   Publisher
   Thorndike Press
   10 Water St., Suite 310
   Waterville, ME 04901